THE FIFTH BOOK OF UNEXPECTED ENLIGHTENMENT

THE UNBEARABLE HEAVINESS OF REMEMBERING

Wisecraft

Praise for the Books of Unexpected Enlightenment

"The action is non-stop, with child's play, schoolwork, and danger all churned together. Lamplighter introduces many imaginative elements in her world that will delight...."
>—*VOYA*

"The British boarding school mystery meets the best imagined of fantasies at breakneck speed and with fully realized characters."
>—Sarah A. Hoyt, author of *Darkship Thieves*

"L. Jagi Lamplighter, a fantastic new voice and a fabulous new world in the YA market! Rachel Griffin is a hero who never gives up! I cheered her all the way!"
>—Faith Hunter, author of the *Skinwalker* series

"*The Unexpected Enlightenment of Rachel Griffin*, a plucky band of children join forces to fight evil, despite the best efforts of incompetent adults, at a school for wizards. YA fiction really doesn't get better than that."
>—Jonathan Moeller, author of *The Ghosts* series

"Rachel Griffin is curious, eager and smart, and ready to begin her new life at Roanoke Academy for the Sorcerous Arts, but she didn't expect to be faced with a mystery as soon as she got there. Fortunately she's up to the task. Take all the best of the classic girl detective, throw in a good dose of magic and surround it all with entertaining, likeable friends and an intriguing conundrum, and you'll have *The Unexpected Enlightenment of Rachel Griffin*, a thrilling adventure tailor-made for the folks who've been missing Harry Potter. Exciting, fantastical events draw readers into Rachel's world and solid storytelling keeps them there."
>—Misty Massey, author of *Mad Kestrel*

OTHER BOOKS BY L. JAGI LAMPLIGHTER

For an up-to-date list, see http://ljagilamplighter.com/works.

THE BOOKS OF UNEXPECTED ENLIGHTENMENT

The Unexpected Enlightenment of Rachel Griffin

The Raven, The Elf, and Rachel

Rachel and the Many-Splendored Dreamland

The Awful Truth about Forgetting

The Unbearable Heaviness of Remembering

Guardians of the Twilight Lands (*forthcoming*)

... and more to come.

THE PROSPERO'S CHILDREN TRILOGY

Prospero Lost

Prospero In Hell

Prospero Regained

THE UNBEARABLE HEAVINESS OF REMEMBERING

L. JAGI LAMPLIGHTER

BASED ON THE WORKS OF MARK A. WHIPPLE

ILLUSTRATIONS BY JOHN C. WRIGHT

Wisecraft

Wisecraft Publishing
A publishing company of the Wise

Published by Wisecraft Publishing
A publishing company of the Wise

This is a work of fiction. All of the characters and events portrayed in this book are fictional, and any resemblance to real people or events is purely coincidental or an Act of God.

ISBN: 978-1-953739-12-4 (hardcover)
      978-1-953739-11-7 (paperback)
ASIN: B086GKM896 (e-book)
Second edition
Revision 2.2.1 2022-08-07

First edition, 2020

Edited by Jim Frenkel

Cover art by Dan Lawlis
https://danlawlis.wordpress.com

Interior illustrations by John C. Wright

Typeset by Joel C. Salomon

Cover design by Danielle McPhail
Sidhe na Daire Multimedia
http://sidhenadaire.com

The text for this book is set in Crimson Pro by Sebastian Kosch & Jacques Le Bailly, licensed under the SIL Open Font License, Version 1.1; see https://fonts.google.com/specimen/Crimson+Pro and https://github.com/Fonthausen/CrimsonPro for details.

Chapter headings are set in RM GINGER, © 2009 Ray Meadows, licensed under CC BY-ND 3.0; see https://fontstruct.com/fontstructions/show/258661 for details.

CONTENTS

Dedication

IX

This book is dedicated to:
St. John's College
in Annapolis and Santa Fe,
the real Roanoke Academy.

Because there still is at least one place left
for those who want an education
instead of a degree.

ONCE THERE WAS A WORLD

THAT SEEMED AT FIRST GLANCE MUCH LIKE OTHER WORLDS

YOU *MAY HAVE LIVED IN* OR READ ABOUT,

BUT IT *WASN'T*....

Chapter One:
Redcaps in the Morning,
Sorcerer's Warning

Rachel Griffin was awakened by a tapping on the window of her fourth-floor dorm room. Climbing out of bed, she padded across the cold floor and peered through the open curtains. Outside, above the leafless branches, a faint paleness was visible in the eastern sky.

Something huge and black shot toward her window. Rachel stumbled backward, nearly screaming. The dark shape tapped against the glass. In the light of the few will-o'-the-wisps that had drifted out of their sconce-like nighthoods at each corner of the ceiling, Rachel could make out an enormous raven and the gleam of blood-red eyes.

She clapped her hand over her mouth until she had regained her composure.

"Jariel. You nearly scared the living daylights out of me!" she whispered in her English accent. With a soft giggle, she gestured toward the wayward will-o'-the-wisps. "See, a few of my daylights escaped!"

The Guardian of the World, in his guise as a great black bird, passed soundlessly through the glass of the closed window and landed on Nastasia's vanity. In one talon, it held a crystal vial.

"Rachel Griffin, your blood-brother needs you. He is west of here but not far."

Rachel rubbed her sleepy eyes. When she glanced up again, she was alone, standing with her bare feet on the cold floor. Had the Raven truly come or had that been a dream? On the vanity lay a crystal vial that had not been there before, a familiar vial with a long white sticker on one side. On the label, in Sigfried's spidery hand, were the words: *Chameleon Elixir*.

Losing no time, Rachel stepped into her boots, grabbed her red duffle coat and white snowman hat from her wardrobe, and retrieved

Vroomie, her steeplechaser-model bristleless broom, from under her bed. She slipped on her pouch that was larger on the inside and put into it her wand, a slender length of silver that had once belonged to her grandmother. She also donned the aquamarine pendant her brother Peter had given her for Yule, which he claimed would protect her from paralysis hexes, and put her athame in her coat pocket. Bristleless in hand, Rachel downed the elixir the Raven had left for her, shivering at the slight lizardy aftertaste of chameleon.

Rachel took a deep breath. Luckily, even though Roanoke Academy for the Sorcerous Arts was technically on lockdown, the school was not allowed to keep the building completely sealed by enchantment for more than an hour, due to possible fire hazard, so she would be able to slip out. Opening the window as quietly as she could, she climbed onto her steeplechaser and shot out into the pre-dawn morning.

The temperature had dropped during the night. Snow was falling, and the cold February air felt bracing against her sleepy face. She laughed with joy. Flying made her so happy, especially after having been trapped inside for over twenty-four hours. It drove off all her dark thoughts.

She flew through the air on her steeplechaser, an elegant flying device of polished walnut with handles of wrought iron and shiny brass. Where a normal broom might have bristles spread a tail fan of alternating slats of mahogany and cherry wood. Currently, though, she could not see it. Thanks to the special herbs that her Elf had given Sigfried before she died—which he had put into the chameleon elixir —even her bristleless was invisible.

No one could see her and Vroomie as they flew.

It was Thursday, the eighth of February. The students had been locked inside since Tuesday evening. During a skating party, three unknown figures with black pillowcases over their heads had opened the wards of the school. This had allowed the wild fey, who normally lived elsewhere on Roanoke Island, onto school property. Since then, the campus had been deemed too dangerous for students. Until the proctors could reestablish proper wards, a lockdown had been declared. Classes had been canceled, and students were confined to their dorms. Domestic fey delivered food from the dining hall three times a day.

As she flew, the wind tousled her hair. In the distance, she could hear violin music playing a reel. Perhaps one of the musical groups in Dare Hall, such as The Geometric Quartet or The Ginger Snaps, had decided to rise early and had opened the windows of the room in which they practiced, except they weren't supposed to leave the windows open during the lockdown.

She left Dare Hall and flew south toward the next closest dorm, Spenser Hall. As she flew through the forest west of Spenser, the music grew louder and more boisterous. Rachel darted between trees whose branches were decked out in icicles. Ahead, in the growing early dawn light, she could see stomping footprints appearing from nowhere in the fresh snow. They seemed to be dancing, forming the steps of a jig. Beside the footprints, Lucky the Dragon hovered in the air, making fancy S-shapes to the beat of the music.

Rachel thought back a few seconds, calling upon her perfect memory to show her the scene she had just witnessed. No differences. She sighed. Her method for seeing through obscurations did not allow her to see through the chameleon elixir. If those were Sigfried's footsteps, she could not see him.

Fifteen feet beyond Lucky and the dancing footprints were four small men. They wore red hats with long drooping peaks, heavy leather coats with high cuffs, and shiny black boots with silver buckles. Three of them sawed on fiddles. The fourth whistled upon a flute. *That was strange.* She knew that American redcaps were friendlier than their bloody, vicious Scotland and Ireland cousins, but still, a concert in the snowy forest seemed oddly peaceful.

Too late, she saw that the violinists grinned maniacally, and the eyes of all four danced with malicious glee. More importantly, ruby sparkles swirled in the snow. The air twinkled and smelled of cherries. The birches with their curling papery bark gleamed. The snow glittered with red glints as if a child had spilled art supplies.

"Sigfried?" she called.

"Griffin, back up!" Sigfried's voice called. He, too, spoke with a British accent, though his hinted at his lower-class, orphan upbring-

ing. "They've got magic music!"

Rachel shouted, "That's inspiration enchantment. It makes you dance or fight or laugh."

Then she clapped her hands over her mouth. If she shouted too loudly, it would draw the attention of the proctors, which might be a better outcome than ending her life as dye for a redcap's hat, but it would be a close second.

"Ya think?" Siggy's footsteps spun in a circle to the music.

Three trumpet notes sounded from the direction of Sigfried's footprints, sending out a blast of silvery sparks. However, as he blew, he spun. Instead of sweeping the redcaps off their feet, his wind gust merely disturbed some snow to their left.

Rachel, too, found herself attempting to dance to the lively tune, which was dangerous in mid-air. Her perfect memory made her immune to entrancement, but this was different. This was inspiration. She was no more immune than Sigfried and Lucky. Landing quickly, she jumped away from her bristleless, so that she twirled about on the open snow, far from her broom—and from the nearest birch trunks —in the hopes of avoiding damaging herself.

"The Raven sent me!" she called, annoyed. "What are you doing out here?"

Sigfried blew another blast. Again, his gust missed the redcaps; however, it scooped up Rachel. The sparkly, silver wind tossed her into the air. She flew, head over heels, until she fell face-first into a drift of soft, fresh snow.

Somewhere, outside of the cold, cold whiteness, she heard Lucky's growly voice.

"Er... oops," muttered the dragon.

"Better not breathe flame, Lucks, since you're dancing, too," came Sigfried's voice. "Don't want to accidentally crisp the blood-sister. Or me."

"Yeah, there are probably rules about not eating relations, even if they're crispy," agreed Lucky with great seriousness.

Wonderful, Rachel thought, her face ice cold. *I'm going to die, frozen in a snow bank while invisible. Do elixirs wear off when you die? Or do they stick, and you stay that way forever?*

The trumpet blared again. The violin music suddenly halted.

"Ha! Take that, Red Tops! I knew I'd get you if I timed it right!"

Rachel climbed to her feet, brushing snow from her face and hat. Two of the little men had been thrown some twenty feet and were picking themselves up out of the snow. They did not look happy. Rachel took advantage of their momentary consternation to run to Sigfried, or at least to where his footprints were appearing.

"Quick!" she shouted. "Lucky, ward us!"

"Um... how do I do that again?" Lucky asked. "Wasn't paying attention in that class."

"Run in a circle three times widdershins. Make sure that the silvery part of the bottoms of your feet is touching the ground... er, snow."

"Boss, that makes no sense. How can I run with my shins if my feet are touching the ground?"

"Good grief!" Rachel cried, feeling that she sounded rather like her boyfriend when she said it, which made her happy. "Not with-your-shins. Widder... never mind. Anticlockwise." Rachel moved her finger in a counter-clockwise direction as it was quite possible that Lucky could see her despite the invisibility elixir. "Right to left. Three times. Around both of us, quick!"

"Okay. Got it!"

Lucky swooped down and moved rapidly to trace out a circle in the snow around Rachel and Siggy, his long, sinuous body dancing and swaying as he did so. As the dawn grew brighter, she could see him more clearly, a serpentine *lung* covered in golden fur except for his ruby stomach scales, his long, flame-red, koi-like whiskers, his red horns, and the fluffy, crimson dorsal ruff that ran from between his horns, down the length of his back, to the puffy tuft at the end of his tail.

The music had started again. The little men looked angry. The beat picked up to a spirited reel. Ruby sparks circled Rachel's feet, and her legs began to move faster.

Truth be told, it was rather fun. Rachel loved dancing. It did not feel as if she could not control her limbs, unless she tried to stop. Otherwise, it felt like the urge to move about to music. She began to smile as she twirled and moved her feet, attempting cleverer steps.

"That's it, Lucky," she called. "Just one more time aroun —
umph!"

Mid-leap, Rachel's face collided with the shoulder of the invisible Sigfried. Pain exploded throughout her nose and cheeks, and her arms windmilled. She might have been able to keep her balance had her feet not had a will of their own, but, even as she was falling backward, they insisted on continuing to high-step to the reel. She crashed into the snow, smudging and ruining Lucky's attempt to ward them.

"Watch where you're goin', Griffin," called Sigfried.

"I can't!" she wailed from where she lay in the snow. "You're invisible."

"Ah. Fair point."

Rachel flailed, trying to rise, her efforts hampered by her continued attempt to dance. A crimson stain appeared near her in the white snow. Her nose must be bleeding. As his previous, still-unfinished ward had been ruined, Lucky began again, this time snaking out a larger circle.

The redcaps let out an eerie ululating cry. Hackles rose along the back of Rachel's neck.

"Ace! Two can play at that," cried Siggy, and he let out a similar cry.

That gave the little men pause.

Enough was enough. Pinching her nose, Rachel rolled into a kneeling position. Her feet tried to tap and jig, but with her weight on her knees, there was little her feet could do. Fixing her gaze on the little men, she whistled.

Blue sparks flew from her mouth, striking the flute player, who ceased to move, frozen in place by her hex. Sigfried followed this with a well-timed wind blast, throwing the two he had previously struck back another forty feet. They tumbled head-over-heels, pointed redcaps flying.

The remaining unencumbered redcap returned the favor. He ran his bow across his strings, and the red sparkles swirling toward Rachel and Sigfried changed to blue.

"Not again!" cried Rachel, unable to duck.
She hated being frozen.

With a thud, the outline of a figure in a parka appeared in the snow beside Rachel, where Sigfried had been dancing. It lay motionless. When the twinkling blue sparks reached Rachel, however, they spun oddly and winked out. With a cry of joy, Rachel realized that the aquamarine necklace her brother had given her for Yule had protected her as promised.

Lucky finished his third time around them, widdershins. Like throwing a switch, the compulsion to dance stopped. Her limbs were her own again. Red sparkles swirled around the outside of the circle Lucky had tracked in the snow but could not cross it.

"*Obé!*" Rachel made the accompanying hand gesture in the direction of the body-shaped indentation of snow. Luckily, the Word of Ending cantrip took only one hand; her other was still pinching her nose to staunch the bleeding.

Sigfried both began to move and instantly reappeared as her cantrip cancelled the effects of his chameleon elixir. He had snow in his golden curls and a gleeful look of maniacal delight that almost matched those of their opponents. On his back, he wore Zoë Forrest's red and blue backpack. *That was suspicious.* Zoë's backpack had an entire room inside. What did Siggy plan to move?

"Quick!" Rachel shouted. "Get them!"

"Now I got 'em," Siggy crowed, grinning like a jack-o'-lantern.

Raising his trumpet, he blew. Blue sparks flew from the instrument, accompanied by the scent of evergreens. They swooshed forward, surrounding the remaining redcap. It stopped moving, standing like a violin-wielding statue beside its flute-playing companion. There was no sign of the other two, the ones Siggy had sent flying with his wind blasts. They had fled.

"Lucky, ward them!" cried Rachel. "They're fey! They'll be stuck in the ward!"

Lucky flew forward and circled the two frozen redcaps three times, counter-clockwise. Running to join him, Rachel pulled Zoë's athame from the backpack and drew a circle in the snow with the warding knife, tracing Lucky's path.

"There! That should hold them," she declared.

"Woohoo!" Sigfried whooped, leaping in the air and high-fiving Lucky's taloned paw.

"What are you doing out here?" Still pinching her nose, Rachel put her free hand on her hip and glared at him, even though she knew Siggy could not see her. "You do realize if they catch us out during a lockdown, we'll be punished, possibly expelled. We're still on probation for the time we accidentally fell off campus… into Transylvania."

"Expelled, ex-smelled, I'm not afraid of them!" scoffed Sigfried Smith. "Besides, they won't catch us. We're too wily. And we're invisible."

"That's not the point," Rachel replied, realizing that he did not know that she had made him visible. "What are you doing out here?"

"Getting my loot."

"Loot?"

"From the ogre's cave. I knew if I didn't get it right away, the adults would steal it. They already stole the ogre. By the time I woke up in the infirmary after the beating the ogre gave me and sent Lucky back for it, it was gone. After all my plans to mount the head on our clubhouse wall! I didn't even get any hair so I could make that Anti-Ogre Achilles Elixir."

"The ogre's cave! That's miles from here—on the northernmost point of the island."

Siggy shrugged. "Lucky carried me in the backpack."

"How did you get in trouble with the redcaps from the *inside* of a backpack?"

"I saw them on my way back," Siggy tapped his chest where Rachel knew his all-seeing amulet rested beneath his parka. "I climbed out, so I could investigate. I thought they would offer me something to drink, and I could play ninepins and wake up a hundred years later."

"Valerie would be a hundred and fourteen," Rachel observed wryly. "The Wise often live to be two or three hundred, but that's a long time to ask her to wait."

"Oh, good point! Can't leave my best girl behind!" Looking back at the redcaps, Siggy added, "We'll get credit for catching them, right? Is there a bounty?"

Rachel grabbed her aching head with the hand that was not holding her nose. "Credit from whom? Sigfried, if anyone finds out that we were out here catching them, we'll get into horrid trouble."

"Oh. Right." He slumped, deflated.

Voices called from the direction of Marlowe Hall. Footsteps crunched in the snow.

"I hear the proctors coming," she whispered loudly, running for her broom. "Quick, jump on. And drink another elixir! You're visible!"

"Libra!"

The arched window of her dorm room flew upwards. Rachel ducked her head, soared through the opening, and landed. Once in the safety of her room, she breathed in the pleasant scents of cedar and clean linen. The warmth was wonderful, but it also made her feel the depth of the cold she had escaped. She shivered and chafed her arms.

She had dropped off Sigfried at the window to his dorm room, waiting while he emptied Zoë's backpack of whatever he had found in the ogre's lair. Then Lucky accompanied her back to her own room. The sinuous red and gold dragon followed her through the open window, sniffing around the rug in the middle of the chamber. Her cat, Mistletoe, hissed from under her bed, and Beauregard the Tasmanian Tiger lifted his head from his bed at the foot of Rachel and Nastasia's bunk. Lucky ignored both familiars and snaked off next door to return the backpack to the foot of Zoë's bed, before the other girl could notice it was gone.

Out of the corner of her eye, Rachel caught sight of a pair of silver ice skates with purple laces leaning against the end of her bed, conjured skates that, by all rights, should have vanished over a day ago. The skates had been conjured by Laurel but made permanent, Rachel was certain, by the Raven. A happy feeling danced inside her. She felt as if he had given her a gift.

Lucky returned and slipped out the window, heading back down toward his human. With a sigh of relief, Rachel closed the window and ended her chameleon elixir with a cantrip.

"R-Rachel?" came a small squeak.

She whipped around, looking about. Two dark brown eyes and a shock of curly black hair stuck out from under a blanket on the far top bunk. Her roommate Astrid stared down, her expression a mix of terror and relief. Her normally caramel skin had blanched to a dull gray in the dimness.

"Yes. It's me. S-sorry," she whispered, hoping not to wake their other two roommates.

Now it was Rachel's turn to be afraid. *Would Astrid tell on her?*

Astrid's head came out from under the blanket, a concerned look replacing her fearful one. Quietly, she whispered back, "Is that blood on your hat? Are you bleeding?"

"Oh!" Rachel pulled off her hat. Spots of red now marred its pristine white, blotting out the left eye of the hat's snowman face. Looking in the vanity mirror, she saw that her nose looked a little funny, and blood had splattered her coat. "Yes. Or, rather, I was. My poor hat."

"Let me help."

Astrid slipped down from her bunk, her long limbs clad in lavender flannel pajamas spotted with pink and blue llamas. She always wore her collars turned up in what Hildy from the room next door called a Dracula collar, but which reminded Rachel more of the collar in a black and white poster of an actress named Audrey Hepburn that hung on the wall of Sandra's study.

Taking the white hat, Astrid paused to squeeze Rachel's hand. "You're frozen. Why don't you take a warm shower, and I'll get the blood off?"

Gratefully, Rachel slipped out of her coat and followed Astrid's advice.

In the end, Rachel chose the huge, claw-footed bathtub at the back of the bathroom rather than a shower. She poured bubble bath into the water and climbed into the sudsy tub, luxuriating in the heat. As she stretched a leg to soap it, pointing her toes, she tried to gather the courage to face another day of lockdown.

One day stuck in the dorm had not been too bad, but two? Rachel was not used to being confined with so many people. Being at school with no classes would not have been so bad if she could have spent the free time with her boyfriend. Alas, Gaius was locked away in a different dorm. Sigfried Smith would have had the same problem, except that the proctors had brought Valerie Hunt over to Dare Hall for a few hours. His girlfriend had been so distraught about his wellbeing, after she saw the ogre beat his head against the ice, that the staff felt she should see with her own eyes that he had recovered.

Of course, Rachel had been able to speak to Gaius over their black bracelets, and once, they had talked over their calling cards, so they could see each other's faces. She had loved that. Still, it was not the same as sitting together and holding hands. So she had been forced to make do playing games with her friends, while Gaius spent his time hanging out with....

Rachel bit off that thought and sighed. *What did it mean to be in love with two boys?* Her love for Gaius Valiant burned fiercely in her breast. Just hearing his voice made her feel giddy with joy. This she found reassuring. Yet, every time her thoughts strayed to *the other boy*....

Rachel pressed her palm against her face, her cheek unusually warm. *What a horrid fate!*

She could not help wondering, though, if fate might have had a hand in her current dilemma. Tuesday night, her friend the Raven had—at her request—altered her destiny, giving her the option to choose a different future than what had previously awaited her. As he spoke, Jariel had glanced toward where Gaius and Vlad had been playing hockey. Rachel's heart jumped like a skater clearing a log. Had she mistaken his gaze? *Was it Vladimir Von Dread he had been looking at all along?*

It did not matter. Nothing could come of feelings she might harbor for the Crown Prince of Bavaria. He was six years her senior and in love with her eldest sister, Sandra. Solemnly, Rachel resolved to remain true to her boyfriend. So long as she never spoke of her other feelings, no one need ever know.

Her thoughts returned to the Raven. Normally, he did not interfere with mortals. She wondered why he had warned her about Sigfried's peril. Jariel had become very precious to her. It troubled her that he was under the control of the dreaded Master of the World —the mysterious father of the King of Magical Australia, grandfather of her best friend, Nastasia Romanov—who could command the Guardian, forcing him to commit cruel or reprehensible acts, such as change people's memories or alter their personalities.

A shiver ran through her having nothing to do with the cold. *Cruel acts such as altering Rachel's parents to make them give up their first-born daughter, Amber, and then erasing their memories to make them forget she had ever existed.* Rachel wanted her whole family back together.

She wanted it more than she had ever wanted anything in her life.

What she needed was a wish, Rachel decided as she blew into the bubbles. Of late, so many things had gone wrong—many of them matters that she could discuss with no one. A wish, at least, could be made privately.

That decided it. From now on, she would watch the sky every night at dusk. True, it was often overcast. The storm goblin, the Heer of Dunderberg, had been even more active of late whipping up storms and tossing boulders. If she were patient, however, sooner or later, she would catch the first star of evening which, in her opinion, led to the very best kind of wishes.

As the frothy bubbles slowly began to sink back into the warm water, Rachel sat up and reached for her soft lavender towel.

It was time to face the world outside the shower curtain.

Chapter Two:
Wishing Thrice Upon a Star

Gathering the strength to leave the paradise of the warm bath, Rachel slipped into her fluffy, peach dressing gown and pushed aside the curtain. Astrid stood by the sink working on the hat with a cotton ball and a brown bottle of hydrogen peroxide. The red wool coat lay on the counter beside her. It had a big wet spot where the blood stain had been.

Rachel wiped the steamy mirror with a paper towel. Her nose was swollen and felt tender to the touch, but it did not seem to be broken. She wondered if it would turn black and blue.

As she toweled her hair dry, she said, "Thank you. You're a lifesaver."

"No problem." Astrid gave her a sweet smile, her llama-covered sleeves pulled up to her elbows as she worked upon the hat. "My mom taught me how to do this when I was six. You can do it with soap and water, too, but you have to use cold water, so the heat doesn't cook the blood into the fabric. And a lot of soap, rubbing it in with your fingers over and over. Hydrogen peroxide is much easier. I think she made a point of explaining the whole thing to get my mind off my skinned knee, but it has served me well. My mom sometimes jokes that it was cleaning up after all my skinned knees that led to my interest in science." She held up the snowman hat, which was again pure as snow. "There, see! No harm done!"

"Thank you! Oh, that's brilliant!"

"It's the least I could do after you saved me from the darkness and the pixies on the ice Tuesday night. I might not ever have found my way back, not with my hurt foot. I could have...." Astrid's voice trailed off. She gestured at Rachel's face. "What happened?"

"I hit my nose on Sigfried."

"On Siggy?"

"I couldn't see him."

"Oh. That's a sha—" but Astrid never finished. Instead, a giggle erupted. First one or two, and then waves of giggles. A moment later both girls were laughing, until they leaned over, grabbing their stomachs and gasping for air.

"Rachel," Astrid asked, when they could breathe again, "may I ask you a question?"

"Of course!"

"A few weeks ago, you and the dean were walking in the hallway with a man…."

"And you dropped your books," Rachel recalled, wishing, after she saw Astrid's face, that she had not said that aloud.

"Oh, you saw that." Astrid ducked her head, embarrassed.

"That was Agent Bridges from the London office of the Wisecraft. Why do you ask?"

"Um, no reason." Astrid was quiet for a moment. "I can't believe you remembered that I dropped my books. How embarrassing. Do you really have a perfect memory? Sorry, I overhear a lot because no one notices I'm there."

"No one notices you? I am sorry, Astrid!" Rachel cried. "I will try to do better!"

"You don't need to worry about it. No one else notices me either."

"But I want to notice you! You are one of the most delightful people I know!"

Astrid bit her lip and ducked her head shyly, not knowing what to say. She reached out and pressed Rachel's fingers with her own. Rachel smiled and squeezed back. Astrid drew her hand back, as if that amount of forwardness had been too great an effort for her.

"And yes," stated Rachel, "I do have a perfect memory."

"That's an interesting gift." Astrid leaned forward, curious. "How far back do you remember? Birth? Back into the womb? Before that?"

Rachel shook her head. "The talent doesn't develop until we learn to speak. I only recall back to around age two. Mum's the same."

"I imagine it's an extremely useful talent." Astrid raised her head and met Rachel's eyes. "But it also must be at times quite a heavy burden."

Many people throughout her life had commented on how much they wished that they could have a perfect memory, and a few had acknowledged it might be difficult at times; but no one had ever offered sympathy with such understanding. Rachel eyed the other girl carefully, but Astrid looked sincere.

"I suppose so," Rachel agreed, faintly surprised. "Occasionally it is."

That evening, she stood with her forehead pressed against the cold window of her dorm room. Outside, the rain-drenched paper birches were so wet that their bark glowed a pearlescent pink. All day, the storm goblin had raged, and the heavens had poured down upon the campus. As evening had fallen, however, the clouds parted, revealing a patch of pale blue. The almanac in her mental library claimed it should be dark enough to see the stars in three minutes. If the clouds would only stay parted, she might catch sight of the first star of evening and make a wish.

She waited breathlessly.

Behind Rachel, a gaggle of girls sat in the middle of her dorm room, gathered around a card table playing Chinese checkers. The group consisted of two of Rachel's roommates plus the five freshman girls from the room next door: Zoë Forrest, Joy O'Keefe, Sakura Suzuki, Wendy Darling, and Hildy Winters. While Zoë and Joy usually hung out with Rachel and her roommate Nastasia, the other three were normally part of a different crowd. All the other girls were playing the game, except for Zoë, who sat with her feet up on the table.

"We've been locked in a whole two days!" cried Joy O'Keefe, her mousy brown hair tied up with thin cotton socks. She was a cheerful girl, bubbly to a point that teetered dangerously close to silly. "Does anyone know how long it's going to take before we can go to class? Or, more importantly, the dining hall?"

The young ladies had decided to curl their hair. Some had wrapped their tresses around socks, which were now tied into knots, forming makeshift curlers. Others had used spongy rollers Rachel's older sister Laurel had conjured for them. These rollers would vanish in twenty-four hours, so the girls would not need to put them away.

Rachel's hair was wrapped around rollers, too, though she feared her friends would be disappointed when the curls fell out of her flyaway hair after only a few minutes. Her hair was like that.

"Yeah, nah," Zoë said in her faint New Zealand accent. She sat casually backwards on her chair, popping cheese and crackers into her mouth. "I don't mind having food brought to us. I could lounge here and eat in bed all the time. Plus, we don't have to go to class."

Zoë stretched and stood up. She was the cynic of their crowd. When Rachel first met her in September, she had been cynical yet cheerful. Ever since she had fallen into the darkness between worlds and come back with scars all over her body, however, her cynicism had gained a nasty streak. Zoë's pixie-short hair and her single, long, braided forelock was currently a brilliant Chinese lantern red. Her braid still looked odd to Rachel's eye now that Zoë had lost the feather that used to adorn it.

Bowls of snacks—cheese and crackers, veggies, and fruits—sat on the table beside the thick round wooden Chinese checkers board. The room smelled of grapes and cheddar. Zoë moved around the table to refill her plate.

Joy, who had put aside her fluffy white cat, paused, gaping up at Zoë. "Boy! Talk about a growth spurt!" she cried. "You and I used to be the same height. Now you're much taller than me!"

Rachel mentally compared Zoë as she was now with Zoë back in September and saw that Joy was correct. All the girls had matured a little—even Rachel herself was an inch taller than she had been and had now reached the lofty height of four feet six inches—but Zoë was considerably taller. She now looked like an older teen instead of going-on-fifteen.

On Zoë's shoulder, its nose twitching rapidly, sat her tiger-spotted quoll—a little marsupial like a long-nosed rat crossed with a small spotted opossum. Other familiars were present as well. Beauregard, the Tasmanian tiger, stood with his nose pressed against the table, waiting patiently for treats. Joy and Wendy both held their cats in their laps, and Sakura's tiny fluffy white *shima enaga* sat upon her shoulder stretching its wings and preening. In a wire cage near her bunk, Astrid's red-winged blackbird cheeped and trilled at the unfamiliar bustle.

There was no sign of Kitten Fabian's familiar, the tiny Lion, but Hildy's familiar, a truly gigantic Bernese mountain dog that was larger than Rachel, kept sniffing under Rachel's bunk, where Rachel could feel Mistletoe crouched, hiding from the large dog. Being able to feel her cat, as if it were her arm or her foot, was one of the perks of the familiar-bonding ceremony, which had worked even though Mistletoe was not actually a familiar.

Alas, Rachel now knew that her cat was just... a cat.

The sky outside the window was a faint blue-gray. Then, three tiny silvery lights twinkled in the heavens.

Rachel squinted at the three stars. Closing her eyes, she recalled the last few seconds once and then again more slowly—one millisecond at a time. No matter how carefully she tried this, she could not catch any one of the stars appearing before the others. First, there were none, and then all three appeared simultaneously. *What did that mean?*

She consulted her mental library of books and encyclopedias—both Wise and Unwary. Nowhere was there a mention of what to do about wishing if more than one star appeared simultaneously. She was not sure what to make of it. *Could she wish on all three stars?*

There was no lack of additional urgent matters that needed fixing. Finding two more wishes would not be a burden. The problem was going to be picking only three. To be safe, she would make her most important wish first. She fixed her gaze on one of the three stars: *I wish that my sister Amber, stolen at birth, would be reunited with our family.*

"My brother Ivan says that he heard, on good authority," Nastasia Romanov said, "that the proctors should be done with the makeshift wards by this very afternoon and that the lockdown should be lifted by Saturday morning, if not by dinner tomorrow."

The Princess of Magical Australia was an exquisitely beautiful young woman with a faultless peaches-and-cream complexion. She sat straight, not touching the back of her chair. Even with curlers in her golden locks, she looked as lovely as a dream, a trick few could pull off.

Joy's voice trembled nervously. "But Rachel's sister Laurel says it will be weeks before we are allowed outside again. She says we should all hope fervently that the staff continues to send food—because last time something like this happened, one of the dorms was forgotten and all the students starved to death. When they finally opened the building, only skeletons remained!"

A smile tugged at the corner of Rachel's lips. She was grateful she had taken to heart the Lion's wisdom about forgiveness, as she was again on good terms with her sister, but that did not make Laurel not, well, Laurel.

Over her shoulder, she said wryly, "I would not exactly call my sister a reliable source."

Ignoring her, Joy pressed the princess more plaintively until Nastasia repeated Rachel's words in a slightly politer form. Immediately, Joy gave a cheerful smile and returned her attention to the game.

Rachel sighed.

Gazing out the window again, Rachel thought back over the last six months. So much had happened in so short a time. She had arrived at school in September so full of hope only to discover that the world was much more dangerous than she had realized. In the same way that her World of the Wise hid from the mundane world of the Unwary, there was another more secret world hiding from the Wise. This more mysterious world seemed to be controlled by the Romanov family—though Nastasia herself seemed unaware of this—or at least by Nastasia's unknown grandfather, whom Rachel referred to as the Master of the World.

The new hidden world also included a demon who—possessing first Aleister Crowley and then Mortimer Egg—had repeatedly performed a ritual that brought people to earth from other worlds. The ritual required that a family be murdered in front of the eyes of one member, often the youngest, who was then left alive. Only, as far as the demon knew, the spell had never worked. Each time this ritual brought someone from another world, the Guardian of the World had altered the entire planet so that everyone recalled that the person had always lived here. Of the nine girls in the room, five of them: Zoë, Astrid, Kitten, Sakura, and Hildy, were Outsiders—Metaplutonians, as Siggy called them—who had been brought to earth by repeated castings of this terrible ritual. All five girls had been adults before the Raven turned them into children, though none now remembered her previous life.

Turning her head to the right, Rachel could see these girls and the other three behind her in the mirror on Nastasia's vanity. The group of them looked so friendly, all laughing together, so cheerful and lively. The sight of them seated around the card table made her heart ache oddly.

Rachel loved Chinese checkers. When they set out the board, she had been delighted. The other girls, however, had immediately claimed the colors they normally played during game night at the Young Sorcerers' League. Since Rachel was the only one in the room who was not a member of the YSL, she had not been a part of their previous games.

Not a single girl had thought to ask if she might like to play now, even though she had tried to speak up and ask to play three times.

With so many people present in her room, why did she feel so lonely?

Still gazing into the vanity mirror, Rachel noted that she, too, was visible there: tiny and slender, as if she were far younger than her thirteen years, with the almond-shaped brown eyes she had inherited from her half-Korean mother. She was dressed in a black academic robe with a yoked front. Atop her head, her midnight hair was wrapped around pink, conjured curlers.

She looked fairly ridiculous. In a fit of fancy, she waved at herself. From the top bunk on the far side of the room, Astrid—whose face was peeking shyly out from where she had been hiding under a blanket reading a book—waved back. Rachel smiled at her happily and then turned back to the window.

Over by the table, Rachel's final roommate, Kitten Fabian (whose real name was Jane), finally asked the question that was foremost on the minds of the girls.

"But will the lockdown be lifted in time for the Year of the Dragon Ball?" she cried. She was a short girl, fierce and cheerful, with straight brown hair and freckles, who also spoke with a British accent. "That's the real question. The ball is scheduled for the first day of Lunar New Year, which is Saturday. If we have not yet been released, will they cancel or reschedule it? Can Lunar New Year even be rescheduled? Doesn't it have to be celebrated on the dark of the moon?"

"They could not possibly cancel," Sakura Suzuki insisted quietly. She was Japanese and spoke with careful precision. Usually, she wore her hair in two long pigtails with bells tied into them. Only now, her thick locks, too, were up in curlers. Rachel suspected that her hair would not hold the curl either. "Some of us have been working on our costumes for months."

Despite her sympathy for the staff's attempt to keep the students safe, Rachel fervently agreed with Sakura's sentiment. The school could not possibly cancel the ball. No universe could be so cruel. After all she had been through, she had been so looking forward to this normal schoolgirl activity. She planned to dance and dance and dance. While she had been to balls, she had never been to a masquerade. The very thought of attending one made her shiver with anticipation. Masquerades were mysterious and full of possibility. *Anything could happen.*

"I trust all will resolve satisfactorily," replied the princess, "but if it should not, and we miss the ball, it will only be because the faculty are doing their best to protect us."

"They have to hold the ball!" insisted Joy. "Absolutely everyone would rebel!"

"Not the boys," Zoë shrugged as she sat down again. "I don't think they care."

"Siggy cares," Joy cried loyally.

"Only because Smith thinks the dragon theme was chosen to honor Lucky," smirked Zoë.

"Which is true," said Wendy Darling, who looked a bit odd to Rachel's eye now that her ever-present cloud of hair was wrapped around socks instead of floating around her head like a dark nimbus. Wendy, the daughter of the real-life hero of the famous comic, *James Darling, Agent*, the hero of the Terrible Years, occasionally struck Rachel as the only normal girl in the dorm. "The Sacred Days Club did chose Chinese New Year to celebrate this year because we have an Asian *lung* here at school, and this will be the Year of the Dragon."

"Sakura has an Asian lung," quipped Zoë, patting her own chest. "Two in fact."

"*Lung* as in dragon," Sakura corrected with all seriousness. "Not as in breathing."

Rachel listened with half an ear. With the rest of her attention, she contemplated her second wish. It was hard to think clearly amidst the commotion. It had been this way for two days. She wished she could have even a few minutes to herself.

In the woods below, something moved. Rachel squinted, but she could not make out what it was. Could it be one of the two escaped redcaps? She had casually mentioned to the proctor who brought the mail that morning that she had seen two redcaps outside her window. It was a lie, but at least it alerted the staff to the presence of the mischievous fey in the birch forest.

Behind her, Wendy Darling called over her shoulder. "How's your father, Rachel? Has he recovered from his accident?" To the others, she added, "Rachel's father and my father used to be partners, once upon a time. I was so sad to hear that he had suffered a memory loss."

Rachel gave a noncommittal answer, not wanting to lie outright to her friends. They thought her father's memory had been lost in an accident. Rachel knew better. It had been robbed by the Master of the World.

"Serves him right," murmured Zoë, from where she still lounged by the crackers.

Rachel spun and stared at her wide-eyed. "I beg your pardon?"

"Hear me out, Griffin." Zoë raised a hand, her face serious. "I don't mean that I want bad things to happen to your family. I don't. But you got to admit: If he was doing an experiment with memory-removing magic, he kinda had it coming."

Joy looked up from where she had been jumping her green piece over Hildy's white one. "But Agents need to practice those spells— how else can they hide things from the Unwary?"

Zoë shrugged. "Yeah, nah. Listen, O'Keefe. A couple summers ago, my father sent me to stay with some mundane relatives in Upper Marlboro, Maryland. There's a race track there. Quite pretty. Anyway, these relatives weren't Unwary—well, not when I got there— but they were not sorcerers. They were just normal human beings— a family of four. The mom was really sweet. She taught me to ride a bike and showed me... well, girl things. I was a jerk to her, because I couldn't recognize sweet when it bit my bum, but...." She shrugged again. "Point is: something went wrong in the neighborhood. Wasn't my fault. At least, I don't think it was. I wasn't even involved. The Agents showed up and began wiping people's memories.

"Turns out my little third-cousin-twice-removed, Theo, was at the playground where it happened. They wiped his memory of the incident. Only they overdid it. Removed a whole week. To be safe, they did the whole family. I was lucky to be able to convince them not to do me, too. They wanted to remove my memory of the World of the Wise." She grinned. "Shut up right quick when they found out that my otherwise-worthless father was a lawyer with BB&K."

Her humor drained away. "Gave me a choice. Go Unwary or the family forgets me."

"And you picked remaining Wise?" Joy leaned forward eagerly.

"That's terrible," Wendy whispered. "I am so sorry, Zoë. I wish we had known each other then. I'm sure my father could have set things right."

Zoë swallowed, sitting down in her chair again. "It had been really nice there. If it wasn't for the fact that I would have had to forget Seth and Misty, I probably would have just stayed. They could have made the family forget I wasn't their real daughter."

"Can they do that?" asked Hildy, who had been a cheerleader before she came to Roanoke and who was now broom-crazy. She was a California girl with golden streaks in her darker blond hair. Rachel had only ever seen her in two moods—happy-excited or outraged-excited. "Use magic to give people a family, I mean?"

"Yeah, nah," Zoë said again. "It's not a real family. Point is: changing people's memories sucks. And if someone tries and, instead, changes their own memory, it seems fitting."

"I see your point," Nastasia replied, her brow furrowed as she considered all this. Clearly, Zoë's story disturbed her.

"That's not what happened," murmured Rachel.

Most of the others did not hear her, but Zoë had been looking right at her. Rachel watched her face change as Zoë figured out that the public story was not the real one.

"Right," Zoë nodded slowly, putting her feet up against the table again and interlacing her fingers behind her head. "Don't mind me, then. I was out of line."

Rachel acknowledged Zoë's comment with a slight nod and turned to gaze out the window at the evening sky.

Just under a month ago, Rachel's father had somehow offended this Master of the World, and he stole Ambrose Griffin's memories of the last few years, though, of course, Rachel's friends knew nothing of this. The Master of the World had tried to steal Rachel's memories, too, but a Rune given to her by her dead Elf had protected her—the Elf who had been killed by the storm goblin.

"I am coming to believe that it is immoral to change people's memories," Nastasia spoke with slow, measured words, thinking deeply. "We should not treat others in a way we would object to being treated ourselves. Certainly none of us would want it to happen to us."

"You can say that again," Rachel whispered, glad that she and her friend finally agreed on something.

"But...." Joy looked back and forth between Rachel and Nastasia uncertainly, "what about law enforcement? How else could the Wise stay hidden?"

"Why stay hidden?" countered Hildy. "We're sorcerers. With magic powers." She made a whooshing motion to indicate a broom in flight. "Why cower in the shadows as if we were thugs or something?" She looked at the other girls, her eyes shifting nervously. "Are we thugs?"

Rachel opened her mouth and shut it again. She could not answer without talking about the Wall that protected their world from Outside, and she knew she should not do that in front of so many girls who were not in the know. The very act of drawing attention to the Wall would weaken it.

Meanwhile, the princess was saying, "After all, we don't modify people's memories in Magical Australia, and yet we get by. I cannot feel it is the right and decent thing to do."

Rachel, whose father's memory had been stolen by Nastasia's own grandfather, could only nod sadly. Her hands curled into fists. Her family had been torn apart by this man, and they did not even know it. The more she learned about this Master of the World and how he changed people with magic or removed or altered their memories with impunity, the more angry she became. The memory of waking up in the middle of the night to see him standing in this very room—a silvery path, like the one Nastasia could produce but as wide as a sidewalk, trailing behind him as he coolly instructed the Raven to tamper with her memory—caused chills to run up and down her body.

Ever since they had discovered the Metaplutonians, Rachel had been growing more and more alarmed that the people of her world were being treated so badly, that their lives were being interfered with in such a cavalier manner. Discovering the existence of the Master of the World had given her a target for her hatred. But how did one fight an enemy who could remove memories and change the laws of nature? No one should be able to get away with such a thing! And yet, what could be done?

Rachel felt out of her league, helpless. If only she could... *make a wish?*

The sky was darkening, new stars appearing. Rachel called upon her memory to find the three that had showed up first. Picking one upon which she had not yet wished, she made her second request: *I wish to take revenge upon the Master of the World.*

A collective sigh sounded from the other girls as the princess jumped a yellow piece all the way across the Chinese checkers board. Then they sighed again as Sakura, who went next, jumped her blue piece over even more pieces.

In front of Rachel, clouds rolled in from the west, over the peak of Storm King Mountain. They moved across the darkening sky like fluffy ships under full sail. In a moment, the stars would all vanish again. *What should her third wish be?*

Lightning flashed followed by a crack of thunder. Once again, the storm goblin was throwing tantrums. As long as the Heer was free, the local fey did not feel bound by the covenant that normally kept them from interfering with Roanoke Academy—which was why the students were stuck inside. If the Agents of the Wisecraft could but catch the storm goblin, everything would go back to normal. Before the third star disappeared behind the clouds, Rachel wished her third wish: *I wish someone would catch the Heer of Dunderberg.*

CHAPTER THREE:
HAVE PRINCE, WILL TRAVEL

The next morning, the proctors brought the mail. Rachel and her siblings received a letter from their mother telling them she had asked the dean to give her children leave, so they could come home and visit their father. She hoped this way that they could see that he was still himself, despite his memory loss, and help update him on what he had forgotten due to his accident.

As Laurel read the letter aloud, Rachel's hand brushed the right side of her head where the Rune of Memory lay against her scalp like a silver tattoo. Zoë's Rune allowed her to take other people through dreamland with her. She and Rachel had received their Runes from the same person; could Rachel's affect others, too? If she touched her head to her father's, would her memory-protecting Rune restore his stolen memories?

Eager to try, Rachel wanted to leave immediately. Peter and Laurel laughed, pointing out that they could not ask the dean for permission to travel while locked in the dorm. Peter told her to buck up and not worry, the lockdown would end soon enough. Laurel leaned over and mussed Rachel's hair and told her not to be such an impatient missy. As Rachel glumly walked away, she realized there was someone else who might be able to arrange for her to speak to the dean.

The first two times she tried to call Gaius, he had whispered that he was not available.

Half an hour after her second try, he called her back. "Sorry about that, Rach," Gaius said in his British drawl. "The dean wanted to see us."

"Oh… too bad I didn't know. That's why I was calling." She paused to keep her voice from trembling. It surprised her how frightened she was to ask her next question. "Um. I wondered if Vlad could arrange for me to see the dean today."

"Today? Um... probably. Is it important?"

"Not important per se. My mother asked if we would visit Father, and I thought today might be good as I wouldn't miss any classes. Do you think Vlad would be willing to take me?"

"Take you home? Probably, I'll ask him. Hey, Vlad!"

The black bracelet stopped vibrating. Rachel could no longer hear Gaius's voice. She had not meant for him to ask if Vlad would take her all the way home—she had just wanted him to escort her to the dean's—but the idea of having the prince accompany her to Gryphon Park, terrifying as it was, seemed more appealing the more she thought about it. It would give her a chance to tell him about Amber.

The bracelet vibrated. Gaius's voice spoke in her ear again. "Rach? He says to tell you that he will pick you up at the door of your dorm in fifteen minutes."

"Oh, wonderful!" Rachel cried, rushing over to make sure her hat and coat were dry from their cleaning. They seemed serviceable. "Gaius, what did the dean want with you lot?"

"She called in our people and Abraham Van Helsing's group from Dare—the vampire hunters?—to ask if any of us had violated the lockdown. Seems somebody caught a redcap yesterday and left it frozen in the woods near Spenser. The proctors want to know who did it."

It took all of her dissembling skill not to laugh out loud.

"Really," Rachel managed finally. "How interesting."

"You wouldn't know who did it, would you, Miss-Seems-To-Know-Everything?"

"As a matter of fact, I might," she smirked.

"Really! You *do* find out everything. Even Vlad doesn't know the answer to this one."

"Information loves me," Rachel replied dreamily. "It comes and finds me."

"Apparently, it does!" Gaius replied, amused.

"In this particular case, however, I have a distinct advantage."

Gaius was silent. Then, even more amused, he asked, "As in... you were there?"

Rachel raised her nose primly. Even though he could not see her, she was glad it had not turned black and blue after all. "Let's just say Sigfried Smith deserves at least half the credit."

Dread met her on the porch of Dare Hall, which was empty, except for someone's wolf familiar, which lay stretched out on the flagstones, enjoying the cold weather. The Prince of Bavaria was dressed in a black dreadnought coat with a hood trimmed with wolverine fur, which Rachel recalled was famous for always being frost-free. He looked remarkably distinguished in his winter gear. When Rachel first glimpsed him, her heart skipped a beat.

He took her hand and strode down the snowy path towards Roanoke Hall. Her mitten fit snugly in his heavy leather dueling gauntlet. The firmness of his grip was comforting. She walked beside him in her bright red duffle coat, taking five steps to his every three. Walking with the prince was not like holding hands with Gaius. Vladimir was so tall and imposing that Rachel felt very much like a little sister being taken on an outing by her big brother—her incredibly imposing big brother. She was too filled with joy to breathe.

He would be her brother once he married Sandra. She had even taken to calling him by the nickname F.B.—short for Future Brother-in-Law. Rachel liked nicknames. They were a bit like sharing a secret with someone. It was because of this that she continued to call the being who protected her world "the Raven" or "Jariel" when everyone else called him "the Guardian."

As they walked, she recalled Tuesday night. She and Vlad had been skating on the ice in the falling twilight, beneath wisp sculptures and stars. Carried away by the wonder of it, she had blurted out her true feelings. Rachel continued walking; but her eyes were now locked on the snow. Her cheeks grew so hot that she feared steam would rise from them. Carefully peering upward past her snowman hat, she fixed her gaze on Vlad's face. He appeared as calm and imperious as ever. Her heart rate slowed. If he was going to carry on as if nothing had happened, she would, too. The blood slowly drained from her cheeks until they merely felt a tad warm.

They went into Roanoke Hall and down the corridor to the dean's office. Dean Moth, a short, stocky woman with a shock of ear-length white hair, sat behind her desk. Even seated, she had an air of brisk authority. Vlad led Rachel before the desk, still clasping her hand.

The dean looked at him slightly suspiciously, but after reading the letter from Rachel's mother, she gave permission for Mr. Von Dread to escort Miss Griffin home. The suspicion of the dean pleased Rachel. She enjoyed speculating about what Dean Moth must think of the Prince of Bavaria requesting to escort a random Dare Hall freshman off campus.

The two of them thanked the dean and left. Hand-in-hand, they walked across the snowy lawns, toward the gym, the lily pond, and the tree-lined pathway to the ruined castle. Walking thus, Rachel felt both rather grown up and especially tiny at the same time. She luxuriated in both sensations. She recalled the speech he made back in November about watching the world burn to save Sandra, and, even though she suspected he would not let the world burn, she felt pleased that his devotion to her sister put the two of them in a secret club of people who adored Sandra—a club with the motto: *Sandra uber alles!*

As she opened her mouth to speak, she glanced at the older boy towering above her. In his previous life, Vlad had been a gypsy king who had conquered sixty-five worlds. He did not remember any of this, of course, but Rachel wondered if some subconscious memory of it contributed to his confidence. He strode along beside her, calm and impassive, and yet, the memory of the disdain in his voice, back in September, when he dressed down those whom he claimed had disappointed him, whom he accused of being weak, still loomed large in her mind. Much as she adored him, she lived in quiet terror that he might see through her and finally realize how weak she was. Then he might turn that same disapproving gaze upon her. She closed her mouth again.

Vladimir glanced down at her, asking pleasantly. "Tell me, Miss Griffin, are you looking forward to the ball?"

"Oh, yes!" Rachel declared, her trepidation forgotten. "We've talked of nothing else."

"It is all the ladies of Drake Hall have been discussing, as well,"

Dread stated. "I suspect you are less giddy than some of our freshmen, having previously attended informal dances."

"Perhaps, but I have never been to a masquerade," Rachel replied, adding, "Though my grandmother spoke about them at length."

"The previous Lady Devon? What did she say upon the topic? Did she approve?"

"I don't think she entirely approved of anything." Rachel pressed her lips together. It would be most unlady-like to smirk at her esteemed grandmother.

"As to what she said...." Rachel copied her grandmother's intonation, her voice crisper and more nasal, "'Child, it is wise to be wary at any dance, because even an ordinary ball or a country cotillion can conceal hidden pitfalls. Despite what others may say, however, I tell you from experience that masquerades are an entirely different animal. They are not held in the Fields We Know but rather take place precariously close to the Wood Perilous, where the fairies dwell. Approach a masquerade with the same vigilance you would employ if you suspected yourself to be in the company of a pixie or a phooka. Men are dangerous. Music is dangerous. In combination, they can be deadly, or worse. Be as cautious as a doe and as wise as a serpent.'"

"That is..." Dread paused to help Rachel over a patch of slick ice, "... a most unusual assessment. It differs from my admittedly-limited experience with such festive events, though caution and wisdom are never ill-advised."

Rachel nodded, adding, "I've also read many stories about masquerades, of course."

"Indeed? What occurs in these stories?"

Rachel glanced up at him to see if he was patronizing her, but his expression looked sincere, which made sense once it occurred to her that it was unlikely he had the spare time to read either romances or historical novels.

"Marvelous things. Secrets are uncovered. Friendships are forged."

"Indeed. You seem to have plenty of the first," he mused, "but perhaps you must be ever vigilant searching for fresh secrets if you wish to maintain your reputation for knowing an unexpected number of things, rather as a fisherman must be ever in pursuit of more fish. As to the second, you've been here for nearly six months. Have you not already forged friendships?"

Rachel did not answer immediately. She had friends, or rather she had people whom she thought of as her friends, but, other than Siggy, she was reluctantly beginning to have to admit that they were not really *her* friends. Rather, they were the princess's friends, or Siggy's friends, or Valerie's friends. Except for Nastasia herself, of course, she reminded herself belatedly, and maybe Astrid. She and Astrid could not yet be considered fast friends, as they did not yet spend time together outside of classes, except for during the forced situation of the lockdown.

She thought back over the last few days. Weren't friends supposed to be people with whom she could share her hopes and dreams? Instead, she felt as if she had been thrown into prison with a random bevy of females, and now they had to pull together, whether they liked each other or not, if they wished to escape with their lives.

She did not wish to share any of this with the Prince of Bavaria; however, so she settled for merely replying, "One can never have too many friendships."

"If you say so," he replied mildly in that tone boys used when it was a subject about which they had lost interest.

Rachel glanced around, peering between the snow-dusted shrines in the memorial garden and across the frozen lily pond. Nothing moved except falling snow.

"Is it safe to talk here?" she asked softly. "I have something I need to tell you."

"Relatively safe, Miss Griffin," he glanced down at her, "if we keep our voices low."

Rachel lowered her voice to just above a whisper. "I have learned something else about... the subject we discussed on the ice."

"*Taflu!*" Vlad declared in a deep voice. Holding up his hand in the bull-like gesture, thumb and middle fingers curled, pinky and index finger extended, he put the back of his hand to his mouth and performed the accompanying gesture for the cantrip in the four directions. Then he repeated the whole ceremony around Rachel.

"We are now protected from divination and other methods of supernatural eavesdropping," Vladimir said. "We should be reasonably free to speak. Have you learned more about the supposed Master of the World? I must admit, the idea that the minor kingdom of Magical Australia, a country that the Unwary don't even know exists, is run by the son of the man who gives orders to the Guardian protecting our world is..." he paused, "... disturbing."

"He can make the Guardian change people."

Von Dread halted. "Change... in what way?"

"Their memories. Their whole personalities." Rachel's voice wavered unexpectedly. She swallowed. "To make them... the way he wants them to be."

"Can you give an example?"

"Making family members who would normally sacrifice their lives for each other do things like give up their own child."

"Their child? To what end?"

Rachel stared straight ahead as she spoke, focusing her eyes on inconsequential things, a leafless Japanese maple, a stone bench near the entrance to the tree-lined path. "I don't know. Maybe so he could have a servant with a perfect memory? And then he makes the family forget that it ever happened... forget that they gave away their own daughter."

Von Dread stopped walking, stunned. He stood in the falling snow for some time, saying nothing. Finally, he spoke, but Rachel felt he was not really addressing her. "Is he thinking it is a kindness to make a man forget his daughter? What is he doing?"

Dread turned and regarded her closely. "This 'Master of the World' shall not change who I am. I cannot have someone altering my thoughts. It is a terrible thing and should be used only on criminals or the Unwary. And even then, only in the most dire circumstances."

Rachel nodded, but her thoughts lingered on the word "Unwary." The Wise thought nothing of changing the memory of the Unwary, but was that not exactly what had happened to her family? They—everyone in her whole world—were Unwary compared to the Master of the World. Rachel shifted uncomfortably. Like Nastasia, she was beginning to seriously question whether memory-altering magic should be used on anyone, ever.

Vladimir began walking again. Rachel hurried to keep up. Presently, she said, "She is going to come here. My lost sister, I mean. I may need your help. I want to get her back… but I don't want to do the wrong thing and cause something terrible to happen. I need help unraveling what the situation really is…." Her voice had begun to shake.

Vladimir pressed her hand comfortingly. "As I said last time we spoke on this subject, he is a powerful unknown. He has control over our lives, and we know almost nothing about him. Yet, you have my word. My people shall not be idle. We will avoid open war with this Master, if such is possible—especially as we do not yet know the extent of his powers. But he shall prove reasonable, or, ultimately, we will deal with him. He shall do your family no more harm."

Rachel gave a simple brisk nod. Outside her, the day was unusually cold. Inside, however, she felt as warm if she were standing beside a roaring hearth. Vlad wanted to defend her, to help undo the harm to her family. Between him and Sigfried—who she knew would be on her side—she felt as if she were part of a brave team ready to battle against a terrible wrong. She could not imagine anything more wonderful.

Beside her, Von Dread continued, "If you hear that he will be in our world, let me know. I will try to insert Jenny into his life. She may be able to finagle her way into the confidences of a king. Knowing *where* he will be would be helpful as well."

Rachel's eyes widened, impressed with upperclassman Jenny Dare, if Von Dread thought her capable of accomplishing such a thing. At the same time, she felt dubious that a schoolgirl, even an impressive one, could make headway against such a man.

"I will tell you if I learn anything," Rachel promised earnestly.

"Be careful, Miss Griffin," Dread advised kindly. "Don't needlessly endanger yourself. This will be a very delicate situation at best. I'm hoping it doesn't end with us all thinking we're plumbers living in southern Greece."

In spite of the gravity of the situation, Rachel could not help giggling. She covered her mouth with her free hand, but it did not keep more giggles from escaping.

"The same goes for you, F.B.," she said gravely, a little thrill shooting through her when she used the nickname. "As Gaius said, we need you."

Once on the docks, Vlad tucked her arm through his, and the world turned into brilliant white light. When the light faded, they had jumped to the west bank of the Hudson where they stood on the shore in a small copse of trees between the river and the railway. Taking her by the hand again, Von Dread led her to the small stone cottage that served as the Roanoke Glass Hall.

Pulling off glove and mitten, they laid their bare hands against the blue-tinted travel glasses and stepped through to New York, London, and then Exeter. In Exeter, a smaller walking glass led to the Gryphon's Nest Pub in Gryphon-on-Dart, the town upon the Duke of Devon's estate. To the right, a door bore the ducal crest. Rachel touched her family crest. The door swung open. Behind it was a small closet with a second blue-tinted walking glass.

"This is only for the family's use," she explained, as they pulled off gloves and mittens again and put their palms on the bluish glass. The mirror gave way beneath their fingertips like water. "The door with the ducal crest only opens to family members."

"Would the spell that guards it be a way of testing to see if the young woman who comes at the Raven's behest is actually your sister?" asked Vlad.

"I don't know," Rachel replied, intrigued. "I am not sure if it is keyed to each of us individually, or if it responds to anyone who is of our family's line."

Vlad gave the ducal crest a final glance. "It might make an interesting test."

Chapter Four:
Snowdolls

They stepped out into another, larger closet. Rachel opened the door, which led into a hallway paved with flagstones. As they walked toward the front door at the end of the hall, they passed an arch to their left that opened into a hexagonal chamber.

The room was a life-sized dollhouse. The child-sized furniture was lavender and white, as were the play appliances lining the walls: a stove that baked real muffins, a toy refrigerator, washer and dryer, and other mundane devices, many unknown to Rachel. Around the outside, taped to the angled stone walls, hung pastel hand-drawn sketches of fairies. Each cute, winged, pixie girl in her gauzy, handkerchief-hemline gown had been drawn to express a single clear emotion: clenched fists and red face for anger, bowed head and sorrowful pout for sadness, cheerful grin and upraised hands for joy, and so on.

In the center of the room, dolls sat on heart-backed chairs, positioned around a little lavender table: a baby doll, a Sasha doll, several Witch Babies brand dolls that Laurel had turned into little Goths, and three child-sized dolls that looked like pixies. Painted wooden food lay atop violet plates next to a tiny porcelain tea service. Everything looked a bit dusty.

Rachel headed for the front door, walking by an enormous hearth on her right, but Vladimir paused and looked around the dollhouse.

"Where are we?" he frowned.

"The gatehouse," she said. "We use it as our glass hall."

"It looks…."

"Like an Unwary room? The gatehouse is the only place on the estate where electricity works," explained Rachel. "It was Sandra and Laurel's playhouse. Some of these toys belonged to Mummy and Aunt Melissa, when *they* were children. Laurel lost interest, but Sandra still loves all those Unwary things. She has a study upstairs where she listens to Unwary music and does other Unwary things—or she did, before she began working for the Wisecraft *as a spy!*"

The idea that Sandra, who had only graduated from Roanoke last year, was already an Agent, an undercover one at that—when it took most candidates years just to be accepted into the Wisecraft—still amazed her. But it did not surprise her, especially when she stood right here, her gaze resting on the fairy sketches.

"So this is where Sandra spent her childhood?" Vlad regarded the chamber with interest. He walked around, his hands clasped behind his back, stooping to examine each miniature lavender appliance. "Who drew the sketches?"

"My Aunt Melissa," said Rachel. "My mother's sister."

"They represent a considerable outlay of time. Your aunt has a great love of fairies."

"Um... not exactly," Rachel murmured very softly.

"Why was this Sandra and Laurel's playhouse and not yours?"

"Grandmother forbade Peter and me from playing here," Rachel said airily, as she headed for the front door. "She felt it was a bad influence."

"What toys did she consider a good influence?" Von Dread raised an eyebrow.

Rachel shrugged. "The ordinary playthings of the Wise—toy brooms, play alchemy sets, snowdolls, plushy pegasi with gems for eyes that could fly and play music."

"Snowdolls?"

"Conjured toys that only last a day—a little like snowmen."

"Ah." He nodded. "We call them *Verschwinders*—vanishers. They are rare in Bavaria because we have few conjurers, but there are conjurers among the Romani, my mother's people. I still recall a *Verschwinder* that my Uncle Stefano made for me, shortly before his untimely demise. It was a huge black swan, large enough to fly me through the sky. It could speak and defend me. I was young enough that I did not realize until the next morning that... but that is of no concern," Von Dread finished mildly, returning his attention to the tiny oven before him.

Rachel opened the front door and stepped out under the arch of the gatehouse, where it spanned the gravel drive. To one side, great oaks lined the way that headed out toward the main road. To the other side, the drive ran through the formal gardens to the mansion. Behind her, Von Dread tarried within. Standing in the midst of the playhouse in his long black coat with its fur-lined hood, he looked imposing and impossibly out of place. Rachel suppressed a grin.

Looking back at the living dollhouse, she finally understood a mystery that had puzzled her for her whole life: how her older sister Sandra had come to fall in love with something so alien as the ways of those who lived without magic. The answer had been right here all along—in the living dollhouse that their mother had designed for her daughters.

Rachel and Peter had grown up with only the playthings of the Wise, the things the children of sorcerers had played with for generations. But that was because their grandmother had put her foot down and insisted that the future duke be given a proper upbringing. What had not been clear to Rachel before was: why had Grandmother insisted?

Now, she understood. Their mother, coming to this strange new life after having grown up among the Unwary, had decorated a playhouse for her first two children and filled it with things that were familiar to her from her own childhood. Sandra had spent her early years happily playing with mundane appliances, baking muffins, and doing other things that Unwary children do. Somewhere along the way, Grandmother must have realized that Sandra was starting to prefer the mundane ways to the Wise ones.

Rachel thought of Sandra's flat in London, where her sister lived among the Unwary with electricity and refrigerators. What would have happened to Gryphon Park if Peter, the heir to the dukedom, had decided that he, too, wanted to live that way? With an odd jolt, Rachel realized for the first time that, at least to a small degree, her grandmother might have been in the right.

As she waited for Vladimir to join her, Rachel wondered how Sandra would feel about leaving her beloved Unwary world to marry the prince of a Country of the Wise. Would it be painful? Or did she love Vlad so much that it would not matter? And, what if it were too painful? Might Vlad need to find a different bride? Perhaps one who loved the ways of the Wise and would give almost anything to stay in the world of aristocratic sorcerers and old castles? Blushing, she shoved aside the disloyal thought.

The gravel drive led through snowy lawns and formal gardens filled with topiary figures. Green foxes, rabbits, hounds at chase, deer, dragons, centaurs, and even leafy birds that looked to be in flight all peeked out from among the manicured landscaping. Every fifty feet, yew trees on either side of the drive had been clipped into the shapes of gryphons. Snow crowned some of these magnificent green beasts with little white caps.

To the left, the landscaping opened onto snow-covered moors that stretched away over rolling hills, spotted here and there with wild ponies. Farther away, Gryphon Tor rose above the moors. The ruins of the family's original Saxon castle still loomed upon its peak.

Dread paused, taking in the view. "I had not realized you lived so close to the moors."

"Technically, this is Dartmoor National Park," Rachel replied, adding with a quick half-smile, "But yes, we do. It is part of who we are. Our family has caught phookas and ponies on the moors for millennia."

Ahead, a moat circled the mansion. Once, when only the Old Castle had stood here, it had been a real moat. Now the drawbridge had been replaced by a stone platform some hundred feet wide—with gardens planted to either side of the carriage drive. Handsome stone gryphons flanked the bridge, as if guarding the way.

A short lawn separated the moat from Gryphon Park Manor. The august and impressive main wing of the manor house greeted their view. Its roof was a wonder of narrow turrets and cupolas designed by the same architect who had built Dare Hall. To the right rose the Old Castle of which the modern hall was an extension, the pale stone of its walls half-covered in ivy. Four towers rose above the castle's crenellated roof. The top room in the tallest of these housed Rachel's favorite place at Gryphon Park, her grandfather's library.

They approached the house, gravel crunching underfoot. As they neared the bridge, Von Dread paused and examined the manor. "An impressive edifice."

"Thank you," Rachel acknowledged the compliment with a demi-curtsy, holding up her school robes like skirts. "It's one of the largest private residences in the world. But, of course, most of that is because there is so much extra space inside. Still, the exterior is quite sizable. There is another wing behind the Old Castle." She pointed to the north.

Vlad resumed walking and took her hand again. He had not replaced his gauntlet after passing through the glasses; neither had she put on her mitten. The touch of his bare skin sent tremors of fire shooting up her arm and throughout her entire body. She wanted him to continue holding her hand forever.

"Significantly larger within, you say?" Vlad asked. "Doesn't kenomancy become more difficult the larger the container? Your family's estate must be worth a king's ransom."

"My great-great-great-grandfather, Uther Griffin, Seventh Duke of Devon, was a kenomancer," replied Rachel. "He built the main hall in the seventeen eighties. The seventh duke was quite an interesting character. Apparently, adding new rooms was his hobby. He's the only duke not buried in the family graveyard. It's said he was carried off by fairies."

"And he was never found?"

"Laurel says he did not want to be found, because his wife was a harridan. But Laurel is routinely unreliable. She probably made that up whole cloth."

"I look forward to viewing the interior."

Tennyson, the family's butler, met them at the door. He was tall and sparse, dressed meticulously in a traditional butler's uniform: black morning coat, gray vest, gray striped trousers. He bowed to the visitors. "Lady Rachel, splendid to see you, and Prince Von Dread, an honor."

Von Dread nodded regally. Rachel noted that their butler had picked up from her parents the Roanoke Academy tradition of calling princes by their last names, something Rachel was fairly certain was not usually done in the greater world.

"Lady Rachel, your parents have been hoping you would come. They will be thrilled to hear that you have arrived, I have no doubt. They are in their suites. Will the two of you wait in the Red and Gold

Drawing Room? The Green? The Oriental? The Musical? The Paisley?"

Rachel glanced up at Vlad uncertainly. She had not intended to drag him along while she spoke to her parents. "We have a plethora of drawing rooms. If there is a particular color you would prefer to wait in, F.B., don't hesitate to ask."

"Any drawing room you pick will suit me nicely," he replied mildly.

Tennyson stood beside them, waiting alertly. Ordinarily, he was relaxed and friendly. At the moment, however, he hovered with attentive formality. Rachel puzzled over this until it occurred to her that while she—whose roommate was a princess—did not think traveling with a prince was particularly noteworthy, to Tennyson, having royalty in the house might be a novelty.

Amused, she wondered if it would impress the old family servant if she dismissed Vladimir with cavalier disregard, banishing him to some unused sitting room. That smacked of showing off, however, a behavior beneath the dignity of a lady of quality. Besides, she knew what would happen if she abandoned him. Dread would sit stoically as a parade of footmen and maids attempted to present him with an endless choice of refreshments. It would be better to take him with her; her parents would not stand on ceremony.

Rachel gave the old butler a fond smile. "Why don't you announce us both, Tennyson? Vlad and I can find our own way to the Red and Gold."

Tennyson bowed. "As you wish."

The butler took their coats and departed. Rachel still wore her black academic robes, but Vlad was dressed in dark traveling clothing cut in the Bavarian style, with shoulder braiding and a tuxedo collar. Rachel quickly averted her eyes. There was something about seeing the boys she admired in their street clothes that always seemed mildly improper to her, as if she had come upon them in their pajamas. The fact that she *had* once seen Dread in his pajamas did not help. She thrust that thought aside and set off for the Red and Gold Drawing Room.

They walked through the ornate halls, past marble statues, painted ceilings, and sweeping staircases, Von Dread pausing here or there to examine the décor. Rachel wished that she had thought to keep their coats, as the long halls were chilly. When they reached the drawing room, however, it proved toasty warm.

The Red and Gold was a large chamber carpeted in ornate crimson and gold. The heavy oak furniture was upholstered in dark red velvet. A gilded wrought-iron grate guarded a medium-sized fireplace, behind which a young salamander cavorted, scenting the air with cinnamon. Paintings of Griffin ancestors hung on the walls, men in bright hunting garb and women in wide, pastel gowns—including one of Uther Griffin's eldest son, Dinadan, the eighth duke.

Between these paintings, set against the vermilion damask wallpaper, were mirrors in which the gilt of the molded baroque ceiling was reflected. Over by the windows, scarlet curtains were held back by gold tasseled sashes. Outside, a wrought-iron arbor stood amidst a leafless rose garden. Beyond that was the moat, the water frozen now, with two bridges, one wood, one stone, allowing access to the lawn beyond. To the right of the stone bridge, snow covered the backs of the topiary elephants and the head of the winged horse, its yew wings still visible, bright green against the white of the snow. Beyond, a herd of white roe deer wandered across the snow-covered lawns between the house and the walls of the hedge maze.

To her infinite regret, Dread released her hand, examining the portraits and the outside vista. Rachel watched him, entranced. Or rather, she glanced at him obliquely and then thought back, remembering, so that she could study his face without staring. He was impossibly handsome, standing with his hands clasped behind his back. Even with her dissembling skills, it took significant effort not to sigh.

There was something tremendously intimate about being alone with him, as if they were truly friends. She recalled the story he had told in the gatehouse about the black swan and bit her lip, imagining Little Vlad jumping out of bed the next morning, eager to play with his new swan friend, only to discover that snowdolls lived but a single day. If her heart had not been captured by him already, she would have lost it, here and now, to that tiny sad Bavarian prince.

"Quite impressive," he stated at last. "The décor and furnishings are of comparable age and quality to my home, though Gryphon Park —or the small portion I have seen of it, at least—is brighter and airier than Svartschwanstein Castle."

"My family has lived on this estate for over a thousand years," Rachel replied proudly. "We have had time to collect many fine things."

"I notice furniture from as far back as the Empire. And this table," he gestured at a delicate end table with a crystal knob on the desk drawer, "is a Louis the Thirteenth. It has a twin in the audience chamber in Svartschwanstein. I will have my father send it to yours."

Rachel's voice rose with surprise. "That's very kind of you."

The doors opened, and Tennyson announced The Duke and Duchess of Devon.

Ambrose Griffin, the eleventh Duke of Devon, was an extraordinarily tall and handsome man. Calm and imperturbable, he regarded his diminutive daughter with a twinkle in his eye. Walking over to her, he bent down and lifted her up, giving her a warm hug. Rachel threw her arms around him in return.

Her father's hands moved along the side of her ribs and waist, as if he could not believe how thin she was. He frowned. Too late, Rachel remembered that, before Tuesday, she had hardly eaten. It seemed like a dream now, that time before she talked with Vlad on the ice, when she had been too distraught to eat. Her father did not say anything. Perhaps, he thought it was a growth spurt. She was probably taller than he had recalled her as being, too, since his memory had been set back a few years.

She had thought that it was the loss of her father's memory that had upset her so much. While conversing with Vlad, she had realized it was not that. Rather, she was tremendously angry at Gaius. Only, it was not Gaius, per se, that had been causing her to feel so despondent, but rather the fact that her "most important person" had been less than supportive. She had known, when she chose Gaius as the person to whom she gave her greatest allegiance, that picking a teenage boy as the keel of her soul was a bad idea. He was well meaning, but he was just a boy. Once she realized this, she had forgiven Gaius easily—for *nearly* everything—but, much as she adored him as her boyfriend, she had felt that she could no longer keep him as her "most important person."

That title now belonged to the Raven.

She hugged her father for longer than was perhaps socially polite. She had not seen him since her disastrous visit to his office in Old Scotland Yard—after which he had lost his memory, and the Raven had, apparently, restored him to closer to what he had originally been, before the Master of the World had forced the Raven to change him, decades ago. Rachel peered at him carefully and was relieved to see that he looked exactly like the father she remembered.

Her mother still stood in the doorway. Ellen Griffin was as tiny as her husband was tall. Straight dark hair fell around a pixie-like face with up-tilted eyes betraying her Korean ancestry. She was a vision of loveliness in a soft, blue-ribbed turtleneck and a skirt of Black Watch that complemented her beauty and extraordinary shapeliness. Ordinarily, a gentle merriment danced across her face, but now she appeared as emotionless as a China doll. Knowing her mother as she did, alarm bells began to ring in Rachel's mind.

Like Rachel herself, her mother looked utterly calm only when hiding some strong emotion. Rachel's heart thumped oddly in her chest. Was Father worse than she had been led to believe?

Von Dread stood a short distance away, patiently waiting to be introduced.

Back on her feet, Rachel gestured toward him and announced properly, "Mummy, Father, this is Mr. Von Dread, a friend who agreed to accompany me here. Vlad, these are my parents, Lord and Lady Devon."

Clicking his boot heels together, Vlad inclined his head, performing a greeting bow in the very proper style of his father's Bavarian court.

The duchess glided into the room to stand beside her husband. She spoke unusually stiffly, "Thank you for bringing our daughter to visit us, Your Royal Highness. I am sorry we do not have a more fitting welcome for you."

Beside her, her husband bowed to the Prince of Bavaria. "Your Royal Highness, welcome to Gryphon Park. As my wife said, we apologize for the less than appropriate welcome."

Vlad looked slightly uncomfortable.

Rachel frowned, gazing at her parents through narrowed eyes. *Your Royal Highness?* Not even just *Your Highness?* Her parents knew that no one stood on ceremony at Roanoke. Out here in the real world, they dealt with nobility on a regular basis, and she had seen her father chat easily with the King of Magical Australia. Why treat the Bavarian royal family so differently?

Oh. Of course. Her father *despised* the King of Bavaria, whom he believed to be a tyrant and a danger to the stability of the World of the Wise. He did not know that Vladimir was different from his father, or rather, he did not remember. In her eagerness to let her father know that the King of Bavaria's son was not a young tyrant in the making, as Vlad had once put it, Rachel had written her father long letters during the school year, telling him all that Vlad had done to protect her, including: giving her the black bracelet; the business card that would bring help if she crushed it; and even the time he offered to fight the Agents to protect her. With a pang of sorrow, she now realized that her father had forgotten those letters, along with everything else from the last few years of his life.

Rachel found this notion tremendously disturbing. Just thinking about forgetting made her feel light-headed. She wished she could sit down.

Meanwhile, Von Dread spoke gravely. "There is no need to apologize. The decision to accompany your daughter was a last-minute one. It was my pleasure to bring her."

A warm flush spread through Rachel. She kept her face calm, but, inside, her spirits danced like tipsy butterflies. Just being near Vlad was intoxicating. Sadly, this did not help her feel less dizzy.

Glancing at her mother quelled her giddiness. She had seen her mother at formal affairs, particularly while her grandparents still lived. The duchess had always been graceful and composed. Now she seemed almost rigid. Rachel glanced sideways at her father. He seemed his normal self, relaxed and happy to see her.

Rachel moved to her mother's side. "Mummy, don't be so cold to him," she hissed under her breath. "He's a friend!"

Her mother's demeanor did not change. "Excuse me. I must speak to the servants about refreshments."

Lady Devon turned and departed, leaving Rachel staring after her in hurt surprise. She frowned, wondering why her mother did not use the bell pull to call a servant. Why did she have to go herself? Grandmother would have severely disapproved.

The duke gestured for the young prince to take a seat on one of two crimson divans that stood across from each other, separated by an antique coffee table. Vlad did so, sitting with his back to the window—though he could still see the area behind him in the gold-speckled mirrors. Rachel speculated that Dread probably would have liked to sit facing the windows, the most likely direction by which danger might approach, but that he had ceded such a position to her father, figuring that the seat of best advantage should go to the master of the house.

Enough of that; this was the moment for which she had come. Rachel asked Vladimir to please excuse her and the duke for a moment. Then, she took her father by the hand and led him to an armchair near the windows. Looking curious, he sat down.

Eager to attempt the idea she had come home to try, Rachel climbed onto her father's lap. Ambrose Griffin smiled, startled but delighted.

"Aren't you worried about our, er, guest?" her father asked softly, indicating with his head the sofa where the prince sat.

Rachel shook her head. "He just came to bring me here so I could see you and see for myself that you were well. He's not expecting us to entertain him. He said so. Besides, we can go talk to him in just a moment."

Her father nodded. "I am so glad you came, Rachel," he said gently. "You must excuse me, sweetie, if I don't seem to remember things you think I should know—such as what you wrote in the many wonderful letters you sent me. I have them in my pile to get to, but with two years of correspondence to reread, I am still back about a year and a half ago. I'll get to them, though."

"That's all right. They'll be there," Rachel replied, wondering if he might react differently this time to the detailed reports she had sent him back in September.

Reaching up, she pulled his face toward her, smiling into his eyes. Then pressing the side of her head—where the silver tattoo was—against her father's head, she willed it to do something: affect him, shine silvery light, anything.

She peeked sideways, glancing at her father's face. Nothing had changed. Did she need to move more of her hair? Press the silvery Rune directly against his skin?

Burying her face against his shoulder, she murmured under her breath, "Jariel, can you help me use my memory Rune to heal my father?"

The Raven's voice spoke in her ear, over the black bracelet. "I am sorry, Rachel Griffin. I cannot extend the power of the glyph. It is attuned to you alone."

"Oh." She swallowed. She should have asked him before making the trip, though the chances that he would have answered her then were small. "Thank you, anyway."

Rachel sighed. She had known it was a long shot, but she still felt disappointed that her plan had not worked. She should return to Roanoke immediately, as she had already taken enough of Vlad's time. Yet it was so nice to sit with her father, seeing for herself that he looked and spoke as she remembered him. She had not realized how much she missed him.

Misinterpreting her sigh, her father squeezed her more tightly, rocking her back and forth as he rubbed her back in a comforting manner. Rachel gave her father one last hug and slid off his lap.

The two of them returned to the divans and sat down together across from Von Dread. Her father then asked her a series of questions: about her classes, her job assisting the P.E. tutor, how she was getting along with her roommates, and how her cat was doing. Rachel answered as best she could, leaving out the truth about Mistletoe. If her family caught whiff of the fact that Mistletoe was not a real familiar, they would insist she pick another. She felt too loyal to her beloved cat to bear such a thing.

She glanced at the door, wishing her mother would come back, but there was no sign of her. With another sigh, Rachel acknowledged that it was time for her to go.

Chapter Five:
What Are Your Intentions?

Just as Rachel began to open her mouth to say goodbye, her father addressed their guest. "Prince Von Dread, you're a junior at the college?"

"I am, sir."

Rachel, who had been starting to rise, paused. She did not want to impose on Vlad, but if she did not interrupt, maybe her father would discover for himself what a fine and upright young man the Prince of Bavaria was. She took her place demurely on the red velvet beside him.

"And you are studying?" asked Ambrose Griffin.

"Thaumaturgy and warding, with minors in augury, obscuration, alchemy, and canticle."

"Ambitious," observed her father.

Not as ambitious as Sandra, Rachel thought smugly. Her oldest sister—well, the one everyone else believed to be the eldest—had majored in enchantment, conjuring, alchemy, canticle, and warding. Vlad would have two rings of mastery to Sandra's five. It was no wonder Von Dread was impressed with her sister and wanted to make Sandra his queen. The Lady Sandra Griffin was the most accomplished sorceress of her generation.

The duke continued, "Do you have any plans yet for after graduation? Will you compete in the Olympics again? Go into your father's state department?"

Von Dread met Lord Devon's gaze evenly. "I was... hoping to arrange for marriage."

Rachel's heart flip-flopped and then began to beat more rapidly. She felt like a tightrope walker balancing above the pit of total mortification. On one hand, it thrilled her that Vlad's first desire, upon graduating, was to marry Sandra. Very few boys held marriage to be so important. That he held such an old-fashioned goal made Rachel's heart swell with pride and approval. Of course, Vladimir was a prince with a duty to secure an heir.

Countering her delight, however, was a growing sense of anxious embarrassment. What if Father asked the wrong question? Would Vlad blame her? What if the prince decided never to speak to her again? Horrified, she sat rooted to her seat, her eyes wide.

Her father nodded in approval. "Is there a particular princess you have in mind?"

Von Dread turned slightly red in the face. Despite her discomfort, Rachel had to avert her eyes and press her lips together to keep from smiling. He looked so adorable.

The door to the Red and Gold Drawing Room opened, and the Duchess of Devon returned, accompanied by a footman who carried a silver tray containing their very best china tea service, which he placed on the coffee table. Rachel's mother poured out for the prince, who thanked her, and then for the duke, and finally for Rachel. The footman followed behind her, offering each of them cream and sugar cubes. Once tea was served and the footman had departed, Ellen Griffin sat down beside her husband, on the other side from Rachel and gazed at Vladimir calmly—too calmly. Rachel recognized that look. A chill traveled up her spine. *Something was very wrong.*

The duke said, "I was just asking His Royal Highness if there was a princess in his future."

"Really?" Ellen Griffin gazed at Dread expectantly, her back as straight as a fire iron. "I am eager to hear the answer to this."

The prince turned a degree redder. Rachel would have found the cool, impervious prince blushing over Sandra even more adorable, were she herself not so acutely embarrassed. This was a hundred times worse than Father's good-natured questions. Hadn't Mother promised to *help* Sandra convince Father to accept the prince's suit? *Was it her deliberate goal to make her daughter as uncomfortable as humanly possible?*

Rachel could sit still no longer. Jumping up, she circled behind the divan and leaned over next to her mother. Very softly, she whispered in her mother's ear. "Mummy, that's not very polite. Putting him on the spot like this. Maybe we should let him talk to Daddy, alone."

Her mother ignored her, continuing to watch their guest expectantly. Rachel sighed and returned to her seat beside her father.

Vlad cleared his throat. "I have no plans to marry royalty at this time."

The duke nodded. "It must be hard to choose, with such a small group of young ladies."

Vlad gave a terse nod.

"Your Royal Highness." The duchess leaned forward. The intensity blazing in her eyes at odds with her calm demeanor. "What are your intentions towards *my daughter?*"

Ambrose Griffin's eyebrows shot up so rapidly that it was a wonder they did not fly off his face. He did not look amused in the least. He glanced at Rachel and then back to Von Dread. The very notion that her father might think a romantic understanding existed between herself and Vladimir sent shivers of joy throughout Rachel's entire body. She knew that was *not* the appropriate reaction, but she could not help it.

Vlad, meanwhile, threw up his hands. "I have no intentions toward R—"

Her mother cut him off. "I do not mean Rachel."

The duke instantly looked less annoyed. He leaned forward, his expression one of extreme curiosity. Rachel felt oddly deflated. She smothered a sigh.

"Lord and Lady Devon." Von Dread sat even straighter, if such a thing were possible. "I intend to marry your daughter Sandra. She has not, as of yet, given me permission to address you, so I had not previously done so. I wanted this to happen differently, but I will not lie or mislead you. I love your daughter, and I intend that she be my wife."

Shivers of a different sort spread through Rachel. Vladimir held himself so regally as he spoke of his love for Sandra that she could not help rooting for them. She examined her parents' faces, searching for a sign that they recognized what an amazing catch Sandra had made. The duke looked quite surprised, but he did not look angry. Her mother, however, was still dangerously calm. Little cues— the straightness of her back, the rigidity of her pinky—indicated that Ellen Griffin was furious.

The diminutive duchess spoke with icy grace. "I think it inappropriate, Your Royal Highness, that you courted our daughter without first obtaining our permission. For how many years has this behavior go on?"

What? Rachel sucked in her breath. *This was not why she had brought Vlad here!* Her mother was being uncharacteristically unfair. How could parents send their children to school and not expect them to fall in love? The children were eating and attending classes *in the same building.* It was not as if Dread had needed to travel in order to "court" Sandra.

Watching her parents grill this young man, whose friendship she so valued, was more than she could bear. She rose from the couch and darted away, crossing to the windows. Resting her palm against the cold pane, she pressed her forehead against the glass.

Her fingers tracing her black bracelet, she whispered, *"Vlad, should I stop them?"*

Pinned beneath the gaze of both her parents, Von Dread did not reply. She watched out of the corner of her eyes, but he did not so much as twitch his head. He continued to answer their questions with princely reserve. All very well for him, Rachel thought. She herself felt too embarrassed to breathe. She pulled the armchair she and her father had used so that it faced the window and hid her from the others. Then, tucking her knees under her, she covered her head with both arms, pressing her wrists against her ears. *Could people die of embarrassment?*

Her heart was beating so loudly, she feared she was about to find out. First Father and Jariel, now Mummy and Vlad—must her parents go out of their way to embarrass all the powerful people who befriended her? Perhaps her father noted her distress. As Rachel peeked through her fingers while peering back at the others, she saw him give his wife a stern glance.

"You will have to excuse us, sir," he said to Vlad. "I need to speak to my wife."

Rising, Ambrose Griffin offered his arm to his duchess, who rose stiffly and departed from the room without him. Crossing to where Rachel still sat by the window, the duke leaned over and said, "Dear, could you please entertain our guest while I speak with your mother?"

Rachel nodded wordlessly, afraid to speak lest her voice shake with anger.

The duke departed, leaving his daughter alone with the prince. Dread waited calmly until the door had entirely closed behind the duke. Then, he sighed, running a hand through his dark hair, reddish highlights visible where the sun struck it.

Rachel tried to rise, but her legs were trembling. Vlad was going to be furious at her for leading him into this trap. *Oh, she never would have asked him to accompany her had she known!*

Rachel levered herself up from her chair and ran to his side. "F.B., I'm so.... I'm so sorry!"

Vladimir Von Dread leaned back on the divan, crossing his arms. Then, he chuckled. Rachel gawked at him. He was even more devastatingly attractive when he laughed. The force of it hit her like a punch to the solar plexus. For a moment, she could say nothing at all.

"Why are you sorry, Miss Griffin?" Vlad asked with a laugh, unaware of all this. "This is going far better than I expected. I was extremely inappropriate in my behavior toward your sister. Of course, I should have spoken to your parents first. Or had my father speak to them. I feared your father would throw me into a burning hearth or feed me to your hounds. Instead...." He spread his hands and shrugged.

Okay. That was not what she had expected either. Rachel struggled to regain her composure. After a moment, her legs grew steadier, and she found she could breathe.

"As long as you aren't angry," she murmured, tremendously relieved. "I wanted you to have more time before.... I don't even know what my father remembers."

She dropped down onto the couch beside him. Gazing directly into his eyes, she explained, "I asked you to bring me here because I had this idea about how I could help my father regain his memory—I thought it was tremendously clever—but," she sighed and folded her hands in her lap, "it didn't work."

"Such is the way of life, Miss Griffin, but you must keep trying. Although we should, perhaps, wait a bit. We do not want to draw attention to your father. If this Master of the World were to find out that the duke has been cured, he'd most likely look into it. Or, at least, I would."

"Oh. Good point," she whispered, unnerved. "The Raven told me that Father's more like his real self than he's been in years, but he doesn't seem very different from the old him. Maybe it's just that what he knows has changed. "Besides," she admitted with chagrin, "I am out of ideas."

"You will think of something, Miss Griffin," Vladimir laid a warm and comforting hand upon hers. "You're surprisingly resourceful."

When her parents did not return right away, Rachel considered heading back to school. She had no desire to speak with her mother. She considered storming out; however, she remembered the Comfort Lion's lesson in forgiving. If she left now, she would remain angry. Her thoughts would be taken up with what she might have said or hoped to say next time. Also, the Lion had promised to give her a present if she forgave others. Better to speak with her parents now. Perhaps she could find a way to forgive them for their treatment of her guest.

"Please wait here, Vlad," she rose. "The bell pull is beside the door. Do not hesitate to ring for a servant should you need anything."

"Do as you must," Vlad replied with a regal nod. "My needs are met."

Leaving the drawing room, Rachel set out to find her parents. The house was enormous, but it was likely they had not gone far. She tried the Blue Salon first, as it was both nearby and one of their favorite haunts. Sure enough, both her parents were present, seated together on a deep blue sofa surrounded by royal blue curtains and navy damask wallpaper, upon which hung five long wall hangings—paint on silk—one across from each of the wide, arched windows.

Stepping into the room, Rachel glared at her parents. It had been years since she had expressed any sort of temper—not counting her fateful visit to her father's office. She had been a very dutiful child, but now anger combined with embarrassment transformed into fury.

She cried out, "Father, Mummy, h-how could you do this to me?"

Ambrose Griffin looked up, his keen gaze filled with fondness. "Do... what, again?"

"Question Vlad like that! He's our guest!"

The duke raised an eyebrow but not his voice. "If the young man wishes to marry my Sandra, he had best be prepared to answer a few questions."

That his point was valid did not make her less angry. Rachel stomped forward. "He took time off from his very busy schedule to escort me here, and you made him turn red!" she cried with a wild gesture. "He may never have turned that red before. *In his whole life!*"

"A little embarrassment is a small price to pay for my daughter's hand."

Rachel felt her fury faltering. When her father was right, he was right. Embarrassment was a mere trifle if Sandra was the prize. No wonder Dread had laughed.

"True, your mother was short with him, but he has not been as forthcoming with us as he ought to have been." The duke eyed his daughter thoughtfully. "I assume, since you have not acted surprised, that you already knew about the prince and your sister. I am slightly confused—not unusual these days—why you brought him here, if you didn't want him to speak to us."

"Frankly, I forgot about the whole him speaking to you about Sandra thing," Rachel crossed her arms in annoyance. "By which I mean that I wasn't thinking about that matter. Obviously, I didn't *forget*, forget. He's here because I wanted to come see you, and I needed someone who could get me out of the lockdown long enough to speak to the dean."

"You know how we feel about the King of Bavaria, Rachel," her father said. "The man is a tyrant and a bully. When he declared war on Syria thirteen years ago, he not only dropped nuclear warheads on Damascus and Aleppo, he continued attacking with a mixture of mundane and sorcerous weapons until the country was, in his words, 'returned to the sands.' Millions of people died. Millions. The neighboring countries are still complaining about radiation, deadly chemicals, and other horrors. Is that the sort of person you wish your sister allied with?"

"We have at least eight princes in the school," she replied seriously. "We used to have ten—before Remus and Fenris Starkadder were executed by their father, the King of Transylvania." Rachel shivered. "Most of them act like everyone else. Vladimir is entirely different. He's what a prince should be.

"I suppose I don't mind if you give him a hard time," she continued gravely. "Boys do have to climb glass mountains to get princesses, and no one is more worthy than our Sandra—as long as you understand that you couldn't find a better son-in-law." She glanced at her mother, frowning. "Mummy knew, too. She had said she was going to speak to you about it. Maybe she has, and you have forgotten. As to Vlad and Sandra,"—her eyes lit up—"I do know, but only because I saw the look on Sandra's face when she talked about him. Nobody told me."

Rachel thought this last was a very telling point. To her disappointment, her father did not seem bowled over by the fantastic catch his eldest had made.

"The conversation should continue with Sandra present," he said. "I don't want her to think we harassed the poor young man. I will be asking Sandra to bring him by properly."

"Ambrose, please dismiss the Prince," Lady Devon spoke without turning her head. "I am really not up to speaking to him again today."

The duke crossed to his wife and kissed her on the forehead. "You need not fret, Ellen. I'll speak to him. Rachel, dear, why don't you come with me? We'll get you back to school. I think your mother and I both need some rest."

Rachel gazed at her mother. "Could you give me a second to talk to Mummy?"

"Very well," said her father. He paused, looking down at her. "Try not to judge us too harshly, Rachel. Our lives are unusually difficult at the moment."

Chagrined, Rachel nodded. Her remaining fury drained away like water from a tub. The duke smiled fondly and mussed her hair. He turned to depart, then he came back and squatted down in front of his diminutive daughter.

"I don't want you to share this with the other students," her father said, "because the school does not want them to panic, but I think you should be aware, Rachel, that the school's Board of Visitors and Governors, of which I am a member, is considering closing the Roanoke Academy—until the Heer of Dunderberg is captured. Another minor fey-on-campus incident might be swept under the rug, but anything major, and they will send everyone home."

"Oh, no!" Rachel cried. "They can't! At least not before the ball! We've been looking forward to it so!" A sense of panic rose in her chest. If they closed the school, she would not be able to see Gaius or Vlad or any of her friends. How could they save the world if they were not together? "Close for how long? A week? A month? How long will it take to catch the Heer?"

"I don't know, sweetie," the duke replied. "Parents are worried. Some are talking of pulling their children from school. It is wiser for the school to make the choice to shut down for a time than to have too many students withdrawn. They might not come back. Besides, it's a matter of safety."

The duke kissed the top of her head and departed. Rachel stood stock still, shaken. Then she drew a deep breath. She could worry about that later. More immediate issues were before her.

Chapter Six: The Secret of the Fairies

Rachel crossed the room and came to stand beside her mother, kissing her on the cheek.

"I thought you were in favor," she said plaintively. "You told Sandra you'd talk to Father."

Ordinarily, the duchess was the very soul of grace and gentleness, but her mother's eyes were oddly empty. Up close, Rachel could see that her mother was wearing makeup, which was not something she had ever done at home. There were dark lines under her eyes, visible despite the thickly-applied foundation. Rachel's stomach still twisted with fear. *What was wrong?*

The duchess gazed at Rachel as if her daughter were a ghost. She reached out, her fingers barely stroking Rachel's cheek before her arm dropped again. "Are you gone, too? Is that why you're so different?"

"I'm not different," Rachel replied, "just fiercer. Terrible things have happened to me, but I haven't crumbled yet. I've had a few bad days. But don't despair, Mummy! We'll get Daddy's memory back."

Her voice trailed off as the duchess made a soft, sad sound. Perhaps hearing that terrible things had happened to her youngest daughter was not reassuring to her.

"Mum," Rachel asked, lowering her voice, "Did Daddy talk to you between the time when he spoke to me at the Old Scotland Yard and when he lost his memory? Did he warn you that it was going to happen? Did he tell you why?"

Her mother put her finger to her lips. "A little, dear one. You cannot speak about it. If you do, it could happen to you, too. Or to me."

Rachel leaned forward and whispered into her mother's ear. "It can't happen to me. I already have a whole set of fake memories, but they haven't replaced my real ones."

The duchess gasped in relief. Her arms closed around her youngest child, pulling her close. Rachel hugged her back. When her mother finally let go, she gazed at Rachel with great concern, but at least her pixie-pretty face was now animated, rather than blank.

"As long as you will be okay, my child." The duchess's voice was her own again, gentle and caring. Her mother pressed her face against her daughter's hair and murmured absently, "Don't fret, dearest one. This happened last time, too. I will recover. Eventually."

Last time? A chill crept over Rachel. Did some part of her mother still remember Amber? Was that why she was so anxious now? A blinding anger gripped Rachel. *The Master of the World was the cause of all this. Was it wrong to hope that he meet a painful demise?* If Rachel asked her mother about Amber, would she, too, freeze up and forget the thread of the conversation, as her father had?

The thought of her mother forgetting *anything* was tremendously disturbing.

"Mummy?" Rachel's voice trembled, but she could not bring herself to ask.

Climbing onto the blue velvet sofa beside her mother, she leaned against the duchess's shoulder. Her mother in turn rested her cheek on the top of her daughter's head. Rachel sighed, a long, satisfied sigh, and snuggled up against the softness that was her mother. This was more as it should be. As usual, the duchess smelled of gardenias and a touch of lavender.

"Yes, dear?" asked her mother, who had heard her daughter's aborted query. Her voice was not so haunted, but there was still a deep sadness in it that cut Rachel's heart.

She searched for a topic that might cheer her mother, glancing around the Blue Drawing Room as she did so. Her eyes fell upon the five wall hangings draped against the navy damask—lengths of creamy silk set against royal blue silk backings. Upon each, stylized feminine figures had been painted in the ancient Korean style. Each wore a *hanbok*, short jacket and a very wide skirt, and sported one of the unusually large, lumpy hairstyles of ancient Korean tradition.

Ancient Korean artwork usually showed the women with small mouths and very little expression. These works were quite different. They were expressive, as if drawn to represent a particular emotion.

A feeling like electricity spread through Rachel's limbs. She leaned forward, her attention arrested. She had seen these hangings a thousand times, but, only now did she recognize them for what they were. The figures on the wall hangings showed the exact same body positions and expressions as the fairy drawings in the gatehouse. They were a traditional Korean rendition of what her mother and Aunt Melissa called the *five grand poses.*

Rachel gaped, amazed that she had missed this her whole life. What other things might exist in her memory, hidden in plain sight?

The fairy drawings, painstakingly sketched by Aunt Melissa, were a child's primer to the *poses*, both the *five grand poses*—angry, giddy, sorrowful, serene, and fearful—and the *lesser poses*. These were the emotional states that she and Sandra and her mother called The Griffin Girl Secret Techniques, but which were really secrets of the Kim Family. An advanced practitioner could, supposedly, assume any pose at will, not merely the serene pose, which Rachel thought of as her "mask of calm."

"Mummy, where did these hangings come from?" Rachel asked, astonished.

"Your great-grandparents brought them from Korea," the duchess replied. "Legend says that they have been 'in the family since the beginning'—though I don't know what that means."

Gazing at the wall hangings, Rachel recalled being six, standing with Sandra and their mother before a mirror, practicing those same poses. Her mother would tell sad stories, or ghost tales, or funny jokes to make them laugh, and then, suddenly, give the command to assume their mask of calm. Even back then, Sandra could instantly go from weeping to laughing. She could assume any of the grand poses effortlessly.

Aloud, Rachel said, "Sandra mastered all the poses, didn't she?"

"Sandra is especially talented," the duchess agreed, her eyes growing more animated. "She spent summers studying with my aunt. I believe she learned more than even Melissa and I know. That is probably one reason the Wisecraft promoted her so quickly."

Eyes half closed, Rachel recalled Kim Ye Jin—her mother's father's older sister, who was also known by the name Jin Cavendish. Her great-aunt had been a society woman while her husband, a famous diplomat, had lived. Ye Jin's hair was mostly gray now, but her face was still as young as a girl's. She was a spirited and independent woman who still wore gloves and smoked cigarettes in a long black holder, like the women from her youth. Recalling how her great-aunt had both let on very little and seemed to know so much, Rachel had no trouble believing that her mother's aunt was most skilled at the dissembling arts.

That alone had made Ye Jin a superb wife for a diplomat. Thinking back over all she knew of her great-aunt—putting together clues and snippets of conversations heard of the last decade—Rachel realized that Ye Jin shared another of the Kim family gifts—the perfect memory. Rachel, who had given some thought—back in the idyllic days before she discovered that Vlad was in love with Sandra—to how useful it might be to a man of importance to have a wife who could remember absolutely every conversation she had ever heard, thought it was no wonder that Ye Jin's husband had been so successful.

Was that why Sandra was so good at these techniques, because of Ye Jin? Rachel's older sister did not have a faultless memory but that did not seem to slow her down.

The next trick, after dissembling, was to read the emotional states of others from their slightest tells. Having spent much of her childhood with her father's parents, Rachel had only learned a smattering of these advanced techniques. Sandra had spent her time with Mother and Aunt Melissa, and, apparently, with Great-Aunt Jin. She had mastered both dissembling and *kumihotoushi*, the art of reading others. This was what made her such an excellent spy.

"I only truly learned the serene pose," Rachel admitted ruefully. She pointed at the wall hanging with the calm woman, the only one that resembled traditional Korean art.

"You were such a funny little mite." Her mother pressed her cheek against Rachel's. "You were only interested in learning what I tried to teach you if it won you approval from Blaise. What was it you saw in that cantankerous old man? Everyone else was afraid of him, but not my tiny daughter. The sun rose and set for you when he entered or left a room."

Rachel blinked. Her beloved grandfather, Blaise Griffin, the Tenth Duke of Devon, had valued calmness and self-control. He had even had a motto about it. Was that why she had strived so hard to master the mask of calm? Because she wanted to be, as he would have put it: *Calm as a lake in August, and cool as ice.* She had also learned just enough *kumihotoushi* to help her read his slightest expressions—but only his. What other people had been thinking—the tenant farmers, the maids, her parents, her siblings—had remained a mystery to her.

With a sudden start, Rachel realized that there was one other person whose reactions were close enough to those of her grandfather's that she could *sometimes* guess at his thoughts, whether he was pleased or annoyed, even if he gave no overt sign: *Vladimir Von Dread.*

As to what her other friends were thinking, she had no clue. Well, maybe Sigfried. He was pretty obvious. And Gaius was not too hard, though sometimes she could not read him at all. But Joy? Zoë? Nastasia? The princess was the hardest. She hid her emotions the same way Rachel's grandmother had, because she had been taught that doing so was ladylike. Rachel had never learned to read her grandmother, who had been rather a disapproving presence in her life. For the first time, she wished she had tried harder.

In answer to her mother's question, Rachel answered softly, "I loved him because he loved me."

It was the only explanation she had to give.

"Yes." The duchess's lips quirked into just a hint of a real smile. "That he did."

Rachel sat up straight and gazed pleadingly at her mother's face. "Please don't be too hard on Vlad," she begged. "After I got kidnapped, the next time someone tried to take me away from the school, he showed up with his people, instantly, to make sure I was okay. He was going to fight the Agents to protect me—fight Templeton and Scarlett MacDannan! It made me very happy. It was the first time I felt safe since Dr. Mordeau turned into a dragon."

"Trying to show off in front of Sandra's little sister, was he?" The duchess's tone was unusually wry, but her customary sparkle had returned to her eyes.

"Maybe." Rachel frowned, hiding how much that idea hurt.

"Tosh. What else would motivate a nineteen-year-old prince to squire about a freshman child?" the duchess asked, gently brushing Rachel's flyaway hair behind her ear.

"Why would a cantankerous old man befriend a little girl?" countered Rachel.

"You were his granddaughter," Ellen Griffin replied dismissively. "You're not the granddaughter of the Prince of Bavaria. Be realistic, my sweet one. You two can't possibly have much in common."

"But we do!" Rachel countered. She leaned against her mother's shoulder again. "I had already set out to befriend him, even before I found out he was in love with Sandra. I'm not saying that being Sandra's sister hasn't made it easier, but he would have ended up as my friend anyway, eventually."

"W-why?" cried her mother, drawing back so as to look at her daughter. "The son of *the King of Bavaria?* Who will you and Sandra befriend next? Hitler's heir? Stalin's? Aleister Crowley's? What do you and your sister see in that beastly boy?"

"Hitler didn't have an heir," Rachel objected.

Her mother rolled her eyes. "That is not to the point."

Rachel added, "As to Vlad, I like the way he thinks. He reminds me of Grandfather."

Her mother's lips parted slightly. "Ah. Yes, I can see that."

Belatedly, Rachel recalled that, to her mother, a comparison to Grandfather might not be a recommendation.

The duchess drew Rachel in for a last, tight hug. Then she made a low disapproving noise in her throat, her hands moving up and down Rachel's waist, ribs, and back. "Why are you so thin? You were not this thin when you left home after Yule! Don't they feed you at school?"

"I-I haven't been eating." She bit at her lip. "I was upset."

"Ah." Her mother's face softened. "Yes. I... understand that, too."

From the chagrin in the duchess's expression, Rachel wondered if maybe her mother had not been eating properly either.

"And now," Ellen Griffin smiled, "you had better get back to school. It has been a long day already here for us, and I hear you have a masquerade to attend tomorrow!" She laid her cheek against her palm, a dreamy look in her eyes. "I so loved the dances when I was at Roanoke. Strange and wondrous things have been known to happen at a Roanoke masquerade. I am sure you'll have a splendid time! You have what you need for your costume, right? I had Tennyson send everything you requested."

"I have everything I need, thank you," Rachel replied, kissing her mother on the cheek. "And you have a lovely day tomorrow. I hope you can put your troubles aside and enjoy Lunar New Year. Will you be going to see Grandpa Kim?"

"I will, my dearest one. Shall I tell him you send your love?"

"Yes, do!" Rachel suffered a sudden pang of sadness that she would miss the yearly trip to pay their respects to her mother's relatives.

"Goodbye, my dearest," Lady Devon said. "Take care of yourself."

"I will. Goodbye, Mum!"

One last goodbye hug and Rachel ran back to the Red and Gold Drawing Room, where she and Von Dread took their leave of her father. Then she collected their coats from the butler, and they departed.

The two of them traveled back in silence. Rachel wished terribly to take advantage of this private time with Vlad, but she could think of nothing to say. So, she said nothing, except to thank him sincerely when he dropped her back at her dorm.

That afternoon, she wrote a letter, which she gave to one of the proctors to post when they checked on the dorm during dinner.

The letter read:

> *Dear Sandra,*
>
> *I went to see Daddy today. He seems all right, but I didn't get to talk to him very much, because both our parents spent most of my visit grilling Vlad (who had escorted me home). Vlad turned rather red but said afterward that Daddy was much nicer to him than he had expected. Mummy was very cold to him. She did not tell me why.*
>
> *Anyway, Daddy seems to be doing well, but Mummy seemed sad and upset. You should visit her and try to cheer her. Maybe bring her a new hat, from both of us. New hats always cheer people.*
>
> *Love,*
> *Rachel*

Early the next morning, Rachel was awakened from a nightmare by the sound of knocking on their dorm room door. A sleepy Kitten

Fabian climbed out of her bed and went to see who it was. Outside stood Yolanda Debussy, the college resident for the girls' side of Dare Hall. A tall, slender young woman with pale orange hair, Yolanda was neatly attired in the white shirt sleeves, black skirt, and sleeveless robes of the uniform style known as half-academic. Rachel knew that, under the influence of the *Spell of True Recitation*, Yolanda had confessed to kissing an Agent of the Wisecraft named Jack Oliver. Rachel felt that this was wildly romantic.

"Bad news," the upperclassman reported dryly. "Lockdown has been extended. The masquerade has been canceled. Or possibly postponed."

"Surely not!" cried Rachel, sitting up in her bunk.

"Oh, no!" Kitten cried, adding in her clipped British accent, "That's hardly fair. We were told we would be able to go outside today!"

"Sorry," Yolanda shrugged, adding more kindly. "Apparently, two girls from Spenser went out early this morning and were beguiled by a couple of redcaps. They're okay, but the campus has not been declared safe after all."

"W-were they hurt?" Rachel's voice quivered.

Would this be the straw that broke the Board of Visitors and Governors? Would they all be sent home? She dearly hoped not. More importantly, she hoped that the girls were okay.

"No. They are all right, just a bit confused. But they haven't caught the redcaps yet. The proctors are trying to drive them outside of the new temporary wards, but there's concern that something worse could still be around. So we all have to stay inside," said Yolanda. She shook her head regretfully and departed.

As Kitten shut the door and returned to her bed, she murmured anxiously. "I do hope they reschedule the ball! We've been looking forward to it so."

Rachel let her head fall back against her pillow and squeezed her eyes shut. Relief that the school would stay open warred with dismay over the fate of the Year of the Dragon ball. In the grand scheme of things, a canceled dance was not a big deal, so she was surprised how much the disappointment hurt. She had been looking forward to the dance so much. She wanted to dance with Gaius and with Siggy and,

if possible, with Michael Cameron. She felt bad that she had somehow upset the young man the time she tried to speak with him at
the Knights of Walpurgis meeting, the time he stormed out. He had
never come back. A dance might be good neutral ground for making
amends.

Her eyes still shut, she admitted to herself secretly that she
would also have liked to dance with Dread, but she knew that would,
most likely, not have happened anyway. Not only would it have been
physically challenging—he was almost two feet taller than her—but
also she rather suspected that college juniors did not bother with upper school freshmen at dances. Still, perhaps she could have caught
a few minutes alone with him. As she drifted off to sleep, she imagined standing by the refreshments table, blushing with pleasure as
the Prince of Bavaria graciously handed her a glass of punch, their fingertips brushing.

Another day was spent inside, studying and playing games. The Griffin children and the Park brothers, two boys from Korea who went by
the English names of Lionel and David at Roanoke, were particularly
disappointed, as they had looked forward to participating in Lunar
New Year traditions with the Korean tutors on campus. Rachel's sister
Laurel, who was one of the better conjurers in Dare Hall, tried to make
it up to them by conjuring some red Chinese lanterns and a few Yule
crackers to make the day seem more festive. However, since the main
focus of Korean Lunar New Year festivities was the food, and conjured
food could not be eaten, Rachel found the reminder of what they were
missing more painful than cheering.

Nastasia came and gently asked Rachel if she was all right,
adding, "You were moaning last night. I feared you were having a
nightmare. I didn't know if I should wake you."

"I was," Rachel smiled sadly. "It was probably brought on by my
fears for my parents. Particularly, the fear I felt when I realized that
my mother—." She could not explain to the princess how angry she
had been at the Master of the World, Nastasia's grandfather, when
she realized what forgetting Amber must have done to her mother.
"I-I thought something was wrong with my mother when I saw my

parents yesterday. Father seems to be doing well, despite his memory loss, but my mother...."

"She has a memory like yours, doesn't she?" Nastasia asked, insightfully. "I know how much you hate it when anyone's memory is interfered with. Is she the same?"

Rachel nodded. "She... didn't take it well." She made a small snorting sound that was her attempt not to laugh. "She was beastly to Vlad."

"Vladimir Von Dread?" The princess's tone had become decidedly icy. "Where does he fit into this?"

"He escorted me home, so I could see my father."

"Did he?"

"I-I needed someone who could get me out of the lockdown and in to see the dean." Rachel braced herself, waiting for the princess's tirade against the Prince of Bavaria, whom her friend despised. "He was so very nice and took me all the way home."

The princess said nothing for an unusually long time. When she finally spoke, there was a faint note of approval in her voice. "That was quite decent of him."

The weekend passed slowly. Being stuck in an enclosed space with so many other people was very difficult. Ordinarily, she might have relied upon Sigfried and Lucky to enliven the hours, but Siggy and Seth Peregrine had decided to follow the lead of other Dare musical groups and spend their free time practicing for their band, which they were debating calling either *Dragonsmith and Peregrine* or *Skunklaunchers*. Rachel could only bear so much of the scratchy, strangled noises they called music.

A few hours were spent participating in the dorm-wide chess tournament. Rachel won two games before she lost to Astrid. Her brother Peter did quite well, winning sixteen games before he lost to Liam MacDannan. By the end, everyone in the dorm had lost to one of the four MacDannans. Then Ian MacDannan lost to his sister Oonagh, and Conan MacDannan lost to big brother Liam. Liam and Oonagh played each other three times, but all three games between the siblings ended in stalemates, so the Great Dare Hall Chess Championship ended in a draw.

She did learn that she was not the only one whose dreams had been troubled Lunar New Year's Eve. Normally, dreams faded, but this nightmare stayed with her. She had been trapped by a high gate, maybe twelve or fifteen feet high, made of long spears, alternatingly silver and gold, set at regular intervals with crossbars. It sounded pretty, but, in the dream, it had been haunted by a sense of terrible wrongness. Several other people had experienced strange dreams as well, most of them far more intriguing than a frightening gate. Joy had dreamt that she went flying to the North Pole and that a giant *nisse* lived there. Peter Komarek, her brother's best friend, had dreamt that he met the ghost of Caesar, and that they had debated philosophy together. Her sister Laurel had dreamt that she had woken up to discover she was three inches tall and that she had spent the day dancing with the pixies, and Sigfried had dreamt that the sword Excalibur was calling him from a hidden cave, crying, '*Come find me— if you are worthy.*' The others understood that New Year dreams were often portents of the far future rather than of things that were soon to come, but Sigfried refused to believe this. After waking, he had immediately begun using his all-seeing amulet to look for underground caves, but so far he had not found any within one hundred and fifty feet of Dare Hall.

CHAPTER SEVEN:
THE DIE OF BOREDOM
DEBATE CLUB

Wednesday morning dawned bright and sunny. The all-clear sounded, and the campus returned to a semblance of normalcy. The all-clear had previously sounded on Monday night, but the next morning it rained. The Heer of Dunderberg and his imps spent the whole day throwing lightning bolts and giant boulders. The dormitory windows shook from the thunder, so the dean ordered the students to be kept inside for yet another day. Thus it was not until Wednesday that they were actually allowed outside.

Classes resumed, though students were still encouraged not to spend too much time outside. It felt good to get back into the normal routine of things. The thought that the school, which now seemed like such a solid part of Rachel's life, might suddenly close, just because someone—the culprits had not yet been caught—had opened the wards and let in the fey, shook her to the core. During her free period after Language, Rachel went to the library and researched an idea that had come to her for a project for the Die Horribly Debate Club. Maybe she could mobilize her friends to help keep the school open without having to tell them of the danger.

After that, she spent fifteen minutes flying through the seldom-used third floor of Roanoke Hall. As she was heading downstairs again for her next class, she spotted Michael Cameron walking through the halls, carrying his books. A sophomore with spiky brown hair, Michael would have been good-looking were it not for his perpetual scowl. He dressed in the subfusc uniform style—slacks, white shirt, black tie, black jacket, and a half cape—though somehow he made it look punkish. Unlike almost everyone else in the hallway, he wore a baseball cap instead of a black mortarboard. Ever since Michael had volunteered to be Cydney Grave's second when Cydney challenged Rachel to a duel back in early September, Rachel had wanted to get to know him better. She had admired the fact that he had stood by the girl whom everyone else had deserted. That was the sort of boy she would like to have for a friend. She had not had a chance to speak to him, however, since the day he stormed out of the Knights of Walpurgis meeting back in November.

Rachel slowed her pace. She had planned to approach him at the ball, thinking that the music and dancing might make speaking with him easier. The ordinary rules of conduct were relaxed at a ball. People who might never speak to each other could mingle freely. She probably should be patient and hope that the event would eventually be rescheduled; however, she was so frustrated from days of inaction that the idea of waiting any longer seemed unbearable.

Throwing caution to the wind, Rachel headed toward him.

Michael snarled with annoyance when he saw her, but then, he tended to look annoyed no matter who spoke to him. She decided not to take his scowl personally. As she grew closer, however, Michael began walking faster, leaving Rachel's short legs behind. She dodged through the crowded hallway, trying to keep up until she nearly ran into two towering college seniors, Donner Virgil and Veli Hirvela, both of Scandinavian descent and as handsome as Norse gods. Veli, who had a narrower jaw and a more serious expression, scowled at her until she curtsied and squeaked out an apology. Then, he smiled forgivingly. Donner—who looked like a young thunder god with eyes so green Rachel thought they looked like chips of emeralds—merely nodded. His familiar, Solbrudir, an iguana-sized red and blue dragon, as brightly-colored as a tropical bird, peered down at her from the lofty heights of his master's shoulder.

Shouting a second apology to the seniors, Rachel hopped on her broom and shot down the hall, dodging students on their way to class or flying over their heads. When she finally caught up with Michael Cameron, she slowed and glided along beside him.

Gathering her courage, she asked, "So, I spoke to you once, and now you're never coming back to the Knights?"

"Wow, yeah," Michael replied snidely. "Like I'm not going to the meetings because of you. You know, the entire world doesn't revolve around Rachel Griffin. I'm busy. Get over yourself."

"Then... why aren't you coming?" she asked, confused. "Von

Dread told me that, one day, you were going to be a very valuable member of the club."

That was *not* what Vladimir had said, but she felt it was a decent translation from Dreadese to the language spoken by normal people.

"What part of *I'm busy* does your brain not comprehend? Go play with your boyfriends."

"Boy*friends?*" Rachel cried wildly. "Now I have more than one?"

He walked faster. She increased her speed to match his. Her face was calm and cheerful, but inside she was frustrated. All she wanted was to thank him. Why must he make it so hard? Maybe if she tried to think like him? It worked with Von Dread. Of course, thanks to her grandfather, she understood how Vlad thought; with this boy, all she had to go on for how punkish, annoyed kids thought was what she had read in books.

"Of course. You're right. I'm an *idjit*," she snarled back at him, trying to think of something that might hit on what he was actually thinking. "Why would a guy who doesn't care what anybody thinks care what anybody thinks?"

"Whatever." He made a dismissive gesture.

Okay, that had not worked. She looked down as her cheeks began to grow red; however, she did not let him get ahead of her.

"What's your angle, Griffin?" Michael snapped, pausing. "Why do you care *at all* what I think, where I am, or what I'm doing? This is some jerkish Knights thing, right? Freka is really friendly to me all of a sudden, and, now, so is Valiant's five-year-old girlfriend. And the club elections are getting closer, aren't they? Wow, that doesn't seem obvious, does it?"

Michael scowled, looking even more annoyed than usual. Rachel bit her lip. It hurt that he thought she was trying to get something out of him. It had not occurred to her that people might be approaching him about the upcoming election.

"Would you like me to make up an answer or tell you the truth?" she replied. "I should warn you: a made-up answer will only take ten seconds. The truth might take a bit longer."

He paused beside a portrait of an old dean and ran a hand over his spiky hair. "If I ask you for the made-up one, will you leave me alone when you're done telling me?"

Rachel thought about it. "No."

"Whatever. Class time. Bye!"

He ducked into the nearest classroom. It did have students in it; maybe it was where he was actually heading. Rachel moved farther down the hall and waited a moment, to see whether he reappeared. When he did not, she sighed and headed on to her own classroom, rebuffed but all the more determined to someday break through his defenses.

The weekly meeting of the Die Horribly Debate Club was held that afternoon in their clubhouse in the back leg of the third floor of Roanoke Hall. Posters covered the walls: singers, Australian landscapes, newspaper clippings, reproductions of woodcuts by Darius Northwest, and huge posters of a grinning Siggy. The woodcut of the ogre had a red X across it.

Rachel, Joy, Zoë, Salome, and Valerie sipped ginger beer and sarsaparilla that Sigfried had bought for them as they waited for Nastasia, who had been called away to speak with her family. Payback sat beside Valerie, who was spinning an empty sarsaparilla bottle around her fingers as if it were a knife. The Norwegian elkhound thumped her tail against the ground as she waved it happily, hoping for a treat. The air smelled of the sharp, synthetic odor of nail polish. All the girls had painted their nails. Rachel's were black with silver and gold sparkles that reminded her of a starry sky. She was quite pleased with them and kept glancing down and wiggling her fingers.

Rachel was eager to present her idea for the group's next project. Three times, she nearly started, but she held off. She wanted to wait for Nastasia, so that she could speak to everyone at once. Hopefully, with the princess's support, the two of them could convince the rest.

Siggy sat upon the large polished wood table in the center of the clubhouse with one shirtsleeve pulled back, exposing his bare arm. Lucky was draped beside him. Salome Iscariot lay stretched across the table with one foot propped up so that she could paint her toenails, though currently she had pushed aside the open bottle of Blushing Out Loud Pink and was ogling Sigfried's arm along with the other girls, except for Rachel, who found such behavior unladylike.

"Do it again!" Joy squealed, bouncing in her seat.

Valerie, Salome, and even Zoë joined Joy in looking on with interest as Sigfried flexed his biceps. Rachel, who thought of him as a brother, continued to admire her sparkly nail polish.

"See," Sigfried chortled. "Perfect workmanship. Know why? Because I was made by an emperor. Only robots made by emperors are this flawless."

"You weren't actually made by an emperor," scoffed Salome.

"Actually, he was." Rachel made an elegant, nail-displaying gesture. "The Emperor of All Things Seen and Unseen. The Lion told me it was true."

Salome goggled, gazing at Sigfried with new interest.

Siggy's girlfriend Valerie quipped, "I wonder what my father will say when I tell him I'm dating a robot."

"He'll say you have good taste, of course," replied Sigfried, slipping his sleeve back over his arm. Several girls made an *awww* noise.

The door opened, and Nastasia glided gracefully into the clubhouse accompanied by Beauregard, her Tasmanian tiger. Joy jumped up and ran over to Nastasia, and Payback leapt up and padded over to greet Beauregard. The two touched noses. They had finally become friends.

"You're back! You're back! How did it go? Did you have fun? Can I carry anything for you?" Joy bubbled over with enthusiasm.

"No, thank you, Joy," Nastasia replied graciously. "I have nothing to carry but my coat."

She sat down next to Rachel, accepting a ginger beer when Valerie passed her one. Zoë tossed Beauregard and Payback each a quoll treat from her backpack, which they gobbled down.

"Nail polish?" Salome gestured lazily toward the collection of twenty colors.

Nastasia gave an involuntary shudder.

"You don't like painting your nails?" Salome gawked. "Are you even human?"

"I appreciate your generosity," the princess replied, "but I prefer my nails pristine."

"How did it go?" Rachel asked. Despite Nastasia's lack of enthusiasm for the subject, she held up her fingers, showing off her night sky nails.

"Oh, how pretty, Rachel. They look very becoming upon you," her friend replied with a kind smile. "There is news, though it's not mine to announce. It does not involve any of us. As for myself, my father put his foot down and declared that I could not be married off until I turned fifty. So my engagement to Wulfgang is off."

"Aw, too bad." Salome wiggled her blush pink toenails. "I thought that was romantic."

"Romantic!" Joy burst out. "That jerk? He's so rude, not like our sweet princess!"

"How do you feel about that?" Rachel asked curiously. She moved her arms about trying to push away the stray hair that had fallen into her face without smudging her nail polish.

Nastasia looked a little sad. "I don't have an opinion either way about Wulfgang, but I do long to be useful to my family. I am not sure that the alternative is...." She sighed.

Rachel, who also longed to be useful, felt her sorrow keenly. The two girls exchanged sympathetic smiles.

"What have you been doing?" Nastasia asked pleasantly.

"Not much," Zoë quipped. "We were waiting for you."

"Princess," Joy asked, "I've been thinking about Hildy's question. Why do we hide? Why not tell everyone about magic and the World of the Wise?"

"I wish we could," Rachel replied sincerely, glad to be able to speak openly, since everyone here was already in the know, "but we need to protect the Walls. There are dangers Outside. If what people believe in here changes too quickly, the Walls fall down."

"I am still not entirely certain these Walls are a good thing." The princess frowned.

Rachel, who was the one who had seen the *tenebrous mundi*, the beings who maintained the Walls, and who had stopped Azrael from ordering them to take the Walls down, resisted the impulse to grab her head or perhaps slam it against something. Then a thought struck her.

"Nastasia, why don't you ask your family?" she suggested. "Your father must know whether the Walls are good or no."

"Ah, that is a splendid idea." The princess nodded regally. "I believe I will."

"Okay, enough of this boring stuff," cried Siggy. "What's next? I say we go after the storm goblin! He's a menace. We would be doing everyone a service if we caught him."

"We would," Rachel began cautiously.

She tried never to contradict Sigfried's crazy schemes until after she had initially agreed with him. Ideally, she would prefer to suggest a safer way rather than to say no. "It would redound to our glory, to be sure. But only if we succeeded. Even the Agents have trouble with that one."

"That Heer is becoming quite a nuisance," agreed Nastasia. "If only he would limit his activities to between classes. If one is not in Roanoke Hall when a lockdown is sounded, one misses class. He is interfering with our studies. This must be stopped."

"Are you for real?" Salome Iscariot burst out laughing. "You think the Heer should stop—so we can go to class?"

"Canceling classes is a feature, not a bug," murmured Zoë. Using her magical talent, she ran her hand over her pixie-short hair and long forelock braid until they matched her poppy red fingernails. On her shoulder, her familiar, Aardvark, backed away, as if he feared that she would not be satisfied to stop with her hair and might move on to changing the rusty orange and white spots of quolls.

Valerie snorted with laughter. Rachel and Joy exchanged glances and shrugged.

Nastasia continued, unruffled. "However, we must leave this matter to the tutors and the dean. The storm goblin is far too dangerous for us to face ourselves. We are but students."

"Which is why," Rachel held up her clipboard, "I've come armed with tasks we can do."

"Tasks?" Joy looked dubious.

"Does it involve free food?" Zoë yawned.

"No one knows if the wild fey on campus have been caught," Rachel began. Her father had asked her not to talk about the threat to close the school, but he had said nothing about motivating them to proactively solve the problem. "I have made a list of the known fey—at least known to Mr. Tuck—that live on the island," she gestured at the portion of their clubhouse wall covered with blowups of woodcuts—originally drawn by her hero, Librarian Adventurer Daring Northwest—of various fey creatures: *each-uisge*, woodwose, et cetera, and the crossed-out ogre.

"That's right!" cried Siggy. "I need to be able to cross off more beasties. Bring out more red paint! Or would it be better to have Lucky just burn their pictures? We could hang the charred remains on the wall as a souvenir."

"Do you think if we catch the woodwose or the water leaper that they will let you keep the head this time?" asked Salome, from where she lay on her back, looking up at her fingernails.

"Let me!" Sigfried bristled with indignation. "I'd like to see them *try* to take them away. They will have to pry them from my cold, dead hands!"

Rachel sighed. Someday, if the gods were gracious, she would be able to voice an idea without constant interruptions, but today was not that day.

"You were saying, Miss Griffin?" the princess asked kindly.

Rachel threw her a grateful glance. "Below each fey, I listed the more obvious signs associated with its presence. Shall I read them aloud? I wrote out a copy for each of you."

She pulled the sheets off her clipboard and prepared to hand them out, but Nastasia stopped her with a raised hand.

"I believe we have this information already," the princess said, "in our textbooks."

"True," agreed Rachel, "but the rest of us don't have one book that magically contains all the school textbooks, Nastasia, and we probably don't want to lug six different books with us."

"Lug with us...." The princess gave her a puzzled frown. "I admit to being confused."

Rachel stared at her friend as if she were daft. "Take it with us as we search the campus. We can hunt for evidence as to whether the wild fey are still here."

"But we are forbidden from going outside the new wards."

"I wasn't suggesting that we go outside the new wards," Rachel replied, restraining her frustration. "We can canvas the area *inside* the new wards, looking for signs of fey the proctors might have missed. There were redcaps inside the new wards—two of them may still be here. There may be other dangers, as well."

"That's an interesting idea," mused Valerie, tossing the empty bottle she was playing with and catching it. "I could bring my camera. If we find anything, I could take a photo, and we could show them to the proctors, once I develop them—crazy, computerless campus!— who would know if what we found was actually dangerous."

"Exactly!" said Rachel, pleased that Valerie had caught on.

A furrow appeared on the princess's perfect brow. For a moment, her features underwent a subtle tug of war between puzzlement and something else. Then her lips settled into a moue of disapproval. "I do not believe that the proctors will appreciate our interference."

"We are trying to save the world." Rachel slid her mask of calm into place to hide her surprise. She had been certain that her friend would come in on her side. "That does occasionally involve facing danger. I figured helping protect the campus is a good first step."

"But we are not to seek out danger," the princess reminded her.

Rachel, who yearned to seek out danger the way other girls yearned to find their favorite boots on a massive sale, puffed out her cheeks, exhaling.

"Very well, staying on campus is too dangerous," Sigfried announced dramatically with that gleeful gleam in his eyes that meant he was deliberately provoking the princess, "because all the fey are here. Perfect time, then, to sneak off campus and explore the ogre's cave. There were some interesting things in there that were too large to haul away."

"Certainly not!" the princess replied, her voice becoming stern. "We have been forbidden from leaving campus. All of us. We are on probation. We could face severe consequences."

Sigfried shrugged. "Only if we get caught."

Rachel took a shaky breath, her bottom lip trembling slightly. She had to find some way to derail the escalating Sigfried-Nastasia feud and get her friends' help to patrol the campus, so that the school would remain safe and stay open. Should she obey her father and not tell them why it was so important to find the rest of the fey? Or did she trust her friends?

She hated having to keep secrets, and she hated having them kept from her. Father had not asked her to give her word. He had merely made a request, and his reasons were rather flimsy. Not panic the students? *Really?*

She opened her mouth to tell her friends. Before the words had left her lips, however, the princess drew herself up and declared regally, "Sigfried Smith, such talk is unworthy of a one who wishes to be a knight. Knights keep their word."

"I never gave my word not to leave campus. It was an order," objected Sigfried, adding, as if it excused everything, "from adults."

"Those adults are my family's friends! I see no reason not to follow their wise counsel."

"But if we listen to them, we can't go out and do knightly things," objected Siggy.

"As it should be," replied the princess folding her hands primly in her lap. "We are students. Our role is to learn. Maybe, when we are grown, we will have an opportunity to do great deeds, but now our task is to learn the skills we shall need when that day comes."

"But that's boring," Siggy scowled.

"When Sig's right, he's right," Zoë yawned and rose to her feet. "Being good is boring. All this talking has left me knackered. I'm going out to throw snowballs. Who's with me?"

Salome, who had been looking so bored that it was almost painful to behold her, perked up at the thought of getting out of the meeting and doing something else. She jumped up, raising one hand. "Me! Oh, me! Let's go!" She leapt off the table, grabbed her fur-trimmed coat, and ran. "Last one to the commons is a rotten egg!"

Zoë and Valerie also began gathering their things. Payback barked happily. Sigfried had not yet moved, but he had an ugly scowl on his face. Joy remained seated beside the princess, but she looked cowed and uncertain. When Nastasia rose and began putting on her winter cloak and white muff, Joy jumped up, too, and began putting on her coat. Beauregard followed slowly. Apparently, the Tasmanian tiger, who was used to the balmy weather of Magical Australia, was not keen on returning to the snowy cold.

"Wait!" cried Rachel, jumping to her feet, still clutching her carefully-drawn up plan and all her notes. "We just started! Everything on my list is something we can do without breaking any rules! Patrol the campus for fey, for instance. I heard the kappa in the Oriental Gardens was spotted moving among the decorative rocks. Maybe it knows something. Or we can question Mr. Badger. There are loads of things we could still do together...."

But they were out the door, except for Sigfried and Lucky, who still sat on the table.

"Think they'll mind if Lucks and I finish their ginger beers?" asked Sigfried, downing someone's half finished drink. Beside him, Lucky finished off another, bottle and all.

"Not at all," Rachel sighed, dejected. She sat down on the table beside him and took a sip from her own bottle of fizzy, ginger goodness. "They've already forgotten them."

"Some days, it's hard to save the world," opined Sigfried, downing yet another half-finished soda.

Rachel sighed again. "And the days when we don't need to save the world are even harder."

Chapter Eight: She Knows About the Exclamation Point!

Thursday the fifteenth was Lupercalia, which ordinarily was one of the biggest holidays of the year. There would be a huge festival back at Gryphon-on-Dart. With the Year of the Dragon Ball just around the corner, however, the Sacred Days Club, in consultation with the faculty, had decided not to hold a formal ceremony.

A few observances of the day were still held. The dining hall served corn cakes and goat meat stew. Some of the boys dressed up as goats and ran around whipping each other with paper streamers, but, all in all, it was a rather muted affair. Rachel missed the *yeomso tang* that they ate at home. It was lighter than the heavy tomato-based stew served by the campus cooks. As she was too young to participate in most of the Lupercalia ceremonies—and some of them were rather awful—she did not mind missing them. Remembering how she and Gaius had discovered that Saturnalia was actually the celebration for a particularly horrible demon named Moloch, Rachel shivered and wondered if the god Lupercus were also a demon.

Thursday night came and with it the Knights of Walpurgis. The previous week's meeting had been canceled, due to the lockdown, and everyone was eager to stretch and duel. With this in mind, Vlad kept the opening portion short. After the announcements, Von Dread raised his wand and waved it over the table. Glasses appeared in front of each seat. Then Urd Odinson and Naomi Coils rose, carrying bottles of red wine, and poured a small serving into each glass.

When everyone had been served, Dread raised his. "I would like to toast our brother, Romulus. Congratulations on the announcement of your marriage."

Romulus rose and addressed the gathering. "Thank you, brother prince. For those of you who have not yet heard, I am engaged to the Princess Alexis of the Kingdom of Magical Australia. We have not set a date yet, but I will make sure each of you receives an invitation."

Glasses clinked, and well-wishers shouted. Rachel gaped at Nastasia. It stung that the princess had not told her, but then, Rachel had not told Nastasia about Sandra and Dread either.

"This is the other news I mentioned that I did not feel was mine to disclose." Nastasia whispered as the Knights sipped their wine.

Not hers to tell. That was how Rachel felt about her sister's secret romance, too; so maybe she should not blame Nastasia for keeping their secret.

"Why is someone in your family always engaged to someone from Transylplania?" asked Sigfried.

"It is pronounced Tran-syl-va-nia," Nastasia corrected him crisply. "You know how my father put our country on the pink monopoly money standard? To him, it's a lark, but my mother's a more serious person. She's tired of our country being a laughingstock. She wants to trade with other nations. She has an arrangement with Transylvania where King Adolphus will help us establish a real currency upon the marriage of one of us to one of his children."

"So, instead of you marrying Wulfgang, your sister will marry his brother," said Rachel.

Nastasia looked glum. "My father's quixotic decrees confuse me. I was willing to do my part for the family. I am not sure why he suddenly changed his mind."

"Maybe he thought you were too young?" asked Rachel.

"Perhaps. But Alexis is only three years older than I. She is hardly fifty. Singling me out gives the impression that he's playing favorites. Either way, I believe this new arrangement is much more satisfactory to our parents. Romulus is the crown prince, not seventh in line."

"Is Alexis happy about it?" asked Rachel.

She did not know the princess's older sister, but the bookish princess struck her as kind and thoughtful. She glanced at the cold, standoffish Crown Prince of Transylvania and felt sorry for Nastasia's older sister.

"Why should she not be?" replied Nastasia.

Rachel pressed her lips together, not wanting to voice anything negative about the young man who was now to be the princess's brother-in-law. "Does she love him?"

"I don't see how that enters into it," Nastasia said. "Alexis will do her duty admirably."

Rachel fought three duels, winning two and losing one spectacularly to the flamboyant Ethan Warhol, who caught on that she could spot him casting the cantrip that let him move extremely fast and busied her with other spells first, so that she had no time to prepare.

After that, she decided to walk off her bumps and bruises by circling the floor and watching some of the upperclassmen duel. She paused to watch a duel between Jenny Dare and Urd Odinson's younger sister, a sharp-eyed, statuesque blond named Skuld. Just before their duel began, Rachel noticed Skuld shooting Vladimir a smoldering look. Rachel's eyes narrowed. That was the problem with Vlad and Sandra keeping their relationship secret. Other young women thought they still had a chance. With the specter of the hopefully-to-be-rescheduled Year of the Dragon Ball looming, they were intensifying their efforts to draw his attention. After all, he had to dance with someone. Rachel sighed. It was hard not to envy his lucky dance partners.

Which girls were interested in Dread? She reviewed her memory of earlier Knights' meetings, recalling which girls had made cow eyes at Vlad. A number of college girls seemed to be equally enamored of Vlad and Romulus Starkadder. She mentally divided them into the "Drake Girls" and the "Dee Girls." As she recalled the last five and a half months, she realized that not a single one of these girls had shown interest in only one of the two princes. All those who strove for royal attention tried equally to draw the interest of both elusive princes.

No wonder Vlad had been so taken with Sandra. She had not thrown herself at Romulus.

Turning back to the duel, Rachel's gaze fell upon Jenny Dare, the young woman whom Dread thought skilled enough to ingratiate herself into the court of the Master of the World. She knew Miss Dare was the medic of Dread's group, but she knew very little else about her. Suddenly, she found herself wanting to speak with her. As Von Dread strode by her, Rachel ran up beside him and tugged shyly on his robe. "F.B., would you introduce me to Miss Dare? I have spoken with her occasionally over lunch, but we've never been officially introduced."

He nodded. "Of course."

As the two of them crossed the chamber, they passed close to where Romulus Starkadder instructed several younger students. The two crown princes gave each other a frosty nod. Rachel watched with interest, wondering about the meaning of their interchange. She thought back over the many duels the two royal heirs had fought against each other. Vlad and Romulus dueled regularly during the practice periods, probably because no one else could keep up with either of them, except maybe Gaius or their friend, William Locke. Vlad never won these duels. He never seemed angry afterwards, but neither did he seem particularly delighted. She recalled Salome telling her during her first Knights of Walpurgis meeting that, the previous year, Romulus's right-hand man, Simon Komarek, had challenged Vlad for the leadership of the Knights and lost. She wondered for the first time what else had gone on between the two princes of which she knew nothing, and how much, if any, of their mutual coolness had been caused by the women around them?

Dread brought Rachel to where Jenny Dare was talking animatedly with several young men, all of whom stood like tame deer eating from her hand. Rachel looked with interest at the young woman of whom Dread thought so highly. She was a college sophomore with straight, shoulder-length chestnut hair. Compared to many at Roanoke, Miss Dare was not particularly pretty, but she was so vivacious that Rachel suspected the young men never noticed.

When Jenny saw the prince, she excused herself from the young bucks and came over.

"Miss Dare, this is—" Dread began stiffly.

Jenny raised her hand, palm forward. "Stop, please. It's about time you introduced me to her! I don't need your long-winded, super-formal introduction. I know her family!"

She smiled at Rachel in the same way a cat might smile at a

saucer of milk. There was definitely a great deal of affection in the look. Rachel just was not sure if it was a kindly affection or one more like that of her older sister, Laurel the prankster.

"I'm happy to finally get a chance to meet you officially, Rachel. I've heard great things about you from so many different people I can't even keep track. I'm Jenny, by the way. Please feel free to call me whatever you wish—though if it's not Jen or Jenny, you might want to throw something at the same time, so I know you're speaking to me."

"Um... hi?" Rachel said, buffaloed.

Jenny cheerfully barreled on. "So, how do you like the Knights? No, no, I don't mean specific ones. I can see how much you like our dear Gaius. And, of course, everyone loves Dready, because he's a bag full of kittens on a plate of puppies. Have you had a chance to speak to William at length? You should ask him about *SCIENCE!* Yes, I did say it with an exclamation point. You have to, when talking about *SCIENCE!* where William is concerned.

"No?" Jenny continued. "You look confused? Or maybe gassy? Can I get you a cup of water? As I was saying, the Knights, do you like the group? Or are you here because you don't like it, but you want to punish yourself by going to meetings you have no interest in? If that's the case, you should punish yourself with exercise. It's tough but good for your butt."

It took a moment for Rachel to recover her aplomb, startled as she was by the other young woman's cheek. The reference to gassiness—in front of Vlad—was embarrassing, and the last comment was so outrageous in mixed company that Rachel was not sure how to respond.

Beside her, Von Dread rubbed the bridge of his nose as if he had suddenly developed a headache.

There was something oddly familiar about Jenny's behavior. Well, two could play at the game of quick banter and a barrage of questions. Rachel took a deep breath and dived in.

"Hello, Miss Dare. It's ever so nice to meet you. I understand you are related to the Dares of Dare Hall? I live in Dare Hall, but I hear you live in Marlowe. Should that even be allowed? A Dare in Marlowe? Is there something particular I'm supposed to know about you, such as that you are super smart? Or super good at conjuring? Or super athletic? Or something like that?

"As for your other questions. Yes, I love Gaius, but the other members are growing on me, too—but not like moss or lichen. And, yes, I jolly well do know that *science!* requires an exclamation point, because I have talked to Mr. Locke about *science!*" Rachel emphasized the word without practically shouting it, the way Jenny had done. "And hope to do so again—as often as possible in fact. So, yes. I like the Knights. Loads, in fact."

"She knows about the exclamation point!" Jenny turned on Dread. "Who told her? You? Way to keep a secret, Vladimir!"

Vladimir Von Dread remained stoically silent.

"Vlad never reveals secrets," Rachel staunchly defended her hero. "As for how I know, you shall have to accustom yourself to me knowing unexpected things. I know an alarming number of unexpected things." She paused. "Information loves me. It comes and finds me."

Jenny raised an eyebrow. "It is true. I'm directly descended from Virginia Dare, the founder of Roanoke Academy. But the fair school, founded by my illustrious ancestor, is not a dictatorship. So nobody can force me to live in Dare! And I decide—not to!" She threw up her arms victoriously. "Even though my older brother did—live in Dare, that is—when he was a student. As to the second half of your question: I choose all of them. Yes, I am super smart, super good at conjuring, and super athletic! And also, something like that!"

Rachel kept a cheerful smile on her face, but inside her head, alarms blared. Since arriving at school, she had grown wary of giving out information and receiving nothing back. Miss Dare was unquestionably entertaining, but she was tripping dangerously close to the line of sucking up knowledge without sharing anything of value in return. She had not actually answered any of Rachel's questions.

Giving the older girl a look so arch it was catapulted into the running for most-arch-look-ever-given-by-a-thirteen-year-old, Rachel crossed her arms and said a proper English voice. "All you did is repeat what I said, which is the same as having told me nothing at all."

"That's the short of it!" Jenny gave her a big grin. "Say so much, yet say so little? It's an art form. You should learn it."

Rachel drew herself up with an elegant Victorian formality that would have gained the approval of her great aunt Nimue or even her grandmother.

"Thank you," she replied, "but I have better things to do."

"Probably for the best," Jenny shrugged cheerfully. "Sorry to gab and go, but I must return to my dear admirers. Simon, darling, are you ready to duel?"

Simon Komarek, the very same dark-haired friend of the crown prince of Transylvania who had once dueled Von Dread for control of the Knights and the older brother of Peter Komarek — Rachel's brother's best friend—stepped forward and awaited her on a dueling strip. Jenny joined him at the other side of the dueling mats, and the two bowed to each other. Jenny raised her fulgurator's wand. Simon fought with a large sapphire dueling ring.

Turning away, Rachel discovered that Von Dread actually looked embarrassed.

"Um, was I rude?" Rachel asked, blushing at her attempt to match Jenny's spunk. "I-I tried not to say anything impolite, but she was so funny and yet...." She sighed. "It was unexpectedly difficult not to be snide."

He shrugged. "She is used to being spoken to... inappropriately. She is very useful, though. I would not have her as part of my circle were she not."

"Useful in what way?" Rachel asked carefully. "That's what I was trying to find out."

"She can walk in circles others of us cannot," replied Von Dread. "I try to keep my thoughts regarding her to myself, for fear that too many people knowing her strengths might reduce her usefulness. She hears things. People speak to her, and they speak around her. Do not speak of her to others. Her most valuable power is social and not magical at all."

Rachel thought of her mother's warning not to tell anyone about her perfect memory. She understood exactly why a person might wish to keep their talents to themselves and how some talents were far more useful if nobody knew about them. She nodded.

The prince stepped slightly closer and lowered his voice, "Jenny Dare is a confidant of your sister's. That should tell you something about her character."

Intrigued, Rachel turned to glance at the charming older girl with renewed interest. Suddenly, the last few minutes fell into perspective. Jenny's stances, her motions, her expressions, and most of all, her non-stop barrage of questions had all seemed strangely familiar. Now Rachel realized why. It was almost as if the young woman were copying her body language from Aunt Melissa's wall of fairies. Only Rachel did not think Jenny was dissembling, not in the technical way that the Griffin Girls used the word. Rather, it was as if she were imitating the *giddy pose* by a deliberate choice, as if she had learned from Sandra just enough to keep other people off kilter by assuming this cheerful, excitable front. But why would anyone do such a thing? Unless Sandra had also taught her....

A cold shiver traveled up Rachel's spine. Because suddenly she was certain that this was exactly what her sister had done. Sandra had taught her friend *kumihotoushi*. Why else would Jenny Dare be so valuable to Von Dread? The secret art allowed its practitioners to read the reactions of others, giving them tremendous insight into those around them. Jenny Dare threw out a huge number of questions and stray comments, all the while watching her target like a hawk and thus learning a great deal from their responses to her barrage.

All of which meant one thing: Rachel would have to be tremendously careful, or Jenny Dare would see right through her. *Might she figure out that....*

Rachel very carefully did not so much as glance at Vlad.

At that moment, Jenny, who was still in the midst of her duel, noticed Rachel watching her. Very grateful that she had resisted the urge to glance at Dread, Rachel smiled and waved. Jenny shot back a big smile of her own, just as a swirl of blue sparkles—from Simon Komarek's dueling ring—hit her in the chest. She froze, her hand still up in a cheery wave.

Rachel cringed and called out, "Sorry!"

The duel was called in Simon's favor. Even after he released her from his spell, Jenny kept her big grin. As Rachel walked away, she concluded with a tiny bit of relief that Sandra had chosen to teach Jenny the giddy pose because the young woman was sincerely a cheerful person.

Chapter Nine:
The Snow-Fairies Incident

Friday morning, as the Dare Hall students walked through the chilly February air on their way to lunch, Valerie Hunt came running toward them. She had stuffed her ubiquitous camera under her bulky pink parka to protect it from the low temperatures. Her golden locks were covered by a fuzzy pink hat.

"Guess what? Guess what?" Valerie jumped up and down, clapping her hands and kicking up her feet behind her. "They've rescheduled the ball!"

Rachel exclaimed with joy. She spun to grin at Nastasia who happily smiled back. Beside them, Siggy and Lucky high-fived each other. Only Zoë looked unimpressed.

"Thank the gods!" Joy squealed with glee. She jumped and clapped, too, the pompom on her hat bobbing, though she was not nearly as graceful about it as Valerie. "I swear I would have died if they hadn't. After all the work we've done on our costumes!"

Joy grabbed Zoë's hands and the two began to spin. Delighted, Rachel stretched out her arms. The princess, who stood watching, merely smiled, but Valerie impetuously grabbed onto Rachel. The two girls spun across the snowy lawn, leaning away from each other, laughing joyfully. Rachel's hair streamed behind her like a banner. The forces pulling upon her were both terrifying and exhilarating, as if, at any moment, she might lose her grip and go barreling into the forest. Out of the corner of her eye, she noted a pink blur as Valerie's hat went flying.

"Quick, Lucky!" Sigfried cried. He held his fingers, bent like talons, in front of his face. "Claw out my eyes! Too much cuteness! Brain exploding!"

One of Rachel's hands slipped free of Valerie's, causing them both to lose their balance. The two of them crashed into Joy and Zoë. All four girls collapsed into the snow, where they lay on the ground giggling and moving their arms and legs to form snow-fairies.

"How did you come to hear this, Miss Hunt?" Nastasia inquired pleasantly, gazing down at the supine Valerie. "No word of this has yet reached us."

"Salome told me," Valerie called up from the snow.

"How'd she find out?" inquired Joy, still lying on her back.

"Vladimir Von Dread announced it to Drake Hall," Valerie drawled, waving her arms to increase the wingspan of her snow-fairy. "Apparently, the Lord of Evil has connections."

"Because he's evil?" Joy asked, sitting up and brushing snow from her hair.

"Most likely," Valerie quipped.

Nastasia nodded. "We are aware that he has a method of spying on the dean."

"No, we aren't!" Irritation crept into Rachel's voice. She sat up and shook her head, sending snow scattering. "We found out that the dean had told him that information, remember?"

Rachel rose to her feet, exasperated that her friend continued to hold to a poor opinion of Vlad. She was grateful she and Nastasia were on good terms again, but it frustrated her that her friend was so focused on her rigid idea of good and evil that she made no allowances for Rachel's feelings. Neither for that matter did Joy or Zoë. Even Sigfried, who was much easier to get along with, fundamentally did not care how Rachel felt about things.

At least she had Gaius! Though, secretly, she could not help noticing that while Gaius was kindly solicitous of her well-being, he did not actually care what she felt.

Boys were like that.

Rachel ducked her head. No one was obliged to sympathize with her. She could not by right object, but it would be nice, just once, to have someone to whom she could confess all that was within her heart. *If only her Elf had lived.*

A motion in her peripheral vision caught her attention. When she glanced at the forest to her left, there was nothing there. Even when she examined her memory, she could not determine whether she had seen something move inside the forest or if it had been a stray motion nearby.

"I am very happy the ball is on again," said the princess, "When will it be held?"

"February twenty-fourth. Not this next Saturday, but the one after," said Valerie. She leaned over to retrieve her hat.

"The last day of Lunar New Year," Rachel said, "The official festivities take two weeks."

Joy moaned in mock despair. "Sooo long? How can we wait soooo long?"

"It is frustrating," Nastasia acknowledged, "but there are silver linings. For instance, those who plan to wear conjured outfits have extra time to practice their conjurations."

"Do people wear conjured costumes?" Valerie's eyes grew large.

Rachel nodded, "Many of the college students do, and some offer to conjure costumes for younger students. My sister will be conjuring hers."

Joy nodded her head enthusiastically. "Four of my sisters are in Marlowe. Three of those are in college. They'll be conjuring our costumes. They've been practicing for months. I've had to go let them get my size right and such several times."

"I'd love to learn that!" Valerie exclaimed. "I've been interested in it ever since Mrs. Heelis told us about it last fall. Conjuring garments, I mean. You could conjure a new outfit every day. You'd never have to do wash. It would just vanish before twenty-four hours was up."

"Many do," replied Rachel. "Conjure their outfits, I mean."

"Wouldn't they end up naked the next day?" asked Sigfried, puzzled.

Joy rolled her eyes. "No one wears the same outfit for twenty-four hours, silly."

Siggy and Lucky exchanged glances. Rachel recalled that when he arrived, back in September, Sigfried had only owned a single robe. She suspected that, even now that she had helped him buy a larger wardrobe, he did not change his robes as frequently as Joy might deem appropriate.

They resumed walking toward the dining hall.

"Are you looking forward to dancing, princess?" Joy asked.

"Not I," sighed Nastasia. "I've been to too many formal dances. They are always a bore, and grown men step on my feet."

Rachel asked, surprised. "Balls of state? Even though you are not of age?"

"My father believes that waiting for a debut is old-fashioned," Nastasia replied gravely. "He says the exercise is good for us."

"Have you ever had to dance with...." Rachel waved a hand vaguely.

Nastasia discerned the train of Rachel's thought. "An emu or a kangaroo? Indeed, I have. Once, it was an elephant seal who Father insisted was a dignitary of some importance. We all had to take a turn around the floor with it... which was difficult, because it waddled so very slowly. The cassowary bird was the scariest. They can disembowel a man with a single kick."

"And your father trusted it to dance with you?" Rachel's voice rose in surprise.

Nastasia shrugged. "For all I know, it was an officer of the Privy Council that Father had transformed for the evening—perhaps as a punishment for a petty offense."

"Does he do that often? Transform his courtiers?"

"Not to my knowledge," the princess opined, "but with Father, one never knows."

Gliding along beside Rachel, the princess announced, "I have just had a most charming idea. Why don't we do each other's hair for the ball? I am only just learning about hairstyling. Rachel has been helping me. We could teach each other new styles."

Rachel smiled. Before coming to school, Nastasia had never done her own hair. She had relied on servants. When she had first arrived here, she had been helpless. It pleased Rachel that her efforts to help her friend learn to be more independent were appreciated by the princess.

"That's a great idea. All your ideas are the tops, Princess, even better than peanut butter and chocolate," burst out Joy. "But, just this one time, I've got an even better idea! Why don't I ask one of my sisters? After all, there's no point in having six older sisters, if I don't put them to use. They can come do our hair—or one of them can. It will be great fun! What do you all say?"

The girls all agreed eagerly. As they continued along the snowy path, Rachel realized, chagrinned, that she had been too hasty. She should have waited after all and spoken to Michael Cameron at the ball; maybe it would have gone better. On the other hand, if it had gone badly, it would have been far more embarrassing to have her partner stomp off mid-dance, leaving her alone in the middle of a crowded ballroom. With a sigh, she dismissed the matter. It was over and would never trouble her again.

There it was again, a motion to her left. Rachel turned and squinted into the forest but could not make out what was moving between the hemlocks. Was it her imagination? No, looking back in her memory, she definitely saw a motion there. It was something large, not a squirrel or someone's cat. Was it a student? A familiar? *Or something else?*

What should she do about it? If she told her friends, Nastasia would tell the dean, who might decide that the campus was too dangerous after all. The same went for the proctors. She could not do nothing; however, what if it were a fey and someone were to get hurt?

"So, about the ball, boyfriend," Valerie declared behind her, hooking her elbow through Sigfried's, "I'm not happy with my costume. What are you wearing?"

"My sisters and I have our costumes all planned!" Joy declared, bursting with excitement. "We're all going together. What about you, Zoë?"

Zoë yawned. "Not my scene."

"You could come in black and make your hair red in honor of Year of the Dragon," suggested Rachel, who, try as she might, could not imagine not wanting to go to a ball.

Zoë shrugged.

"What about you, Princess?" asked Joy.

Nastasia strolled beside her, one hand stroking the back of her Tasmanian tiger, who trotted alongside her, pausing now and then to sniff at icy puddles. "While I was at home, my family gave me a most lovely dress. Apparently, it's been in the family for generations."

"I can't wait to see it." Joy sighed happily.

"I am going as my familiar," Rachel said. The idea had been inspired by a comment Valerie had made months ago, when Sigfried suggested calling the Die Horribly Debate Club Zoë and the Pussycats. "You can help put my hair up in cat ears. Or Joy's sisters can."

"You have a familiar?" Valerie asked, surprised.

Rachel called upon her dissembling skills to keep from blushing over the disgrace that was the situation surrounding her "familiar."

"Yes, Mistletoe," she said. "He's a black and white cat. I have a bodysuit, ears, tail, and paint-on whiskers. Mum sent it at my request."

Sigfried was faux-boxing with Lucky with his free hand. "You should dress your familiar up in a small cat-sized version of your robes. Then, you can go as it, and it can go as you."

Valerie gave her boyfriend a friendly punch. "You didn't answer my question."

"Well," Sigfried stroked his chin. "I'd like to dress up, but I don't own any clothing except robes, one torn and dirty shirt from St. Dismas's, and pair of trousers two sizes too large that I stole off a neighbor's clothes line before my trip into the sewers. Oh, and the t-shirts Goldilocks gave me for Yule. Thanks, G.F. I used to own a pair of underwear from that trip, too, but it... well, it's unfit for the ears of girls what happened to that."

"He means I charred it by accident," murmured Lucky sheepishly. He snaked around his boy's body like a fancy, furry boa.

"Can I buy clothing from a catalog?" asked Siggy. "Can we sneak off school grounds and go shopping? I have been dying to go to the city and spend some of my ill-gotten gains."

Joy nodded enthusiastically. "You can *definitely* order clothing from a catalogue. I think you should dress up like a dragon. Or a ninja. Or a ninja dragon."

"Ninja dragon's not bad," Siggy replied thoughtfully, giving Valerie the eye. "Or I could dress up like a police officer."

One of Valerie's eyebrows arched seemingly on its own. She blushed slightly. "Well, that might be nice...."

Any further comments were interrupted by a peal of thunder, heralding another atmospheric temper tantrum by the Storm Goblin and his imps. The whole group broke into a run, eager to reach the doors of Roanoke Hall before they could be barred from the dining hall and their lunch.

Rachel slid into her customary lunch seat at the center table in the plus-sign-shaped dining hall and placed her tray beside her boyfriend's, breathing in the savory fragrance of chicken and rice soup. It never failed to thrill her that she was allowed to have lunch with these impressive upperclassmen. Peter and Nastasia disapproved of her sitting at Vladimir Von Dread's table, but she was determined not to allow them to rob her joy.

Gaius was mid-conversation with William Locke and Topher Evans, discussing the overlap between alchemy and thaumaturgy. Von Dread presided over the table, listening. Across from Rachel and Gaius sat the two college juniors, William, his girlfriend, Naomi Coils, and the younger Topher. Jenny Dare swung by to say hi, before taking her tray off to go sit with some friends, and the elusive Lucy Westenra stopped by briefly to hand Dread a manila envelope, which he accepted with an appreciative nod, before she, too, moved on to sit with other girls from Dee Hall.

The fountain at the center of the dining hall had been turned down, so that, instead of the usual roar of water, there was merely a gurgle. Rachel was grateful. It meant she could hear the others speak without straining.

"Hallo, you lot," Rachel said, at the first lull in the conversation. In her hand, she held the sheath of papers she had put together for the Die Horribly Debate Club meeting. She set them on the table in front of Gaius and his friends, "I wonder if this would interest you."

William Locke was the first to pick up a paper. Brushing his straight dark hair from his eyes, he examined Rachel's notes with cool scientific curiosity.

"Fascinating," William stated. "A rather thorough analysis of fey tells." He scanned the page, one eyebrow arching. "Particularly, I note, for fey who live here on Roanoke Island. Is this for a class assignment or is something afoot?" He lowered the paper and gazed at Rachel over the top of it, one eyebrow still raised.

"I was just thinking that if enough of us knew these signs, it might help the proctors secure the campus," she said casually.

Topher Evans, a good-natured but awkward young man with a large Adam's apple and glasses, picked up a page, glanced at it, turned it over, glanced at the other side, and set it down again. Then he tipped his head up slightly, eyes narrowed. Rachel knew that look. He was searching his memory, which was like hers, to see if he had spotted any fey signs.

"This is a pretty thorough list," said Topher. "Some of these things I have seen, like leaves blowing in the wind. But I think there was actual wind, so I didn't see leaves blowing without wind, which means, in retrospect, that I don't think I've seen any of these yet, but I will keep my eye out." He paused and gave a kind of half shrug, adding. "But, really. This is a good idea. The school should give a list like this to everyone."

College junior, Naomi Coils, was less impressed with Rachel's efforts. She was a serious young woman with dark red hair whom Rachel had only ever seen smile when she was speaking with her boyfriend, William. She glanced at a page briefly and dismissed it, either because she was not interested or because she wished to eat her lunch—Rachel could not tell.

Rachel began eating her own lunch, meanwhile recalling, again and again, the motion in the forest that had caught her eye. She tried to determine something about it. Had it been a person? A large familiar? After fifteen attempts, she realized that she recognized the motions.

Horse. It was a horse. *That was not good.*

Suddenly, what had seemed like a lark became a very serious matter indeed. Rachel lowered her voice, "If I tell you all a secret, can you keep it to yourselves?"

"Not if it endangers the world, the school, or my country," Vladimir replied quite seriously, "but if it is not a matter of immediate security, of course."

Rachel swallowed. "You will have to decide for yourself whether it is such a matter or not. If you deem it to be that important, you can tell someone."

"Very well," Vladimir inclined his head, indicating to the rest of his people that they were to keep the matter among themselves unless he said otherwise.

Rachel leaned forward and gestured to others to come closer. They did, except for Naomi, who leaned back, looking coolly disinterested.

"When we were at Gryphon Park," she whispered, "my father told me that if the fey caused another major incident, the Board of Visitors and Governors would close the school."

Eyebrows leapt. A gasp or two rang out, and even Naomi leaned forward in consternation.

"That's not good," blurted out Topher Evans. He pulled off his glasses and wiped them with a cloth from his pocket. "Not good at all. It's February, and I live in Alaska. Do you know how much I don't want to go home? I would be lucky if I could even get to my home. The bush jockey would probably just abandon me on the side of some frozen river, and I'd have to go live with wolves until the spring thaw."

"Come on, Evans. It's not that bad," Gaius drawled, reaching behind him to fill his cup from the fountain. "Wolves are warm, and they smell better than foxes."

Dread stated, "We cannot allow Roanoke to close. The campus must be made safe."

"That's where this comes in." Rachel gestured at her papers, lifting and smacking them on the table again for emphasis. "As William pointed out, I have noted down the known signs for the fey thought to live on this island. If we can find them, we can make sure they are captured before any more incidents occur."

"Wise, Griffin, very wise." Gaius elbowed her in the ribs fondly. Leaning over, he whispered, "You look especially cute today. It's the snow-in-your-hair look, I think."

Rachel blushed both from delight and from embarrassment. She must look a mess. She should have straightened herself up more after the snow-fairy incident. All the snow from when they had been lying, waving their arms and legs on the ground, was still melting in her hair. Glancing sideways through her lashes at Gaius Valiant, Rachel gave silent thanks for the good fortune of having such an adorable boyfriend. Gaius's old coat was frayed, but his eyes were bright. His hair, a chestnut brown, was drawn into a queue and tied at the nape of his neck. He was short for his nearly-seventeen years, but he was still much taller than she. Gaius, too, had once been an Outsider. In his previous life, he had apparently destroyed an interstellar community —though neither Rachel nor Gaius knew how he had accomplished such a thing.

"Has anyone seen anything yet?" Topher asked. "I haven't. I've checked."

"There's an *each-uisge* in the forest north of Roanoke Hall," Rachel said, her voice low.

"*Each-uisge!*" Naomi placed her cup back on the table with a bang. "Have you any idea how dangerous they are? Far more dangerous than nixies or kelpie. This one was only allowed to stay on the island because it promised never to stray farther than its marsh. If it is confirmed to be on campus, they will close the school down for certain." She frowned severely but then glanced towards the end of the table. "Vladimir, what can be done?"

Dread covered his tray with a napkin and slid back his chair. "I will assign watches. We start patrolling immediately."

Despite diligent searching, by Friday night, they still had not found the *each-uisge*. Dread decided that since the proctors were actively patrolling at night—and the school staff were already on notice that these fey might be on the grounds—their group could risk the presence of the dangerous fey for one more day. Vladimir set up watches for them, starting the following morning. If they could not locate and apprehend the creature before nightfall on Saturday, however, they would need to inform the proctors.

CHAPTER TEN:
GROUNDED

The morning of Saturday the seventeenth dawned bright and mild. The weather was so beautiful that Rachel, who was not scheduled to patrol until the afternoon, decided to tempt fate and fly outside. Apparently, fate did not appreciate her taking such liberties, because this turned out to have been a huge mistake.

The permanent wards of Roanoke Academy were obvious; they were constructed of trees that grew trunk to trunk, forming a solid wall of bark. But the temporary wards that the proctors had constructed hugged the campus and consisted of only a wire fence, too low to see from the air. Rachel did not know where these new wards were—until she flew over one.

She was sailing along on Vroomie at a nice clip, enjoying the wind through her hair on this relatively mild February day, when the steeplechaser cut out and dropped like a stone. Rachel tried to kick-start the tail fan. When that did not work, she tried casting a cantrip. That did not work either. Instead, she plunged through tree branches, wishing that her cat really was a familiar, as then the gift a sorceress receives from her familiar would have protected Rachel from being hurt by falling.

But Mistletoe was just a cat.

Rachel slammed into the ground and lay dazed in the snow for about fifteen minutes. At least the cold helped numb some of the pain. Her cheek was scratched, and her knee hurt a great deal. Eventually, she was able to move enough to reach for her wand. She had stored a simple first aid charm that Jenny had cast for her; however, the purpose of high-strength wards such as these was to stop all magic and render anyone who crossed powerless. Sadly, wards of this kind did not differentiate between people trying to break into the school, and people crossing in the other direction. Even her wand was not working.

Eventually, she managed to climb back to her feet and limp back to the campus propre. Once on the right side of the wards, her wand woke up, but, Jenny's charm was only able to mitigate a small amount of the damage she had suffered. Worse, once back on the right side of the wards, she still could not get her steeplechaser to start.

Feeling dazed and panicky, she went in search of the one person who she thought might be able to help, her boss, the P.E. tutor. Only when she found him in his office in the gym, Mr. Chanson greeted her with a frown. Rachel balked. The two other times had she seen him frown at someone, and it had not gone well for those people. She hoped that his expression was merely a response to his seeing the scrapes on her face and the needles in her hair.

Sadly, this was not the case.

"Miss Griffin," Mr. Chanson said sternly. He was an extremely handsome man with hair so black it almost appeared a steely blue. Ordinarily, his glasses gave him a mild-mannered appearance, but at the moment, he did not seem very mild. "I have received a disturbing report about your behavior."

"M-me?" cried Rachel, aghast, clutching her inert bristleless to her chest.

"I hear that you have been stalking students through the hallway on your broom."

"Stalking!" she objected shrilly.

Michael Cameron had ratted her out.

"You are a bright young woman, Miss Griffin. Have you noticed anyone else riding their bristlelesses inside the buildings?"

Rachel gazed at him, as wide-eyed as a phooka trapped by a flash hex. *Did they?* She had never once thought about the subject.

Mr. Chanson tried again. "Would you fly your broom in your own house?"

"Y-yes! I fly in my house all the time," she exclaimed. "We all do. The hallways are very, very long. It can take five or ten minutes to cross from one location to another."

He said nothing for a brief moment. Then, his face softened. "That's true. I've been to your house. I see what you mean."

Rachel's head bobbed up and down several times, nodding. She felt so mortified that she was having trouble concentrating. She suspected her face was as red as conjuring sparks. The world seemed to buzz in her ears, despite her being reasonably sure that such a concept made no sense.

Why had these complaints been brought to her boss, of all people? She would have much preferred to be dressed down by the dean or one of the assistant deans. Mr. Chanson held such a good opinion of her, believing her to be a competent and reliable girl. It broke her heart that he might feel she had let him down. Would she be able to regain his good opinion?

On top of her abject embarrassment came a dose of self-loathing. It was her impatience that had brought this upon her. If she had just waited for the dance, she could have spoken to Michael Cameron without having to chase him. *All this just because she had wanted to thank the ungrateful rotter.*

Mr. Chanson stroked his chin thoughtfully. "Nonetheless, I cannot allow you to be flying through the hallways of Roanoke Hall or out through the dormitory windows."

Rachel felt as if she had been struck through the heart by an arrow. It hurt more than the wounds from her fall. She tried to swallow but did not succeed.

"I want you to give me your word: you will not fly in buildings or through windows."

Her eyes stung. She blinked rapidly to keep from crying.

"Miss Griffin?"

"I... give you my word," she stated sadly, when she finally found her voice.

Making that promise felt like amputating a limb. She felt too heartsick to bring up the fact that her broom was not working. Maybe she could ask Mr. Fuentes to help her with it.

As she started to limp away, however, Mr. Chanson called after her in a consolatory tone. "Miss Griffin, have I ever mentioned my parents used to own a broom-manufacturing company? They were put out of business by O.I., but they still make the occasional broom, special order."

"Chanson's Quality Bristlelesses!" Rachel turned back to face him, surprise temporarily eclipsing disappointment and pain. "Of course, I have heard of them! I read a whole book about their brooms.

Their flying enchantments were said to have been excellently done. I-I didn't realize you were part of that Chanson family."

"Would you like me to ask my parents to take a look at your broom? To see if they can soup it up, so to speak?"

"You mean, make Vroomie even better?"

He nodded.

She thought back quickly, recalling where she had run into trouble with Vroomie in the last few months. "Would they be able to reduce the drag caused by the becalming enchantment?"

"Oh, without question! My family's becalming enchantments are the best in the business! I could ask them if yours could be improved."

"Oh, would I!" The hard lump in her throat melted. She imagined being able to maneuver while becalmed. It would have kept her and Sigfried from being blown across the wards the time they tried to fly to the top of Storm King Mountain and the Heer sent them tumbling across the wall of trees that warded the campus. That time, Jariel had restarted her broom, but Rachel knew that if he had not done it already, there was no point in asking the Raven.

Another thought struck her, and she hugged Vroomie to her again. "H-how long w-would it take? How long will I be without it, I mean?"

"A few days. Maybe a week at most. You should have it back before the Year of the Dragon Ball. You can borrow a school Flycycle until then."

Rachel clutched Vroomie all the more tightly. "And have they worked on other steeplechasers, your parents, I mean?"

"Quite a few," he replied. "Back in the day, Chanson's Quality Bristlelesses was famous for its steeplechasers."

"I would like that very much," she said politely, "O-only, I seem to have broken it. I... flew over a ward."

Mr. Chanson tsked fondly. "Miss Griffin, what shall we do with you? But no worries. We'll have that problem solved in a jiffy."

He put out his hand. Very slowly, Rachel surrendered her beloved steeplechaser.

"Very good, Miss Griffin. I will take good care of it," he said, smiling. "Now, I suggest you visit Nurse Moth and see what she can do about your face and your leg."

Rachel smiled wanly and limped off toward the infirmary, grateful to Mr. Chanson for his help and that he had been willing to take her back into his good graces.

That afternoon, Rachel and Gaius tromped through the paper birches following hoof prints in the snow. He wore his threadbare jacket. She stood out, bright as a cardinal, in her red wool coat and her white snowman hat.

"This is where you saw the kelpie-thing yesterday, right? What's it called: *each-ooski*?" Gaius asked. "I know Naomi and William started here when they were patrolling, but I figured we have a better chance of finding it if we start at a place we know it's been."

Rachel nodded. "Vladimir mentioned that, occasionally, the prints stop, picking up again elsewhere. I wonder if the *each-uisge* can sink into the snow as it would a loch? Or is it only snow dolphins that can do that?"

Gaius's head shot up. "Are snow dolphins truly a thing?"

"They truly are," Rachel nodded seriously, adding dreamily, "I have seen them in the glaciers of Thulehavn."

"Hang on. Is that...." Gaius raised his hand to indicate silent. A moment later, he let it drop. "Scratch that. It's only Merry's reindeer."

"Ooo. I've seen her in the wood before. All the animals come and talk to her."

"Really?" Gaius peered through the forest, but it was just the reindeer munching on bark. "I'd like to see that."

Rachel noted that Gaius casually called Merry Vesper by her first name. The upper school junior from Marlow was not in his class or in the Knights, but, apparently, he knew her. She wondered how they had come to know each other.

Gaius drawled, "Topher and I took the advice you'd written on the sheet you gave us and went to speak to the kappa in the Oriental gardens this morning."

"Oh, did you?" Rachel cried, delighted, though she was little disappointed that she had not been there to meet the kappa.

"We played good cop, bad cop. He had the cucumber, and I brought the ginger," Gaius explained.

"So now you're bad cop," Rachel asked with only the slightest of giggles, "threatening the poor kappa with ginger?"

He shrugged. "I wasn't very effective. I hoped to do the thing from stories—you know the one I mean, where you bow to the kappa and it bows back, spilling the water in the cup on its head? Then, you refill it, and the kappa offers you a boon? But this one was too savvy. It put a plate over its head cup before it bowed. I guess through the years other students have tried the same trick."

"Did you learn anything useful?" asked Rachel.

"It was very cagey and would only answer three questions, and Toph and I didn't think them out as thoroughly as we should have —but the short answer is: There are two large fey on campus that are not supposed to be here and an indeterminate number of smaller ones. And one of the bigger ones is definitely the *each-uisge* from the marsh on the northwest corner of the island. And the kappa basically confirmed that the water horse is dangerous to touch."

"Right, because you get stuck to it." Rachel nodded. "What was your third question?"

Gaius colored slightly. "Er... better not repeat it. Except to say, kappas can be gross and weird. Poor Topher was traumatized."

Rachel laughed at that. Then, she glanced up at him. "Is Topher really going to be stranded if we get sent home?"

Gaius burst out laughing. "No, he lives in a town with a walking glass. He's joking, Rach. He just wants to be the Alaskan Farley Mowat." He paused. "Though, it is cold in his hometown this time of the year. He's right about that."

"I wondered," replied Rachel. "It didn't make any sense at all for a broom jockey to be limited as to where he landed his bristleless."

They marched on through the snow, the occasional papery curl of birch bark crinkling in the wind. Gaius was slightly ahead. Rachel gazed at his back speculatively. She was wildly curious about his costume for the upcoming ball, but, somehow, she felt too shy to ask.

They he stopped atop a slight rise. The tracks had vanished again, but Rachel caught sight of them about ten feet away.

"By the way," Gaius drawled as they continued walking, "the only time Michael Cameron has ever spoken to me was this morning, when he grabbed my arm and said, and I quote, '*Hey, cradle robber, could you get your annoying girlfriend to annoy anyone but me?*' You... wouldn't happen to know anything about that, would you?" When he spoke the words "cradle robber," he sounded very English, even to Rachel.

By some miracle, she managed not to blurt out that she found it totally adorable that her much-older boyfriend had been accused of robbing the cradle because he was dating her.

"If he asks you again," she snorted with laughter, "you may tell him that it has nothing to do with you, and you know nothing about it."

"If you say so," he said, a bit skeptically.

Double rotter! Rachel ground her teeth. Not only had Michael Cameron complained to her boss, he had also heckled her boyfriend. Rachel's hands curled into fists. The more he resisted, the more her resolve strengthened. She was not going to let Michael's ill-temper defeat her. He could be as obnoxious as he desired. Sooner or later, she would get her chance. She was going to thank him for his part in the duel, back in September, if it was the last thing she did!

Speaking of Michael Cameron reminded her that she had not yet told Gaius about the day's earlier disappointments.

She sighed. "My boss dressed me down today."

"You?" Gaius asked, surprised.

She went on to explain how Mr. Chanson had restricted her comings and goings. She did not tell her boyfriend how she had flown over the ward or how Michael Cameron had snitched on her—she did not wish to cause even more trouble between the two boys—but she did explain about no longer being allowed to fly down hallways or in and out of windows.

"You know," Rachel perked up suddenly as she clambered over some deeper mounds of snow, "this broom nonsense has one good aspect."

"And what might that be?" her boyfriend paused for a moment and bopped her on the nose with his finger.

Rachel giggled. Then she replied thoughtfully, "I've had some trouble obeying orders. But I don't think I will have trouble obeying Mr. Chanson, even though I quite regret not being able to do the things he's told me not to do."

Gaius leapt to a place where the footing was smoother, offering his hand to Rachel. He helped her to the softer snow and then released her. "And do you think that's a good thing?"

"I think it is," she replied, a warmth radiating through her from the touch of his hand. "The world is a more harmonious place when people obey rules, and children are supposed to obey their elders. Imagine what a bad precedent it would set if everyone disobeyed."

"Good point, I guess," Gaius mused, looking around for the prints, which had vanished again. "Though I don't think a little disobedience here at school is necessarily so terrible. Some of the rules make sense, but others...." He rolled his eyes.

"But you wouldn't disobey Vladimir?" Rachel prompted.

Gaius rocketed back on his heels. "No! Never."

"See. It is important to *be able* to obey people."

"How come this time you can make a proper job of it?" he asked curiously.

Rachel turned slowly in a circle and then pointed at where the tracks picked up again, some twenty-five feet away. "Hmm.... Part of it is that I like Mr. Chanson, and I do not wish to disappoint him. But there must be more than just that, because I admire the dean, too, but not wanting to disappoint her never seemed to help."

"Let's look at this logically," Gaius said, applying his scientific bent of mind. "Was it ever really about not being able to obey any adult? Or was it some specific issues. For instance, do you do your homework?"

"Always!" Rachel responded instantly. Then she winced. "Except practicing the flute, which I hate."

"Can't fault you there," Gaius drawled. He paused and gazed upwards at where the bare branches met the blue, blue sky. Rachel gazed up with him. He reached over and took her hand in his, which made her heart dance a jig of joy. "That's why I dropped enchantment after Sophomore Chorus. Sick ducks are more melodic than I was on that oboe."

"Six sick ducks?" Rachel quipped, grinning at him.

"Especially six of them," Gaius replied smoothly. "Back to you and obeying orders. You didn't disobey about homework, or where to put your tray in the dining hall, or not littering on campus, right? What kind of orders, specifically, did you find problematic?"

"Hmm, good question, Mr. Scientist," Rachel replied, smiling, as they walked on hand in hand. She thought back. "I think there are only two kinds of orders I have trouble obeying."

"Don't throw yourself into danger and, oh, don't throw yourself into danger?" Gaius quipped, teasingly.

Rachel giggled. "No, it wasn't that. Throwing oneself into danger is a side effect."

"What's the main issue, then?"

"Orders that interfered with gathering information or helping those in need."

Gaius thought about this as they came to the wire fence that marked the edge of the new wards. "Shall we go over or just walk along the fence and peer through it?" he asked.

"Better do the second," Rachel replied, trembling slightly as she recalled the force of her fall earlier that day, after she accidentally flew over this very fence. "I'm not sure how to get over these wards without our magic stopping."

"Oh. Good point." Gaius clutched his wand convulsively with his free hand. "So, you can obey Mr. Chanson because his orders were about neither of those things?"

Rachel tipped her head back, thinking. Overhead, a flock of small birds flew across a few white puffy clouds and the perfect blue sky behind them.

Presently, she said, "Not entirely. Because flying in and out of windows could be related to either—and I'd still do it if someone's life were in danger. I think it's that he listened."

"Listened?" Gaius released her hand and jumped over a fallen tree trunk, skirting the edge of the makeshift, waist-high wire fence. "I don't follow."

Rachel jumped onto the fallen tree and walked along it a few steps, her arms out like a gymnast, before she leapt back to the snow. She also recalled their trek in the snow so far but did not note anything new in her memory that she had not seen the first time. She checked for signs of other fey, too, but saw nothing that seemed out of place.

"He listened when I wanted to explain why I had been doing it," she said. "So when he told me not to do it anyway, he did it with all the information. When I ignored the orders of adults, it was because I knew something—about a danger, for instance—that they did not. And they would not listen to me. So, a part of me thought: well, they would do X if they listened, but they are not listening, so I had better do X—before someone gets seriously hurt."

"And seeking information?" asked Gaius.

"If we don't have sufficient information, we won't know when X needs to be done."

"I can see that." Gaius leaned over the fence and peered through the pale trunks, trying to see which way the hoofprints had gone. "Basically, you didn't trust the supposed authority. I feel that way about many people but not about Vladimir, which is why I can obey him just fine."

"Exactly that. Yes," Rachel replied, gazing over the fence as well.

Gaius put his arm around her shoulders, making her feel snug and warm. Guilt jabbed through her. It was not right that her heart should be so conflicted. *This* was the boy who deserved her love and devotion. She resolved to find a way to wrestle her feelings for *the other boy* back into hero worship and adoration.

She closed her eyes, basking in the unexpected warmth of the February sun. She felt so comfortable with him. If only there were a place where they could actually curl up together—nothing inappropriate, just stretch out and snuggle close. Maybe the couch in her....

"Oh no!" she cried suddenly.

"Something wrong?" Gaius squeezed her shoulder.

"I'm locked out of my secret hideout—that room I took you to!" Rachel moaned. "If I can't fly through windows I can't ever go back to my secret room."

She glanced over her shoulder towards Roanoke Hall, where the hexagonal tower that held the room which only she seemed to visit rose among the many other spires and towers on the roof, but trees blocked her sight. Sighing, she gazed glumly at the snowy ground. *How would she ever get back her peacock pillow and her plushy lion?*

Gaius gave her a sympathetic smile and tightened the comforting arm around her shoulder. She leaned against him and then tensed suddenly as something dark moved among the pale trunks.

"Gaius," she whispered hoarsely, grabbing his arm. "There it is! The *each-uisge*!"

Chapter Eleven:
The Horse
Come from the Marsh

Rachel and Gaius sprinted alongside the fence, trying to keep up with the cantering *each-uisge*. As they ran, Gaius spoke over the bracelet to the rest of Dread's team, sharing information and receiving instructions. Occasionally, they could catch a clear glimpse of their quarry. The water horse was a handsome animal, coal black with a flowing mane and tail. To an ordinary observer, it probably looked like a mundane horse, but Rachel kept noticing little things that were not quite right, an odd fluidity to its motions, the wrong proportion of its neck.

Speaking over the bracelet, Dread told the two younger students to just keep an eye on the water horse and not to take any action against it until the others arrived. After about five minutes of moving through the evergreen branches of the hemlocks, Gaius and Rachel rendezvoused with the rest of Dread's group just north of the Watch Tower. With Vlad were William, Topher, and Naomi.

The six of them spoke together quietly, deciding how they would encircle the *each-uisge* and who would perform what attack. Once they all knew their parts, they spread out to encircle the black steed. Creeping through the hemlocks, Rachel came upon a stick to which someone had pinned a four-petaled flower made of silver foil, the edge of each petal having been cut a number of times, forming flaps. It looked like something from a lower school art project. She glanced at this curious object for a moment, but it did not connect with anything in her memory. She wondered how long it had been out here, hidden among the hemlocks.

Creeping onward, she came to a boulder that made a great hiding place and waited for the others to move into position. Whispering over their black bracelets, they each indicated with a single syllable when they were ready. Eventually, Von Dread, William, Gaius, Topher, and Naomi stood poised, wands ready. Rachel prepared to whistle.

"Now!" Dread's voice sounded in her ear.

As one, they leapt forward and fired at the *each-uisge*.

Nothing happened.

The entire group of them stood, pointing their wands or, in Rachel's case, whistling, but nothing occurred—no sparks, no scents, not even a glint of a wand gem.

Too late, Rachel's memory dredged up an image of a four-feathered silver pinwheel, tall and thin with delicate, needle-like protrusions — *a quatre plumes d'argent* or, more colloquially, a plume-silver. It was a device used for sensing sorcerous or supernatural influences. It did not look much like the fat, flower-like, hand-made version nailed to a stick, but she was suddenly certain it was the same thing. Plume-silvers were often placed on temporary wards.

"We're on the wrong side of the wards!" shouted Topher, who apparently had come to the same conclusion at the same time. "Our magic doesn't work."

"Retreat," commanded Dread.

But it was too late.

The sleek black steed began to elongate, its proportions becoming less horse-like, more distorted. Its mane and tail grew longer, floating in an impossible fashion, almost as if it were under water. Moving with astonishing speed, it kicked backward, its leg extending over twelve feet. Its hoof struck Topher in the stomach, throwing him through the air.

Then rearing up, it tossed its head with a loud whinnying cry and charged directly at Rachel. She wanted to move. She thought about moving, but the horse struck her before she could act on that thought. It was like fighting Ethan Warhol, only a hundred times worse.

It struck her with its shoulder, throwing her hard against the snowy ground and then trampling her stomach with one of its hooves as it escaped off through the hemlocks. Rachel lay gasping on the ground. The whole world had receded to just her body and the sky. She did not even feel the pain yet, though she knew it was coming. Her head felt oddly heavy. The lower part of her body did not seem to exist at all.

She wondered obliquely if she would ever feel her feet again.

All around her, there was motion. Gaius was beside her, kneeling by her head. She heard William calling Topher's name, and Vlad calling for Jenny, which might have been her imagination, because Jenny Dare was not even with them.

Then, she closed her eyes, because keeping them open no longer seemed like a good idea.

"Rachel, honey?" a girl's voice was calling her. "Rachel, can you hear me?"

Rachel slowly became aware of her surroundings. She held her breath, but no pain came. She felt strange. Her head still felt heavy. Her legs felt wobbly, but the important part was that she could feel them. Something was between her and the snow. It felt like a blanket.

She opened her eyes. Above her were blue sky and the feathery evergreen branches of hemlocks. To either side, Gaius and Jenny Dare knelt beside her, staring at her face in concern.

"Try another dose," Gaius was saying. "She doesn't seem to be responding."

"No, let's let this one work," Jenny replied. "Too much is as bad as too little. Oh, look! She's opened her eyes!"

Jenny smiled at her, a cheerful, almost-gleeful smile. In her hand, she held a slender length of elm wood inlaid with gold and tipped with an emerald—the gem used by healers.

"Rachel, honey, can you sit up?"

Rachel slowly sat up. She felt very unsteady, but there was no pain. She touched her stomach, where she remembered feeling the water horse's hoof. Everything seemed fine, although it was a bit sore when she pushed on it.

"Hey." Gaius was kneeling very close to her, looking at her with great concern.

"Hey," she murmured back, smiling at him.

His eyes searched her face carefully. "How do you feel?"

Rachel thought about this. "Wobbly. But okay."

Gaius broke into a big grin. Straightening, he reached out and gave Jenny's shoulder an appreciatory pat. "Good work, Dare. Thanks."

"Any time, Valiant," replied Jenny, who was running a pair of scrutiny sticks, two rounded lengths of wood inset with gems and carved with runes, up and down Rachel's body. Two gems lit up. She looked at them and smiled. "All right, Rachel, honey. You should be good to go. Just take it easy for a while. I'm going to go check on Topher again."

Gaius sat down on the blanket next to Rachel and pulled her onto his lap. He held her very tightly, as if he was very happy to have her there. She smiled sleepily and laid her head against his chest. Out of the corner of her eye, she could see Vlad talking seriously with Naomi. Behind Gaius and to his left, she could hear William's calm, serious tones, and Topher, sounding rather wan, trying to crack a joke.

"Glad you're still with us," Gaius murmured into her ear.

"Me, too." She snuggled up against him. "Where are we? I don't recognize that tree."

Gaius started to laugh and then stopped. "Wait. You're serious. You actually remember every tree?"

"Don't you?" she asked, still feeling slightly fuzzy-headed.

"We had to move the two of you to a place where sorcery worked, so Jenny could heal you. I was afraid to move you—we Unwary worry about that—but Jenny explained that any damage done by moving you could easily be undone by magic. We all carried you back across the wards."

Rachel nodded slowly. That made sense. With magic, one could heal mundane damage. It was magical damage that gave the nuns and monks of Asclepius pause.

Somewhere behind Gaius and to the right, Jenny was talking to somebody.

"Oh, aren't you beautiful!" her voice came gaily. "What a pretty thing you are. Can I pet you? Ride? Sure, that sounds like fun."

Wait... what? Rachel struggled to sit up and see over Gaius's shoulder. Jenny stood a little distance from the rest of them, gazing at a magnificent black steed with slightly wrong proportions. Her expression was cheerful, and yet she looked very slightly dazed, as if her eyes were not entirely focused. As if in a dream, she moved toward the *each-uisge*.

"Rach. You don't have to get up. You should rest," Gaius began.

Only Rachel was out of his arms and lunging to her feet. "No! Don't touch him!"

But, for the second time that afternoon, it was too late. The water horse knelt, and Jenny was on its back, even before the others turned to look.

"Jenny!" Naomi cried, racing forward, drawing her wand.

"Stop!" Vlad pointed his ebony and gold wand, sending a steam of blue sparks toward the black steed. The sparks flew straight and true and then petered out, as the attack crossed the make-shift wards.

Without hesitating, Dread ran to the right, as if to bodily block the creature from leaving. William and Gaius were both on their feet as well. Topher started to get up and then had second thoughts and lay down again. To Rachel's relief, he seemed only a bit pale, and he did not move as if he were in pain.

The black steed took off like an arrow. As one, the others were after it. Rachel ran with them, too caught up in her fear for Jenny to notice how shaky she was. Even Topher had clambered to his feet and was running, albeit slowly. Dread was in front, moving rapidly in an attempt to surround the creature and perhaps herd it. With almost no effort at all, the water horse leapt twenty-five feet through the air, sailing over Vladimir, whose brows shot up as he watched it pass over his head.

"Wha—" Jenny suddenly came to herself on the back of the black horse. "What am I doing up here! Um...." She tried to lift her hands, but they were stuck to the neck of the each-uisge. Her legs, too, were stuck. "*Vladimir! Help!*"

"We need to herd it back to where our magic works," Dread stated as he ran. He spoke quietly. His words sounded in everyone's ears over their black bracelets. "And we have to cut it off from the river. If it gets anywhere near the river, I will jump. To do so, I'll have to put the wards down momentarily, and then I shall have to explain myself to the proctors. But being caught at this is better than risking her life."

Running back to the closer side of the wards, he drew something from an inner pocket of his robe, some kind of cloth or blanket of brilliant blue satin. As he ran, he shook it out. To Rachel's astonishment, it was his cloak of black swan-feathers, the one she had seen hanging in his bedroom back in September, the one he had been wearing in the vision Nastasia saw of him, in his past existence as the Dread King.

Vlad paused, reached into the lining of the cloak, and pulled out a bristleless. It was a custom-made, sleek, black racer with a gold racing stripe down the side. Leaping upon it, he stuffed his swan-feathered cloak back into his robes and took off. Meanwhile, Gaius, William, and Naomi were ahead, running. Rachel was running, too, but she could not keep up. Her legs were short, and she could not seem to catch her breath.

Gaius and William were in the lead. When the water horse leapt the makeshift wire fence, which had reappeared here, and ran onto the campus, they pointed their wands and fired, but the water horse was too fast for them. Jenny's familiar, a yellow-beaked mynah bird, dived at the water horse, crying like an eagle, screaming like a crow, and even clanging like the bells that marked a change of classes. When Jenny shouted for it to back off, afraid that it would become stuck to the black steed, the bird began circling high above her, crying, "Bad dog! Bad dog!"

His wand outstretched, Gaius tried again and again and again. Suddenly, Jenny cried out, delighted, waving her right foot, which had come free from the horse's sleek black pelt.

"You freed my leg," she cried, "Now do my hand!"

Vlad, flying at high speed, came up beside Gaius and instructed him to hop on, which was not an easy task, because the racer's seat was not meant for two.

Vlad spoke calmly, though there was a tension in his voice that Rachel had not heard before. "I am going to fly you closer. See if you can free her!"

"On it!" Gaius replied.

The two of them shot forward, lightning quick. They moved toward Jenny's left side, trying to stay between the runaway steed and the outer ward. William ran after them with Naomi on his heels, but only the two on the racer had a chance of keeping up with the *each-uisge*.

Trying desperately to catch up, Rachel wished that this had not happened while her broom was with Mr. Chanson's parents. She was breathing in ragged gulps like a sick sheep. Topher had given up entirely and stood panting, his head down, his hands resting on his thighs. Should she stop, too? *No.* Drawing as deep a breath as she could, she ran faster.

Vlad and Gaius both pointed their wands at the *each-uisge* and fired off spell after spell to no avail. The thing seemed able to leap away from the effects of the magic. Rachel was impressed. This creature was leagues ahead of the kelpie they had fought in Transylvania. It was as if it were partway into the fey realm and could dodge the effects of their magic.

Flying alongside the creature, Gaius pointed his wand at Jenny. She cried out in joy and waved her left hand freely. She kept it up so it would not get stuck again.

Vlad commanded, "The beast is evading our sorcery. Concentrate on Jenny! Our spells can affect her."

Gaius cried, "Can you get me closer?"

The racer darted forward. Gaius waited, poised. As Vlad came up alongside Jenny, the younger boy fired again. With a whoop, Jenny's left leg came free, and her body flew away from the horse. Only her right hand was still attached. Suddenly, she was flying freely, being dragged through the air by her arm alongside the black steed.

With a loud smack, Jenny's leg slammed into a tree truck. She screamed in pain.

"I've got this," Naomi announced in her calm, clipped voice, though she was breathing heavily, followed by, "*Tiathelu!*"

Casting the cantrip directly gave her more control than if she had used her wand. She levitated Jenny's body upright, away from the *each-uisge*. She could not pull Jenny free, as the other girl's hand was still stuck to the neck of the black steed, but she could hold Jenny's outstretched body away from the creature's sleek coat so that she would not accidentally touch its hide again. Also, she attempted to maneuver Jenny around obstacles, such as tree trunks; however, this required that Naomi run fast enough to keep Jenny within her sight.

It did not help that they were running on snow, and twice Rachel slid, though she caught herself and kept going. She hoped desperately that Naomi would keep her footing.

"Bad dog! Bad dog!" screeched the little bird, circling Jenny's head.

The wake of the racer spooked the black horse. It whinnied angrily and dashed southward, down an incline. Ahead, through the trees, Rachel could make out the boardwalk that ran beside College Creek. She could hear the faint rush of water that had not frozen. Luckily, the horse was now running parallel to the river, but who knew when that would change. As soon as the fey steed smelled the water, it would make its final dash toward the creek.

They had to free Jenny or stop the horse before it reached the river! If it reached water, it would become much more powerful and try to drown its rider. Vlad had sped up, but to free Jenny's other hand—her final place of contact with the steed—required coming around the horse, which might scare it toward the creek.

Rachel ran as fast as she could pump her legs. Her thighs burned. *There must be something she could do to help.* In the stories she had heard from the servants as a child, fey who were immune to sorcery always had a weakness, a spot or place where they intersected with the mortal world and were vulnerable to its laws. For the kelpie and phooka of Dartmoor, it was their hooves, the spot where they touched the earth of this world.

She would have liked to share this, but she was panting too hard to talk. She changed direction, running southwest. As she ran, she triangulated, guessing at the black steed's current trajectory. She ran downhill at a diagonal, heading for a spot that, if she planned it properly and the creature did not change course, should put her ahead of it, if only for a moment.

"Vlad! We've got to get to the other side!" Gaius called. "I can't reach her from here."

"I do not wish to herd the creature toward the river," Dread replied. "If we can force it to run back towards the west, we can fly up beside it on its other side."

"I-it's get-ting away fr-from me," Naomi gasped, her breath coming in ragged hacks. "Wil-liam. B-be re-ady to take ov-er."

"Understood," William replied. He, too, sounded breathy, though he was not yet panting. Rachel was impressed. She had not realized that William was in such good shape. Or was it because his mother was an elf?

Rachel slowed, sliding down a steeper hill sideways, hemlock branches in her face, then put on another burst of speed. She did not know if she could keep up. Would she make it close enough to try her idea? As she ran, she pulled her silver wand from her neck pouch, holding it tightly in her hand, sliding most of it inside her sleeve, so she would be less likely to drop it.

"It's turning," Gaius said triumphantly. "Just a little more, and we'll have you, Jenny!"

Sure enough, the black steed swerved away from the racer, heading back toward the west, which was perfect for Rachel's plan, if she could just get a little closer.

"Any time, now," said Jenny. "I appreciate everything Naomi's doing, but... this flapping like a banner in the wind behind the evil horsey is getting a little old, and a little cold. *Brrr.*"

"Doing our be..." William began.

Naomi screamed. Rachel glanced sideways in time to see the red-haired upperclassman tumbling down the hill, head over heels.

"Naomi!" William cried. His wand was in his hand and pointed at her, catching her before she could come to a hard landing.

"Yikes!" cried Jenny, as her body began to fly free, falling.

"Got you!" cried Gaius, pointing his wand at her. "We..."

The water horse swerved and began running straight for the creek. *This was the closest Rachel was going to get. It was now or never.* She stopped, braced herself, pointed her wand with both hands, and concentrated on the horse's hooves. Even though she was using her wand, she shouted out the word component of the cantrip. "*Turlu!*"

Concentrating with all her might, she cast the spell she had used against the lightning javelin the night of the skating party. Performing it exactly as Gaius had taught her, she did not try to stop the runaway steed. That might be bad for Jenny. Instead, she moved some of the water horse's speed from the creature and into a copse of saplings father down the hill. If she pulled this off, it would slow the *each-uisge* enough that Gaius and Vlad could rescue Jenny.

She performed the spell. An unseen force blew her target saplings over until their branches brushed the ground. The thickest of them creaked and cracked with a report like a rifle. The other saplings sprang back up again once the force of the spell had dissipated. Meanwhile, the black steed was suddenly moving at the speed of a slow walk.

Vlad darted around the closer side of the water horse, Gaius stood on the footrests, no mean feat on a racer, one hand steadying himself on Vlad's shoulder, the other holding his wand. And then Jenny was free and floating through the air until she came to rest gently on the ground. Her familiar landed on her shoulder where it jumped around, agitated, alternating between quacking like a duck and making kissy noises. Jenny rubbed her cheek against its black and gray feathers and closed her eyes, sighing.

Bereft of its victim, the *each-uisge* bellowed in anger. Again, it lost its appealing shape and elongated, until it looked like a bony monster with enormous fangs and seaweed for mane and tail. Its whole body was now a deep kelp green.

"Shoot at its feet!" Rachel shouted, finally able to breathe.

"You don't have to shout," Gaius's voice came wryly in her ear. "In fact, my ear drums would prefer if you didn't."

He spoke lightly, but his attention was on the water horse, sparks flying from his wand. Just as the sparks began to swirl around its hooves, it leapt, arcing a dozen feet above their heads. It landed next to where Naomi still lay in the snow and lunged, its muzzle elongated until it was twice as long as it should be. Its fangs opened to clamp on her leg. Only William was in the way. Quick as a flash, he had leapt between the monster and his girlfriend. The water horse's awful teeth closed on William's arm. He grunted in pain but did not scream.

"Gotcha!" Gaius shouted, firing again.

Before the spell arrived, the creature had released William and leapt away, moving up the hill at such speeds that Rachel's eyes could hardly track it. One more leap and it was over the makeshift wards again, vanishing among the hemlocks.

Dread watched it depart, frowning. "How disappointing."

"You didn't have to do that, William," Naomi said sternly from the ground.

"Actually, I did," William replied evenly.

"Didn't know you were the play-the-hero type," she said, disapproval in her voice.

William replied calmly, though his face had taken on a slightly green cast. "I am an employee of Ouroboros Industries. The school has granted me permission to come and go, as my father needs me. The bite of a kelpie, of which *each-uisge* are a subset, contains virulent poison as well as diseases—which the medics at O.I. are quite skilled at dealing with. If any of you had been bitten, you would have had to report to the infirmary and explain to the nurse how you came to be injured. I do not."

"Ah." Naomi lay back on the snow and closed her eyes. "Good point."

"Do you want one of us to come with you?" asked Dread. "I could probably get clearance to accompany you."

William shook his head. "I will be fine, but I am leaving now. I leave the rest to you."

He winked at Naomi, who had opened her eyes again, and departed, walking at a brisk but unhurried clip toward the campus and the docks.

Chapter Twelve: The Lark, the Lily, and the Thorn

The remaining five students headed back to the glade where they had been before the *each-uisge* had trapped Jenny, so that Jenny could pick up her dropped scrutiny sticks and a few other supplies. As they went back up the hemlock-studded hill, a gorgeous black and white magpie with an iridescent sheen along its wings flew down out of the branches and landed on a large boulder to their left, staring right at them. Rachel gawked at this behavior, but the others treated it as if they thought it was an everyday occurrence. The bird cocked its black head and spoke in a voice that sounded like a slightly higher version of Topher.

"Hide, quick. Proctors!" called the bird. "Hide, quick. Proctors!"

"Bad dog!" replied the mynah bird from Jenny's shoulder, causing her to giggle.

The five of them crouched behind the boulder. Sure enough, voices — two male and one female — drifted through the forest, though they were too far away to make out words. After a few minutes, the magpie, which Rachel deduced was Topher's familiar, announced, "The coast is clear! The coast is clear!" Rachel found it was amusing that both Jenny and Topher had familiars that could imitate human speech. She knew that Gaius and Vlad did not have familiars. She wondered about William and Naomi.

Continuing, they met Topher, who came slowly limping toward them. He had slipped on the slick snow while running and twisted his ankle. Jenny fixed it with a flick of her wand and then checked it with her scrutiny sticks, which she also ran over her own leg. Apparently, she had already repaired whatever damage she had suffered when she struck the tree.

"We've got to get moving!" Topher warned them. "I think Bifrost warned you—at least I asked him to," he glanced at the magpie, who was seated on a branch, paying no attention to the humans, "but two proctors were just up here along with Urd Odinson, checking on what had disturbed the *plumes d'argent.* I ducked behind that outcropping over there, and they didn't see me by sheer chance because they didn't realize how far the thing could jump. They interpreted the hoofprints to mean that the water horse came onto campus and left again. But they'll be back shortly. I heard Fuentes telling Mr. Scott that the new fencing had come in, so they could now fence off the last part of the campus. They asked Urd to thank the DeVere students who had apparently helped them and Master Warder Nighthawk make the old-fashioned wards that they had put in this area while they waited for more fencing. Also, they said they would be patrolling this whole area after they got the new fencing."

The group of them started downhill, heading through the hemlocks back to the campus *propre.* Rachel was so tired, she could hardly open her eyes, and her legs trembled like plucked violin strings. Gaius kept an arm around her to keep her from swaying.

"Would you like to ride, Miss Griffin?" Dread asked, gesturing toward his racer.

Rachel's face lit up. Gaius scooped her up and deposited her gently on the bristleless. She blushed with joy, seated up on the sleek, black device that had so recently carried her two favorite boys. A warm glow filled her, caused by Dread's care for her and Gaius's gallantry.

"I am glad to hear that the proctors are aware there was a disturbance. We will have to inform them of the *each-uisge,*" Dread said regretfully. "This beast is too dangerous for us to pursue. I have fought numerous magical beasts. I have never encountered anything like it."

Naomi replied in her calm, clipped way, "Roanoke Island itself is a magical place. The fey who live here are steeped in sorcery in a way that those in the rest of the world are not."

"I never want to be in that situation again. Over a ward and without magic." Gaius shook his head. "When we were chasing the horse, I kept thinking of things we could do to restrain it, but it was so fast. It was out of the area each time before I could try it."

Topher said, "That was really scary, crossing a ward and not having any magic. Can we just do that to each other all the time? Have our familiars ward somebody and, *zoop*, all their magic is gone? How come pranksters don't do that to each other every day?"

Naomi gave him a skeptical glance. "Familiar wards would not do this. They are flimsy things compared to permanent wards, good for blocking certain cantrips and lesser supernatural entities, such as woodland fey. Even these make-shift wards took the proctors several days to lay properly."

Rachel's head dropped, dejected. "I'm just sorry that, after all this, they're going to have to close down the school."

"Maybe they won't close it down," Topher offered. "Maybe they'll just lock us up for a few days, bring in an expert, and catch it."

"Or maybe they will have to finally abandon the campus for good and rebuild Roanoke Academy on a new spot," Naomi replied sternly. "My parents have always held that this was a dangerous place for a school."

"There's no helping it," Vladimir replied, "Magic attracts magic. Any place you brought so many different disciplines together would attract fey. At least, here, they are a known quantity and, if they can recapture the Heer, things should quiet down again."

"What I don't understand," Jenny said as she marched cheerfully beside Vladimir, "is: how come the horsey-thing's magic worked on both sides of the wards?"

"That's because those were makeshift wards," Naomi relied. "I lived in DeVere in my upper school days. As anyone who has ever lived there knows, from every time they try to open a door, different things stop different kinds of supernatural creatures. Some are stopped by cold iron, some by straw, some by red thread, some by bread. Makeshift wards try to combine all the common elements to create a general catch-all barrier. But some things slip through."

Rachel nodded from where she floated beside them. "Many old and powerful fey have special gifts that grant them exceptions to the ordinary restrictions. Sometimes they have traded a normal vulnerability for an abnormal one. The annals of the supernatural beast hunters are filled with tales of the efforts they had to go to in order to find the specific weakness of some ancient supernatural menace." She paused and then added, "The kelpie we fought in Transylvania also crossed the wards Xandra drew."

Gaius stepped closer and laid a hand on her forearm. "You were really brave, Rachel Griffin, getting out there and running toward the thing that stepped on you."

Rachel lowered her lashes, blushing at his praise. Gaius walked beside her, rubbing her back gently and whistling a familiar tune.

Naomi cocked her head. "Ah, 'Lark, Lily, and Thorn.' I have not heard that song in years."

Gaius replied airily, "When my mum was ill, we had a nurse from Devon. She used to sing that. I was reminded of it because the events in the ballad were a bit like our situation here."

"And what is that?" Vlad looked up. "I am not familiar with the tune."

Gaius stretched and then took Rachel's hand as he walked. "It's an old ballad about three siblings, a boy and two girls, who catch a phooka on the moors. It just reminded me of our day."

"Did they catch it?" Topher asked. "Did they live?"

"Yes, and yes," Rachel said softly, "though they were all cut down a decade or so later during the Wars of the Roses."

"Wait." Gaius's eyebrows rose. "They were real people? I didn't realize that." He looked at Rachel's face, his eyes narrowing. "Were they Griffins?"

"No, another branch of our family. They...." Rachel paused, reflecting on the ballad, and then blurted out, "I can catch the *each-uisge*!"

"Rach, you are in no condition to catch a cold, much less an evil, vindictive horse," Gaius said with some concern. "You're wobbling."

Sighing, Rachel slid from the racer to prove that she was capable of walking. She stumbled at first, to Gaius's alarm, her knees nearly giving out, but then she caught herself and was able to walk chipperly alongside the rest.

"I feel much better," she said truthfully, though her legs were still a bit wobbly, "and I will feel even better soon. Please. If we tell the proctors, that's it. They'll have us locked in the dorms again and probably cancel the ball for good. I can't stand being locked in again. I'll go batty. I truly will."

"If Rachel isn't using it, can I ride the bristleless?" Topher asked plaintively.

"No," Dread said mildly. He unfolded his cloak and slipped the racer back into wherever it had come from.

Seeing Topher's crestfallen face, Gaius burst out laughing. "Suffering builds character, Evans."

"I'll suffer you!" Topher muttered, trying to elbow Gaius in the ribs, but Gaius was too quick for him.

The older boy ducked away, chuckling, "That makes no sense. Don't you mean 'I'll build you some character?'" which only made Topher try harder to hit him.

"I can do this!" Rachel insisted, ignoring the roughhousing boys.

"Rachel, honey," Jenny said gently. "I don't think trying again is a good idea. What happened to you, Topher, William, and me was bad enough. What if someone really gets hurt? Something a student like me can't fix?"

"It is too dangerous, Miss Griffin," Dread declared. "I cannot risk another person getting injured. I will tell the proctors about the *each-uisge* without mentioning any of you. If they close the school...." He looked grim. "We can hope it will not be for very long."

"Please! I can do this!" cried Rachel. "I can!"

"What, specifically, did you have in mind?" Gaius asked.

"Exactly what happens in the song. You can be the Thorn."

Gaius got a kind of half grin on his face. "That's not very hard. My part, I mean, but...."

"What makes you think you can do better than the rest of us?" Naomi asked, her voice particularly dry.

"You've heard the song," Rachel replied, "I am from Dartmoor. My family has been luring in kelpie and phooka, and worse things, for thousands of years. Gaius and I can do this. I just need to gather some supplies and consult an expert."

"There are experts?" Gaius quipped.

"There are," Rachel replied firmly, her eyes dancing, "and, as it happens, one of them is on campus."

"Are you sure we should try it here?" Rachel looked dubiously around the clearing in the paper birches behind Dare Hall, close to where she and Gaius had first started their patrol earlier that afternoon. The sun was near the horizon, and the warmth of the day was gone, the February cold returning. "It's not very big."

"Any farther into the woods, and we'll cross the wards again," Gaius replied, his arms full of blankets. "Besides, with all the hoof prints coming in and out of this clearing, it looks like the thing has come here a number of times."

"Okay." Rachel turned slowly in a circle. "I guess it will do."

"Vlad, William? You hear that?" Gaius lifted his head slightly as he spoke over the black bracelet." He nodded and turned back to Rachel. "They are in position. Far enough away to be out of scent range but close enough to rush to our aid if everything goes pear-shaped. Vlad says he can always jump in an emergency—but the staff and the proctors will know, of course."

Rachel nodded solemnly. "It's okay. We won't need them."

"What now?" Gaius glanced around the snowy glade. "We hang out and hope it comes back?"

"Not exactly," replied Rachel.

Gazing up, she could see the peak of Storm King rising above the trees with the sun just above it. She consulted an almanac in her mental library.

"Do you know the time?" she asked.

Gaius said aloud, "Vlad, what time is it?" and then repeated what the prince told him.

Rachel nodded. Reaching into her pockets, she brought out a stoppered vial. "Here. I am going to go grab some supplies... and our expert. Drink this and get wrapped up comfortably in the blankets. You have to stay still or it won't work, so you had better be warm."

"I admit to being intrigued," her boyfriend replied. He took the vial, read the label, opened it, and sniffed. Then he shrugged and downed the contents. His whole body shivered. "Ugh. Chameleon."

Then he faded from sight.

"This is excellent Chameleon Elixir. I can't see myself at all." He must have leaned over, because the snow disturbed itself and a stick rose up into the air. "You've been holding out on us, Griffin! This is the good stuff. See, even when I hold the stick, you can't even tell where... yikes!" The stick had vanished, too.

"Wh-where'd it go?"

"You're holding it, aren't you?" asked Rachel.

"Y-yes. Yes, I am. I can feel it, but why did it disappear?" There was a slight edge of panic to Gaius's voice, though he quickly recovered. "Ahem. I mean, what is going on here?"

Had she never told Gaius about the existence of the Elf herbs? No, apparently, she had not. It had not been on purpose, though now that he did not know, she felt reluctant to reveal Sigfried's secrets.

She grinned and replied mysterious, "No secrets can be revealed."

"If you say so. This is some impressive stuff."

Random objects, such as rocks or snowballs were vanishing and reappearing.

Rachel nodded serenely. "I will be back in less than twenty minutes. Before the sun sets. See you then. Or rather, you'll see me. I won't see you. You're invisible."

It took her only a few minutes to race down to the menagerie and gather the supplies she needed, but it took her much longer than she had expected to find her sister. She was about to give up and go back on her own, as she did not want to miss sunset, when she found Laurel sitting in a common room with several other upperclassmen.

"*Unni!*" Rachel gasped, out of breath for running. "Do you have a minute?"

"Sure." Laurel rose and stretched. She was dressed in her subfusc uniform: white blouse, a slender black double tie, black leggings, and a skirt that Rachel was pretty sure was shorter than regulation required. To her friends, Laurel said, "Don't do anything I wouldn't, you lot. I'll be back when I'm done boxing the ears of my sister."

The two of them walked to Laurel's room, a double which she shared with her best friend, Muffy Calico. The walls were plastered with posters, and the curtains were a purple velvet damask. A sword rack mounted on the wall held two clarinets.

Rachel eyed her sister suspiciously. "And why would you box my ears?"

"I'm sure you are up to no good about something."

Rachel did not respond to that. Instead, she turned to face her sister, blurting out all in a rush, "Tell me again how you catch a phooka. Don't leave anything out."

"Oh, ho! A test is it? Can't be that you didn't study. Did they go over this a day you weren't in class for some reason?"

Rachel ignored her barbs. "This is what I have so far." She laid her supplies on her sister's desk, pushing aside a half-written essay. "But I want to make sure I know all the steps."

"Is this serious?" Laurel frowned slightly. "Well, to start with, this looks good." Laurel went over the steps. "The real key is how you handle the come-hither. If you resist it, the phook will know and run. If you cannot remember yourself, you will be lost and drown horribly. It's that second part I sometimes have trouble with. That's why we have the Thorn, of course."

Rachel puffed out her cheeks and exhaled. She glanced out the window. "It's almost twilight! I've got to go."

"Wait!" her sister commanded. She leaned down with her hands on her thighs, gazing at Rachel. "This is for real, isn't it?"

Rachel bit her lip and said nothing.

Laurel grabbed her coat. "I'm coming with you."

"Tell me again why Daddy told you about this supposed school closing?" Laurel asked as they arrived in the snowy glade. "He didn't say a word to Peter and me."

"Because I went home to see him, as requested," Rachel replied.

"Without us?"

"You said you didn't want to go."

"What? I never did!"

Rachel glanced up at the sun, which was practically touching the peak of the mountain. "Do we start when the sun falls behind Storm King or when it goes below the horizon?"

"Storm King. Magically, it is just as significant, and it gives us more light." Laurel gazed up with her. "Not much time left! *Brrrr*! It's cold here! Ready?"

"Okay," Rachel walked to the middle of the glade and held up her supplies.

"Sugar cubes," commanded Laurel.

"Sugar cubes," Rachel echoed as she laid down a line of sugar cubes—she had found a few in her trunk—and horse feed she had fetched from the menagerie.

"Apple," said Laurel.

Rachel put the apple down carefully parallel to where she had last seen Gaius.

Laurel glanced around. "Your Thorn is well hidden. Are you sure he's here?"

There came a very faint sound of a throat being cleared from behind a leafless bush. Laurel stared into the bush but, of course, saw nothing.

"Wow. That's well hidden." Laurel leaned toward her sister, grinning, "Who is it, Sigfried Smith?"

"We're running out of time," Rachel said, primly.

"Okay, whatever. Keep your little secrets." In a louder voice, she said, "Thorn, you do your stuff when the beastie is eating the apple. That's what makes him vulnerable to the mortal world. When he eats the apple. Not before. Got that? Try it before and something bad happens. Probably to me. Okay," she turned to Rachel, "Now, choose: Lark or Lily?"

"Lark," Rachel said without hesitation. Despite her brave words, she still felt a tad wobbly. Well, okay, massively wobbly, but legs were not needed to play the Lark's role.

"That's wise, but, *dongsaeng*—" Laurel leaned over, hands on her thighs again, and gazed directly into her sister's eyes. "You realize that if this goes wrong, I am going to die, right? Just want to make sure you are taking this seriously."

Rachel's head bobbed up and down, her heart suddenly beating unnaturally fast.

"Good, because I'm serious. A number of the women in our family have died this way down through the ages. There are ballads about two of them, and a third is still used as a cautionary tale to frighten children in the Lake Country."

Then Laurel straightened and grinned, tossing her hair. "But it won't go wrong. I could tell you a lot more stories about Griffin and Wyllt women who have pulled this off. Come on. Let's do this!"

She turned and faced the west. Rachel stepped up beside her, so that the two of them stood side by side at the eastern side of the glade, facing west.

"Hair down," Laurel instructed.

Reaching back, Rachel took the clips from her hair and stuck them in her coat pocket. Laurel, whose hair was significantly longer than Rachel's shoulder-length locks, did the same.

"Combs out," her sister called.

Both Griffin girls extended a hand holding identical tortoiseshell combs inset with mother of pearl. They paused, thus posed, watching the sun.

The sun began to disappear behind the mountain peak.

Laurel barked out. "Begin!"

As one, the two Griffin girls began to comb their dark locks. As they combed, they sang, their voices rising and mingling in beautiful melody. Rachel loved to sing. She had started formal voice lessons at age eight and had sung quite a bit back at home. Laurel only had a smattering of formal training—she had preferred dancing and vaulting—but she still was a lovely singer. The sisters sang together, their voices soaring, filling the evening with melody and beauty.

Together, they sang a ballad called "A Wind in the Heather" about a young woman who pined for the love of a horse, singing of how she wished to leave her old life behind, to wander the windy moors, and to ride and ride and ride to the sea. They sang and combed, matching their motions together. As the song ended, they both sank down, one hip against the cold snow, the other leg over the first one, their heads bowed and their hair over their faces, in what Sandra and Laurel had dubbed the "sorrowful girl pose."

As she sank into the cold snow, Rachel heard the *clomp* of the *each-uisge*'s feet as it entered the glade. Glancing through the curtain of her black tresses without moving her head, Rachel could make out the magnificent black animal with its long mane and sleek coat.

Taking a very deep breath, she lifted her voice to sing.

Laurel spun to her feet and began to dance. Moving with wild yet graceful steps, she danced towards and away from the *each-uisge*, tossing her hair like a midnight mane. The black steed, too, began to toss its mane, rearing on its back feet at the same moments that Laurel, with fierce abandon, threw herself backward, coming down and bowing over its foreleg when Laurel bent forward, her hair cascading to brush the snow. Laurel spun, lunged, and sprang back, hair whipping like a banner, in perfect timing to the almost dance-like motions of the water horse.

Meanwhile, Rachel sang and sang and sang. Not a song with lyrics, such as their earlier ballad, but a wordless song that had been sung by women of her family upon Dartmoor for thousands of years, long before even the Griffins had come to Briton. This music came from their Wyllt ancestors, the family line whose most distinguished member, Myrddin Wyllt, was known to history by a much more famous name. It was not Myrddin; however, but his female ancestors who had used this song to call phooka, kelpies, and ponies on the moors.

Making the most of her wild child persona, Laurel danced with the water horse, leaping and turning and tossing her long, sable locks. She threw off her coat, dancing in her white shirt and black leggings and her too-short skirt. She was hampered slightly by the fact that she had not attempted this in some years. There were moments when Rachel could tell her motions had been choreographed for a shorter girl with a more willowy line, but Laurel quickly modified her steps to adjust to her taller, more-womanly shape. The steed, too, pranced and tossed its mane, moving to the melody of Rachel's wordless song.

Only this dance was not meant to be danced on snow. As she twirled around the central place where the apple stood, Laurel slipped on the slick ice and lost her footing. As she wind-milled her arms, falling sideways, Rachel's mind's eye showed her the *each-uisge's* teeth champing down on William's arm. Without knowing how she knew, Rachel knew absolutely that if her sister hit the ground, she would die.

But this time, Rachel did not freeze up. Her wand was already in her sleeve from their earlier adventures. Without even moving, she flicked her wrist, bringing the length of silver into her hand. A charge of *tiathelu* was all she needed to catch the wind-milling Laurel and nudge her gently back onto her feet. Laurel's eyes grew wide for just a moment, but she did not hesitate, picking up her dance right where she had left off.

Finally, as the sun sank farther behind the mountain, Laurel arched her head way back and then, with a last leap and twirl, collapsed all the way to the snow, one leg pointed behind her, in an elaborate, extended version of the "sorrowful girls pose," her head down, her arm flung across her eyes, as if overcome by sorrow.

The black steed moved slowly forward, nibbling upon the horse feed and sugar. When it reached the apple, it stopped. Silent as *Wilis*, Rachel and Laurel rose to their feet and slowly, gently, came to stand beside the neck of the huge black beast, who believed that the beguiled girls were about to mount and be carried to their doom.

When their hands hovered just above the sleek, satiny coat, the *each-uisge* bit into the apple. Blue sparks surrounded the water horse, and it was all over.

Gaius did not stop with the paralysis hex, which Rachel realized, to her delight, must have been one that she had cast for him. He put at least half a dozen glowing golden Glepnir bands around the beast and also had vines grow from the snow and entangle it for good measure.

"Well, that was fun." Laurel stretched to one side and then the other. "But I have friends waiting and homework calling." She paused and peered into the darkness. "That's not Siggy; the Glepnir bands are too precise for a freshman. That's your pervy boyfriend, isn't it?"

"Hey!" Rachel objected. "He just saved you from certain watery death. Besides, I don't make fun of your boyfriend."

"That's because Charlie is practically perfect in every way," retorted Laurel.

"Charlie... Fairweather?" came Gaius's dubious reply, followed by a derisive snort.

"What's wrong with Charlie? He's a gentleman. Not like some people. Come on! I just helped you out here."

"You started it," Gaius replied blithely.

Laurel paused for a moment, followed by peals of laughter. "Oh, right. So I did." She departed, waving behind her as she went. "Ciao!"

Gaius called Von Dread, who strode into the clearing, surrounded by black swan feathers. It was the first time Rachel had seen him wear his cloak. He looked magnificent, almost more impressive than the water horse. Removing the cloak, he flipped it to the brilliant blue satin lining and opened the same middle seam from which he had drawn out the racer. With a gesture like a stage magician, he threw the cloak over the *each-uisge*. The water horse disappeared into the kenomanced space inside, and the cloak fluttered to the ground.

Chapter Thirteen:
The Difficulty with Forgiving

Sunday afternoon turned out to be unexpectedly mild for a New York winter. Bristlelesses floated everywhere as their riders enjoyed the lovely weather. Rachel spotted college senior Laura Diggle, whom everyone called Kiki, darting among the bell towers on the roof of Roanoke Hall. A group of students stood on the shore of the lake *oohing* and *aahing* as they watched her soar. Even Rachel was impressed by her grace and speed.

Unable to take advantage of the perfect flying weather, as she had surrendered her broom, and tired of listening to her dormmates gripe about how the ball should have been postponed one week instead of two, Rachel had donned an olive green sweater over her robes and headed toward the gymnasium. The sky was blue with an occasional fluffy cloud, but water dripped from previously snow-laden branches. Students and familiars squelched about in the melting snow, leaving deep, wet footprints everywhere they went.

Laughing girls were leaping from the roof of the gym, plummeting spread-eagled toward the frozen ground, screaming inarticulately as they fell. Rachel's heart leapt into her mouth. Not seeing any floating harnesses or any sign that they had swallowed a hover elixir, she threw up her hands to perform a cantrip, hoping to save one of them, when the first two girls who had struck the ground stood up, untouched except for the wet snow that clung to their clothing. After a moment of incomprehension, Rachel realized that these were students with cat familiars taking advantage of the fact that they could fall safely from any height.

Shaking her head at their antics, she continued around the brick building, walking down the well-trodden path that ran behind the gymnasium to the school's track, which was situated in the woods east of the gym. Low wooden bleachers sat to either side of the wide track that circled around a sports field. The Track and Broom teams were taking turns using the facility. The racers paced the outer circle while flying polo players practiced above the inner field.

Rachel climbed onto one of the bleachers and found a place that was not directly beneath the dripping branch of a hemlock. She still felt shaky from the previous day's exertion, so she had chosen an activity that would mainly involve sitting. She watched the racers take turns at the various events: the hundred yards, the thousand yards, a relay race that included both flyers and sprinters. She only half paid attention until the upper school boys' team paraded out onto the field, led by their captain, John Darling.

Rachel's lip curled up into a sneer. He looked so smug and self-satisfied, just the way he had looked when he had laughed at her back in September, the time Cydney Graves had drenched her in orange juice. She recalled cruel things she had overheard him say, about her and about other girls. Just seeing the arrogant rotter made her skin crawl. She sighed.

She was *not* off to a good start.

Forgiving Ivan Romanov had been easy, even though she had been very angry with him. She had hoped she would be able to apply the Lion's advice to John Darling as well. She thought back to what the Lion had told her about forgiveness. He had spoken of giving a gift to the one who had offended her and how that felt. Could she do something kind for John Darling? She balked at the notion. Grimly, she watched the dark-haired upper school senior preen and strut around at the starting line. She looked for some positive action, some good quality she could use to help herself overcome her disdain of this annoying boy.

The bleachers shook. Beside her, a female voice asked in an accent that was halfway between Kenyan and British, "Come to try out?"

"Excuse me?" Rachel looked about, startled.

Ameka Okeke had climbed onto the bleachers beside her, a navy blue parka left open over her rose-colored track suit. Daughter of a Nandi chieftain and a Chinese mother, Ameka had high cheekbones, dark bronze skin, and beautiful, almond-shaped eyes, much like Rachel's own. Rumor had it that she was an ace at every sport the school had to offer, though Rachel had never seen her in action.

"We have an opening for a number 3 on our junior flying polo team," offered Ameka. She rested the shaft of her bright blue racer with its white racing stripe on the next highest step.

"No thanks," Rachel replied cheerfully. "Last time I went to a flying polo game, I was six, and a ball hit me in the face. I haven't been back."

"Too bad," Ameka sat down beside her, adding, "I am the Maenad Whip."

Rachel stared at her blankly.

"Like in a parliamentary whip?" Ameka squatted down on the step Rachel was seated upon. With a big grin, she quipped, "I'm supposed to whip our freshmen members into shape and get them onto the field."

"Oh! I'm a Maenad, aren't I?" Rachel said, finally grasping the situation. Freshmen were assigned to one of the sports teams, whether or not they ever bothered to show up. "So you're the heavy whose job it is to pressure me into playing?"

"My friend, I pressure no one." Ameka held up a hand, as if to forestall any false ideas. "All I do is breathe upon the flame of desire already raging in the breasts of budding young athletes. Tell me the truth." She pointed a long finger at Rachel's face. "Don't you *want* to come out and fly with us? You are said to be very good."

"I am good," Rachel replied honestly, "but not necessarily as good as they are." She waved at the group of college flyers who had just yielded the field. "Besides, I ride a steeplechaser. It's great for maneuvering—but I couldn't outfly a racer."

"So don't race. Go out for flying polo."

"I like flying polo," Rachel admitted, or she did now. She had spent so much time reading up on the Windcolts, a professional team, and the Lake Michigan Falcons, a college team, in order to chat with her favorite proctor, Mr. Fuentes, that despite her childhood ball-to-the-face incident, she now found the sport interesting. "Would I have to fly a polo broom?"

"Probably."

Rachel shivered. "I would feel disloyal, like cheating on a boyfriend."

Ameka rolled her eyes. "Fine, my friend, be that way. Can you do anything else? Dance? Swim?"

"I can," Rachel replied slowly, "but I doubt I'd win any contests. I don't know proper strokes or that sort of thing. At home, we just dive in the water and go. Swim to the raft or the island. That sort of thing. We don't have to do the crawl or the butterfly or whatever. Really, I don't think sports are quite my cup of tea." Rachel paused a moment, a thought occurring to her. "Unless you have broom ballet. Does Roanoke have a broom ballet team?"

Ameka blinked. "Broom ballet is a thing?"

Rachel laughed gaily. "It surely is. Rather a bit more like Cirque du Soleil in the air, though, than like a real ballet."

"Oh, broom circus! That I have heard of. No. At least, I do not think we do. Some things are too quirky, even for Roanoke."

Rachel pressed her lips together at the disrespect being shown to her beloved sport. She had a poster of the Pinswallow Broom Ballet on the wall of her room, back at Gryphon Park. She used to stare at it every night as she fell asleep, recalling, as she drifted off, the daring swoops and synchronized maneuvers of the broom dancers.

"Why are you here then... *kah!*"

Ameka's whole expression changed; her eyes narrowed, and she glared off to the left. Following her gaze, Rachel saw a college girl chatting with Ameka's older brother, who had shucked his parka due to the warmth of the day and stood in his sweats with a bright blue towel slung around his neck. Opeyami was darker than his sister and took after their father. Ordinarily, he wore a charismatic grin, but, right now, he had that stunned look boys sometimes acquired when they were talking with a girl whom they considered to be out of their league.

Rachel recognized the young woman, too. She was Jasmine Grimaldi, a Knight of Walpurgis and the leader of the cabal that Rachel had dubbed the Drake Girls. Looking at the young woman's dark complexion and long, silky black hair, Rachel would have guessed that she was some exotic islander, but apparently she was a countess from Bohemia.

A shiver went through Rachel. Countess Jasmine Grimaldi was the elegant young woman who had screamed when, during the first week of school, Rachel had shot over her head on Vroomie while flying through Drake Hall. Rachel could hardly blame the countess for screaming, as the wake from the steeplechaser had probably blown the older girl's hair and books all awry, but Rachel had been in pursuit of the wicked Dr. Mordeau in an attempt to save the lives of Gaius and Mr. Chanson, so she could not feel too bad about it. Still, Miss Grimaldi has never forgiven her and scowled when Rachel came too close.

Jasmine Grimaldi had also been one of the names that Dr. Mordeau had mentioned in Nastasia's vision. Rachel recalled that the countess had been one of the students under the effects of the evil tutor's geas.

"She's prince hunting," Ameka said bitterly, rising to her feet. "Trying to schmooze up to him, so that she can move in for the kill at the ball. But Ope doesn't see it. He's smitten."

"Oh, right. He's a prince because your father's an *Orkoiyot*?"

"*The Orkoiyot*."

Rachel consulted an encyclopaedia in her mental library. "A book I read said that the last *Orkoiyot* died some time ago."

Ameka shook her head. "You must have read an Unwary source, my friend, because we've been alive and kicking in the World of the Wise for generations. Back in the twentieth century, the British incarcerated my great-grandfather. Kept him locked up for forty-two years. *Forty-two years!* They believe that our line ended with him. But my people had moved into the World of the Wise. Disappeared right under their noses!"

"Really?" Rachel asked, intrigued. "One doesn't hear much about people joining the Wise on purpose."

Ameka shrugged her shoulders. She reached her right arm over her head and leaned to the left, stretching. Then she did the same thing again to the other side. "The tribes live in those gray areas—between the Wise and the Unwary—since many have shaman or witch-doctors or the like. When my great-grandfather was captured and my grandfather went into hiding, he managed to reach the Wisecraft, in Prester John's Kingdom. They brought in obscurers to hide a large number of our people and a portion of our lands. They even hid an entire age-set. That is why the Unwary think that the Nandi skip *Ko-*

rongoro—because the entire set moved into the World of the Wise, and the Unwary forgot their existence."

"I... um..." Rachel began, but the encyclopedia article she had just recalled explained that all men of the Nandi tribe were divided into groups by age. Each of these age-sets had a particular name. According to the unwary article, many tribes in Kenya had seven such sets, but many neighboring tribes had eight. Rachel nodded slowly, indicating that she understood.

"Your father's with the Wisecraft, right?" Ameka's eyes sparkled with the intensity of her interest. "I would love to be an Agent! I own every issue of *James Darling, Agent!*"

"My father is Merlin Thunderhawk," Rachel grinned. "Er... I mean... the character in the comics is based on him."

"He's so cool!" Ameka jumped with glee, kicking her bottom with her heels while she was in the air. She landed lightly, bouncing on the bleacher step. "Does he really fall from the sky and land on people like that?"

Rachel recalled her father coming through the window after Mortimer Egg, the first time she and her friends were kidnapped, and how impressive Agent Griffin had looked with his Inverness cloak floating behind him like wings. "Yes, he does."

"That is awesome, my friend! I want to do that!"

"You could. Be an Agent, I mean."

"I suppose." Ameka frowned thoughtfully and sat down again. "I am hoping to get onto my country's football team—whatever it is called here. Soccer? I might follow the lead of Von Dread and take a year off to pursue sports. Possibly between the upper school and college."

"You mean a professional football player? Wise or Unwary?"

"There's only one football," replied Ameka loftily. "I want to play real football, not some namby-pamby magic version. It is a dangerous sport, but I feel I am up to the challenge."

"A dangerous sport?" Rachel blinked.

"In Africa, we take our football very seriously. A friend who plays for a team in Kinshasa, in the Democratic Republic of Congo was in a game where his team was losing. The team owners became nervous and called a witch doctor, who decided that the best way to victory was to sacrifice my friend. The witch doctor gave him an elixir that poisoned him. He fell to the ground in agony, but his team kept playing and started making goals. He only lived because there happened to be a nun of Asclepius in the crowd, who saved him. But because he lived, the final score was only a tie."

"That's really hardcore!" Rachel gasped, horrified. "What happened to him?"

"The next week, he was back on the field. Brave kid." She shrugged. "But, for me, that is the advantage of being a Roanokean. I can learn to ward my teammates from harm." Eyes narrowing, she glared at her brother and the countess again.

"Miss Grimaldi seems quite attentive," said Rachel. "I might think she rather liked him—if I hadn't seen her show the same kind of attention to Vlad and Romulus Starkadder."

"Yeah, I...." Ameka gave Rachel a very strange look. Leaning over, she laid a hand on Rachel's shoulder. "My friend, did I just hear you refer to the lord of evil himself, as 'Vlad'?"

"My boyfriend works for him," Rachel muttered, suddenly too embarrassed to voice the more truthful "he and I are friends." That sounded too much like boasting.

"Vlad like Vlad the Impaler? I cannot decide if that makes him less scary or more." Ameka chuckled. She rested her elbow on her knee and her chin on her palm. "But back to Jasmine: Everyone knows her father is desperate to make some kind of important connection. He is the second cousin of the current Archduke of Bohemia. He married for love when he was quite young, an actress from the Philippines. Now he regrets that this marriage brought him no political connections, so he wishes to make up for this by hitching his daughter to a prince."

That explained Miss Grimaldi's exotic coloring. Rachel gazed at the elegant young woman. She could understand why Ameka's brother was so tongue-tied. The Bohemian countess looked like a daughter of an actress whose beauty won her the love of a count.

"Thing is," Ameka said darkly, "apparently, a lowly *Orkoiyot* is not important enough. Jasmine hardly gave Ope the time of day until Father was elected to Parliament."

"You mean, your father's a delegate, is he?" asked Rachel, impressed.

There was no Okeke on her mental list of the two hundred delegates to the Parliament of the Wise, but people occasionally stepped down and were replaced. Perhaps, there had been a special election she missed hearing about, while she was here at school.

Ameka shot her a brilliant grin. "Father just won the African seat.... He's a councilman!"

Rachel's eyes widened. She straightened, impressed. There were over two hundred delegates, but they were all members of the Lower House that met only occasionally. The real business of the Wise was done by the Parliamentary Council, which consisted of the Chancellor, the head of the Parliament, and eight councilmen, representing, respectively: North America, South America, the Far East, India, Africa, Australia, Western Europe, and Northern Europe—the latter of which included Eastern Europe. Along with the Grand Inquisitor of the Wisecraft, these were the people who truly ran the World of the Wise. Ameka's father had just become one of the most powerful men in the world.

"The seat vacated when old Mr. Bello died?" Rachel asked. "Congratulations!"

"Thank you." Ameka continued to grin. "A councilman from Kenya is a first. Usually that seat has gone to someone from Prester John's Kingdom. Father had to campaign very hard. He wanted to be of some real use. You see, his duties as an *Orkoiyot* are light, as he is not called on to run day-to-day matters—and there hasn't been much call of late for going to war. Also, Mother helped. She's the daughter of a famous Chinese alchemist."

Rachel nodded. "And this catapulted your brother onto the shiny list for the Bohemian countess?"

"Yeessss," hissed Ameka, her eyes narrowing again as she regarded the distant conversation. "I cannot believe that he does not see her for what she is: a fortune huntress."

The countess was squealing and leaning forward, her hair draped across Opeyami's shoulder. The young man, usually so composed, looked completely smitten.

"Can't you tell him?" asked Rachel, following her gaze.

"No," sighed Ameka. "Or rather, I have, my friend, but who listens to a little sister?"

Rachel sighed as well. Out of the corner of her eye, she caught a motion in the forest across from the bleachers. She held very still, letting her eyes track it as it moved from tree to tree. A frisson ran up her spine to the top of her head. It was a fey; she was sure of it.

Or was it a student, approaching the track through the trees? She watched the spot, waiting to see if anyone emerged from the forest.

There was a roar of approval from those ringing the track. Ameka jumped to her feet and shouted.

"Look, my friend!" she cried, gesturing at the track. "Dash Darling has won his race!"

Rachel tried to school her expression, but something must have betrayed her true reaction, because Ameka's face fell.

"You don't like him?" she demanded. "Why is that?"

Rachel sighed and traced a pleat of her black robe. "I used to fancy him, for three years. His father and my father used to be partners, so the families all get together at Yule and such. I called it my 'crush from afar.' But since I came to school...."

"Yes?" Ameka leaned forward, watching her face intently.

Rachel bit her lip. Ameka would not believe her, any more than Opeyami believed what Ameka had to say about Countess Jasmine. All that would happen if she explained would be that Ameka would dislike her in the future. "Let's say, I've been disenchanted."

"He wasn't what you expected, my friend?"

Rachel gave up on watching the woods out of the corner of her eye—no one had emerged, nor had she seen the movement again—and turned to gaze at where those below were congratulating John Darling, clapping him on the back.

"He laughed at me when I was humiliated. And...." Rachel winced, recalling some choice things she had heard him say about Merry Vesper. "I don't like the way he talks about girls, one girl in particular."

"Is it me?" The look on Ameka's face was excruciating, as if she could not decide which answer would be worse.

Rachel shook her head, regretfully. "No. H-he hasn't mentioned you in my hearing. But he says very rude things about what he wants to do to… another girl."

Ameka gazed out at the forest, blinking back tears.

"I'm sorry," Rachel whispered, feeling horrible. Apparently, Ameka had believed that she and "Dash Darling" were almost an item.

She had expected Ameka to brush off any complaint, but the other girl seemed to be taking her seriously. Could she have suspected but not wanted to believe it was true?

"Don't be, my friend," Ameka's voice caught, but it grew stronger as she spoke on. She drew herself up; a light came into her gaze. "My father says that it is the most important thing in the world to be truthful and humble. I have a ways to go with humble—call it a work in progress—but I do value truth. I would rather know the truth and be unhappy than believe a lie."

"That's quite admirable," murmured Rachel.

From below, another Maenad called to Ameka that it was their turn. Ameka threw Rachel one last watery smile, grabbed her blue and white racer, and ran down the steps of the bleachers to join them. The Maenads grabbed their brooms and headed for the track. As they passed the boys, who were leaving the training area, the two teams high-fived each other. Only, when Ameka reached John Darling, who greeted her with a big grin, she walked right by without so much as acknowledging him. He stared after her, hurt and surprised.

"Why, she gave him the cut direct!" Rachel exclaimed quietly, delighted.

It felt good to be believed, and, much as the news hurt, Ameka's father was correct about the value of truth. It was better that Ameka know the truth about John Darling—that he was an immature, callous rotter who did not truly care about anybody but himself. It was only as she rose to leave that Rachel remembered that her purpose in coming had been to forgive John Darling.

Chapter Fourteen: Fire and Salmon

Leaving the sports area, Rachel crept quietly through the woods, wishing she had her broom. She called up her memory of the movement she had just seen to make sure she stood in front of the exact tree where it had taken place. Then, she peered around, wondering if she had seen an animal, a student, or something supernatural. If she were wrong, and it was just athletes from the boys' and girls' teams who had sneaked off for some snogging, she was going to feel rather foolish.

Then she looked down. There, in the snow, were the prints of bare feet, enormous bare feet. When she put her own heel into the heel of the print, her whole foot only reached the middle of the footprint. *The woodwose.*

Rachel stood very still, recalling what she knew about the woodwose, the wild man of the woods of Roanoke Island. Some wild men of the wood were deadly to encounter. Was the Roanoke wose dangerous? Mr. Tuck had mentioned the woodwose as one of the island's creatures with a "charmed life," but that term was used rather broadly. It might mean that it was immune to harm like the ogre; it might mean something else.

She recalled sitting on her father's lap looking at his photo album of his time at school, as he told stories of sneaking into the Woseforest with his brother Emrys. In Father's stories, the two of them had been more worried that the school officials would catch them than that they would come to harm from the forest's master. Peter had asked once if Father had met the woodwose, and Father had replied that he had seen it twice, but never up close.

Rachel began to breathe a little easier. She looked at the prints and gulped; how massive they were compared to her foot. Should she follow them?

"Gaius," Rachel touched her black bracelet and spoke aloud.

"Er… not now, Rach. I'll have to call you back. It may be a while."

Gaius's voice was cheerful, so whatever he was in the midst of was not life threatening.

Should she wait? How long would he be? Should she call Dread, or was he part of the same project Gaius was involved in? She would look the utter fool if she disturbed Gaius and then disturbed Vlad during the same activity. She reviewed what she had learned from Daring Northwest and other sources. He claimed that there were two kinds of wose, gentle and vicious. He also claimed that most were "resistant to the arts of Circe." Rachel did not know what that meant. She also reviewed what he and others had said about Himalayan yeti, Mongolian *almas*, Chinese *yeren*, and North American Sasquatch.

One old legend claimed that they were attracted to campfires, as they had forgotten how to make fire, and that they would sit and gaze into a fire until it turned to embers. Another told stories of the creature being drawn into a trap by the smell of roasting seafood. A third claimed that they became lonely and pined for the comfort and friendship of a female, as there were no female woses. Not everyone agreed on this last point. Northwest reported that some areas of the world seemed to have wild women of the wood and others did not. But either way, the stories she had read about woodwoses interacting with women and children had been promising.

An eerie shiver crept up Rachel's spine. *Theoretically, she could do this alone.*

She found a flattish boulder amidst the hemlocks, brushed off the tiny bit of remaining snow, and broke off some branches from a dead beech, which she laid in a pile until she had enough for a campfire. Then she stood wondering how to light it and what to offer it to eat.

She had read a story of a Bigfoot that came to where alder-spit salmon was cooking around the edge of a fire. Maybe the woodwose would like that, too. They were supposed to eat fish. But where could she find a fish? Even if she had been a proficient fisher, which she was not, she had no equipment for ice fishing. If she went to the dining hall, which was not open at this hour, it was unlikely that she would be able to convince the cooks to give her a raw fish or even a cooked one. Either way, she was, at the very least, going to have to find a match, as she had not yet learned how to call up fire. Maybe Zoë would have one.

Returning to her dorm, she found Sigfried and Lucky stomping in the snow in front of Dare Hall. There was a well-tracked path running from the porch of the dorm towards the main campus, but almost no one had headed west toward the woods. Thus, the two of them were leaving fresh footprints in a nigh-pristine field of wet, squishy snow.

"Hallo," she called, waving.

Sigfried stomped toward her, the motions of his feet sending up a spray of slush.

"Goldilocks won't fly to the tor with us," he complained.

"Does she know the way?" asked Rachel.

"See," Siggy turned to Lucky, who was practically swimming through the wet snow, leaving a long snaky wake. "That's what I like about Griffin. '*Does she know the way?*' Not like some princesses, whose names we shall not mention." His voice grew higher and more Magical Australian as he continued, "'We cannot leave campus. We're on probation. We must remain zombie slaves to the adults. All praise the adults!' Bah! If the adults told her to jump off London Bridge, would she advise us to listen to that, too?"

There were a few minor differences between leaving the protection of Roanoke Academy and jumping from London Bridge, but Rachel did not bother pointing out such quibbles.

"Wouldn't be so bad," Siggy grumbled, "if she hadn't talked my girlfriend into being afraid to escape campus. Even for a good story!"

Rachel's ears perked up. "There's a good story?"

Sigfried and Lucky nodded simultaneously, Lucky popping out of the snow at just the right moment.

Siggy asked, "Did you know that the Here and There of Iceberg can create explosions?"

"Explosions?" Rachel paused and looked at him carefully. "How so?"

"Take me out, and I'll show you," offered Sigfried.

Rachel considered this. If she caught the woodwose, she was going to need to fly it back to its wood. Continuing around the rest of the island at that point would not be difficult.

"Okay," she began, "but first I need you to... Oh! I can't. Mr. Chanson has my broom."

"He stole it from you, eh? That thief!" cried Sigfried. "We'll get it back for you!"

Lucky added helpfully, "I could burn his left foot!"

"Trust an adult to act like an adult!" cried Sigfried.

Rachel pressed her lips together, trying not to laugh. "You'll be an adult some day, too."

"Not me!" Siggy objected hotly. "I've decided. I'm going to be a knight instead."

Rachel decided that pursuing this line of thought would prove unproductive. Instead, she said, "Actually, he's helping me. He's making my broom better. But he did say I could borrow a broom from the broom closet in the gym if I wished."

"Let's take 'em all!" declared Sigfried. "Maybe we can make them follow us as we fly. Whole flock of brooms! When do we learn to make multiple objects float like Misty Lark does when she's playing the drums in secret? How many objects can we make float at once? Five hundred and two? I'm planning to buy more knives and then make them all fly at people. Hey, what if we make all the brooms fly at people? We could attach bayonets to the front and bombs to the back. It would be like *The Sorcerer's Apprentice*, but with explosions!"

Rachel sighed, shaking her head. Lucky zipped through the snow, bounding like a snow dolphin. Watching him, she had a thought.

"Sigfried," she began casually, "do you happen to have any food?"

"I knew it!" Siggy crowed. "I told you this day would come! The adults are starving you, aren't they? They're trying to get you to cave. Don't give in! Here, you can have this meatball sandwich I picked up last night at dinner. Some idiot was trying to throw it away." He pulled a ziplock bag from his pocket and held it up upside down, so that the meatballs had fallen out of the goopy bun. "I wouldn't normally give it up, mind you, but it's for my blood sister. A brother has to make allowances."

Rachel tilted her head, peering at the bread and fighting off an attack of nausea. Actually, the bun was not as wet as she first thought.

Spread out, it was almost the size of a salmon filet.

"Come on." She grabbed Siggy's arm and began to tug. "Come with me to the alchemy labs. I have a brilliant idea!"

Sigfried and Lucky followed her to the second floor of Roanoke Hall. The alchemical supply closet did not disappoint. Rachel found an entire jar filled with salmon scales and bones. Using a tricorne mirror and other ingredients to help indicate that she wished to transfer odor and taste, Sigfried was able to move the essence of salmon into the bun from his meatball sub.

"Perfect," Rachel grinned. "Come on, Lucks! We have a fire to light!"

"We get to catch a *what?*" Siggy cried rambunctiously as they tromped through the snow. "Ace! Its head will look great in the clubhouse! Is there magic for preserving it? Because, if not, you girls will just have to put up with the smell."

"Or I could eat it," Lucky offered, "before it starts smelling too much. I could eat that salmon for you, too, if it gets too heavy. It smells tasty."

"No!" Rachel objected. "Not unless it turns out to be violent."

"Why would the salmon be violent? It's dead," Lucky asked, puzzled.

Siggy said, "It's not dead. It's bread." He turned to Rachel. "What are we going to do?"

"You can be the Thorn, so to speak. Drink a chameleon potion and, when the woodwose comes close, freeze him with a hex from your wand. I put some in there for you the other day, so I know you have one... unless you and Ian have used them all up freezing each other again."

"Not this time!" Siggy crowed. "I got him on the first try. Then, I forgot him and left him there until Enoch happened to return to the room about twenty minutes later and set him free. Kind of almost feel bad about that, but not really."

"Is he still talking to you?" Rachel blinked. "Being frozen by the paralysis hex for too long can hurt. If it had been me, I would have been spitting mad!"

"Ah, it's okay. He said this was nothing. He has brothers. Once when he was... he said 'wee'... they were supposed to babysit, only they just hexed him and left him there, all day, until his parents found him that evening. But he said he didn't mind so much, because his parents were so angry, his brothers couldn't sit down for a week."

Rachel pressed her fingers against her mouth to keep from giggling. It only sort of worked. She had a feeling that Ian, or maybe Sigfried, was exaggerating, but one never knew.

"Are you ready?" she asked.

His brow beetled, "What are you doing again?"

"I'm part of the bait."

Siggy's eyes goggled. Then he threw back his head and laughed long and hard. Finally, he wiped his eyes, murmuring something about how he thought that only happened on something Rachel could not quite catch. She tried recalling it three times, but it still sounded like *Scooby-Doo*.

"Wait." He stopped laughing. "My part is to do nothing except point a stick?"

"Can you do that?"

"May-be."

"Please."

"Oh, all right," Sigfried stamped his feet in the snow. To Lucky, he whispered, "So boring. I might have a dying-of-boredom attack."

Rachel took a deep breath. "Remember, if you are *helpful*, I will take you to the tor to see the explosion. Or whatever it was. Also, there's something I want to discuss with you. I have someone who I want taken down."

"Yes! *Ma Capitaine*! Whatever you say, Dark Mistress! We are at your service!"

Rachel sighed. She most certainly did not want to be anyone's dark mistress, but some days, there was just no winning with Sigfried.

Sigfried drank the chameleon potion and hid. Rachel returned to the pile of sticks. She had not been able to find an alder on quick notice; it was not a common tree on Roanoke Island. Hopefully, a branch from the dead beech would do. She carefully opened the bun, stuck the stick through it, and stuck it into the snow, so that it stood open and upright, as close to looking like a flayed salmon filet as a piece of bread could. She then moved the pile of sticks at the edge of the rock closest to her make-shift alder-spit salmon.

"All right, Lucky," she announced, "light it up!"

Rachel squatted down by the fire and pretended she was cooking salmon. It smelled like salmon, and it reminded her of salmon, but if she looked right at it, it still looked like a bun from yesterday's meatball sub, except now it was starting to get toasty.

Lucky had not disappointed. He had lit the pile of sticks with a gout of his breath that nearly consumed the entire fuel supply at once. Rachel had to wait for the fire to die down and add more wood, but now it was burning nicely. She sat beside it feeling a bit foolish, as there was nothing except the scent of fake salmon to draw her prey. She wondered if she should sing again. Did woses like singing? Or was that only ponies?

The sound of snow sloshing interrupted her musing. Rachel looked up and froze. A tall and shaggy figure was stepping through the hemlock branches thick with green needles and white snow. The woodwose came into the clearing, sniffing. It was enormous, even taller than the Raven. It was covered from head to toe in a coppery brown fur, with thick hair and beard flowing from its head and face, more man-like than beast-like. Its eyes were a deep dark brown. It wore a deerskin covering its front and back, but its sides and limbs were unencumbered.

The wose shuffled forward and leaned over, its massive hand reaching slowly toward her face. It seemed as fascinated by Rachel as it was by the fire, as if it could not decide which one to feast its eyes upon. Rachel wanted to scoot backwards, but her limbs refused to move. A hand that big could probably break her neck with a single gesture—whether it meant to or not.

Blue sparks danced in the air from over her shoulder. The great hairy creature froze mid-reach. Rachel breathed a sign of relief.

"There, that did it," Sigfried's voice crowed.

"It did!" Rachel clapped her hands. "Lucks, be a dear and fetch Zoë's backpack."

"Sure thing, Dark Mistress!" called Lucky.

Rachel sighed as Lucky zipped away. Siggy, still invisible, stomped around yodeling, no doubt performing his version of a Peter-Pan-style war dance.

"Well," Rachel said cheerfully, "That was easy."

By the fire, the woodwose moved. Its first motion was a bit jerky, but then it was moving normally again. *And it looked angry.*

More blue sparks and the scent of evergreens encircled the creature as Siggy shot it again, and Rachel whistled. This time, the woodwose hardly even slowed down. Rachel tried a Glepnir band, but it did not form properly and was nowhere near the intended target. She fired off two other cantrips and whistled the bedazzling hex, but to no avail.

Siggy blew a blast on his trumpet. Silvery sparks swirled through the air, accompanied by the faint fragrance of vanilla; however, the gust of wind did not push the shaggy beast-man but curled around him as if it had met up with an old friend. The woodwose opened its yawning maw, displaying massive, yellowing teeth. Very big teeth. It lunged directly toward Rachel.

She scuttled backwards, waving her arms and shouting, "Wait! Wait! We just want to bring you back to your forest!"

"*Home?*" The beast paused mid-charge and slowly cocked its head, its voice rough and awkward. It reached out toward her with its huge hand.

"*Aaiii!*" Behind her, Sigfried let out an ululating shout that grew closer and then rushed past Rachel. *Thud.* She could not see him, but it sounded as if his body had struck the hairy mat that was the woodwose.

"*Ouuawwweeee!*" The shaggy brute let out a terrible bellow, an earsplitting cry of anger and pain. Rachel screamed and grabbed her ears. Brilliant scarlet blood dripped down its leg. Sigfried's bowie knife, the one Valerie had given him, stuck out of the creature's hip. Whatever charm protected the woodwose's life did not protect him from knife blades. Looking at the crimson blood and the protruding knife hilt, Rachel suddenly felt lightheaded. She took a wobbly step back, reaching out for support and getting a handful of spindly hemlock branches.

They had sent Lucky away, but the dragon would know that his boy was in trouble. Rachel hoped he was rushing back.

The woodwose bellowed again, grabbing the still-invisible boy in a bear hug and squeezing. There was a crunching sound that Rachel feared might be some important part of her blood-brother. She let out a frightened squeal.

"Let go of me, you brute!" Siggy shouted, followed by a much more muffled shout. Much relieved to hear the robustness of his voice, Rachel wondered what in the world could be filling his mouth.

She did not have to wait long for the answer. Siggy began to fade into view. First, splotches of him—a section of his back, a hand—then all of him, his hand still clutching his knife. Somehow, the woodwose, by its very presence, was countering their sorcery. Rachel wondered if that was what Northwest had meant by "resistant to the arts of Circe."

Sigfried was now fully visible. The wose had him trapped in its deadly embrace, but that had not slowed the boy down. His teeth were clamped onto the wose's shoulder, his mouth full of titian hair and possibly flesh. His body jerked, as he tried to push the knife farther into the wild man.

With a roar, the great beast-man cast Siggy aside, throwing him through the air like a dog's squeeze toy. The boy landed with a thud. He started to rise, but his breath had been knocked out of him. He fell back onto the snow, struggling desperately to breathe. The woodwose pulled the Bowie knife from its hip and cast it aside. Then it charged forward, baring its huge, yellowing fangs and covering yards with every lumbering step.

Before she could think it through, Rachel was across the glade. She leapt in front of the charging brute, standing between the wose and her blood-brother, her arms outstretched.

"Home!" she shouted fiercely. "We can take you home!"

The woodwose thundered to a stop, standing so close that she could smell its fetid breath, its brow drawn together as it examined her face. Rachel gazed fiercely back, her arms spread. The terror that had left her lightheaded earlier had vanished. She did not feel any fear whatsoever. Behind her, to her relief, she heard Siggy scrambling to his feet.

"You shouldn't protect me, Griffin," Sigfried objected. "It is un-knightly to hide behind a damsel. Whatcha tryin' to do, ruin me?"

Rachel raised one hand, indicating that Siggy should halt. He slowed down but kept walking toward her. Then, seeing his knife off to one side, he dashed through hemlock branches, until he could grab it from where it laid in the now-crimson snow. Sigfried then leapt to his feet and charged back, ready to attack again.

Meanwhile, the woodwose towered above her, at least twice her height. It squatted before her and, very gently, patted her head. Rachel stood very still, gazing into its hairy, expressive face. Its other hand held its bleeding hip. It had a thick musky smell. Rachel tried very hard not to imagine it snapping her neck.

"Food?" she asked softly, gesturing toward the fire.

"*Fooood?*" it asked curiously, tilting its head to gaze in the direc-tion indicated.

Rachel gently stepped backwards and then walked around it to the fire. The beast-man followed her, one hand pressed against its hip wound, the other rubbing its arm where the pesky boy had bitten it. Rachel held out the toasted bun on a stick, which, she had to admit, smelled pretty good. The alchemical properties would vanish even-tually, but since losing taste would not harm the body, the bread was safe to eat.

The wose took the stick with the flayed bun, examined it, sniffed it, and gave a big toothy grin. Then it tore into the bread with the same relish as if it were actually fish. Rachel wondered if it understood what it was eating or if it was fooled by the alchemical illusion.

Suddenly, the woodwose put down the half eaten mock-salmon and disappeared behind the lacy, needled branches of the hemlocks.

"Oh, he's gone!" Rachel cried. "We failed."

"Let's hunt him down!" Siggy crowed. "We can mount his head on the wall!"

Rachel shook her head rapidly. "Sigfried, we can't kill fey—not unless they harm us first, and in a big way. Not just turn us in circles or make us dance."

"Why not? I can take 'im."

"It's not about taking him. It's about treaties — between the Wisecraft and the fey. There are seven treaties, with the Five Elf Lords, the Solitaries, the King Beneath the Mountain, the Wild Hunt, and the rest. There are all sorts of clauses, but the gist of them is this: If we obey the treaty, they won't beguile the Unwary, who have no protection against them. It's of utmost importance...."

With loud clomping footsteps, the woodwose returned. In one hand, it held a mess of moss and bark which it pressed against its wounded hip. Retrieving the bread, it squatted down and stared into the fire as it chewed, as if entranced by the leaping and dancing flames. Rachel had to admit that the flames were beautiful, flickering and crackling.

"*Want go home,*" the beast grunted.

"We can do that," Rachel promised her shaggy visitor. She slipped around to kneel beside him and, using snow, washed the blood from the fur of its thigh. The beast-man grunted, grateful.

"*My forest misses me. Ancient oak is angry. Great willow weeps.*"

"Why did you come? Why did you leave your forest and come onto the campus?"

The woodwose cocked its head, possibly thinking.

"*Have dream. See man in mask. He say to come.*"

That was unexpected. Rachel wondered if he meant the figures with the black cloth over their heads who had opened the ward-lock. "What did this mask look like?

"*Like winter. All spirals and ice.*"

"I... don't know what that means," murmured Rachel.

"*Want go home,*" the great, shaggy man pouted.

Rachel glanced back at Sigfried, who nodded grimly. She reached forward and laid her hand cautiously on the beast-man's hirsute arm. "Yes. We'll take you home."

CHAPTER FIFTEEN:
MEMORIES OF BATTLES LOST

Rachel and Sigfried shot out of the tree-lined path, through the arch in Bannerman's ruined castle and out over the docks. The sky was overcast and gray. The air was moist and almost warm and smelled of melting snow. Ice covered the Hudson. Snow blanketed the fields to the south, and the rocks to the north dripped with hoarfrost. Rachel turned the borrowed bristleless toward the snowfields. *Oh, it was a glorious thing to fly!*

Lucky sailed along behind them. The woodwose, who had not seemed to understand the question "what is your name," was snug in Zoë's backpack. Rachel had decided not to ask Lucky whether he had asked permission before he snagged it. Best not to know.

She had meant to borrow the cherry-colored Redbird model Flycycle she occasionally used for demonstrations when assisting Mr. Chanson, but an old O.I. Starling model, black with a brown stripe, kept falling off the rack. Finally, she gave up trying to get it to stay on the hook and took that one instead. The Starling was much longer than Vroomie and ended in a horizontal peacock fan of three fat blades, instead of the steeplechaser's ten narrow ones. It felt odd to be sitting upright and steering with handlebars, but at least the levers seemed to be in working order. Still, she hoped that she would not be called on to do any fancy maneuvering.

Usually, Rachel flew north, but the Woseforest was on the southeastern shore of Roanoke, so she headed south, flying by flat, snowy fields that, during the fall, had been covered with flowers. Farther inland, the bare trunks of oaks and birches covered a low knoll. Atop this low rounded hill stood standing stones, like a mini Stonehenge. Rachel gawked, surprised. Then she recalled Mr. Tuck, during his History of Roanoke speech, mentioning that a wight lived by the standing stones. Maybe these were the stones he had meant.

They swooped around a copse of leafless maples and oaks, the wind whistling in their ears, and found the coast was now heading eastward instead of south. Farther east, the wall of towering trees growing trunk to trunk that made up the wards of the school came almost to the shore. Only a narrow strip of land ran between the bark wall and the ice of the river. Here and there enough snow had melted for them to see the sand beneath it.

"I say!" Rachel exclaimed in delight. "I think this stretch is a beach. I'd seen photos of the beach—from back when my parents were in school. I had no idea where it was. I used to look at my parents' photos all the time when my siblings were here, and I was still at home."

She flew up high enough to see over the ward-wall, even if she dared not fly over it. Beyond a stretch of forest, she glimpsed the tall spire of the central tower of the lower school, an attractive building. The top half had dark beams of wood against a whitewashed background, Tudor-style. The bottom and the tower were white and cream brick. Around it were snowy fields, forests, and, to the eastern corner, a lake upon which young children skated.

"What's that?" asked Sigfried, leaning dangerously to peer closer. He made a gesture to Lucky, who flew right up to the edge of the wards, but even the dragon did not dare cross.

"That's the lower school," said Rachel.

"Lower than what?"

"Lower than the upper school."

"You mean magic elementary school? Ace! Wish Lucky and I could have gone there," he said wistfully. "My roommate went there. Lucky git."

"Hey!" chimed in Lucky.

"I didn't mean you, Lucky," Sigfried clarified. "I meant Ian. His mum was in law enforcement, so she put her kids in boarding school. Now she works here, so they get to see her all the time," he sighed, a slow, drawn out sigh. "Must be nice. Having a mum."

"It is," replied Rachel. She paused a moment and then added. "Why don't you come home with me over spring break? It will be ever so much more fun than staying on campus by yourself. You can even have your own pony, if you like."

"Pony could be tasty," offered Lucky, who again snaked along beside the Starling.

"Not to eat!" exploded Rachel. "To ride. We can pick one from the herd. Or you can pick one from the moors if you wish."

Though probably not the way Laurel did it. The mental image of Siggy throwing his head back and forth as he danced, his blond curls rippling in the wind, nearly caused her to giggle out loud.

They dropped down to fly closer to the river. Rounding the southeast corner, they flew northward along the eastern shore of the island. The Starling left a larger wake than the steeplechaser, and several times she was startled when the wind of their passing sent snow and chunks of ice skittering across the frozen surface of the Hudson. To their right, a train rattled along the eastern shore of the mainland. Beyond rose the high, rocky slopes of Breakneck Ridge. To their left, on the eastern shore of Roanoke Island, a few trees spotted the snowy beach until they came to where Roanoke Creek emptied into the river. After that, the ward-wall receded from the shoreline, and they were flying by forests again.

Rachel peered at the forest. The trees were thicker here, welcoming and mysterious at the same time. It was the sort of forest one wanted to creep into in search of something marvelous and to flee from at night. It was the sort of forest that likely concealed a number of riding trees. Perhaps, she and Sigfried could sneak out here some twilight and see if they could find one that would be willing to give them a ride. Rachel tilted her head and thought back, adjusting in her mind for twenty-five years of tree growth. She recognized this wood from her parents' photo album. *It was the Woseforest.*

They landed and released the woodwose from the backpack. It jumped out and shouted with joy, leaping up and down and thumping the ground with its great feet. Rachel thought this was funny until an odd, deep thrumming, almost too deep to hear, sounded around her.

The trees were answering him.

The forest smelled wonderful here; the thick odor of evergreens perfumed the air. Rachel looked at the woods more closely. Tall tulip poplars, straight as fire pokers, towered over them. Stately hemlocks and white pines, which Rachel had always found a funny name for the greenest of pine trees, gave the forest its festive color. Willows grew along the riverbank, their branches arching downward, even in their leafless state. Above them all, there rose one massive oak. Rachel wondered if this was the oak that had been angry at the absence of the wose.

Nor was it just the trees who welcomed their master's return. Squirrels chattered in the branches, and a deer peeked out through the feathery hemlock branches. Even though it was midday, an owl let out a long low hoot. The wose, in return, stamped its feet again and laid its hand on the trunk of the nearest tree. Already, it was moving more easily, as if merely returning to its forest was helping its wound to heal. Perhaps, that was part of its charmed life, too.

Suddenly, Sigfried exclaimed in dismay. Rachel glanced over to see him holding the parts of his fulgurator's wand, which had been snapped in two. Lucky hovered in the air beside him, looking on in consternation.

"Aw! Must have happened when the bear-ape hugged me!"

Rachel walked over to take a look. "The gem is intact. That's what really matters. And one of the older students can probably fix it for you with the Word of Mending."

"Really?" He grinned. "Ace. Magic is so useful."

"*I help.*" The beast-man held out its great paw-like hand.

Very gingerly, Sigfried handed the wose his broken wand. Lifting the two pieces near its mouth, the master of the Woseforest began whispering to the fragmented cherrywood, cooing or humming softly. The sound was strange and sad and made Rachel's heart ache, and yet it also made her feel more solid, more wholesome, as if she and all the world were intertwined, and all had their proper place from which they never need fear that they could stray.

Before the astonished eyes of the two students, the two pieces of the cherrywood grew and moved, entangling around each other, like roots seeking earth. And then the wand was whole.

The woodwose returned it to Sigfried. The boy peered at it carefully. There was a little ring of thicker wood around the spot where it had snapped, and there was still a break in the gold tracery that lined its length. Other than that, it looked as good as new. Siggy whooshed it through the air and even fired off a spell or two. It worked. Grinning, he spun it around twice and slipped it back into its spot on the bandoleer that held his elixirs.

"Thanks, Mr. Wose." Sigfried stepped over and, reaching into his pockets, offered the beast-man the bag containing the meatballs that had originally been in the sub. "That was right decent of you. Sorry I called you a bear-ape."

Rachel curtsied to the great shaggy man. "Glad we could be of service."

"*Come again,*" said the woodwose. "*We can sing the song of evening together.*"

Rachel ran forward and hugged him, though she could only reach its leg. The wose put its massive hand gently on her head. Then Rachel ran back to her broom, hopped on the Flycycle, and when Sigfried had mounted, too, flew up and away, waving until the woodwose disappeared beneath the evergreens.

"And now, we're going to see the crater, right?" asked Sigfried.

"Oh, right!" Rachel replied. "A promise is a promise."

She flew north, along the shore. Soon, they rounded a narrow promontory that ended in a series of tiny islands that were little more than large boulders extending into the Hudson. On the far side was a deep cove. The ward-wall was visible again, just beyond the edge of the shore. In the cove was a large flat rock, forming a small island, maybe forty feet wide. Gazing at this idyllic, snowy cove, a strange sensation—half-eerie, half-nostalgic—passed through her.

"Hang on! I recognize this place!" Rachel cried. "I've seen it in photographs!"

She glanced up and down the shore, matching what her eyes showed her with photos in the library of her memory that showed the same shore, except some of the trees were more slender and others were not yet there.

"Yes! This is the place," she cried. "It's Merrow Cove! There are pictures of it in my parents' photo album."

"Why would they have pictures of these places?" Siggy frowned. "No one comes here."

"They used to, before the Battle of Roanoke. Before the Terrible Years. Students were given a lot more freedom then. And the wardlocks? Some of them used to be gates. People could come and go. My father and my Uncle Emrys snuck out the eastern gate and into the Woseforest a number of times. I've heard stories about their adventures. Mum and her best friend Ambie once came to this cove with Ellyllon MacDannan—now Mrs. Darling—and met the merrow who live under these waters. Well, under the ice at the moment."

"You have an uncle, too?" Sigfried asked, with a sniff. He grumbled. "Some people have all the family luck."

"Actually, my Uncle Emrys is dead." Rachel's voice caught. She pointed a shaky finger at the flat rocky island. "He died... right there."

Siggy turned and stared at the boulder in morbid fascination.

"He died during the Battle for the Eastern Shore," Rachel continued. "Emrys was part of a cadre of students backing up Scarlett MacDannan in her fight against Morgana Le Fay. Morgana could cast a deadly black fire. Scarlett blocked it with the shield Mr. Fisher made for her, but during the fight the shield was knocked from her hands. Scarlett ran to retrieve it. She was protecting a whole group of students on the shore. Morgana raised her hands to strike her dead, only...." Rachel's voice caught. This story had never struck her so hard before. "Uncle Emrys flew between them. He deflected the fire. Saved her life. But it struck him," she swallowed, "a-and h-he died. Ambie was there, too. They were engaged—that's how my mother met my father, because her best friend was marrying his brother. Emrys and Ambie both died that day, along with dozens of other students."

For once, Sigfried had nothing to say. His expression had become serious. Lucky snaked over and wrapped himself around his boy, his chin resting on the crown of Siggy's head.

"But Scarlett won," Rachel attempted a cheerier tone, despite the constriction of her throat. "Morgana was turned to sludge, right there. On that same rock."

"Sludge?" Sigfried peered hard at the rock, as if searching for a remnant of what had once been Morgana Le Fay. "Get some of that, Lucky. Sludge Le Fey must be good for something alchemical."

Rachel turned her broom toward the north again. As they headed onward, she briefly reviewed her memory of the last few minutes.

Then she gasped. In her memory, the rocky island was not empty. Standing atop the island's flat surface where her uncle and Morgana Le Fay had died almost twenty-five years ago, watching her the whole time she had paused in the cove, was an eight-foot-tall figure with enormous, black raven wings.

Rachel shouted with joy. Turning the Starling around, she shot back into the cove.

"Hey, what are we doing?" Sigfried asked.

Lucky slithered off him to land on the rock, as well. Then his golden fur stood straight up, like a cat's. "Um... boss. There's some-thi—"

Mid-word, he stopped moving. His body hung in mid-air, a slen-der red and gold ribbon. Sigfried froze in the act of climbing from the broom. He had one arm out and one leg up, halfway over the bristle-less, but he was so motionless that he could have been a sculpture.

"Oh!" Rachel spun around.

Everything had stopped: water drops dripping from branches, birds in mid-flight.

She came to a stop, gazing up at the Raven. He stood before her in all his majesty, his black wings spread. He was shirtless and bare-footed but wore pants of black poplin. In one hand, he held a golden hoop. His face was inhumanly handsome; his eyes were as red as fresh blood. Rachel stood humbly before him, her heart beating like the wings of a frightened bird.

The Guardian towered three and a half feet above her. He was now the most important person in the universe to her, but he was not a tame Raven. Truth be told, she was a bit scared of him, terrified even. She was not afraid that he would hurt her. Rather she feared that she might disappoint him. She would do or say the wrong thing, and he would not speak to her again. And then she truly would be just an ordinary little girl—and not the girl who mattered to the Raven.

Come to think of it, it was rather the same way she felt about Dread and for very similar reasons.

The Raven gazed at her steadily. The red faded from his eyes until they were as gray as the wing of a dove on a stormy day. He spoke in a voice that was beautifully melodic.

"I brought you here, Rachel Griffin, because I wished to speak with you."

"Brought me here?" Rachel stepped back, startled. "I thought we came becau…."

The Raven replied, "The proctors have the school brooms ensorcelled to alert them if the devices are taken outside the wards. On one, however, this spell was failing."

"Oh!" Rachel whispered, awed. She pointed at the black and brown O.I. Starling, which currently hung motionlessly in mid-air. "You made it fall into my hands!"

"I decided that it was likely that you would come. When you return to school, give that device to your friend Carlos Fuentes and tell him that the spell needs refreshing." He gazed off into the distance. "I see few futures where he questions you."

Rachel nodded. If she said nothing about why she was bringing the broom, Mr. Fuentes would most likely assume that Mr. Chanson had sent her.

"What did you wish to tell me?" She gazed upward curiously.

"Your sister Amber is aware of any attempt to manipulate her mind." Jariel's inhumanly-perfect lips smiled slightly. "She will arrive searching for that which tried to bring her here."

"I-is s-she coming then?" Rachel's heart thumped oddly.

He nodded solemnly. "Whether soon or no, I cannot say."

"Can you tell me more about her?" she pleaded.

"Her secrets are not mine to tell. You will have to ask her when she comes."

Rachel nodded, resigned. With a sigh, she turned and gazed up the frozen river, past the island and a tug boat that appeared to be stuck in the ice, towards the faint lines of the Newburgh-Beacon Bridge. *A living sister!* It still amazed her. Most of all, however, what reverberated through her mind were the words Jariel had spoken to her about Laurel during the fated skating party that ended with the wards being breached and Siggy killing the ogre: *Your sister was ready to die defending you. I wonder, does that trait run throughout your family? The willingness to sacrifice yourself for another?*

A burst of unadulterated joy had passed through her when she had heard those words. It was true. Her family was like that. It was exactly how she felt in her heart, as if she would give of herself whatever was necessary for her family and friends without hesitation—even to the point of sacrificing her life as Uncle Emrys had done.

She just wished to be called upon to do more. As she gazed out at the ice, she thought not only of Emrys and Laurel's bravery, but also of her father, who, without hesitation, had knowingly risked his memory to protect his youngest daughter—even if it had been a misunderstanding. It also reminded her of her second cousin Blackie Moth, who had apparently given up his entire memory rather than endanger those he loved. Blackie was not a Griffin, it was true, but his grandmother, Great-Aunt Nimue, had been born a Griffin.

If a willingness to die for each other was a Griffin family trait, how badly must the Master of the World have warped her parents to make them the kind of people who would agree to give up their infant daughter? The absence of this sister, of whom she had previously been unaware, now felt like a gaping wound.

She hated the Master of the World with an everlasting hatred. Why had he done such a terrible thing to her family? Recalling her earlier thought on the matter, she turned to the Raven.

"My missing sister," she asked slowly, "she's like Mother and me, isn't she?"

He nodded solemnly, his eyes as vast and deep as the night sky. "Her mind is like yours. She forgets nothing."

"I can imagine many reasons why a ruler might want a servant with a perfect memory," said Rachel, who had thought about this subject at length. With a shiver, she gave thanks, again, that this monster who stole her sister, the Master of the World, did not know about her own memory. His ignorance on this topic may have saved her life.

Jariel nodded. "She was taken when it was confirmed that she, too, shared your mother's gift."

"Thank you," her eyes filled with gratitude. "For telling me all this and for bringing her."

"You are welcome, Rachel Griffin."

Rachel started to turn back towards her broom. Then she paused.

"Jariel," she asked, "why children?"

"I beg your pardon?"

"My friends. Those who came from Outside. They used to be adults, right? Living lives and conquering worlds and such? Why did you turn them into children?"

The Raven cocked his head, as if listening. After a moment, he said, "I suppose it will do no harm to answer your question, Rachel Griffin. It is easier for someone to adapt to a new life from the beginning. In each case, I saved the person from the ruin and destruction that had come upon them—either caused by Azrael's spell or by some other means. I offered them a new life. In return, they agreed to my terms. A few, such as Illondria, asked to remain as they were. A number requested to remain adults even if they must forget the details of their past. The rest agreed to help."

"To help... with what?" she asked, intrigued.

"There will come two great undertakings. The time is not yet, but it will come soon—in a few years." He glanced off into the distance, narrowing his eyes as if peering at something, and then added, "... most likely. I have gathered together those who were willing and have placed them here, together, at Roanoke—so that they might come to know each other and be ready to work together when the time comes."

"What are these two undertakings?" Rachel asked, now burning with curiosity.

The Raven smiled ever-so-slightly. "One is the quest of the Keybearers. You have already volunteered to aid that effort. Of the other..." he turned, glancing over his shoulder, back toward the campus, "... I dare not speak. It involves a dangerous and brave undertaking that can only be accomplished by one who is a student here—someone who must be protected."

Rachel tilted back her head and thought of everything she had learned since September, all the secrets she had learned about her friends and other students, all the prophecies and conversations that might possibly be related. A memory returned to her of the spirit voices that spoke through Xandra Black apologizing for failing to protect....

Straightening, she asked, "Evelyn March?"

The Raven's eyes widened. "How could you.... We must not speak of this!"

Rachel nodded solemnly, saying no more. But, inside, she was tickled pink that she had come to the correct conclusion. She wondered who Evelyn March had been, back when she lived Outside, and what dire task awaited her.

Time started. Birds flew. Water dripped. Wind blew. Sigfried climbed from the broom.

Lucky was still speaking. "—ng's here so watch out. It's.... Aaa!"

The dragon let out a screech. He skittered backward, hiding behind his master. Sigfried stepped in front of Lucky to protect him, swaggering forward.

"Hello, Mr. Raven-Brute. You should be ashamed of yourself, frightening poor innocent dragons!"

The Raven looked faintly amused. "I mean my little brother no harm." He gazed off into the distance, his eyes again turning red. "I must depart. We shall speak again, Rachel Griffin."

He curled his wingtips forward. Then a large black bird wheeled away, dwindling quickly into the distance until it could no longer be seen.

Chapter Sixteen:
The Force of Lightning

The jagged, C-shaped broken top of Stony Tor loomed above them. They flew over hemlocks and spruces, passing the steep, rocky valley on the east side of the tor that she had only glimpsed once before—back in September, the very first time she had taken Sigfried flying. Beyond this valley, to the north, were snowy fields, the lake where the water panther was rumored to live, and the northern shore of Roanoke Island.

Her thoughts kept returning to the idea that her missing sister had been taken because of her perfect memory. She recalled Astrid's comment the morning she helped Rachel wash the blood from her hat: *I imagine it's an extremely useful talent, but it also must be at times quite a heavy burden.*

Was it a burden? Was that why she had been so much more affected by the terrible things that had happened in September and October than her friends? Because terrible events never faded from her memory? The idea that her gift of a perfect memory had a downside was not one that she had previously taken very seriously. But if people were kidnapping her family members because of this gift, maybe she should revisit the subject.

"What was it you wanted to talk about?" asked Siggy innocently as they flew. "Someone you wanted killed? That Valiant fellow?"

"What?" shrieked Rachel. "I don't want you to kill my *boyfriend!*"

He continued with mock innocence. "Thought maybe you had a tiff. Who do you want us to take out?"

"The Master of the World." Her voice vibrated with fury.

"The Master-Who-Sits-On-The-World," Sigfried threw some potato chip dust, from the bottom of a bag, into the air and with a sense of satisfaction watched it rain down. "Very well. I shall kill him for you. What's he look like? A bat? A frog? An evil monomaniac who lives in a skull-shaped castle? Can I keep the castle? Lucky and I could use a lair."

"We need a place to keep the treasure that doesn't fit under the bed," agreed Lucky. "Especially once the warm weather melts the ice up north and we get the additional treasure that the ghost promised the brainy sister back on Halloween."

"There's the ogre's cave," suggested Siggy.

"Too wet and too icy," said Lucky.

Rachel glanced over her shoulder to see Sigfried nod sagely.

"I appreciate your support," Rachel said, sighing, "but I don't think it will be possible. He controls the Guardian."

"The newspaper?" asked Siggy.

Rachel giggled. "No, the Raven."

"Who?"

Rachel took a deep breath, struggling to restrain her exasperation. "The being that maintains the Walls around our world—the Walls that keep the darkness and evil things from Outside from getting in? The giant winged man we just spoke to?"

"Oh, the black bird of ill-omen," Siggy said knowingly. "The one that killed the Elf."

"No!" Rachel let go of the bristleless to grab her head in frustration. "The storm goblin—the Heer of Dunderberg—killed our Elf. When a demon let him out of his prison. The Raven is good."

"He's good, but you want his boss to die."

"Well," Rachel faltered, the fight draining out of her. "I am not sure I want him to die, exactly. But I want him stopped."

"No problem. I'll bash his head, and Lucky will burn his face."

"Burninate him!" Lucky agreed, plummeting down towards the ground far beneath them and then swooping up again. "Till there's nothing left but a flaky black crisp." The dragon snaked back down and paused. "Who are we burninating?"

Rachel replied grimly. "The person responsible for everything our world has forgotten."

"You mean all the secrets we don't know?" Sigfried cried. "You didn't tell me that!"

"Orphaned words," she continued, "like 'steeple' or 'saint'? They represent something that's been erased from history. The Master of the World is the one who decided that we should forget these things."

"He made the *whole world* forget?" He gawked. Sigfried was so shocked that he was actually serious.

Rachel nodded. "He ordered the Raven to do it. He can make the Raven do things. He's also the one who erased my father's memory. My father didn't have a magical accident. He did something he had promised not to do—because he thought he was protecting *me*—and the Master of the World took away the last couple years of his memory."

"That's horrible! That's it. He deserves a horrible death for his crimes against humanity, doesn't he, Lucky?" declared Sigfried.

Flying beside them, Lucky nodded knowingly. "He hurt orphan words, boss. As a former orphan, you should make him pay."

"So, we're taking this Master of the Word out for mangling orphan words and erasing your dad?" declared Sigfried, recovering his normal aplomb.

"That's not all...." Rachel began, her voice hardly above a whisper.

"Stealing your father's memory and killing the language isn't enough?" asked Sigfried. "That's verbicide!"

"And trying to steal my memories," she added.

"Yours! But you can remember everything!" cried Siggy.

"Once you remember it, it's never forgotten," declared Lucky, loyally.

"The Master of the World doesn't know about my perfect memory," Rachel said. "He made the Raven give me fake memories. Thanks to my Elf Rune, the fake ones didn't work."

"That's good!" Siggy declared. "We'd be lost without you. And by we, I mean the Die Horribly Debate Club. It would be like chopping off our head, if the Die Horribly Debate Club were a chicken—where the body keeps running, even though it's dead. That would be us."

"That's right!" agreed Lucky. "We couldn't do anything without our genius sister-creature to tell us what to do! Unless we could eat the chicken. Chickens are delicious. I guess we could do without a head if we got to eat it."

"Thanks, you lot... I think," murmured Rachel, smiling.

Soaring down the slopes of Stony Tor, Rachel thought back to the imposing form of the Master of the World standing in her bedroom, his face lit by the silvery light that shone from the moonlight path at his feet. With a shiver, she recalled how close she had come to dying. The Master of the World did not know about her Elf Rune or about her still-perfect memory. If he had, he might have ordered the Raven to circumvent them.

Suddenly, she was again extraordinarily grateful that her mother had warned her to keep her memory private. Luckily, very few people knew, even among her larger circle of friends.

Aloud, she said, "But that's not why I am so angry."

"There's more?" Sigfried asked dubiously. "What could be worse?"

She was quiet for a long moment. "He kidnapped my sister."

"What?" he cried, outraged. "The hot one with the legs that just keep going? Or the gorgeous older one who's a female James Bond?"

Despite the seriousness of the topic, Rachel burst out laughing at Siggy's descriptions of Laurel and Sandra. Quietly, she told him about Amber, about how her family had been manipulated and then made to forget.

Sigfried had a strange look in his eyes. "They have magic that can do that to parents? Do you think that could have happened to mine? Magic made them forget they had a baby, so they thought, 'Oh, what's this bundle?' and just tossed me in the trash?"

"Um... maybe. But aren't you an android?"

"Oh, true." He thought about this. "But was it the Emperor of All things Mean and Unmean who threw me in the dumpster? Or did he give me to parents who were supposed to raise me, and *they* forgot me and threw me in a dumpster?"

"I, er, rather doubt it was the Lion's Father who forgot you."

"But back to this stolen sister of yours," said Sigfried. "We can get her back if we find his name, right? Is it Rumpelstiltskin? What about Stumplerilskins? How many tries do we get? Oh, I know! Just point me at him! I can stand over a hundred feet away and just watch him with my amulet until someone says his name." Siggy raised his voice slightly. "'Oh, Mr. Wonderpunpkin, here's your coffee.'" His voice returned to normal. "Then we get the kid back, and then we kill him."

"I'm not sure it's going to be that easy...." Rachel chewed on her lip, reluctant to make even more trouble between Sigfried and Nastasia.

She gazed down at the snowy landscape and the pale green tops of the blue spruce. *That was the rub, was it not?* In fairytales, when a child has been stolen, the problem was always solved by diligence and devotion: learning a fairy's name, or knitting sweaters out of nettles, or refusing to let go of a shapechanging loved one. But real life seldom so simple.

True, fairies did exist, and one could deal with them in just such a manner. But Amber had not been taken by the fey. It almost would have been better had she been spirited away. Their chances of recovering her, without harm to themselves or their loved ones, would have been higher.

As she flew, contemplating the Master of the World and his heinous acts, it was as if a sliver of ice lodged in her heart, driving deeper and deeper, spreading numbness and hatred through her soul. Somehow, she was going to get her sister back.

"This *monster* took a child from its parents," Sigfried's voice had taken on a dangerous edge. "He must die! Who is this blighter? Do we know where to find him?"

Grimly, she answered, "He is the grandfather of our friend the princess, the father of the King of Magical Australia. Only Nastasia didn't know about him. This monster even stole his own granddaughter's memory of him."

"We can't ask her about him. She might squeal." Siggy sounded disgusted. "Never wise to keep a snitch in the group. Where is this stolen sister now?"

"Another world. The Raven has promised to make her come here. So we can meet her."

Siggy was quiet for a remarkably long time. Lucky had slunk over and was now wrapped around his boy, the dragon's head resting on his master's shoulder. Rachel could feel the warmth of his body, where it touched hers, even through her coat.

Finally, Sigfried spoke grimly. "We are going to stop him, right? It's not just talk."

"Right." Rachel nodded, glancing back at him.

"And if we can't stop him?" His blue eyes bored into hers intently.

Rachel swallowed. "We do whatever is necessary."

Siggy spit in his hand. Rachel winced, but she spit in hers as well and reached behind her. They shook on it.

Near the foot of the western slope, burnt spruce trees surrounded a bowl-shaped indentation. The trees nearest to the center had been blown flat, splaying outwards from the point of impact, all their branches burned away. Rachel flew the Starling higher, up over the evergreen forest, until she could see the affected area more clearly. At the bottom of the snowy crater were several broken pieces of stone. As she gazed down at it, an eerie sensation crawled up her spine, like a thousand tiny insect feet.

"Here it is!" cried Sigfried. "Where the Heer tried to blow up the tor. Do you think he bombed it from orbit? Hit it with a meteor? Lucky, go check it out!"

Lucky slipped down and circled around the crater, sniffing things.

"Don't smell any gunpowder, Boss," he called.

"Must be storm goblin magic! That Heer's a lot scarier than I thought he was!"

Rachel bit her lip. "I don't think that was the Heer."

"Who was it? Dread?"

The wind blew. Snow melted. Rachel stared at the crater. Eventually, with great reluctance, she admitted, "I think... I did that."

Siggy's jaw dropped open. He looked her up and down, as if taking in her diminutive size. He spread his arms with an expression that accused her of having held out on him. "You?"

She nodded sheepishly.

"Ace!" Siggy whooped. "Let's bottle that! We could kill a lot of ogres! Or storm goblins! Tutors! Visiting lecturers! That Steele bloke in math class! Blaggards who look wrong at a guy's girl! The nuns back at the orphanage! The orphanage itself—after we get the other blokes out, of course! Then they'll never be able to send me back!"

Rachel flew closer and circled the crater. The wind was biting cold. Landing the Starling at the bottom of the bowl, she jumped off and examined the broken stone, looking at it from different angles in an attempt to match it to the boulder she remembered seeing as it flew through the night sky, illuminated by lightning. It was hard to be certain, as it had shattered into several pieces, but she was reasonably sure it was the same boulder.

The air was warmer here, beneath the lip of the crater. Rachel sat on the largest piece of the boulder. Her face pale, she murmured, "Did my cantrip really cause all this?"

Siggy eagerly kicked one of the smaller pieces of stone around in a circle. "Don't know. Didn't see it. I was busy slaying an ogre. How'd you do it?"

"I was about to be shot with lightning by one of the Heer's imps...."

"Don't you have that oak key I made for you? With that, no lightning could hurt you!"

"I'd given mine to Astrid. She was really scared."

"You should've asked me." Sigfried threw out his chest proudly. "I carry extra!"

"Oh! I... didn't know that. I did get it back from her later."

He reached into his robes and pulled out another oak key. "Here, take an extra one. This way, you can share next time someone else needs help. You can have another nettle cake, too."

Rachel accepted the key graciously, slipping it into the kenomanced neck pouch in which she kept the emergency card Vlad had given her. The nettle cake was wrapped in a napkin. She slipped that into the pouch, too. "Anyway, I didn't want to get zapped, so I used a trick Gaius taught me that allows a person to move inertia from one object to another," she explained. "Somehow, when I moved the inertia from the lightning javelin to a flying boulder... it made the boulder go very, very fast. The boulder flew off in this direction and then, boom!"

"Ace!" Sigfried declared again. "I have got to learn how to do that!"

Rachel sighed. "I doubt it's going to happen again." She tilted her head thoughtfully. "But I wonder if knowing about it would be useful to my cousin Blackie. He makes munitions. The principle might apply. I'll write him a letter about it." She paused, eyeing

Sigfried speculatively. "You'd like Cousin Blackie, I think. I should introduce you."

"There must be a way to store it and pull out the explosion when you needed it," Sigfried repeated, "like when True Hiss class becomes particularly boring. Or when girls are droning on about boys or about their fingernails. The possibilities are endless!"

"I... don't think I could do it again. It was rather a fluke."

"Hmm. That's a problem." Siggy stroked his chin thoughtfully. Lucky imitated the gesture, his talons running along his golden chin and red chin tuft. The two of them turned simultaneously and nodded at each other. "What we need is a hustler."

Rachel's head shot up. "I beg your pardon."

"An expert billiards player," continued Sigfried, "someone who could set the boulder up like it was an eightball. Or is the eightball the one you don't want to put in the pocket?"

Rachel sat on a cold remnant of the boulder, her chin resting on her palm. It was probably better not to mention to Sigfried that she, herself, was an ace billiards player who occasionally hustled adults down at the pub in Gryphon-on-Dart. It was one of the side effects of her perfect memory that she could predict motion in three dimensions with greater ease than most. It was this same talent that allowed her to judge distances at high speed when flying.

It was also practically the only game she was any good at whatsoever. She could play chess and bridge, but not with any brilliance, and she was horrid at the sorts of games played with balls.

"Where's my lightning javelin?" Sigfried asked suddenly. "The one I stabbed the ogre with? I sent Lucky back to look for it, but it was gone."

"The proctors wouldn't have left a dangerous thing like that lying around."

"Lying around! It was mine! I wouldn't have left it behind if I had been conscious. Whoever took me to the infirmary should have collected it."

"Sorry, boss," Lucky hung his head. "I should'a looked out for our treasure. I was... kinna worried about you."

"You're forgiven," Sigfried declared magnanimously. "But don't let it happen again. In the future, treasure comes first."

Lucky nodded sagely. "Gold is thicker than water."

Rachel grinned at the two of them. She decided not to point out that, as the person who had caused the javelin to fall, technically, it should have been hers. Siggy had been brave enough to pull it from the ice and use it to stab the ogre, after all.

Instead, she said, "Von Dread carried you to the infirmary. Take it up with him."

"Dread took me?" Siggy's voice grew wobbly with hero worship. "Whoa!"

Rachel did not answer. Von Dread was a dicey subject for her at the moment.

"Bet you could kill whomever you wanted dead with this!" Siggy rested his foot atop another chunk of the boulder. His grin was so large, it threatened to consume his entire head. "You know, the Smasher of the World? Or at least turn him into sludge like S'more-gana."

Rachel gave a mirthful snort. "If I could get him to stand still during a storm, while I lined up a flying boulder and a lightning imp. Come. Let's go."

Bristleless in hand, she climbed up the bank and gazed at the crater from above, still shocked by the size of it. Sighing, she climbed back onto the Flycycle.

A wind swooshed and, catching her robes and the Starling, flipped her upside-down. Spinning head over heels, Rachel toggled the levers and kicked the tail fan in exactly the way that would have brought her steeplechaser out of this kind of a spin.

Only this was not Vroomie. The Starling bucked and spun, carried by the strong gust of wind. Rachel clutched the handle, desperately trying to figure out how to regain control. Her hair flew everywhere, making it even harder to see. Never in all her years of flying had her broom proved so wildly ungovernable. As she flipped backwards and the ground approached rapidly, terror gripped her.

Then, she stopped. Upside down, half falling off, a curtain of hair obscuring her vision, she glanced cautiously through the dark strands to see Sigfried pointing his wand at her, a concentrated expression on his face. Slowly, he lowered her toward the ground at his feet.

Rachel hung on, battered by the torrential winds. The moment he moved her beneath the lip of the crater, however, the strong wind stopped. Rachel slid from the Starling to the icy ground, landing awkwardly, limbs sticking out in embarrassing ways. Quickly, she rolled onto her feet and stood up, dusting off her robes. When she stood, her head rose above the crater's edge, and she could feel the wind again.

"You forget how to fly?" Siggy asked. "It can't be that. You don't forget."

"There's a wind," she gestured wildly, as if she could point to the breeze. Her voice rose. "It knocked me off the eejit gym broom!"

"Huh." He held his hand up. The wind was so strong that it pushed his fingers back. Then he lowered his hand below the edge of the crater. The wind continued to whip his golden curls around, but no wind touched his hand. "That's weird."

Rachel looked up the slope toward the peak of the tor. The spruce growing on the side were motionless. No breeze moved their branches. Only near their position did branches move violently, as if tossed by a gale.

"Come on. Get on." Rachel picked up the Starling again and gestured to Sigfried. "With both of us weighing it down, we should be able to fly out of here."

They both climbed on, and Rachel tried again. She headed straight up from the center of the crater, hoping to shoot through the wind gust and get above it. If the spruce trees up the slope were untroubled, the air should be still at that level.

It would have worked on the steeplechaser.

A whirlwind struck them, spinning them in a circle. Rachel flipped the levers rapidly, but she could not reconfigure the large three-bladed tail fan to handle this much turbulence. The bristleless and its two hapless riders spun sideways, whirling through the air at an unpleasantly high speed. Just as the branches of an oak loomed before them, they jerked to a stop. Then they began to drop like a rock. Behind them, Lucky had grabbed the tail array in his mouth and was tugging. This saved them from the unpleasant fate of ending their days impaled on an oak branch like marshmallows waiting to be toasted, but it also stopped the operation of the broom. The ground grew rapidly nearer.

"Let go!" Rachel screamed. "Lucky, let go of the fan! Come pull from up here!"

Rachel was afraid that he would not be able to hear her over the roar of the winds, but he released the broom and snaked toward the front of the device. His body stretched from the handle, whipping in the wind like a ribbon in front of a fan; however, he managed to keep them steady. Rachel concentrated on righting the device, figuring that they would be out of the effect of the unnatural wind soon, as the trees ahead of them showed no sign of a breeze.

Whoosh. The whirlwind changed directions, striking them in their faces and pushing them backwards. They spun wildly. To Rachel's great chagrin, she screamed.

"What's going on?" cried Siggy.

"I don't know!" Rachel called back.

By calling to Lucky, getting him to pull in a way that was helpful, Rachel managed to maneuver back to the crater. Once below the lip, the air was entirely quiet. The whirlwind spun just above them. Both of them leapt from the Starling and threw themselves face first on the icy dirt. Sigfried kissed the earth. Rachel, her body trembling, pressed her cheek against the frozen ground, grateful to be alive.

Eventually, the whirlwind dissolved. Yet, rising to his feet, Sigfried was nearly knocked flat by the wind that still blew above the crater.

"What is it?" he asked, sitting down again. "Storm goblin?"

"Maybe." Rachel sat up, cold from contact with the frozen earth beneath her. "Only, he hasn't caused this kind of trouble before. Also, it's not raining. I don't think the storm goblin does a limited gust like this. I'm not sure what does."

She thought back over the supernatural creatures that inhabited this part of the island. Nothing came immediately to mind.

"Let's try walking out," she said finally. "Maybe we can get out of the area of the effect."

As they started up the side of the crater, out of the ground popped a creature. It was dressed in bark with wild hair that looked a bit like dried leaves. The thing was nearly as large as they were. Its face was brown as a nut. It grinned at them with an angry, maniacal grin that reminded Rachel a little of Sigfried. She recognized it from Daring Northwest's books.

"Spriggan!" shouted Rachel.

"Wait!" Sigfried spun around from a sitting position, pointing his wand at the creature. "I know what that is! I met one in London. Lucky blastified it. Get 'em, Lucks!"

"On it, Boss!" Lucky yelled cheerfully.

The dragon swooped forward, up the crater, and over the lip, fire blooming from his mouth. The spriggan sank into the earth, vanishing before the plume of flame struck. Moments later, it popped up on the other side of the crater. Siggy blew his trumpet. When silvery sparkles of the wind blast crossed the edge of the crater, they swirled and joined the gusts coming back their way. Effectively, his magic had just increased the force of the wind trapping them.

"Traitors!" cried Sigfried, shaking his fist angrily at the sparks. "If being a wizard wasn't so wizard, I'd give it up." He spun the horn on his finger like a gunfighter with a six-shooter before hooking it to the baldric he wore. With his hands free, he performed a cantrip gesture. "*Argos!*"

A shining golden band swooped into existence in mid-air, but the fey was not there. The spriggan had vanished into the earth again.

When it popped out next, Rachel was ready. She whistled and blue sparkles lit the air, dancing toward the fey creature; however, it was gone again before they reached it. Sigfried let out a growl of frustration.

"It's like a game of magical whack-a-mole!" he declared.

Rachel gave him an odd look. "I... don't know what that is."

Siggy started going through his things. "Spider-climb elixir? No. Chameleon elixir? Maybe. Water Baby elixir? No. Floating elixir— probably make things worse. What can we do? Should I turn invisible and try to sneak up on him?"

"Might work. Might not. Some fey can see through those kinds of elixirs."

"Any other ideas?"

"Well," Rachel thought about it as she chewed on her lip. "Turning our clothing inside out is always a good first step. Many smaller fey creatures cannot come near you if you do that."

Siggy shrugged. "Can't hurt."

Rachel turned her sweater inside out and put it on again. Sigfried stared in consternation at his bulky parka. Making a face, he pulled the thick, puffy sleeves through the arm holes and then frowned, trying to figure out how to put it back on. He managed to stick his arms into the inside-out sleeves.

"Okay." Rachel looked him over and nodded in approval. "Let's try walking out. If he gets close enough to hit us...."

"I'll burninate him!" Lucky vowed.

Rachel said, "The spriggan moves too quickly...."

Lucky said, "Burnination *always* works! It's the greatest nation there can be!"

Rachel said, "Flames cannot reach underground. We have to try something else."

Lucky said, "Let's try incineration!"

Rachel said, "Isn't that the same thing?"

"Cremation!" said Siggy.

"Scalding!" said Lucky.

"Flame-broiling!" said Siggy.

While they jabbered, Rachel picked up the Starling. The three of them marched up the slope of the crater. No wind rose to stop them. Whether this was because of their inside-out clothing or for some other reason, Rachel did not know.

"Spriggan," cried Sigfried, "why are you bothering us?"

Rachel looked around. "Where?"

"There!" Siegfried pointed at a spot behind them, then he pointed underfoot, then ahead of them. "Now over there. The blighter just zooms through solid earth. Cute trick."

Sigfried was pointing at the ground before them when the leaf-headed fey rose out of it.

"You have destroyed my trees." Its voice sounded like a wailing wind. It pointed at the flattened spruces around the crater. "You have stolen a part of my home."

CHAPTER SEVENTEEN: WINDSWEPT!

The two students gawked at the wild-haired fey.

"Stolen? How?" asked Rachel.

The spriggan moaned, wind kicking up snow all around it. "I cannot go there."

"What does he mean, Lucky?" asked the dragon's boy.

Lucky said in his growly voice, "I think he means he lost authority."

"So, when the boulder struck the earth here," asked Rachel, "he lost his ability to pass through it? Is that why he did not pop up down there and attack us?"

"Pretty much," said Lucky.

The three of them stared at the spriggan. The spriggan stared back.

"Um... can we return it?" asked Rachel.

The spriggan tilted its head. "Would you?"

"It depends on what is required."

"Renounce your claim."

It was not hers. Rachel could think of no reason not to return it to its rightful owner.

"Very well," she announced, "I will if you answer my questions."

"What questions?" asked the spriggan cagily.

"What questions?" Sigfried's head snapped around so that he could stare at her, too.

Rachel rolled her eyes. To the spriggan, she said, "Did you go with the others onto the campus when the ward-lock was opened?"

A wind blew snow into the air all around the wild creature. "No."

"Why not?" Rachel asked curiously, wondering if it were lying. Of course, it was here and not stuck inside the warding wall, so maybe it was telling the truth.

"I care not for the Morthbrood."

A tingle of excitement spread through Rachel. She thought back to what the ogre had said before Sigfried killed him. The Morthbrood would qualify as "an old enemy seeking revenge."

Aloud, Rachel asked the spriggan with great interest, "Was it the Morthbrood who let the fey through the ward-lock?"

"No," replied

"I... am confused," Rachel admitted, a bit disappointed.

"Mortals are often confused," replied the spriggan.

Rachel resisted the urge to give into exasperation. She searched for other questions, "Did you dream about a man wearing a mask made of winter?"

The spriggan let out a horrible hiss. "I know not by what art that came. It was not Seelie."

"Was it Unseelie?" Rachel asked.

"What's that?" hissed Sigfried.

Rachel whispered back, "Dark fey, evil fairies. We've only covered that in class," Rachel paused and counted, "twenty-six times."

The spriggan merely repeated, "I know not."

"What about the Heer?" Rachel asked, "What can you tell us about him?"

The spriggan ducked into the ground. Rachel waited patiently. He popped out again and sat on the rim of the crater, crossing one leg over the other, knee to the side.

"It is better when the Heer is in his prison," the spriggan said. "He hurts us. How we all cheered last time he fell, plummeting through the sky like a shining comet."

"Did you see that?" Rachel asked.

"How'd they catch him?" Siggy leaned forward eagerly.

"The Lantern-Lords came. They wrapped him up in glimmering gold," replied the spriggan, "made of the noise of a cat's foot-fall, the beard of a woman, the roots of a rock, the sinews of a bear, the breath of a fish, and the spittle of a bird."

"That's Gleipnir." Rachel recognized the description of the chain the gods wove to hold the great wolf Fenrir. "I think he means Glepnir bands."

"What's a Lantern-Lord?" asked Lucky. "Are they tasty?"

Rachel replied. "It's a slang term for the Agents of the Wisecraft used by the fey. The Wisecraft's symbol is a lantern surrounded by seven stars."

"I have answered your questions," the spriggan moaned as if in pain, throwing itself back and forth in the snow and sending little whirlwinds flying away from itself in three directions. "Do as you have promised; return what is mine!"

Rachel raised her hand. "I, Lady Rachel Jade Griffin, created this crater. I renounce any claim of ownership to it, returning the affected land to its previous owner."

There, that should keep her from making some terrible blunder and giving the spriggan authority over something she should not.

With a cry of victory, the spriggan disappeared, reappearing at the bottom of the crater, next to the broken boulder.

"There," said Sigfried, mock dusting off his hands. "Problem solved."

"Come quickly," Rachel gestured to the seat of the Starling as she jumped on. She wanted to get out of there before the spriggan noticed it hadn't actually agreed to let them go.

That afternoon, another lightning storm struck. The school was locked down again for two hours. This time, Rachel was stuck inside Roanoke Hall. She tromped downstairs to the Storm King Café, where she was waited on by the ubiquitous Fort Thorn, the boy who apparently took a shift at every job on campus. She sipped a rose cream soda while listening to her friends whine about the weather. Tired of their complaining, Rachel pulled out a pen and paper and decided to take action. She penned a long letter to her father documenting their problems with the Heer of Dunderberg, whose image mocked her from the mural beside her on the café wall. She asked her father to mobilize the Wisecraft to do something about the irksome storm goblin.

She did not mention that she knew that the Agents had tried once already to capture the Heer. To do so, she would have to admit that she and Sigfried had left campus during a lockdown last November and had flown to Storm King Mountain, where they most certainly were not supposed to be. She did, however, mention that perhaps the American Agents, despite their illustrious reputation, were not equipped to deal with the problem, and maybe Father's Shadow Agency should come to America to aid them.

Of course, he was not in charge of the Shadow Agency, due to his "memory accident," but the acting director, Agent Bridges, was his best friend, so she knew her father would be able to pass along her message to him. She concluded by pointing out that since the person who had captured the Heer of Dunderberg last time was now the head proctor here at Roanoke, maybe the Agents trying to apprehend the storm goblin should request the help of Maverick Badger.

The tone of her letter was light, but she wrote it with grim seriousness. The Roanoke Compact between the school and the local fey hinged on the fact that the school kept the fearsome storm goblin constrained. This recent trouble with ogres and redcaps was because, with the Heer free, the fey were growing bolder. Theoretically, the school had a year and a day to catch the storm goblin before the terms of the agreement were violated, but the longer he remained free, the less the local supernatural creatures felt that they needed to keep their word. She also wrote a letter to Blackie, telling him about the lightning javelin and the boulder.

Secretly, she hoped the London office of the Wisecraft would become involved, and her father would come, too. There was so much she wanted to say to him. Some of it would have to wait until he recovered his memory. There was no point in telling him what happened that night at Beaumont, how she and the ghost of his half-brother Myrddin saved the world from the demon Azrael, until he recovered enough of his memory for that to matter. There were other things she could tell him now, such as how the Prince of Bavaria was not the "young tyrant in the making" her parents seemed to believe him to be. She had told him some of this in a letter last fall, but then he lost his memory. He had many letters to reread and had not gotten to hers yet, and she had only had a short opportunity to speak to him about this during her most recent trip. She could write him again, but given a choice, she would rather tell him again in person.

If only she could make clear to him all that Vlad had done for her.

The rest of the week went by quickly, as everyone prepared for the Year of the Dragon Ball. In Math, Scarlett MacDannan spent a whole class teaching about the value of red thread and how to tie knots to befuddle trickster fey. Students made hundreds of these befuddlers, which were then spread around campus, both inside and outside the temporary wards. According to the proctors, at least four fey had since been trapped by these knots of red thread. The proctors had captured them and put them back outside the wards *propre*. Nobody knew whose knots had done the job, but Joy told anyone who would listen that all four fey had been caught by knots made by the princess.

Saturday, February twenty-fourth, the last day of Lunar New Year, dawned crisp and cold. It had snowed the previous day, and outside the dorm windows, the world shone a fresh, gleaming white. Turning from the window, Rachel opened the big trunk that sat next to her bed and drew out the traditional cream and lavender *hanbok* folded at the bottom.

She put on the long lavender dress with its painted floral patterns and then slipped into the cream-colored *jeogori*, so short that the bottom of the long-sleeved jacket came only to the middle of her chest. Her *otgoreum*, the wide ribbon that hung down from the short jacket, was a pale shade of lilac. It dangled down in pretty contrast to the brighter lavender of the puffy skirt.

Rachel stood in front of the mirror on the princess's vanity and gave herself a lopsided smile. She looked like one of the dolls her mother kept on a shelf in the Oriental Drawing Room. She glanced at the clock. Too bad it was so early. She seldom saw Gaius around before noon on Saturday. A shame. She would have loved to have him see her in her *hanbok*.

The door to her dorm room opened. Rachel turned quickly, hoping to see Nastasia who, along with her siblings, had gone home to Magical Australia the previous evening for some kind of family meeting, but it was Kitten Fabian returning from the shower. Kitten wore a bathrobe and was toweling her hair. Looking up from underneath her hair towel, she saw Rachel standing before her reflection and declared, "Ooh! Lovely!"

"Thank you." Rachel curtseyed.

Bending back over the trunk, Rachel pulled out her thick, warm *beoseon* and embroidered silk *kkotsin*. The white socks had pretty green and pink flowers. The embroidered slippers matched the lavender silk of her skirt. She slipped both onto her feet.

"Every morning, I wake up and give thanks we are no longer on lockdown. David Jordan's lucky he moved out of Dare Hall while he could." Kitten threw the wet towel onto her bed and then let out a little squeak as the length of damp pink terrycloth fell on top of her familiar. Rushing over, she removed it from the tiny Lion and put it in her laundry hamper. Untroubled, Leander batted at the towel as it withdrew, all the while gazing fondly at his mistress. Kitten continued speaking. "I might have changed dorms on Moving Day, too, had I realized what was coming. I bet Raleigh's a much more interesting place to be stuck."

"Probably is," Rachel sighed, straightening up. "But not as interesting as Dee. Can you imagine! Having free time with all those books!"

"Oh, my!" Kitten tilted her head and sighed, too, a dreamy sigh. "Will you be going to the dancing lessons this afternoon? The princess is organizing them, assuming she returns in time. She promised she would."

Rachel threw Kitten a smile. "I've had loads of dancing lessons, so I don't need to go. But call me, if someone needs an experienced partner."

As she slipped on her hairpiece, a purple and cream silk flower with an embroidered centerpiece set onto a hair band, Rachel recalled that, before heading home, Nastasia had quietly confided to her that she hoped to question her father about the Wall and to discuss the need to continue removing the memories of the Unwary. Rachel was quite curious to hear how her conversation had gone.

"Are you all ready for tonight?" asked Kitten.

Rachel nodded. "Really looking forward to seeing what everyone else comes as. Especially Gaius. I've been wanting and wanting to ask him about his costume. But he didn't bring it up. Or take my bait when I talked about mine. So I decided to wait and be surprised."

"I am in awe of your patience," Kitten smiled. "I'd have asked him outright and botched the whole thing."

Rachel laughed. "Will you be coming to our hair-arranging party?"

Kitten nodded enthusiastically. "Who did Joy say would be helping us?"

"Her sister Hope and a few of her friends. They say they can show us lots of fancy hairdos, plus pin up my hair to look like cat ears—to go with my costume."

"Sounds like a jolly time. I wouldn't miss it for the world!"

Rachel said, "I've studied some older fashions, and I've found one that I think will be perfect for Nastasia! I can't wait to try it on her."

"Lovely! Speaking of cat-ears and hair — " Kitten paused from gathering her robes and underthings and tilted her head half-sideways, gazing at Rachel's outfit. "Is that your costume for tonight? Don't get me wrong! It's quite fetching. But I thought you were dressing as a black and white cat and going as the irrepressible Mistletoe. Not sure cat ears will quite go with that."

"I am." Rachel flashed her roommate a cheerful smile. "Going to the ball as my familiar, I mean. This is for performing *sebae* greetings."

"Oh? What is that?'

"It's a Korean Lunar New Year tradition—though usually it's done on the first day of Lunar New Year, rather than the last. Young people perform a formal greeting before the eldest members of the family, to show respect. Then the elders give them *sebae don*—New Year's money. Only here, at school, we go bow before the oldest Korean tutors—because in ancient Korea, many of the students at the alchemical academies were orphans who lived there year-round. So their professors were the only family they knew—oh, and they don't give us money here. It's just ceremonial. They do give us food, though."

Rachel did not add that her brother had explained to her that it would not do for the wealthy Griffin children to request money from their modestly-paid tutors.

"Special New Year's food!" cried Kitten. "That doesn't sound too bad. Can I come?"

Rachel gave her an apologetic smile. "Only if you can find a *han-bok.*"

"Probably not on such short notice." Kitten laughed. "Do you do other New Year's things? Like play snapdragon? And drink eggnog?"

"Not on Lunar New Year. Back at home, when we went to pay our respects to Grandpa Kim, there were special games, like *yut nori* and *jegichagi.* But at school, Peter says the *sebae* greeting's just a brief affair. Just a formality."

"But with food," sighed Kitten.

"I'll try to sneak something out for you."

"Oh would you?" Kitten cried, peeking out of the head hole in her black robe as she donned her clothes. "That would be grand!"

Chapter Eighteen:
Feasting and Forgotten Family

The day was very bright, sunlight gleaming off the newly-fallen drifts. The three Griffins flew across campus to protect their handmade silk shoes from the snow. Rachel flew on Vroomie, which had returned from the Chansons the previous night. Peter rode his blue and gold racer, while Laurel glided along on a pink and black flying polo bristleless.

Peter looked dashing in his traditional garb. His wide-brimmed, high-crowned, black *gat* was tied under his chin with long ribbons that came from either side of the transparent hat. His long, sleeveless jacket *jeogori* and his baggy-legged pants were of navy blue silk with silver dragon and chrysanthemum brocade running through it. Underneath his long silk jacket, his full sleeves were a light blue. His black silk shoes were embroidered dark blue and red.

Laurel was a world away from the wild child who had danced with the *each-uisge*. She wore a brilliant red *hanbok*, with bright red roses painted on the white collar and cuffs of the royal blue silk of her short jacket. The ribbon dangling down her front was a shiny black, and she had braided and wound her hair into a huge *tre meori*, a traditional hairstyle that surrounded her head like a solid black nimbus. Rachel thought her sister looked like a Korean princess or, perhaps, a *tian*—or like one of the hangings in the Blue Drawing Room.

Outside, the campus bustled with activity. Skaters raced along the west side of the reflecting lake, while a hockey game had erupted to the east. Skiers and snow gliders zipped across the snow-blanketed commons, followed by barking familiars. Enchanted snowmen stepped from their moorings and lumbered down the paths. A game of snowball lacrosse sprayed icy white powder over everyone that ventured near the shouting players. Cold snowy wetness struck Rachel in the face as their path took them too close to the game.

As the Griffins glided toward Roanoke Hall — passing an ice palace, complete with towers and crenellations, behind which a snowball battle was commencing— Rachel felt particularly glad that she had risked facing the *each-uisge* and the woodwose to keep the school open so that today could come, with its ceremony and its ball. It was so nice here at Roanoke, particularly now that she was finally getting along with both Peter and Laurel. Having her siblings flying to either side of her made her feel like the baby sister again. She did not mind. It was nice to have someone looking out for her for a change. Of late, so much had seemed to rest upon her own slender shoulders.

The last time the three of them had been together for Lunar New Year was the winter before Laurel left for Roanoke. Rachel had been seven. She remembered gazing up at her siblings as they stood to bow. How tall they had been! Her traditional garments were blue and red that year, and she had clutched a Hello Kitty doll dressed in a matching *hanbok*. She recalled the bright colors, the conversation, the taste of the broth of the ceremonial soup.

They were a harmonious family. True Laurel and Sandra might fight occasionally — and Laurel and Father, and Laurel and Mum —but for the most part there was great concord among them. Together, they would find a way to recover Father's memory. Then Amber would arrive, and the Family Griffin would finally be whole.

What would she be like, this lost waif, stolen at birth? Of course, she would not be a waif now. She was older than Sandra. The Raven had said that Amber had been taken because she shared the family gift of a perfect memory. Was Amber a clerk or a librarian? Those careers would benefit from total recall. *Oh, please let it be librarian! We could have such fun together!*

Had Amber lain awake at night, wondering where she came from? Had she feared that she might not have been wanted, as Siggy did? Did she even know that her name was Amber? Rachel imagined their first meeting. They would look into each other's eyes and recognize each other at once, as if glimpsing a missing part of their own souls. She pictured them running to each other, embracing, the laughter, the bliss.

Rachel could not wait to bring Amber home. She imagined her long-lost sister's delight upon first glimpsing Gryphon Park. Would the girl who had not known a family's love be overwhelmed by how massive the mansion was? Perhaps not, if she had been in the service of a Romanov. She might have been living in a palace. Of course, it would not have been *her* palace.

What joy awaited them all!

Tempted as Rachel was to tell her siblings about Amber, she held her tongue. Until this missing sister appeared, Rachel had no proof that such a sibling actually existed. True, the hallmark on the silver baby rattle in her mother's traditional Korean jewelry box proved that, two years before Sandra was born, Great Aunt Nimue had bought the rattle for a girl whose name started with A, but that did not mean that such a baby had been born and was still alive. Besides, with all the anxiety regarding Father's "accident," she did not want to disturb her siblings further. After all, Jariel had said that her sister was coming but not when. It might be months before the real Amber appeared, or years.

Maybe Amber would be here by next year, and they could all take off from school for Lunar New Year, to introduce their long lost sister to their extended family. Maybe Sandra could come, too. They could get Amber a *hanbok*, and they could all bow before Grandpa Kim, all five Griffin siblings together. Maybe they could even convince Great Aunt Ye Jin to attend.

"*Oppa, unni*," Rachel raised her head and addressed her siblings with the Korean terms for older brother and sister they used at home. "Do you think Grandpa Kim will be sad that none of us are coming with Mummy to see him this year?"

Laurel shrugged. "Maybe, but it's not like he'll be alone. Aunt Melissa and Uncle Frederick will be bringing Ferdinand and Orlando and little Lilly. And Uncle Robert has a grandson who is old enough to bow, I believe."

"How come we never see Uncle Reginald or Uncle Robert, except at Grandpa Kim's for New Year's?" Rachel mused.

Peter and Laurel looked at each other.

"The rest of Mummy's family doesn't approve of magic, *dongsaeng*." Laurel peered down at her sister, as if explaining something to a two-year-old. "They were angry at Mother and Aunt Melissa for coming to Roanoke. They didn't talk to them for years."

"Angry?" Rachel cried. "Why?"

Peter said bluntly. "They think magic's bad."

"Bad?" Rachel blinked. "That's...."

"They wanted them to be ordinary, mundane girls, to pretend to be Unwary," said Laurel.

"But... why?" cried Rachel again.

Peter shook his head. "We have no idea."

"Grandma Kim was a stick-in-the-mud." Laurel shrugged.

"Actually," said Peter, "I think it was Great-Grandfather Kim who was the sticking point—Mother's grandfather."

"Was it because his wife died mysteriously?" asked Rachel as they reached Roanoke Hall.

The other two looked at her oddly.

Peter dismounted and opened the door for his sisters to enter the building. With a sigh, Rachel stepped down from her broom, so as to keep her promise not to fly through the halls.

"Nana Kim did not die a mysterious death," said Laurel as they headed for the stairs.

"No. Not her," said Rachel. "His first wife, Sun Li. She died in her sleep for no reason, according to Grandpa Kim. Maybe it was a hex or a curse, and they didn't tell him."

"Sun Li?" asked Peter. "Who's that?"

"Grandpa Kim's mother. Our real great-grandmother. He showed me a picture of her." Rachel did not add that he had given her the picture, and she now kept it under her bed.

"Oh. I... didn't know her name." Peter had an odd look on his face that Rachel recognized as the disorientation of discovering a fact you should have known all your life.

Laurel scrunched up her face. "Sun Li doesn't even sound Korean. I think that's Chinese. Are you sure you heard the name right?"

The mouth-watering aroma of Lunar New Year delights wafted down to them even before they reached the second floor. The classroom chosen for the occasion was near the Alchemy labs. The central table had been pushed to the back and hidden behind a row of small potted orange trees laden with bright fruit. Round crimson paper lanterns hung from the ceiling, and the domestic will-o'-the-wisps had been replaced with an exotic Asian breed that twinkled red and gold. On a pushcart to one side a wok sizzled, surrounded by large bamboo steamers.

In the middle of the room, three tutors, two old men and one middle-aged woman, sat cross-legged upon brightly colored silk cushions. Park Hojou, the head of the Alchemy Department—a gentleman well past his two hundredth year—was dressed as a traditional Korean scholar: black *gat* like Peter's on his head, long powder blue silk *durumagi* falling to his knees, and baggy ochre pants visible beneath its hem. Mr. Park's fellow alchemist, Song Jinwook wore his dress academic robes, heavy black poplin cut with the orange of Alchemy, with a mortarboard cap on his head. The third tutor, whom Peter whispered to her was Yeong Jaeeun from the Art Department, was much younger than the men, both of whom had long white beards. She was dressed in a traditional *hanbok* of red brocade. Miss Yeong's hair was done up with elaborate, gilded, and lacquered hair sticks. Her fingernails were black, and her shockingly-red lipstick contained golden glitter.

Other students were gathering, all from Korea or of Korean descent. The boys were dressed in pants and a sleeveless jacket over a full shirt, like Peter, or in the much longer robes, like Mr. Park. The girls wore brightly colored *hanbok*, except for the silvery-haired Silke Coriander, who was dressed in the slender, split-skirted, flowing, painted silks of the traditional costume of the Republic of Cathay. Hers was red, peach, and white.

Rachel wondered why Miss Coriander was present, as she understood the college sophomore from Drake Hall to be a native of Cathay. Rachel did not see Topher Evans, but maybe he was too removed from his Korean ancestors to be familiar with the *sebae* ceremony.

The two Park brothers from Dare hurried into the room. This must have been everyone who was expected, because Mr. Song nodded, and one of the older boys closed the door. The gathered crowd of two dozen students lined up before their elders.

As one, the students bowed. The young men knelt, put left hand over right, and bowed their heads to the ground, their silks rustling in unison. The girls were less organized. Some, like Laurel and Silke, did a simple version of the feminine bow, hands at their sides as they knelt and bent low. Others, like Rachel and Priscilla Kim—one of the three Kim siblings from Dee Hall—put their hands before them, right over left as they bent, performing a more formal version of the feminine bow.

Together, they all chanted Happy New Year: *"Saehae bok manhi badeuseyo!"*

The tutors responded to their happy new year greeting as tradition dictated, offering a blessing and wishing the students a prosperous year. In conclusion, they lit the first incense stick of the Year of the Dragon. The sweet scent of Many Treasures incense curled through the air.

Next came the feasting. The three tutors and two dozen students broke into four groups and gathered around low tables where they sat down on red and gold silk cushions. Silke Coriander, who turned out to be the representative of Cooks' Broth, the cooking club, there to prepare the food, began laying out the traditional delicacies. Rachel's stomach rumbled as she watched eagerly as dish after dish appeared on the table before her.

Most important of the dishes was the *hin ddeokguk*—a soup of pheasant broth and thinly sliced rice cakes, that was served only on New Year's Day. Around it was arrayed a cornucopia of tasty delights: *pyogo beoseot-jeon*, mushrooms stuffed with bean curd, minced beef, and onions; *dwaeji galbi jjim*, specially-prepared braised pork ribs; *jeon*, Korean pancakes containing shrimp or asparagus or other delicacies. There were also fried dumplings and three kinds of kimchi. There was even kimchi *mandu*, which was another kind of dumpling but filled with kimchi. It was like having the best of everything in one little dough-covered wrapping.

The Griffins sat between two sets of siblings. On the right, the Kims were from Illinois. Priscilla was a senior at the Upper School, in Peter and Gaius's class, and her twin brother and sister, Jenna and Jordan, were in Rachel's class. The Kims all wore glasses, which was unusual in the World of the Wise. Rachel wondered if they had decided against having their vision repaired by magic, or if the glasses were talismans, offering some special enchantment.

Sitting on her left were the Park brothers. Lionel Park—who was in the same year as Laurel and Silke Coriander—played the viola for the Dare Hall musical group, the Geometric Quartet. He was dressed in a long garment that resembled a Korean court official's uniform from an earlier era. His *gat* had a square brim, a more ancient form of the hat. His younger brother David, an Upper School sophomore, was dressed in peach and salmon-colored silks. Rachel could not help noticing David's snub nose and very pleasant smile because he kept snorting with good-natured laughter at things the others said.

They ate and ate and ate. Every time Rachel felt she was so full she could not possibly eat another bite, Silke whisked yet another tray of delicious-looking goodies onto the table, and Rachel found herself popping yet more into her mouth. One time, it was mango in a thick, sweet gelatin. Another time, it was tiny confections filled with cream and coated with powdered sugar served on a silver tray. Yet a third time, it was *taraegwa*, a twisted ribbon-shaped traditional Korean confection made from wheat flour and flavored with cinnamon, ginger, rice syrup, and pine nuts and dripping with honey. On top of this, there was a never-ending stream of hot plum tea and cold *sujeonggwa*, a cinnamon and persimmon punch.

The whole experience was made more surreal by the fact that as their hostess, Miss Coriander, leaned over to present each tray, Rachel could clearly see that the older girl had silver irises and strange vertical pupils. In her bright Cathay silks, she looked like some sort of fox maiden or naga. Her silver hair, which fell well past her thighs, seemed to move with a life of its own, as if it had its own unfelt wind or danced to its own unheard music.

As they gorged themselves on yet another tray of pork and leek dumplings, Jordan Kim whispered to the Griffins and the Parks, "Did you know that her hair is prehensile?"

"Certainly mooks mike it," murmured Laurel, whose mouth was full.

Priscilla Kim shook her dark hair and laughed at her brother. "Jordan, don't be so naïve. You believe every story you hear."

"No, really, *nuna*!" Jordan insisted. Rachel saw Peter flush slightly. *Nuna* was the proper address for a boy to his older sister, but Peter often forgot and used *unni*, the way Rachel and Laurel did. "I hear she made it reach out and strangle a squirrel! Then, she brought the squirrel to the next meeting of the cooking club, and they fricasseed it with lemongrass! A friend of mine's in the club. She tasted some. She said it was good!"

"Are you sure that's true?" Peter gave him a skeptical look.

"It is true." Silke leaned over Rachel's shoulder, placing yet another pot of steaming, tart plum tea on the table. "Squirrels are tasty fricasseed with lemongrass, though a little butter and garlic also do wonders. And, of course, I always believe in adding a pinch of coriander."

Silke winked and departed for the still-sizzling wok. Her sheath-like gown fit glove-tight, so that each sway of her hips was held in its own parenthesis of scarlet silk. The young men all watched her depart, identical stunned expressions on their faces. Back at the cooking cart, Silke devoured three dumplings, a pork rib, and several pieces of confectionary, all of which she ate with a pair of long cooking chopsticks.

Looking at the bewitched expression on Lionel Park's face as he gazed at their hostess, Priscilla's expression became sour as she muttered, "How can she eat so much and keep that figure?"

"No idea." Laurel popped another *taraegwa* into her mouth.

Priscilla threw a pointed sideways glance at Laurel. "We know where you put it."

Laurel's mouth was full, but her cheeks puffed out from her effort not to laugh. Casually, she leaned back and stretched. Putting her hands behind her head, she arched her spine, as if to best display the portion of her anatomy that Priscilla had just implied was overly ample. This did not have the effect upon poor Lionel Park that Priscilla might have desired.

"That's a pretty *hanbok*," drawled Laurel, when she had finished swallowing. Her eyes danced with mischief. "Can I borrow it sometime? Oh, wait." She looked Priscilla up and down. "I don't think it would fit. Looks like it's tailored for a twig. You could borrow mine, though. I could lend you six or seven pairs of socks to help you fill it out."

Peter nearly spit his hot tea all over David Park. Rachel had long ago become resigned to being embarrassed whenever Laurel was around, but she still wished she had some place she could hide. Rosy color blossomed in Priscilla's cheeks. Behind her glasses, her eyes grew shiny, as if she were about to cry. Rachel, who was herself even more deficient in the indicated department than Priscilla, felt for the other girl. Her own cheeks burned so hot that she absently wondered if Silke could fry a dish on them. Sometimes, having Laurel for a sister was a trial.

Peter elbowed Laurel in the ribs and gave Lionel a sharp look. When Lionel blinked like an animal caught in a flash hex, Peter glared at him and then darted a glance toward Priscilla. Comprehension dawned. Taking Priscilla's hand, Lionel bowed over it.

"Some men prefer intelligence to more earthy charms," Lionel Park declared in his Korean accent. "Such men are most blessed when they discover a woman of both intelligence and beauty."

Priscilla blushed, delighted.

"Oooh. Nice." Laurel chuckled, still looking entirely amused. "That put me in my place!"

Peter sighed and rubbed his forehead.

Rachel, sipping her tart tea, wondered what Amber would look like.

"I'm stuffed," Peter declared half-an-hour later. "You girls'll have to roll me home."

"No good," Rachel gasped, holding her stomach. "Ate too much! Round as a ball now!"

"Oh, you two. Can't take you anywhere," Laurel smirked, pouring herself another cup of the cinnamon and persimmon punch.

"It is good to see you, Falconridge, Lady Laurel." The Alchemy Department Head, Park Hojou, looking distinctive with his long, wispy, white beard, stood by Peter's shoulder. "How is your family? I hear your father is ill. May the new year bring a return of his health."

Despite his claim that he was too full to move, Peter leapt to his feet and bowed—from the waist this time, not a *sebae* bow.

"Thank you, *seonsang-nim*. I will pass your kind words on to my parents." Peter addressed the older gentleman using the most respectful version of the formal title for teachers.

"And whom have we here?" Mr. Park gazed down at Rachel.

Peter straightened. "Mr. Park, may I please present The Lady Rachel Griffin."

Mr. Park regarded Rachel kindly. "And how many bowls of *ddteokguk* have you eaten?"

Rachel called up her memory of previous bowls and began to count.

Peter leaned over her shoulder and whispered, "He means how old are you?"

"Oh!" Rachel rose, despite feeling unsteady from overeating, and curtsied to the venerable tutor. "Thirteen."

"Ah! A young age to be at so august an institution." The venerable tutor tilted his head. "I see your mother in you. She was quite a scholar herself when she was not much older than you."

"How did you know my mother when she was young?" Rachel asked, curiously. "I thought the tutors from the time when Mother was here were gone—except the dean and Mrs. Heelis, who had left but came back. They either ran away during the Terrible Years or they stayed and were killed by the Terrible Five. I know that none of those who fled were allowed to return. Did you teach here, leave before the Terrible Years, and then come back again, like Mrs. Heelis?"

"I was one of your mother's instructors during the semester she and her younger sister spent at Jeju Alchemical Institute. In fact, it was your mother and her sister who recommended me to Dean Moth, when Roanoke was searching for new tutors when the school reopened."

"Semester at...." Rachel blinked. "Where is Jeju?"

Even as she asked, she found a reference to Jeju in an encyclopedia in her mental library. Apparently, it was an island off the southern tip of South Korea.

Mr. Park replied, "Ellen and Melissa originally enrolled in the alchemical academy at Cheongsung, but the students there were not... overly friendly to half-bloods. So your mother and her sister transferred to Jeju. It is an international city, where anyone of any nation can live."

"I had no idea that Mother had studied in Korea," cried Rachel, her mouth agape.

"She and her sister came hoping to find the rest of their family." He smiled kindly, revealing missing teeth. "Life at Jeju was a shock. She did not even eat kimchi when she came."

Laurel, who had stood up and come to join them, said, "That would explain why Mummy and Aunt Melissa act so much more Korean than their brothers. I've wondered about that."

"I had no idea," Rachel repeated, blinking rapidly as she tried to process this new information. "Did she find them? Our family, I mean?"

"Yes," the tutor nodded sadly. "Or rather, she found where her father had come from, but it was far north, near Tianchi. She could not travel through North Korea to such a remote spot."

"Tianchi?" asked Laurel.

"It is a crater lake, a famous place of beauty, on the border between North Korea and China," said the tutor.

"Right next to China, you say?" Laurel turned to Rachel, poking her in her overly-full stomach. "Hear that, *dongseang*. Maybe our great-grandmother's name really was Sun Li."

Chapter Nineteen:
Mortalized in Snow

Floating on her steeplechaser, Rachel wobbled slowly across the snowy commons. Maybe gorging herself had not been such a good idea. She felt ill.

A cold wind blew down from Storm King, over the treetops and across the open, snow-covered lawns. Shivering, Rachel wished she could close her red coat against the biting cold, but her arms overflowed with little packages of leftovers wrapped in bright red napkins —treats she had procured for Kitten and her other friends.

"Ouch! Ooch! Ouch! It's coooold!" came a pained cry from behind the snow fort. Rachel turned Vroomie and zoomed in that direction.

Behind the turrets of the fort of snow was a hooded figure that seemed to be dancing. Coming closer, Rachel recognized Xandra Black, only she was not dancing. She was barefoot in the snow, yelping in agony from the cold.

Rachel rushed up beside her. "Here, jump on! I'll take you somewhere warm."

"Th-thank y-you!" Xandra slid up onto the broom and sat sidesaddle on the back of the long seat. "Cold! Cold! Cold! Cold! Cold!"

Rachel flipped on the new becalming enchantments, which made the ride warmer, and set off for Dare at high speed. She was immediately impressed at how well the steeplechaser handled despite the drag of the enchantment. The Chansons had done an excellent job.

"*Libra!*" she cried as she approached her dorm, performing the accompanying gesture with some difficulty due to the huge stack of red-wrapped treats in her arms.

The great oak doors of Dare Hall flung themselves open. The wolf, who so often slept on the porch, had been resting regally. It yelped and scampered backwards.

"Sorry!" Rachel called, as she sped by.

The beast shot her a most unwolflike glare.

Once inside, Rachel flew over to the golden grate behind which the black and red salamander cavorted. With a cry of delight, Xandra leapt from the broom and moved forward holding up first one foot and then the other before the hot bars. Rachel figured Mr. Chanson would not object to her helping another student, but she then dutifully climbed off, holding the still floating Vroomie with her elbow.

"Ahhh. That feels good," Xandra sighed. "Stupid spirits."

"Did they take you out there?" asked Rachel. "The voices that speak through you? What did they want?"

Xandra lifted a corner of her hood and glared at Rachel with one lavender eye. "They were looking for you."

"What? *Me?*"

"Yeah," Xandra sighed sardonically. "Just my luck. They borrow my body, walk it into the snow, and then bug out."

"Bug... out? Is that related to ladybirds? Or cockroaches?"

"No. They got scared and bolted. I think they went into hiding."

"*Hiding?* The supernatural beings who use you as their mouthpiece ran and hid?" Rachel blinked. "Aren't they like fairies or demigods or ghosts of ancient prophets or something? What could possibly frighten them?"

"Not what, who." Xandra leaned her head back, enjoying the heat on her legs. It was the happiest Rachel had ever seen the normally-pessimistic young woman. "The princess brought back a bodyguard from Magical Australia. The dude's some kind of spirit killer. My spirits split, but before they left, they wanted to warn you that they foresaw that this bodyguard poses a grave danger to some powerful supernatural being in our area."

"Why tell me?" asked Rachel, puzzled. "Unless...."

Jariel!

She swallowed. "D-did they say anything specific about this supernatural being?"

Xandra shrugged, continuing to hold her foot near the salamander's grate. "I didn't get much, and most of what I did get was driven from my head by the extreme pain in my feet. And then by the fear of lack of pain in my feet, as they began to go numb, because, you know...

frostbite. I don't know how much help I would be to my bossy crowd if I were stumbling around on frozen stumps." She sighed, morosely. "All I got was something to do with thunderclouds or night air."

Thunderclouds or night air? That could be the Raven. He smelled like the ocean winds and summer rain. Or it could be the storm goblin or the Headless Horseman or a lot of things, but if it was not the Raven, why had these spirits wanted to tell *her?*

"Here," Rachel maneuvered one of the red napkins from her towering pile into her fingers and extended it towards the upperclassman. "Have a *taraegwa*. Very tasty. It'll make you feel much better."

Handing over the treat, she departed by gently pushing the floating bristleless until she reached the door, where she hopped back on, leaving Xandra before the salamander enclosure, munching happily on the crunchy confectionary.

Heading out into the winter chill again, Rachel noticed that the great oak doors were still partially open. She paused on the porch, hopped off her broom again, and closed them carefully with her shoulder. The dark brown wolf still sat on the porch, looking disgruntled.

Rachel bowed politely to the creature, barely managing not to drop her red-wrapped packages. "Sorry to have troubled you, Mr. Wolf."

The wolf flowed like water in a dream and stood up. Wulfgang Starkadder glared at her through his longish, dark brown hair. Rachel backed up, startled.

"Bug off, Griffin," Wulfgang growled. "And I *do* mean the cockroach kind." The Transylvanian prince brushed past her and into the dorm.

"Eavesdropper!" she called after him, but it was too late. The great doors had closed with a gonglike *clang*.

Rachel scowled after him and mounted her broom again. Had the wolf on the porch been the Transylvanian prince all along? If so, he had managed to use his alternate shape to sneak outside during the lockdown. That was so unfair.

As Rachel headed back to the commons in search of Kitten, she saw, in the midst of the snowy lawns, Lucky the Dragon perched upon a gigantic snowball—probably originally the bottom of a snowman. To one side, laughing students attempted to sculpt him in snow.

As Rachel flew up, Siggy waved. "Look!" he shouted. "It's the Year of Lucky! He's being mortalized in snow!"

"Mortalized?" asked Rachel, slowing down.

"Immortalized is when they make something that will last forever, right? So, what do you call it when they make an image that won't last past the first warm afternoon?"

"Oh, good point," said Rachel. "Would you like a treat?"

"Food!" Siggy looked around. "Quick, before anyone sees."

Sighing, Rachel maneuvered her pile of red paper-covered treats, until she was able to slide four into Sigfried's hand. "Two for you. Two for Lucky."

"Great! I'll toss 'em into his mouth while he's modeling."

Sigfried threw two treats to Lucky, napkins and all. The dragon opened its mouth and swallowed them whole, burping happily. The students working on Snow Lucky all applauded.

Three young women approached Sigfried. Rachel recognized them as the pink-haired Kris Serenity Wright and her two roommates.

"Mr. Smith, I have not properly thanked you for saving my life during the skating party," Kris announced seriously, though her eyes danced with their customary mirth.

"Yeah!" piped up her friend Rhiannon. "That ogre's-breakfast look would not have suited Kris."

Beside her, Hekpa, the dryad's daughter, nodded solemnly; the tiny mouse peeking from her hair eyed Lucky speculatively.

"No need to thank me. I am a hero. Rescuing maidens who are being carried off by ogres is my job."

"Grand-da is impressed, too," said Kris. "You slew his mortal enemy!"

"Well, you can tell him he owes me one," crowed Siggy, thrusting his thumb at his chest. "That's me, Sigfried the Dragon and Ogre Slayer."

"I'll let him know." Kris grinned mischievously, her pink hair falling in her eyes.

"And me!" cried Lucky, "I'm an ogreslayer, too!"

"So you are!" cried Kris, clapping her hands.

She was correct, Rachel noted to herself; without Lucky to break the charmed life enchantment upon the ogre, Sigfried would not have been able to stop it. The ogre would have killed Rachel—and probably Valerie and Nastasia, too—and then carried Kris away to his ogre cave. Lucky the Dragon had made all the difference.

Siggy struck a pose. "Ogre killer. I'll be signing autographs for anyone who pays me in food."

"Siggy," hissed Rachel, "'tis not done! Asking payment for autographs."

"Actors in Hollywood do it," objected Rhiannon.

"Do they?" Rachel asked, shocked. "How gauche!"

"I'll be happy to bring food… later, when I can find some," said Kris. "It's the least I could do for my rescuer. Right, girls?"

"I make a mean linguine," volunteered Rhiannon.

Hekpa offered, "I can… boil tea?"

"Ace! I'd love…." Siggy paused. "Wait, when you say 'mean,' that's just a turn of phrase, right? It's not an actual living but angry linguine, is it? That would be wicked brilliant, but I'm not sure I'd want to eat it. Lucky would, though. He's an equal opportunity eater."

"That's right," offered Lucky, without moving his head. "I eat both joyful and angry noodles."

"Maybe we could eat the noodles with the ogre. Or wait, the Agents stole the ogre before we could cook him up, didn't they?" scowled Sigfried.

"Ooh!" Kris cried. "Look what they're doing. Let's help with Snow Lucky!"

The three young ladies ran off to join the snow sculptors.

A distant crack of thunder caused all the students on the commons to look up nervously, fearing another lockdown would be sounded. When it was not repeated, they returned to their festivities. Sigfried, however, continued to squint off into the deep blue of the sky.

"So this Heer?" asked Siggy, bending down and scooping up some snow, which he began forming into a snowball. "Is it a here-

and-now? A hear-me-call? And what exactly is a storm goblin? Is it something that gobbles up storms and then pukes them on people?"

"Not exactly," laughed Rachel. She wished she could form snowballs, too, but her arms were still filled with treats. "First of all, it's heer—h-e-e-r. It's a Dutch title, like lord or earl or duke. Second, a real storm goblin's much like a lightning imp or a *strömkarl* or *venti*, creatures that help whip up the ferocity of a storm or throw the thunderbolts or the like. But this one, he's a bit different. No one's quite sure why. Maybe he's a combination of more than one kind of being."

"Is that why he looks like a little kid?"

"That may be the influence of John Colman, a sailor with Henry Hudson on his original voyage up the river, over four hundred years ago. Colman was the first European killed in America. According to that book the library put on display last October, *Legends and Lore of Sleepy Hollow and the Hudson Valley*, some people think the Heer of Dunderberg is Colman, whose ghost merged with or transformed into a storm goblin and tried to use his storms to convince other Europeans to turn back, so they would not die in a foreign land."

"Can ghosts become goblins?"

Rachel shrugged. "That's the theory. On Dartmoor, we had a great black beast that was said to be the spirit of a particularly evil mayor from the nearby town of Okehampton."

"Creepy," shivered Sigfried, who feared only ghosts.

"Oh, and his name is Dwerg. The Heer, that is, not the mayor."

"Dwerg? What kind of a name is that?"

"I believe it's Dutch. He's dressed as a Dutch boy."

"I wish I were a storm goblin," Sigfried declared, throwing his snowball and beaning an upperclassman in the back of the head.

When the angry boy turned around, Sigfried was casually looking the other way. The young man looked right over him in his quest for vengeance. Finally, he threw a snowball of his own at another upperclassman who stood nearby chatting up a young woman. The second young man yelped in surprise before angrily retaliating. Soon a snowball war erupted.

"My work here is done," Siggy beamed.

Rachel snorted and rolled her eyes. "Oh, Sigfried."

Her arms were growing tired from holding the precariously-balanced treats. She glanced back at the crowd surrounding Lucky, but she did not see any of the other Dare students.

"Where's the princess? Did you see her new bodyguard?"

"Who?" Siggy cleaned out one ear with his pinky finger, pretending to be unable to hear that she asked about Nastasia.

"Where are Joy and Zoë?"

"The others are in the gym practicing." Sigfried lobbed a snowball at a mobile snowman someone had sent lumbering across the commons, knocking off its head. The body trembled, waving its stick arms wildly until another student picked up the head and returned it. "I didn't hear anything about a bodyguard, but there was a really big, buff guy over by the gym. Maybe that's him."

Rachel leaned forward and lowered her voice, "Whoever that bodyguard is, Xandra's spirits—you know, the ones that usually embarrass her by using her mouth to speak prophesies at the worst possible moments?—those spirits are so frightened of this guard person, they ran away."

"Ran away?"

"Yes. In hiding or something."

"Who knew spirits were such sissies."

"Apparently, the bodyguard can kill spirits."

"Really? Can he teach me? Does he use a spirit-killing knife? Does he wrestle them with his teeth? The problem with wrestling spirits with your teeth is getting them to stand still. Tried to bite that wraith we fought back in September, but it wouldn't stay in my mouth so I could chew on it. Lucky can chew on spirits sometimes," said Sigfried. "He's blessed that way."

Rachel leaned forward and whispered, "Before they 'bugged out,' they gave her a prophecy. They said some powerful spirit is in grave danger while the bodyguard is here."

"Ace! Can we watch while he rips it apart with his teeth?"

"Siggy! What if it's the Raven?"

Siggy shrugged. "No water off my duck."

"Ooh! Sigfried Smith!" Rachel would have stomped her feet, but she was still sitting on Vroomie, so she was reduced to just kicking her legs. "Sometimes, you're so exasperating!"

Siggy shrugged and popped one of the Korean sweets into his mouth. He tossed another to Lucky, who opened his jaw where he posed in the snow and swallowed it in one gulp. Turning to Rachel, he spread his hands. "I'm all out of food. Can you resupply me? After all, I did lend you my meatball sandwich last week."

Sighing, she handed him some more.

Walking through the gym hallway, her arms still overflowing with red, wrapped treats, Rachel passed a tall, hulking man in a gray pinstripe suit who stood speaking with her boss, Mr. Chanson. She glanced at the figure and looked away quickly, not wanting to draw attention to herself and, by association, to the Raven. She examined the man in her memory. He certainly looked fearsome. *Was this the spirit-killing bodyguard?*

She found her friends in a large practice chamber. Coming into the room was like entering a garden after a fresh rain. Rachel breathed deeply of the enchantment-perfumed air. She smiled cheerfully at the princess, whose face lit up as she waved back.

A group of their friends and classmates stood in a line, playing their instruments. With a *toot* and a *twang*, silver sparkles danced through the air, accompanying short blasts of wind. Their gusts pushed the wheeled sewing forms that the students used for practice dummies. Most of the dummies rolled three to six feet, but two of them went further. Joy's dummy rolled over twenty feet. Nastasia's rolled fifty feet, hit the back wall, and flopped over.

As the others went to retrieve their dummies, picking up the sewing forms and wheeling them back to the nearer side of the practice area, a short, cloaked figure stepped in front of Nastasia. With her face hidden beneath the voluminous hood, Rachel might have mistaken her for Xandra, except that this girl was significantly shorter.

"Allow me, princess." She spoke so softly that Rachel could hardly hear her.

"Thank you, Miss Praetor," Nastasia said graciously. "That would be most kind."

Starlight glistened like glitter around the cloaked girl. It grew more substantial, fluttering, until it coalesced as silvery-white butterflies. Rachel had never seen such magic. The butterflies shimmered like living opals. They reminded her of the mother-of-pearl decorations often found on traditional Korean furniture. Chasing each other and twirling, the butterflies flew by the other students toward the princess's fallen sewing form. Comet tails of starlight trailed behind the flittering forms, swirling around the fallen object and then flying upward. Slowly, the practice dummy righted itself.

The students clapped, but Rachel narrowed her eyes. That was not earthly magic. The butterflies looked innocuous, but they had lifted an object many times their weight. *What else might they be able to do?*

"Oooh! Treats!" Kitten cried, catching sight of Rachel and her armful of red bundles.

The others thronged around, snatching up the many treats. Rachel handed them out, trying not to drop any.

"Who is that?" she murmured to Joy, gesturing with her head toward the young woman who was surrounded by butterflies.

"The princess brought some servants back from Magical Australia," replied Joy, before she popped a Korean confectionary delight into her mouth.

Oh, no. Rachel's heart fell. It was not that she objected to servants per se. They had many at Gryphon Park. But servants were frowned upon at Roanoke where the students were encouraged to do things on their own. The princess had arrived at school not knowing how to do all sorts of essential things, such as brush her own hair or fold her clothes, because previously she had relied entirely on servants. This lack of competence contributed to the apparent aloofness that kept her apart from the other students. Nastasia claimed she wanted to overcome this distance between herself and the others. Having a servant waiting on her here at school, where nobody else had such a thing, was not the way to accomplish this.

Much as she loved her friend, Rachel was again grateful that Nastasia was not *her* princess, even if Magical Australia—the home of the family of the Master of the World—had turned out to be more significant than expected, considering that almost no one had heard of it, even in the World of the Wise.

Rachel handed out most of the treats, bringing the last few to where the princess stood. She handed one to her friend and then turned to offer the last one to Nastasia's new servant.

Time slowed. Under the hood of the cloak was Rachel's mother's chin. *What was her mother doing here?* No. *That was not her mother.* It was a young girl, maybe fourteen or fifteen years old. A girl who had *Rachel's father's eyes.*

"Rachel, this is my new bodyguard, Miss Praetor." The princess, her face calm and solemn, turned graciously to the young woman. "Amber, this is my dear friend, Rachel Griffin."

Chapter Twenty: Sorrow in Steam

Rachel stood frozen in timelessness.

The outside world continued, but, inside, all was motionless. At some infinite distance, she could hear her friends' voices. Joy babbled inanely about how the Romanovs had decided the princess needed more protection. Farther away, other girls said other things, their voices like the moaning of the wind. Through it all, Rachel stared into the face of Nastasia's new bodyguard.

She knew, in a distant kind of way, that her own face was blank, expressionless, but it was not because of her mask of calm. Rather, she was so stunned that no expression had yet passed from her soul to her features.

It did not help that she still felt nauseous from overeating.

When her limbs began to respond to her commands again, Rachel willed her heart and soul into her words and gazed directly into the eyes of her lost sister.

She bowed. "Thank you for coming."

The young woman in the cloak gave no reaction. She did not smile. She did not nod. Her eyes did not shimmer with unspoken emotion. Her face did not grow joyful in recognition, as if a missing part of her soul were suddenly whole. She did not even pause to acknowledge Rachel's greeting. She followed Nastasia expressionlessly, as the latter departed from the practice room.

The other students followed the princess, but Rachel remained behind. Alone in the practice chamber, she wondered vaguely if someone had punched her in the heart. It would explain the pain.

"Come into my parlor, said the upperclassman to the freshman," purred Jenny Dare, as she gestured from the gymnasium corridor through a doorway into a chamber Jenny requested.

The girls, mainly freshmen from Dare Hall, but also a few friends from other dorms and grades, trooped through the door Jenny had opened. With Miss Dare were two of her friends, Iolanthe Towers, and Joy's older sister, Hope. Rachel followed the other girls in a daze. *Was that girl in the cloak really her missing sister? Why did everything seem so blurry and far away?* The girl looked fourteen, not twenty-five. Why was she acting like the princess's servant?

Why had she not instantly recognized Rachel when they met? Rachel had been so sure that the sisters, torn apart by cruel fate, would know each other. Oh, maybe they would not know that they were biological sisters, but she expected there to be a connection, a sudden recognition. Instead, Amber had said nothing. She had not even acknowledged Rachel's greeting. She had merely walked away. This was nothing like Rachel had dreamed it would be.

She wanted to run up and speak to Amber, to ask her questions, to hug her, but she was afraid. What if doing so drew the attention of the Master of the World? Could she openly acknowledge that she knew about their connection without some dire occurrence following? Was that what Xandra's spirits had tried to warn her about: that, if she were not careful, Jariel would be blamed for bringing Amber here and held accountable?

Ahead of her, the other girls stopped abruptly, eyes wide, surrounded by steam. The warm mist was too thick to see through, but they could hear flowing water, as if someone were running a very big bath. The air had the fresh tingle of eucalyptus oil. As the girls moved forward again, three rectangular pools arranged in tiers with water pouring from one to the next became visible. Steps of deeply polished dark wood led down into a Japanese-style bath. Brick-sized blocks of the same dark, polished wood tiled the floor beneath their feet. The steam apparently came from heated rocks in the corners of the room.

"Oooh! Nice!" Hildy Winters spun in a circle, her golden ponytail bobbing behind her.

"Hot tub, here I come!" Salome cried gleefully.

She stripped down and walked into the pool naked, sighing with pleasure as the hot water touched her skin. The other girls chose to don bathing suits, which they picked from lockers to which Joy's sister Hope led them.

Hope O'Keefe was lovely and statuesque, with hair the color of ripe wheat and a surprisingly kind smile. She helped them find suits that fit. Kitten and her best friend, sophomore Amalthea Kern, chose red one-pieces. Joy, Valerie, and Hildy's friend Rowan each chose green. The others chose blue or black with a white racer stripe. All the freshmen from Dare were there, except Astrid and Zoë. Rachel had specifically invited Astrid, but the other girl had declined shyly, murmuring something about her hair being unmanageable. Zoë had mumbled that communal baths were "not her scene." Rachel understood that this was because Zoë was self-conscious about the scars that were, reportedly, all over her body, ever since she had fallen into the darkness between worlds.

Still in a daze, Rachel had followed the others. Ordinarily, she would have been too modest to undress in front of other people, but stunned—and not a stranger to communal baths—she disrobed, slipped into a dark blue one-piece, and slid into the hot pool.

Once the girls had their bathing suits on, it was time to tackle their hair. Jenny, Hope, and Iolanthe directed three girls at a time to the benches and the others into the rectangular baths to wait their turn. Wendy and Hildy had convinced Sakura Suzuki to change her hairstyle for the occasion. No one had ever seen the Japanese girl in anything except long pigtails with bells tied in them—outside of the episode with the curlers. With careful fingers, Sakura undid her long braids and sat serenely surrounded by the cascading fall of her black locks, waiting for the older girls to give her a new hairstyle for the dance. Her friends watched eagerly.

Rachel took all this in as she floated in the bath, but she could not seem to process it. She did not know why she could not blink away this strange heaviness that seemed to be obscuring her thoughts. She could perceive the actions around her, and yet nothing made sense. This was foolish, she told herself. Nothing had really changed, right?

Her life was still as it had been; it was just now she had a new sibling....

She told herself these things, but it was as if her mind was not accepting instructions from her. She wondered obliquely if she were going into shock. What did one do for shock? Raise the feet? At least, here in the heated bath, no one would need to wrap her in a blanket.

As she soaked in the hot water, her memory recorded the conversations around her, but their words had no meaning.

"I didn't realize that the gym could do Japanese bathhouses," Hildy Winters's voice was exclaiming, as Iolanthe Towers worked on her golden mane. Beside her, Hope started on Sakura. "I may never leave this room."

"This gym can do anything. It's amazing," replied Iolanthe, her fingers moving nimbly and rapidly. She was of Japanese descent but spoke with a midwestern accent. She was usually in the company of her familiar, but right now the Australian Shepherd was nowhere to be seen. Perhaps, the dog did not care for the humidity. "It's head and shoulders above what they have at the local academy back home, or in my mother's home in Hokkaido. In those places, they can only produce pre-set rooms exactly as they were originally conjured. Nothing like this."

"There have only ever been three places like this in the world," said Jenny, who was dressed in a blue suit that matched her eyes. It was demure in the front, but the back was cut so low as to be almost scandalous. She had sat down behind fiery-haired Rowan Vanderdecken, granddaughter of the captain of *The Flying Dutchman*. Occasionally, Jenny drew a treat from the sleeve of the robe lying beside her and threw it up to her familiar. The mynah bird—who might have a real name, but whom Jenny called "Mynie"—rested upon a rafter, perhaps trying to avoid the steam. "And one of them was lost long ago when Alexander the Great threw the Island of Tyre into the sea. Pearl divers have searched for it for millennia, but if anyone has ever found it, they have not reported it."

"There are still three," stated Nastasia, gliding around the bath to the far side. She gestured for Amber, still in her floor-length cloak, to put down her bag and towel, which Amber had been carrying for her mistress as she walked behind her. "We have such a chamber in Magical Australia. We call it the Chamber of Whadeweye."

"Wa-do-i?" asked Kitten, poking her toe into the water. She yelped. "That's hot."

"As in '*What-do-I* want today?'" Nastasia sighed. "Yet another of Father's little jokes."

The others laughed merrily.

The princess took a seat on the far side of the wide steamy baths, in front of a large mirror. Seeing her, Rachel recalled, as if from a distant dream, how eager she had been to show her friend the hairstyle she had found for her. She shook her head twice, as if trying to dislodge the cobwebs that attempted to ensnare her thinking, and rose, moving toward Nastasia. In one hand, she clutched a little bag in which she had stashed all the right bobby pins and clips.

Rachel sloshed through the hot water. Before she could reach the edge, however, Amber stepped up beside the princess. "Shall I do your hair, milady?"

"Please, call me Nastasia," the princess replied graciously. "And, yes. My hair. That would be lovely."

The princess leaned back, and Amber began to brush out her glossy, flaxen locks. Rachel stood at the edge of the bath, clutching her little bag, her spirits slowly sinking. She felt too startled and too foggy-headed to move forward. She was not going to get a chance to teach her friend the new hairstyle. Maybe she should have showed it to Nastasia ahead of time, instead of trying to keep it as a surprise.

Joy, who was splashing across the baths to take her turn with her sister, stepped beside Rachel, pouting. "Wasn't this party the princess's idea? I'm surprised she's having her servant do her hair rather than one of us."

Her sister, a servant? The words echoed in Rachel's head over and over. The eldest child of Ambrose, Lord Devon, a duke of the realm, reduced to the status of a servant of a princess of the heretofore unknown kingdom of Magical Australia, a kingdom so insignificant that it issued pink monopoly money with kangaroos and emus on it instead of a real currency?

Rachel's hands slowly curled into fists. Resentment roiled inside her like the brewing of a hurricane. The princess's family had stolen her sister—*and turned her into a servant.* At that moment, she hated the princess more than she could put into words. Somewhere, deep down, she knew this was not Nastasia's fault. Yet her heart still told her that the princess had betrayed her.

Joy went to take her turn at having her hair done. Rachel sat down hard on the side of the bath and gripped the little bag of bobby pins, trying to arrange her face so that she did not look as if she had been kicked in the stomach by a mule. In fact, she had once been kicked by a mule, and it had not hurt as much as this.

Kitten sat down on the edge of the baths beside Rachel, her straight brown hair plastered against her face. She gestured at the princess. "Weren't you going to do...."

Rachel held up her hand to stop her, murmuring softly, "Another time."

"You can do mine, if you like," Kitten offered, her face full of sympathy.

Too despondent to talk, Rachel just shook her head.

Rachel sank deep into the hot, scented water, until the world beyond was engulfed in steam. Her dissembling mask had finally slammed down over her features, but, inside, she reeled. She did not understand why. Or maybe she did. Maybe the reality of her situation was settling in: Her family had been ravaged by Nastasia's grandfather, and there would be no easy fix. What would it do to her mother—the realization that she had *forgotten* one of her children?

Would any of the Griffins ever be the same? She felt so lost, as if she were falling and could not manage to grasp anything to stop her descent. She missed Gaius. If only she could still fly through windows, the two of them could curl up on the couch in her secret room in the hexagonal tower on the roof, where no one would disturb them. As she soaked in hot water, she imagined the two of them there, her head against his strong chest, his arms around her, keeping her safe.

Eventually, it was her turn.

She rose and moved woodenly to where the upperclassmen sat. Jenny put her hair up into two black cat ears, chattering happily the whole time but saying nothing.

Towards the end, however, Miss Dare asked, "Why does Nastasia Romanov's bodyguard—as if she needs a bodyguard—look so much like you?"

Iolanthe Towers, who was standing nearby, perked up. Her eyes narrowed, peering at Amber. "I was going to ask the same question."

Lowering her head, Rachel intoned, "The world is much more evil than we think it is."

Both upperclassmen gave her an odd look, but as other girls were clamoring for their attention, neither of them pressed the matter.

Left alone, her hairdo done, Rachel sank back into the bath. The heated water did feel good, she finally acknowledged. It was not hot enough to melt the frozen parts inside her, but it was relaxing. She closed her eyes and soaked.

Bundled up in their coats, the bevy of girls poured from the gym and across the snowy lawns. As they reached the path that ran down the center of the commons, Amber held up a hand.

"Princess, wait." She spoke calmly from under her voluminous hood. "It's not safe."

Nastasia paused dutifully, indicating with a gracious nod of her head that the others should do the same. "Carry on, Miss Praetor."

Praetor? Nastasia had said that before but why? Amber's last name was Griffin.

Amber moved her head slowly, as if gazing into the forest. Her eyes began to glow with starlight. Silvery butterflies formed a cloud about her, rising into the air. The fluttering forms dissolved into glitter that then gathered together into glowing points directly in front of her eyes.

Two angular starlight-colored beams that crackled like lightning shot from her eyes, zig-zagging into the distance. They crossed the commons and entered the forest to the west, swerving around the trunks of birches and disappearing from sight. Moments later, the beams retracted. Wrapped in the crackling lengths of starlight was a redcap.

The angry fey struggled and scowled, its dry-blood-colored hat askew on its head. The silver-white beams wound tightly around its chest. Amber drew the little man to her and examined him. What could be seen of her expression was calm and pitiless.

"You caught it!" Joy cried with delight. "Bet that's the one that ensorcelled those girls!"

The silver-white bands around the little man's chest began to contract, growing tighter and tighter. The redcap made an odd strangled sound. Then it popped like a soap bubble. The sensation was strange, like waking from a dream. The Roanoke girls all gasped. No choreographed chorus could have gasped more simultaneously.

"Oh my," whispered Kitten Fabian, reaching out wildly as if grasping for something with which to steady herself. "D-did you kill it?"

"It will not trouble you again, princess." Amber inclined her head toward Nastasia. She ignored Kitten as entirely as if the other girl had never spoken. "Shall we continue?"

Rachel stared in horror at the place where the little fey had been. Her sister had murdered it in cold blood. True, the redcaps were annoying, but the treaties between the Wise and the fey required that the two groups obey certain rules. Trickery, enchantment, and beguilement were allowed, under certain circumstances, and killing the ogre during a fair fight fell squarely within the rules. Slaying a fey who was not endangering a human life did not.

It was murder.

Rachel wanted to shout at Amber, to tell her that killing the fey endangered the treaties that kept them from harming the Unwary, but no words came from her mouth. In her mind's eye, she kept hearing the redcap's last gasp over and over again. She felt as if she were falling. Darkness encroached upon her vision. She wanted to fight back, but, to her surprise, she could not. Between feeling nauseous and the shock of the callousness of her lost sister, it was as if all the careful work she had done to knit herself back together, after the tragedies that had battered her at the beginning of the school year, was coming apart: finding Valerie bleeding in the bathroom, fighting ensorcelled classmates and friends, being asked by Azreal to kill her friends and family, being kidnapped and nearly sacrificed to Moloch, the horrendous meeting with her father that ended with him losing his memory, and, worst of all, the death of her Elf. It was as if beholding the murder of this fey had snapped something inside of her. *It was like watching a tapestry unravel, a tapestry of sanity.*

A voice whispered to her that the trials she had faced over the last six months had been too difficult. There was nothing and no one who could save her now. She would be lost.

Only there was one tiny thing.

Rachel felt as if she stood suspended before two doors. Through one lay darkness. Madness lay that way, and oblivion—calm, quiet oblivion—that called to her, promising an end to all her troubles. Through the other, it was as if storm winds blew from that door, pushing her back, resisting any effort to go in that direction. Beyond the storm, barely visible, shone a light.

The darkness whispered to her. *It's not your fault. It was too much for you. All you need do now is let the darkness envelop you. Nothing will ever be your fault again. You do not need to approach the light, do not need to make that huge effort. It probably could not help you anyway.*

Enticing as those promises were, Rachel slowly turned her attention toward the second door. The storm winds seemed to blow her backwards. It would be easy to turn away. So easy to slip into the darkness and drown. And yet, would whatever followed truly not be her fault if she failed to make this one last effort?

In her imagination, she stepped forward. The storm winds parted, and she stood in a memory—the very memory that, moments before, it had occurred to her might offer one last, minuscule shred of hope. It was the first of November, and she stood in the Memorial Garden. The odor of ash from the previous night's bonfire still hung in the chilly autumn air. Before her rose the shrine of the Unknown God, and at its foot sat a Lion.

The Lion was tiny, but it possessed all the dignity of a great beast, one greater than the world itself. It glanced up, and their eyes met. A strange feeling came over her: like the way she felt reading a book while curled up in the comfort of her favorite chair.

That part was a real memory. It had happened last fall. With bated breath, Rachel waited. Sometimes, when she remembered this event….

"Help them," the Lion spoke gravely, *"for they are like sheep not having a shepherd."*

Then, the Lion was gone, and the storm winds closed round about her again.

CHAPTER TWENTY-ONE: THE DOOR AND THE MASK

Them?

With the slowness of a dream, Rachel opened her eyes. The girls stood in a semi-circle around Amber, motionless, like a tableau of shock. All the blood had drained from Kitten's face, and she looked close to tears. Amalthea was clutching her friend's shoulder. Hildy, who knew little of the way of fey, was glancing around, frowning, but her friend Rowan's face had turned a faint green. She looked as if she might be ill. Wendy stood with both hands pressed against her mouth. Sakura clutched her chest in horror. Salome looked uncharacteristically frightened. Only Valerie did not seem shocked, but she looked angry, very angry.

Joy, her bottom lip trembling, turned to Nastasia as if expecting her to take the lead, but the princess did nothing. Nastasia looked even more like a rabbit before the jaws of a wolf than the rest, or like a little mouse who had discovered that the new friend she had invited to tea was a cat. *They are lost*, Rachel thought, *almost as lost as I am.*

She waited for one of them to take the lead, but no one did. Unless someone did something, at least two of the girls would burst into tears. Yet no one moved. Panic rose in her chest. Surely Leander could not expect *her*, the most disoriented of them all, to take the lead? How could she do such a thing? She could barely stand.

Poised before the doors in her mind's eye—which now looked like an open gateway into memory on the right and, on the left, a gaping drop into absolute darkness—Rachel beheld a lone lost star hanging just above the precipice of darkness. It was a porcelain mask resembling a China doll with shoulder-length, straight black hair.

The face was her face.

It was her mental image of her Mask of Calm. Wisdom told her that using her mother's dissembling techniques to avoid emotional pain was a bad idea. But what else could she do? Surely, Leander did not expect her to be able to handle this on her own?

She could not falter now. Too much was at stake.

In her imagination, Rachel seized the mask and placed it over her face. Immediately, an outward calm descended. She stepped forward into the semi-circle of girls, slipping her arm through Nastasia's.

"That was unwise," she stated coolly to Amber. "It will cause trouble for the Master Warder. Someone had better report this to the proctors." She looked around. Amber showed no response, but the other girls were looking to her. "Valerie, you're good at making full reports. Would you go?"

Valerie shrugged. "Um... sure. Come on, Salome."

The spell was broken. The tears remained unshed. Valerie and Salome headed off for Roanoke Hall. Led by Amber, the other girls turned towards Dare Hall and struck out across the snowy lawns. Then, they were chatting cheerfully, as if nothing had occurred.

Rachel was not entirely sure that putting aside the horror that they had just experienced was the best outcome, but it was better than having them dissolve into tears and anguish in the middle of the commons. When they reached the porch of Dare Hall, Rachel detached herself from the princess and remained outside, leaning over the railing, staring into the woods. Her heart beat alarmingly as she considered the ramifications of what she had just done. Donning her mask had shoved her doubts and fears off into the distance, but she knew that, like a swinging wrecking ball, they would return unexpectedly, striking with an even greater force.

Gazing at the papery curls of the bark of the birches, Rachel resolved to face that problem when she came to it. If nothing else, today's actions had granted her a brief reprieve.

But as she turned back towards the great oak doors, the thought came that, maybe, when the tidal wave of doubt and terror did return, if she were very lucky—if providence were on her side, if she were dauntless and brave—she would be able to outrun it.

Rachel gazed into the mirror as she completed the last touches of her cat costume, drawing whiskers on her face with a black grease pencil. The shock of having met her missing sister—and her being nothing like what Rachel had imagined—was beginning to wear off, but she still felt hurt and saddened, as if her heart had been rubbed raw.

She shuddered. This whole thing was still too new, too horrible, to truly comprehend. When she tried to imagine her parents holding a baby and then giving it up—a real member of her family—it was still too much. Would she be able to put on a bright smile and bear the crowds and noise tonight? Or would the inner torment be too much for her? Perhaps, she should remove her costume and spend her evening in her room in quiet contemplation.

And miss her first masquerade ball?

She had never been to the sort of fancy dress ball where the dancers came in costume, and she and her friends had been looking forward to this event for months. She had worked so very hard to ensure that the campus was safe so that this evening's festivities could take place. She wanted to enjoy it, without the Master of the World, curse his name, casting his dark shadow over her every thought.

Was she truly going to let him ruin her evening?

The whole situation was tremendously disturbing, but it had existed for Rachel's whole life, even if she had not known about it until very recently. It would not be resolved tonight. The ball, on the other hand, would last but a single evening. Couldn't she put aside her worries and just bask in the joy of the event?

She would not let the monster ruin her happiness. She was going to go with her head held high, and she was going to dance. Just as she might tuck away a stray lock of hair, Rachel tucked away her shock and pain and resolved to have a splendid evening.

She completed the whiskers. Stepping back, she looked at her whole ensemble in the mirror. She was dressed as her familiar Mistletoe, a tight black bodysuit with an occasional white spot sewn on, a long tail with a wire inside so that it stuck out behind her in an S curve, her cat-ears of hair, and, now, black makeup on her nose surrounded by black whiskers.

She twirled, appreciating the way the tail flared out behind her. "Cute as a button," her grandfather would have declared. Rachel grinned. She could not wait for Gaius to see her.

Almost as if he had known she was thinking of him, Rachel's black bracelet vibrated. Her boyfriend's voice spoke beside her ear.

"Hey, Rach. Vlad has a question for you."

"Yes?" Rachel asked eagerly.

In the mirror, she could see her whole face light up at the mention of the prince's name. She scowled fearsomely at this, wagging her finger sternly at her reflection as she reminded herself that she had decided to merely admire Mr. Von Dread and had no reason to light up like the air above a sorcerers' orchestra.

Gaius drawled in his airy manner. "He wants to know if you know anything about some cloaked figure that is following the princess."

"Oh." Rachel thought rapidly. "Tell him that I think it's the person I told him about."

"Exchanging secret messages with Dread, eh?" Gaius's voice grew slightly fainter, as if he had turned his head. "Interfering with my girlfriend again, are you, Vlad? Hope you are ready for round two. I shan't go so easy on you this time."

Round two? Oh, of the Dread vs. Valiant duel! A giddy sensation assailed Rachel, akin to rapidly downing a glass of sweet wine. In the mirror, a pretty shade of rose crept across her face, from her cheekbones upward to her hairline and downward across her neck, except for where the whiskers were painted, of course. She pressed her hands against her hot cheeks as she blushed with embarrassed delight.

The sensation was followed by flashes of hot and cold as Rachel worried for the first time about what Dread might have told Gaius. Had the older boy mentioned their conversation on the ice? This thought made her heartbeat race. She did not want Gaius to be hurt, especially as nothing could possibly come of her fancying his friend. Then, she reassured herself, Gaius would not be joking in this manner if he thought she did. Besides, Vlad was not a tattler.

Letting out a breath of relief, she fanned her face with her hand in an attempt to cool her embarrassed glee. Her heart rate slowly returned to normal.

"Did she really capture a redcap?" asked Gaius.

"Killed." The animation drained out of Rachel's reflection. "She killed the redcap." Rachel's voice broke. She paused until she felt more collected. "Beams of starlight-colored lightning came out of her eyes, sought through the forest, and came back wrapped around the redcap. When she constricted the beams, the redcap just kind of... popped."

William's voice came over the bracelet, thoughtful and curious. "Can you describe these 'beams,' this star-lightning, in more detail?"

Rachel described them as best she could, repeating everything she had noticed. Over the bracelet, Gaius, William, and their young friend Topher Evans speculated about the nature of the beams, but none of them drew any definite conclusions. If Vlad were present, he was not contributing to the conversation.

"Isn't that going to cause trouble for Master Warder Nighthawk?" asked Topher. "According to Article VII, Section 10 of the Roanoke Concords, the tortious interference...."

"Yes, yes," Gaius interrupted. "You don't need to quote legalese at us, Evans. We all know that matters between the fey and us humans are tricky."

"Actually, it should not be a great trouble, since that redcap was already in a place it should not have been and had recently ensorcelled two young women," Vlad's voice came, cool and impassive. "I am more interested in knowing how she did it, how to reproduce it, and how to defend ourselves against it. But that matter must be shelved for another time. The ball awaits."

The others signed off. Gaius promised he would see her in an hour at the ball.

Rachel looked around her room. Her friends had gone on downstairs to dancing practice. After fixing a smudged whisker, she ran down the stairs to join them, in case someone needed an extra partner. As she headed down the great staircase, voices drifted up.

"I brought along a few extra fellows," Wulfgang Starkadder was saying. "Will we have enough ladies?"

"Oh, I think we shall," Nastasia's voice floated up the stairs, pleasant and gentle, "and we can always take turns. But if not, I could ask Rachel."

Wulfgang made a noise of disgust. "Not Griffin, she...."

"Hey, are we going to dance here or not," interrupted Sigfried's voice, "I am ready to clomp around and step on people's feet."

"Okay, Princess, we're ready!" cried Joy. From the giddiness of her voice, Rachel guessed that she had snagged the—in Joy's mind—plum position as Siggy's partner. "Oh, this is going to be so exciting! Ready, Ginger Snaps?"

Violins and flutes struck up a waltz, as Rachel frowned down the stairs. What had Wulfgang been about to say? He had dismissed her so disdainfully. What was it that he did not like about her? Her family? Their standing in society? Her father's position with the Wisecraft? Was it that she was dating a commoner? Was it that she ate lunch with Von Dread, Wulfgang's brother's rival? Did she annoy him personally? Talk too much in class—though she had not done that recently. Was it her person? Did he think her ugly? Clumsy?

Rachel *tsked* impatiently, dying to know what he had been going to say. The worst part was, she would probably never find out.

Her enthusiasm gone, she sat down on the stairs. Through the bars of the banister, she could smell the faint cinnamon-scent of the salamander playing behind the hearth grate. Below, her friends paired up to dance. The cloaked figure of Amber stood motionless to one side, guarding the princess. The sight of her lost sister waiting on her friend made Rachel feel so ill that she feared she might be sick.

It would be extremely embarrassing to throw up on the stairs, particularly if everyone below heard her.

Rachel hunched over, balled her hands into fists, and dug her fingernails into her palms. Seeing her sister—a member of the Family Griffin—following the Princess of Magical Australia around like a lapdog filled her with a heinous wrath.

And just when she and Nastasia had finally been getting along. The night of the skating party, the two girls had cleared up some misunderstandings, put aside some differences, and the princess had even gone so far, the day after she went home to see her father, as saying something almost nice about Von Dread. Rachel had hoped that everything would go back to normal, and they could just be best friends again.

And now? Could she be friends with someone who treated her sister as a servant? Of course, Nastasia probably had no idea that Amber was Rachel's sister, so it was unfair to blame her. Still, it was difficult to be friends with her, especially with her disapproval of Vlad and Gaius. If only Rachel could just walk away. She could spend all her time with Dread's people and be best friends with Astrid.

The thought was mesmerizingly enticing.

But then, she would no longer have access to the princess's visions or her ability to leave the world. Oh, there was that.

Rachel's cheeks grew hot. That was hardly a good reason to remain friends with someone—because the person had useful powers. There were words for those kinds of friends, and they were not kind words. If she were going to remain friends with Nastasia, she would have to be a real friend. What could she do to make things better?

Through the bars, Rachel could see the princess and Wulfgang as they twirled lightly around the grand foyer, demonstrating the waltz to the other students. Was that a flicker of a smile on her friend's perfect lips as she danced with the young prince of Transylvania? If it had been, it had vanished again.

Rachel gazed at the brooding young prince and recalled how rude he had been to her earlier in the day. She scowled. He was so annoying, as annoying as Nastasia, though in a different way. He and the princess almost deserved each other.

That was not nice, but there was an odd truth about it. Rachel recalled how happy Nastasia had looked as they skated back together at the end of the ice skating party, after Sigfried had killed the ogre, as the princess talked about her conversation that evening with Wulfgang. Then her face had fallen as she explained that she had, once again, rebuffed his offer of friendship, because she was frightened that if she became more friendly with him she might accidentally spill dangerous secrets. It was such a pity. Nastasia needed a friend of her own rank with whom she could be candid. Perhaps Wulfgang needed a friend, too. He almost never spoke to anyone. Maybe if he had a friend, he would not be so nasty to other people. They would be ideal companions, if only there were not the matter of all the secrets Nastasia needed to protect.

Gazing down at where her friends twirled elegantly across the squares of black and white marble, Rachel sat up suddenly, a slight smile on her lips as the germ of an idea began to form.

Chapter Twenty-Two:
The Year of the Dragon Ball

The gym was a riot of noise and wonder. Hundreds of red paper lanterns hung from the rafters of the immense ballroom with its hundred-and-twenty-foot ceiling. Giant paper dragons—red bodies with gold frippery, like reverse Luckys, except that their heads were bigger and more cat-like—graced the walls and floated overhead. In each corner of the ballroom, a huge dragon lantern hovered in the air, fire spouting from its mouth. In the back-left corner, a red gate stood between the dragon lantern and a gigantic crepe gold and white koi.

To the right of the gate, in the center of the back wall, a raised dais supported the musicians—a quartet consisting of tutors from the Music Department on strings and a fifth tutor, the world-renowned enchanter, Mr. Zuckerman, on the piano—who were warming up, adding to the general cacophony. The two refreshments tables—one to the southwest, near the musicians, the other to the northeast, near one of the doors out into the gym hallway—were decorated with giant lotus blossoms and whiskered fish that shone with their own inner glow.

Potted trees stood at intervals along the walls, their branches thick with oranges, medallions bearing paintings of Asian fey, and dangling red paper envelopes. Chairs had been arranged along the walls, between the orange trees. Students had already gravitated to them, animatedly chatting with one another or morosely slumping, alone.

Rachel and her friends slipped cautiously into the ballroom, gawking at the beauty of the hall and the costumes of their fellow students. Kings and harem girls, porcupines and pandas milled about the dance floor. Historical characters chatted with storybook ones. Rachel counted three fulgurators in their white leathers, conical helmets, and lightning-throwing staffs; four Agents in Inverness cloaks and tricornes; and at least twelve girls dressed as Witch Babies dolls. She spotted unfamiliar figures from Unwary movies and familiar ones from the comic books of the Wise: five separate James Darling, Agent costumes, three Scarlett MacDannans—including one of her sons who had come, to the horror of his little brother Ian, dressed as their illustrious mother. There was even one person dressed as Merlin Thunderhawk, the character based on her father.

Nastasia glided across the ballroom, practically floating in a gorgeous antique ball gown with a dainty, glittering, domino mask covering her eyes. Amber stalked behind her in her black hooded cloak. Sigfried and Valerie strode in handcuffed together. He was dressed as a cop; she wore a black and white prisoner's jumpsuit. Lucky rode in draped over them both, but when he saw the decor, he shot into the air to fly with delight among all his paper likenesses.

The O'Keefe girls had come as a fruit bowl, each sister dressed as a different fruit. Faith was a bunch of cherries. Mercy looked adorable as a raspberry. Joy was a bright yellow banana. Rachel would have died of shame to be in public in such garb, but Joy smiled brightly and waved from inside her rubber suit.

Zoë showed up even though she had claimed she would not. Dressed in a short skirt and multicolored leggings, she yawned, already bored. Rachel was unsure if this was a costume or her street clothes. She blinked and examined Zoë again. Was it the effect of her current outfit, or had the other girl grown even taller? She hardly even looked like a high school student.

"This is amazing!" Amalthea Kern was dressed as a popular Witch Baby with a wig of pink yarn and a patchwork skirt. "The room looks so different. It's entirely different from the way it looked during last year's Spring Cotillion."

Joy bounced up and down with excitement. "That's because of my father's friend, Mr. McGillicuddy. He's that really big, hulking guy who was talking to Mr. Chanson earlier. He's an architect who specializes in acoustics. He came and helped them design a better ballroom for the magic of the gym to conjure for them—the same magic that made the Japanese baths and the pool and the practice rooms and the other stuff we use all the time. This way, they were able to get a chamber with much better acoustics. Apparently, at some earlier dances, it's been hard to hear the music properly."

Rachel thought back to the moment when she had seen Mr.

McGillicuddy speaking to her boss and feared that he was the spirit-slaying bodyguard. Could that have only been a few hours ago? It seemed like an event belonging to a lost, idyllic age—before her stolen sister had turned out to be nothing like what she had expected.

"I understand paper lanterns shaped like dragons," said Kitten, who was still looking up. Her eyes followed Lucky as he floated, "but why giant fish?"

Rachel pointed at the red gate in the back corner. "There's a legend that if a koi swims far enough upstream, there's an enchanted gate. If the fish jumps through it, it turns into a dragon."

"Oh, how charming!" Kitten then pointed to simple lanterns sitting under the chairs. Like Rachel, Kitten had come dressed as her own familiar. She looked adorable in her tawny lion costume. "What about the little lanterns?"

"Lantern festival!" Rachel clapped her hands with delight. "Maybe they will let us light them later. They float upwards when lit."

"What's a lantern festival like?" asked Joy, from inside her banana peel.

Rachel shrugged. "I don't know beyond what I have read. At home, we always celebrated the first day of Lunar New Year, because we would visit my mother's family. But by the time the Spring Lantern Festival came around, fifteen days later, we had long since gone back to our normal British lives. Though my mum and I have lit a sky lantern or two, just the two of us. But if there's something special you were supposed to do, we didn't."

With a high-pitched squeak of violin strings, the tuning finished. Rachel and Kitten grabbed each other's hand, trembling with anticipation. The ball was about to begin!

The first waltz of the night was upon them. The musicians opened with Strauss's waltz from "Die Fledermaus." As its lilting notes swelled throughout the gymnasium, beautiful and stately—bringing with them a legacy of a thousand ballrooms, gaily-decorated and brightly-lit—a strange sensation came over Rachel, half-nostalgia, half-the-promise-of-things-to-come. All around her, the scene of festive cheer had suddenly transformed into something enchanted, wondrous. A horripilation of awe passed through her body. *No wonder her grandmother felt masquerades took place beyond the Fields We Know.*

The girls split up; several of them being immediately snapped up by boys for the opening dance, while others ran off to the refreshments table. Left alone, Rachel swayed to the music, her spirits soaring as she watched the twirling couples in their masks and finery.

"What have we here?" a casual masculine voice drawled charmingly behind her. "A pretty little kitty?"

"Gaius!" Rachel squeaked with sheer delight.

Gaius Valiant sauntered toward her. He looked quite dashing in a gray pin-stripe suit, a black ribbon tying his hair into a queue. Rachel's heart skipped a beat. She lowered her lashes, glancing at him sideways, overcome by the secret joy of belonging to such an adorable boy.

"Didn't know you knew who Catwoman was," he quipped.

"Who?"

"Um… who are you dressed as?" he asked.

"Mistletoe, my erstwhile familiar." Rachel turned her head and gestured to show off the cat ears. "Aren't they adorable? Jenny did them for me."

Gaius looked her up and down with obvious approval. He made a little twirling motion with one finger, and Rachel eagerly obliged, spinning slowly enough to allow him to admire her entire costume but fast enough that her tail flared out behind her. Beneath his admiring gaze, a happy thrill spread through her.

Gaius drawled slowly. "Don't you look good enough to eat."

"Like a topper on a cupcake," she replied.

"Then, there's that." Gaius pressed his lips together with suppressed mirth. He murmured something under his breath but even calling up the memory of it, twice, did not allow her to catch the words.

"Excuse me?" she leaned forward. "'To tea… with cream?' I didn't catch that."

"My apologies. That was most inappropriate." He rubbed the side of his nose, his fingers hiding his mouth as he struggled to stop laughing. Then, he bowed gallantly, his eyes suddenly filled with affection and kindness. "'Twas nothing. Merely lines from an old song."

"So not the Devon and Cornwall cream and jam thing." Rachel's eyes glittered with amusement, recalling their previous debate on that subject.

"No," he laughed and bowed again graciously. "Never that."

He gazed at her again, his eyes following lines of her bodysuit. Only this time, Rachel felt self-conscious. Was he admiring her or was he gazing at her chest—reminding himself that she was flat as a boy, too immature to be desirable? She sighed. She was nearly fourteen. When was she going to develop a womanly figure? Some other girls her age were quite curvy. But then, her sisters had developed late, too, and when they did—well, she had once overheard a relative say that the Griffin daughters had been amply rewarded for their patience.

She, too, must be patient.

"Shall we dance?" Gaius held out his hand.

He led her to the dance floor. Once there, Rachel stepped eagerly into his arms as the musicians struck up the introduction to the second song of the evening, the *Swan Lake Waltz*. They stood for a moment, hands clasped, waiting, poised. Then the dancing began, and the two of them spun around, twirling to the music, her wire cattail waving in the air behind her. Gaius was not an expert, but he was not inexperienced either. They danced together for a time, smiling at each other, except when they had to turn their heads to spot, so as not to get dizzy.

Finally, the time had come to figure out his costume.

"Um," she chewed on her lip as she looked him up and down, worried that an Unwary might recognize his outfit instantly. Ah well, it was not as if it would come as any great surprise to him that she was not up on mundane culture. "Whom did you come as?"

Gaius gave a casual shrug. "I don't go in for that sort of thing."

"What?" Rachel cried sharply. "I spent weeks carefully not asking you about your costume so I could be surprised!"

He shrugged. "Surprise."

"Not quite the kind of surprise I was hoping for." Rachel pressed her lips together and blew air into her cheeks at the same time, puffing them out. Then, she brightened. "Oh, I get it! You're dressed as an Unwary!"

Gaius did not seem particularly keen on her interpretation, but he did not argue. Instead, he indicated the ballroom with a gesture of his head. "How do you want to handle this evening? Dance together every dance? Only twice in the whole night, like a Regency couple?"

Rachel thought about the question carefully as they circled the floor. "Only twice seems unnecessarily old fashioned, and every dance together seems, well, cloying," she said carefully, hoping that she would not offend him, as while she loved dancing with him, she was eager to dance with other partners, too. Dances were more fun that way. She looked around at the other couples, as if she could somehow discern how they handled this question. "What's customary?"

Gaius shrugged. "Usually, couples agree to come back together every so many dances. Say, three apart and the fourth back together. That sort of thing."

"Let's do that, then!" she cried cheerfully. "That way we're here as a couple, but we also have an opportunity to dance with others."

"Agreed," he nodded. "I believe we see eye to eye here, Miss Griffin."

"Very good, Mr. Valiant," Rachel said, her voice filled with suppressed excitement. "This is my first ball here at school... well, unless you count the Dead Men's Ball... and I want to enjoy it to the fullest."

"I do not believe dancing with dead people counts," Gaius replied graciously.

They both burst into laughter.

The music played a lilting melody in three-quarter time. To Rachel, it seemed as if they were flying, floating like feathers among the other dancers as they waltzed. She and her boyfriend spun together, Rachel's heart hammering with joy. It was like stepping awake into a daydream.

The song ended. Rachel let out a little shriek of surprise as—as he had done during the Dead Men's Ball—Gaius dipped her, her head dropping suddenly as he arched her backwards over his arm. Once she recovered from the surprise, she grinned. *Dipped! How elegant!*

"Shall I see you again for the fourth dance?" Gaius said, when he had righted her. He bowed from the waist.

"Fourth it is," Rachel replied airily, curtsying in return.

Bending over her hand, he brushed her knuckles with his lips as he gazed into her eyes. Releasing her fingers, he strode away, whistling as he went. Rachel watched him fondly for a moment. Then she spun about, eager to find her next partner.

Lulled by the music, the bright lights, the beautiful costumes and decorations, Rachel's anxiety, brought on by the day's earlier events, had finally ebbed. As she danced, she considered that maybe she had overreacted to Xandra's warning. After all, she had jumped to the conclusion that the Raven was in danger when she had tried to figure out why the spirits had wanted Xandra to warn *her* about some unknown, hulking bodyguard. Now, however, she understood. They had sent Xandra to her because Amber was *her* sister. So maybe Jariel was safe. Even Amber could not slay an angel. Weren't angels as powerful as demons? No known power could seriously harm one of those.

Rachel's thoughts drifted back to the redcap and how Amber had popped the irksome fey as easily as a soap bubble. Wasn't it more likely that the spirit that was in danger was fey? A local American fey, something associated with the air and night? The Lord of Venti? Of nightstalkers? Lady Cobweb of Underhill? Maybe even a dream warden?

Maybe they could ask Amber to capture the Heer of Dunderberg. That would be amazingly useful, though only if Amber agreed not to kill it. If she destroyed the storm goblin as she had the redcap—rather than returning it to its prison—that would be a dark day for Roanoke indeed. Rachel shivered. Better not to mention it.

Still, she felt more at ease about Jariel.

She danced with Salome Iscariot's oldest brother Devon, who had come as a medieval battle sorcerer; with Ian MacDannan who, in keeping with his costume, kept imitating the Cockney accent his father put on for his Red Rider persona; and with his and Sigfried's other roommate, Enoch Smithwyck, the boy who would be dead, were it not for the kindness of the Raven. After she danced again with Gaius, her next partner was Joshua March. Much as she admired the March siblings, Rachel usually avoided them, because anyone who was too friendly with them would be interrogated by their father, the Grand Inquisitor of the Wisecraft, but she figured Cain March could hardly hunt down everyone who danced with his children at a masquerade ball. After all, she was in disguise.

Joshua March, who looked smashing in his pirate garb, had wavy fair hair and disturbingly intense gray eyes. Rachel suddenly recalled that the princess had seen this young man in a vision—hung by his outstretched arms in the middle of a glacier with his stomach slashed open. An impossibly handsome creature with wings of smoke and flame had been torturing him, the same creature that was apparently hunting his sister. She shivered, feeling pity for Joshua's past self who had undergone such an ordeal.

As she danced and smiled, a small amount of her attention remained locked upon her new sister. As she turned and twirled, she automatically tracked Amber out of the corner of her eye. Her sister shadowed Nastasia or, if Nastasia were dancing, waited off to one side, watching her. She stood inhumanly still, motionless as a statue, neither swaying to the music nor—when Rachel could see her face within the deep hood—showing any emotional reaction.

Rachel tried to watch her sister subtly, letting her gaze fall over her as she twirled by and then examining what she had seen afterward in her perfect memory, but maybe she accidentally betrayed her interest, because, as they spun across the polished floor, Joshua March nodded toward the hooded figure walking behind the princess.

"Who's the death doll following your friend?" asked Joshua.

"That's Nastasia's new bodyguard," Rachel sighed. "Death doll? What's that?"

The strangest expression came over Joshua's face. He blinked twice and then thrice more. Rachel caught her breath, icy claws raking the back of her neck. Her father had looked just like that when she had asked him about Amber—a subject he was not allowed to remember.

"It's a term my mother uses," Joshua replied mildly, his pupils not entirely focused.

The conversation drifted to other things, but Rachel's mind brimmed with questions. Who had blocked Joshua's memory, the Raven or Cain March? Whoever it was, had they done the same thing to Joshua's mother, the mysterious Cassandra March, who seemed to have the same flawless memory as Rachel? Rachel recalled coming upon Mrs. March in dreamland, clad in a skin-tight black bodysuit and cavorting with dream versions of the nine Muses. Sometimes, Rachel suspected that Mrs. March knew more secrets than the rest of the world combined.

What was a death doll? Could Joshua not recall it because there was something forbidden about the knowledge? Or was it just that he had heard the term in his former life, before being brought to Earth and turned into a child again? Of course, considering how he had been tortured in his previous life, perhaps blocking those memories was as much a blessing as a curse.

The more she investigated, the more mysteries she discovered.

Chapter Twenty-Three: Waltzing with Wulfgang

Rachel danced next with Officer Sigfried. He was not bad for a boy who had learned to dance that afternoon. As they spun, Rachel showed him how to spot by picking an object in the distance, such as a painting or paper dragon, and returning his gaze to it after each revolution, so as to avoid growing dizzy. She may have created a monster, for he whipped his head around so rapidly that she feared someone would get hurt, probably her.

"How's Valerie enjoying the dance?" she asked as they waltzed.

"She thinks it's smashing, but girls always love these things. We've agreed to meet every third dance. The rest of the time, I'm supposed to find other cute girls to hold in my arms while I step on their feet. I'm not entirely convinced this is prudent—would King Arthur approve of men and women standing so close?—but so far, I haven't lamed anyone. Well, not permanently."

"You needn't take responsibility for that either way," Rachel explained primly as she laid out the rules for him. "It's the woman's job to keep you from stepping on her feet."

"That hardly seems fair." His brow furrowed as he contemplated this.

"The woman worries about the feet," Rachel explained. "The man's responsible for not bumping into other couples."

"You mean, like this?" Sigfried barreled them sideways so that they nearly collided with two upperclassmen—a samurai and a bobbysoxer in her pink poodle skirt.

Rachel resisted the urge to scream.

"Yes, exactly like that," she growled through clenched teeth.

The very idea of deliberately breaking the protocols of formal dancing appalled her. Siggy grinned like a maniac.

"While I have your attention," Rachel said, suddenly recalling her earlier idea from when she had been sitting on the staircase of

Dare Hall watching Nastasia and her dance partner. "I wanted to ask you a question. Um. Siggy? What do you think of Wulfgang?"

"Who, Skarmadder?" he asked as he squinted upward at where Lucky was eyeing a giant paper lotus flower. "He's all right. For a guy who uses other people as shields."

It took some effort not to laugh. She had been there the time Wulfgang had picked up a paralyzed Sigfried and used him as a shield to block incoming spells. Or rather, she had been there *one* time that Wulfgang had done this. For all she knew, it was a regular thing.

"Does he... have any friends," she asked. "Other than his familiar?"

"Friends?" Sigfried looked entirely blank, as if he had never so much as entertained the idea of paying attention to the behavior of other boys.

"It's just...." She glanced over her shoulder, making sure that neither Wulfgang nor Nastasia was nearby and said in a hushed voice. "I can't help wondering if he's been taught not to fraternize with those of lower rank. In which case, I think the princess is the only person in our year who's his equal."

"You think everyone here is beneath him?" Siggy looked taken aback.

Rachel rolled her eyes. "No, but *he* does."

"Ah. What about you?" Siggy furrowed his brow. "Isn't your family high and mighty?"

"I'm nobility. He and Nastasia are royalty. There's as big a gap between nobility and royalty as the one between nobility and commoners. It's just harder to see from below."

Siggy yawned. "Huh... what? My brain just switched off from boredom."

"The princess could use a friend and so could Wulfgang. They were even getting along rather nicely at the skating party. But she won't be his friend so long as she has to keep secrets from him; she feels she's not good at remembering what to keep secret."

"Must give credit where credit's due." Siggy shrugged, lifted Rachel about the waist and swooshing her out of the way of an oncoming couple. "I'm with her. I hate keeping secrets, too."

Regaining her footing, Rachel leaned toward him and whispered, "What if we told him?"

"Told who what?"

"Wulfgang Starkadder. Let's tell him *everything*. Or, as much as Joy and Zoë know."

"Are there parts of everything Joy and Zoë don't know?" asked Siggy dubiously.

Rachel drew a very deep breath and let it out slowly. "Yeeesss."

"Oh, right. Like that Master-of-the-Whirled-who-I'm-gonna-kill." Siggy nodded at Lucky, as his familiar sailed among the paper dragons overhead. Glancing down, Lucky nodded in reply. Sigfried turned back to Rachel. "Sure. Why not. Blab anything you like to Snarfladder. If it were up to me—if it wouldn't destroy the world—I'd tell everyone."

As Rachel glanced around, seeking possible dance partners, her gaze fell upon Amber in her hooded cloak, standing motionless as she watched Nastasia dance with the handsome Squirrel Fabian. The world around Rachel suddenly seemed distant and surreal. *It had happened. Her long-lost sister had come.* And yet, it was nothing like what Rachel had expected.

Had it only been two weeks ago that she had learned of Amber's existence? When she had wished upon the three stars, Rachel had never imagined that her wish might be granted so quickly. What would happen next? Should she confront her and reveal that she was her sister? Or was that what Xandra's spirits had been trying to warn her not to do?

A strange frisson passed through her as she realized that another of her wishes might soon be granted as well. Two days earlier, her father had replied to her letter about the Heer of Dunderberg. He had informed her that a much larger group of Agents, including some from the London offices of the Wisecraft, would be arriving in a few days to join Maverick Badger in hunting down the escaped storm goblin. If they succeeded, the campus would finally be safe again. They would be able to go outside in the rain and would not have to worry about redcaps and ogres. Even better, her father might come himself as part of the storm goblin hunting party. Perhaps she would finally get an opportunity to speak with him, to speak with him about Vlad and Sandra, if nothing else. It was the least she could do for Sandra after allowing their parents to ambush her beloved.

An eerie chill traveled up her spine. If her first two wishes came true, might there be hope for the third one? Could she possibly be granted an opportunity for revenge against the Master of the World? It was impossible, of course. What could she, a mere girl, do against such a monster? Yet, the thought filled her with a strange and awful glee.

Catching sight of Wulfgang Starkadder as he waltzed with Rory Wednesday, Rachel decided to spend this dance following him around the room, so she could be present wherever the song finished. Rory looked ravishing dressed as the Rhine Maiden in a skin-tight, scaled gown. Rachel found her choice of costume eerie—considering that Vlad had said the statue of the Rhine Maiden in Bavaria looked so much like her—until she recalled that Miss Wednesday was said to be descended from the Rhine Maiden and might have picked her outfit for that very reason.

Wulfgang looked somber yet elegant dressed as a Hungarian nobleman: scarlet jacket, vest, and pants with a great deal of golden braid, fur trim that matched his fur shako, and a golden sash around his middle. An encyclopedia in Rachel's mental library had an illustration of a man dressed in the very same outfit: Wulfgang's grandfather, King Geri of Transylvania.

As the current dance came to an end, Rachel rushed in front of him before he could look for a new partner. Stepping forward, she curtsied, quite low. As she had hoped, even though he clearly did not like her, he was too well-bred to give her the cut direct. The dark, brooding Prince of Transylvania bowed and asked her to dance.

They stood motionless through the unnecessarily long introduction that always plagued waltzes—her hand uncomfortably warm in the hand of this boy who looked at her with barely-concealed disdain—and then began to dance. Wulfgang twirled her around the floor with expert ease to the lilting melody of Strauss's "Voices of Spring

Waltz." He moved with practiced grace but did not initiate conversation other than the simplest pleasantries. He was a pleasure to dance with, but when she recalled why she had approached him, her heart began to pound. Taking a deep breath, she plunged ahead before she could lose her nerve.

Rachel gazed at him sideways, through her lashes. "You like the princess, don't you?"

Wulfgang's back stiffened. "Perhaps."

He managed to make the word sound like a monosyllable.

Rachel straightened her shoulders and assumed the cool, business-like approach she adopted when speaking with Von Dread. "Have you noticed that you're stuck in a holding pattern? That no matter what you do, you can't actually reach her?"

He had been smiling slightly as they twirled lightly around the room. His smile vanished. "The princess is an acquaintance of mine," he said stiffly. "Nothing more. She has made clear that she lives for king and country. I expect no less of her."

"That's not entirely true," Rachel replied, "Or rather, it's true, but it is not the problem."

"Oh? Then what is 'the problem'?"

"A great number of secrets have been given into her keeping. The burden of these secrets is heavy. She's afraid to grow close to anyone who doesn't already know them."

"The secrets of her state are for her to share or withhold as she sees fit," he replied with icy chill. "It would be unlikely that she would decide to accept me as a confidante."

"But she needs friends, desperately."

"You are friends with her, are you not? As is the Dragonslayer. Even the Dolt and Goth. Or are you saying she needs more allies in high positions?"

Rachel nearly burst out laughing at his nicknames for Joy and Zoë. "I am saying she desperately needs friends of her own who are not me and not Sigfried. We are friends, but we are also like comrades under fire, making our relationship... strained."

"And?"

"She needs someone who is powerful enough not to get killed, and yet savvy. None of the princess's other intimates are savvy."

Rachel studied him closely, her heart fluttering unexpectedly as she gazed up at his brooding good looks. She fought the desire to avert her eyes demurely and continued to meet his gaze squarely. "But I think you are."

"These secrets," his dark eyes narrowed, "they are secrets of state?"

Rachel shook her head. "This is not about Magical Australia. I mean secrets related to things such as the safety of the world. If you knew as much as Joy and Zoë know, you would be in an excellent position to befriend her. She would have no reason to keep you at arm's length."

He watched her face. "I am listening."

"The problem is," Rachel sighed, "the price for knowing these secrets is high... very, very high."

Wulfgang drew himself up with grave and almost menacing dignity. "Are you suggesting that the Goth and the Dolt can pay such a price, and I cannot?"

"No! Certainly not. I like your spirit, Prince Starkadder. But the Goth and the Dol...." She bit her lip. Amusing as it was, a lady would not repeat such an insult. "But the others didn't know the price ahead of time. If they had, they might have chosen differently. So let me ask you," she leaned in, gazing directly into his dark eyes. "Are you willing to risk death? Are you willing to risk your life? Your sanity? Losing your memory, as my father recently did? Forgetting what you learned. Maybe even forgetting who you are?"

Without hesitation, he replied grimly. "I am."

A frisson of awe traveled through her. Rachel had to admit, she was impressed. She wished more of her friends would show that kind of commitment.

"Are you willing to know secrets you cannot discuss," she pressed on. "Not with your family or your friends. Maybe not even with us—depending on what you learn?"

He nodded.

Rachel leaned even closer, her eyes burning like stars. "Are you willing to be told information, if the very act of telling you might damage the world?"

He stopped dancing, staring back with wolf-like intensity. "Yes."

Rachel nodded slowly.

Wulfgang began dancing again. "If something horrible happens, I shall not blame you unless it is obviously your direct action."

"Thank you," Rachel said softly. "Tomorrow, then?"

"Tomorrow."

The dance ended. He bowed. She curtseyed and departed.

"I did it," Rachel whispered as she passed Sigfried, who had just parted from his latest dance with Valerie. "Or rather, I got him to agree to hear us out."

"Him, who?" asked Sigfried, confused.

"Wulfgang."

"Slargattor? Hear us about what? Oh, right." He threw up his arms. "No! Don't kill me with your eye beams! I remember!"

Rachel struggled not to giggle and failed. She leaned close to him. "He called Zoë and Joy 'the Goth and the Dolt.'"

Siggy barked with laughter. "Ah, Splergbladder. Good man."

Rachel started to leave and then turned back. "Eye beams?"

"Beams of fire that come out of your eyes and vaporize people." Siggy made a gesture to either side of his head, indicating the beams of fire protruding from one's eyeballs.

"Oh, you mean like Amber?"

He gawked. "The princess's bodyguard? She has eyebeams?"

Rachel realized with a cold shiver that she had not told him. She leaned closer. "That bodyguard. That's my missing sister—the one the princess's grandfather stole."

Siggy's attention went immediately to what he deemed the important things of life. "Your missing sister has eye beams?"

Rachel sighed and nodded. "Hot, jagged, white ones. She killed a redcap with them."

"Ace!" Siggy gazed at the cloaked figure in awe. "How do I get jagged white eye beams?"

Gaius came toward them from the left. At the same time, Peter and Laurel approached from the right. Peter was dressed as a Knight of the Round Table. He wore a helmet, a breastplate, and a silver garment that looked like mock chainmail. Over his left arm, he carried a shield bearing a rampant gryphon gules on a field sable. Laurel had come as a flapper, with elbow-length black gloves, a slender, white, beaded headband with a feather on the front, and a short Art Deco gown with a great deal of fringe. She carried a long cigarette holder containing a brown cigarette that was not lit. Both of Rachel's siblings had odd expressions on their faces.

"I say, *dongsaeng* — ," Laurel spoke loudly to be heard above the music. She pointed at where the princess danced, her bodyguard standing patiently nearby. "Why does that girl following your haughty automaton of a friend look almost exactly like our mother?"

"Um... about that," murmured Rachel.

"Yes?" asked Peter, raising one eyebrow. He looked unexpectedly like their father. "About that?"

Gaius watched her face, curious how she would answer. Sigfried was still gawking at Amber, as if expecting eyebeams to emerge. Rachel drew a deep breath. She did not want to lie directly to her own siblings. Was there any purpose in keeping it a secret any longer?

"She's our sister."

"Our... Hang on! *What?*" Laurel exclaimed.

"Our sister."

Laurel and Peter both gave her identical, skeptical glares.

Laurel also crossed her arms. "Why don't we remember her, this *supposed* sister?"

"Great Aunt Nimue remembers her. Sort of."

"Great Aunt...." Laurel was suddenly paying full attention.

"Hang on." Peter's body went rigid. His gaze moved to the princess's diminutive, hooded bodyguard as if pulled by a magnet. "Is this the missing Amber you asked me about last fall?"

Rachel nodded. "She was stolen away, by magic, when she was a baby."

"Stolen away? You mean by fairies," asked Peter, still staring intently at Amber. "That sounds a bit dodgy to me. Is she a changeling? Are you the changeling, and she's the real thing? Or maybe Laurel? I've often questioned whether she was truly a member of the family. Maybe Laurel's the fairy, and that's our real sister. She looks more like Mummy than Laurel does."

Peter spoke lightly, but his gaze remained glued to Amber. Rachel was not sure he was tracking what he was saying, which was an astonishing state of affairs for her normally conscientious brother. He did not seem to notice when Laurel mock-slugged him in the ear for his slights toward her. He did not even seem to notice that his dreaded rival, Gaius Valiant, was standing next to him.

"I misspoke. Not stolen away. Not exactly," Rachel clarified. "Someone—let's call him the Master of the World—used magic on our parents to change them, to make them into people who would do things that they would normally never do—like give up their first-born daughter."

"Wait? First-born?" Peter blinked. "She can't be older than Sandra. She hardly looks older than you. I'd say she was fourteen, fifteen max."

Eager not to draw Amber's attention, Rachel examined her sister by glancing at her and then consulting her memory. Amber did look as if she were fifteen. She was hardly taller than Rachel, not even as tall as their mother.

"I don't know." Rachel shrugged. "Maybe it's like fairyland, and time ran differently."

"And Mummy and Daddy never told us?" asked Laurel, her voice rising. "They just neglected to mention they had another daughter? Codswallop!"

Rachel shook her head. "They don't remember. I tried to ask Father about it. He…" she shivered, "… could not remember long enough to listen to the end of my sentence. His memory of what I was saying just drained away while I was speaking, like water through a sieve."

"That's awfully disturbing," said Peter, eyes still fixed on their long-lost sister.

"Yes, very," Rachel agreed, shaken just from recalling it. "It was."

"What's the next step?" asked Gaius.

"Do we go talk to her?" asked Laurel, watching their sister intently.

"I…." Rachel moistened her suddenly-dry lips. "I don't know."

"Why shouldn't we?" asked Peter.

"Yeah, why hesitate?" demanded Sigfried. "If my family were nearby, and they were hesitating to tell me, I'd be very angry."

There was a pause. Everyone looked at Rachel.

"I'm afraid," she admitted finally.

"Why?" Gaius reached out and took her hand, squeezing it.

Rachel took a deep breath. She did not want to explain about Xandra's prophecy and Jariel. That seemed too dangerous, too private. She settled for the next-most upsetting issue.

"The man who took her, the Master of the World, he's the one who changed Father's memory. Father didn't have a memory accident in January—the Master of the World altered his memory. H-he changed my memory as well, only it didn't quite work. That's how I know this. I am afraid if he finds out about some... some things I know... he'll kill me."

"For knowing too many secrets?" asked Sigfried, nodding knowingly.

Rachel nodded.

"You're afraid he'll kill you for knowing the secrets you just shared with us?" asked Laurel.

Rachel glanced away, "Not all of them."

"There's more?" Peter looked morose.

"Much more," replied Sigfried, cheerfully. "Griffin here knows so much that she's like a Wise to your Unspary. She's a Wiser than Wise."

"Just her?" asked Laurel, "Not you, too?"

Sigfried made an expansive gesture. "Griffin remembers everything. I forget it. I have forgotten more than the rest of you know."

From behind Rachel, Amber's voice spoke, calm and precise. "Excuse me. I could not help overhearing what you were saying. He won't hurt you. He's not that kind of ruler."

Chapter Twenty-Four:
The Destiny of Amber Griffin

Rachel jumped, her heart thundering in her chest. Gasping, she spun around to face Amber. "You overheard us? You were twenty-five feet away in a loud and crowded room!"

"I have very good hearing," replied Amber.

"I'll say," murmured Gaius.

Rachel took several steadying breaths. Her heart still pounded. That had been a close call. A moment or two later, and she might have blurted out how she had avoided having her memory changed. Amber might be right that the Master of the World did not want to kill her, but if he demanded that Jariel remove her Rune and change her memory, it would amount to the same thing—and he had already tried to change her memory once. Could she hide from Amber that she had perfect recall? She dearly hoped so. She would have to avoid saying or doing anything in front of her that might give it away. It was of paramount importance that she keep her talent secret. *Her life might depend upon it.*

Amber pushed back her hood. They could now see her face clearly. The resemblance to the rest of the family was uncanny, as was the complete lack of any discernible emotion. Rachel wondered if she herself looked like that when she used the family dissembling techniques.

Amber stated, "No magic was used on our parents to change them."

"Really?" Peter asked, combatively. "Why did they give you up, then?"

"They swore an oath," explained Amber. "In return for information about the greater universe, they took an oath of obedience to my emperor. Then, for their part, they were asked to contribute their daughter, me. They freely gave me up as active members of the Cause."

"What kind of oath?" Gaius's eyes narrowed. "Was there a penalty if they had refused?"

"They swore upon the River Styx," said Amber.

Laurel's eyes sparked with outrage. "You mean, they would have *died!*"

Amber nodded.

"But they were changed!" Rachel insisted vehemently. "The Master of the World had them changed at the beginning, so they would do what he wanted. They would never have given away one of their children! They would have died first!"

"What makes you think they were changed?" asked Amber.

Rachel had opened her mouth to retort that she had heard it first hand, from the very being who had performed the changing, when she remembered Xandra's warning. It might not be her life that was on the line tonight but that did not mean that no one was in danger.

"I saw it in a vision," she lied smoothly.

"Your visions may not be reliable," replied Amber. "Not all spirits are trustworthy."

That was frustrating. Rachel gritted her teeth. "They have been trustworthy in the past."

"I didn't know you had visions, Rach," Peter said, pleased.

Rachel felt guilty misleading her brother, but then she had had several visions. The Lion had sent them; at least, she was pretty sure he had.

"Can you perform introductions?" Amber said, suddenly a little shy.

"Oh! Of course!" Rachel blushed, feeling very gauche for having forgotten. "This is our middle sister, Laurel, and this is our brother, Peter, Lord Falconridge."

Amber nodded to Laurel and Peter, both of whom were openly staring back at her. Laurel grinned and smoothed the feather in her flapper headband. Peter's face was grimly serious.

Rachel gestured to the other two, adding proudly, "This is my blood-brother, Sigfried Smith, and my boyfriend, Gaius Valiant."

Amber's eyebrow darted up. "Unlucky name."

"How so?" asked Gaius, curious.

He and Rachel studiously avoided glancing at each other.

Amber stated in her calm, military fashion, as if answering test questions by rote, "Another man named Gaius Valiant was responsible for destroying the starlinks, the interstellar gates at Star Yard. Crashed the entire system, destroying the Galactic Confederacy, an interstellar civilization. It was the second most destructive act ever committed by a mortal being."

"Why?" Gaius asked, his voice rising slightly. His hand that was out of sight of Amber grabbed Rachel's and squeezed convulsively. His face was a little pale. Rachel knew that he had been told some of this before, but it could not be an easy thing to hear. "Was he some kind of crazy maniac?"

Amber replied. "He was trying to carry out an illegal science experiment. It had been banned due to the danger involved—which the consequences of his actions retroactively confirmed. The resulting explosion destroyed Star Yard—an interstellar space station— and killed Valiant."

"So, he's not wanted for anything?" drawled Gaius.

Rachel, who knew him well, could hear the relief in his voice.

"Not for destroying the starlink network," Amber nodded briskly, adding, "Had he survived, he would have been executed."

"Oh?" Gaius swallowed.

His grip on Rachel's hand tightened again, but there was no other outward sign of his discomfort. Peter, who still had not showed any sign of realizing that Gaius was present, was staring at Amber as if in a trance. Laurel looked faintly bored with the current topic of conversation. She was playing with her headdress and looking around the ballroom. Rachel realized with a slight shock that Laurel had no idea that Amber was talking about their Gaius, his past before the Raven rescued him from the explosion, brought him to earth, and turned him into a child. To Laurel, they were discussing some unknown stranger.

Sigfried, on the other hand, understood exactly. He had a huge grin with stars shining in his eyes. Anyone who could do that much damage deserved hero-worship in his mind. Rachel suspected that Gaius had just gone up a notch or two in the orphan boy's esteem.

"In order to perform the experiment," Amber recited, "he indulged in forbidden magic."

"But it didn't help?" Gaius asked.

Amber frowned thoughtfully. "Theoretically, it should have been possible to complete the experiment with the help of such magic. I suppose it was the ill-luck that doomed him."

"Ill luck?" asked Gaius. "You mean he happened to fail?"

"No," replied Amber. "A great scientist had discovered a method to direct the luck that comes from the influence of the stars. He found that beneficent influences could be focused on a subject or planet, and ill-luck, from evil stars, could be directed away—allowing only good influences to strike the subject. It was a sound hypothesis, and he used it to design the first truly operative ringworld and to carry out numerous experiments. Unfortunately, one of his mirrors directing the negative influences away from Ouroboros was inadvertently pointed at Star Yard—some light years away. This led, eventually, to the influences from the stars of ill-omen reaching Star Yard, just about the time that this other Valiant was conducting his experiments."

Rachel's lips parted in wonder. She felt as if stars, beneficent or otherwise, were exploding in her head. Amber *knew*. She knew all the things Rachel herself had so longed to discover. Amber *knew* about the history of the Metaplutonians. She *knew* who Gaius had been before the Raven brought him here, and she might even know about the Dread King or who Zoë used to be or Hildy or Valerie. She *knew* about *what* was Outside. She probably even *knew* what the real laws of nature and magic were. Rachel drank in every word that escaped her sister's lips like a desert beneath the first drops of a summer rain.

Gaius gave Amber an odd look. "Star... influences? You mean like alchemists speak of?"

Amber nodded. "People have known about them since the dawn of man, but it took William Locke to confirm the phenomenon and study it scientifically."

"William...." Gaius bit off his friend's name.

"Locke," Amber replied, as if she thought that Gaius had not heard her properly. "Sadly, he died a few years later in a lab accident. He was trying to invent a new type of starlink to repair the broken network and get all the stranded people home."

Peter frowned, "We have a student here by that name."

Rachel's heart leapt into her throat. Beside her, Gaius's face grew even paler. If Amber realized that other people from Outside were here as well, would she arrest Gaius, or worse?

Amber nodded, unconcerned. "That's normal. Wherever worlds are under the same constellations, they are affected by the same influences. This leads to people being born with similar names and even similar appearances."

Rachel could not help it. Her pent up breath escaped in a sigh of relief. Hopefully, Amber would mistake her emotion for wonder.

"Same constellation?" Gaius drawled, gesturing airily toward the night sky somewhere high above them. "How could two planets be equidistant from the same stars?"

Amber shook her head. "No. The individual stars don't matter, only the constellations."

Gaius cocked his head to the left. "What's the difference?"

"A constellation's a grouping of stars as perceived by the human mind," recited Amber in her same pupil-before-the-schoolmaster tone, to the utter fascination of Gaius and Rachel and the dismay of the bored Sigfried and Laurel. Peter was frowning as if thinking of something else. "Where they are the same, the same ideas occur to men. This is how the many worlds are governed—through the influences of the stars—and why some worlds look like each other."

Gaius frowned. He didn't care for magic in his science, but Rachel's eyes glittered with rapt curiosity. Both star magic and the pasts of her friends promised to be infinitely fascinating.

"Amazing," Rachel exclaimed. "And these influences are good or bad?"

"There's much more to it," Amber replied, "but the short version is that the stars that make up the constellations are either stars of good omen that produce beneficent influences or stars of ill-omen, or dis-asters," Amber paused noticeably between the two syllables of the word, "which cause evil fates."

"What about you?" asked Laurel, who did not care about star influence or Metaplutonians. "We only just found out you existed. What do you do with your time? Are you a servant? A slave? Do they keep you locked up in a cage and only let you out on Tuesdays, in order to clean tables by dancing on them? And who is this 'they' anyway? By which I mean, who took you?"

Amber replied seriously, "I am not a slave or menial servant. I am one of The Twelve. I serve my emperor. He is the one with whom our parents made the agreement."

Laurel asked, "If our parents gave you up freely, why was their memory wiped?"

"I was told that, at first, our mother visited every month, but that this was too difficult for her; she became hysterical," replied Amber. "So it was reluctantly decided by everyone involved that it would be better if she forgot me and moved on with her life."

Rachel thought of her mother during her recent visit and swallowed.

Peter spoke up, "Can you tell us a little of your life? I don't understand what you do."

"I grew up as part of the praetorian guard," Amber replied. "I was trained carefully with the skills needed to carry out my destiny. To...."

"Wait, destiny?" Laurel interrupted. "What destiny?"

"Didn't you know?" Amber looked at Rachel, who shook her head. "There was a prophecy. It said that I would have the capacity to... gain a power that would be a tremendous benefit to our side, and with this power, I would destroy a great enemy and...." She cut herself off. "Another part has not yet happened. I cannot speak of that. But the first two parts have already come to pass. I gained the power, and I used it to kill Belial, the Lord of Lies."

"Oh, that's just smashing," murmured Laurel.

"And that's why the Master of the World took you from our parents?" asked Rachel.

Amber replied stiffly, "His title is the Eternal Emperor, Andre the Second."

"No good," said Sigfried, "We already have an emperor."

"You have an emperor?" Peter looked at him oddly.

"I was not aware that there was an ememperor on this world," said Amber.

"The guy who made me," said Sigfried, "The Emperor of All Things Green and Ungreen."

Rachel winced. Somehow, she did not think Amber would be able to follow Siggy's creative use of language.

Before she could interrupt, however, Amber replied, "Do you mean the Emperor of All Things Seen and Unseen?" Her eyes widened. "How do you know about that?"

Sigfried nodded. "We know his son, the Comfort Lion."

Rachel's lost sister frowned. "I thought all knowledge of that was forbidden on this world."

Rachel's face remained impassive, but in her mind, she recalled the Raven's words to her when they talked on the staircase after the skating party: *Know this, Rachel Griffin: nothing left in this world is as important as the one thing I have caused it to forget.*

Oops. Maybe Sigfried should not have mentioned this subject.

Sigfried leaned forward. "Why? Why was it forbidden?"

"I am not at liberty to say," Amber replied stiffly.

"You say you destroyed the... Lord of Lies?" asked Gaius, "Was that a... demon?"

"Indeed. That is well known by the enemy, so I am not forbidden from sharing that detail," replied Amber. "My power can destroy angels and demons. That's why I was put through such extreme training. So I would to be able to gain this power and become a bane to demons."

Rachel swayed slightly upon her feet. She had thought Jariel was safe because he was an angel. *Perhaps he was not safe at all.*

"How many have you destroyed?" asked Gaius, who was listening intently.

"Publicly known?" Amber replied. "Twenty-seven, if you count two fallen angels—angels who were suitable when they were bound into Guardianship by the former Eternal Emperor but who had since gone bad."

A cold shiver ran through Rachel. *Was this what Xandra's spirits had been trying to warn her about?* So much for angels and demons being invulnerable.

"Guardianship?" asked Gaius.

Amber stood with her hands behind her and again spoke as if reciting. "The Romanovs maintain and protect the worlds under their control by assigning each world a guardian angel."

Guardian angel? An entirely different kind of shiver traveled through Rachel. *What a lovely term.* Just hearing it made her lips part with happiness. Swallowing, Rachel asked as evenly as she could manage, "Wh-what would make a guardian go bad?"

Amber bowed her head slightly. "I cannot address specifics, but generally, no one can command these angels except the emperor and his duly appointed representatives. Even the great demons, the Rulers of Hell, cannot make them break their vows to the Romanovs. But two of them refused to renew their vows to the family when my emperor rose to the throne. My emperor had me destroy them, and he assigned new guardians to those worlds."

Rachel's heart was beating so violently that her whole body seemed to be shaking. She wondered if her siblings could hear it. What if Amber found out that the Guardian had essentially disobeyed the Master of the World, since he knew that Rachel's memory had not been changed? *Would Amber kill the Raven for his disobedience?*

"I'm lost," admitted Gaius. "Earlier, you mentioned 'our side.' Side of what?"

"My emperor has few resources and yet faces terrible enemies, of which I may say very little. He holds back both the demons and the Elysians—those who destroyed the World Tree."

"Wait! You know who destroyed the World Tree!" Rachel cried, her voice full of wonder. "The Elysians? Who are they?"

"At least, I didn't do that," muttered Gaius under his breath. Perhaps, he then recalled how good Amber's hearing was, because he stopped talking and pressed his lips together.

"No one you will ever meet," Amber replied, "so it is of no consequence."

"But...!" Rachel cried in frustration.

She recalled her idyllic daydream that she and Amber would be librarians together. The reality could not be farther from the truth. Amber was even worse than her father. Her new sister knew even more and shared even less. Worse, she knew the answer to the very questions that had been burning in Rachel's mind for months now, and she showed no inclination to answer them. Rachel did not even dare voice many of them, lest by doing so, she should accidentally reveal that she knew something else she should not.

Lucky swooped down and landed on the ground, extending his legs, so that he stood upright, like a dog. Amber's pupils widened as she regarded the handsome furry serpent.

"What have we here?" she asked.

Laurel answered cheerfully, "This is Lucky the Dragon. Siggy's familiar."

"Blood brother," corrected Sigfried.

"Best friend," said Lucky.

"Hello, Lucky," said Amber, intrigued.

"You can pet him. Girls like doing that," said Sigfried.

"I'm like a living plushy," announced Lucky in his gravelly voice.

Amber reached out tentatively and stroked the dragon's arched neck with the side of her finger, touching both his furry golden throat and his smooth ruby stomach scales.

"That is pleasant." A tiny smile appeared at the edges of Amber's lips. It made her look younger, gentler. It was the first girlish expression Rachel had seen on her face. Even her death doll of a sister could not resist the furry dragon.

"Why do you look so young?" asked Laurel. "You must be older than Sandra—our eldest sister, who's not here right now. But you look younger than Peter."

Amber nodded calmly. "The process of gaining the power I mentioned arrested my aging. I was fifteen at the time. That was about fifteen years ago."

"Fifteen?" Rachel leaned forward. "But that makes you thirty years old. Our parents have only been married for twenty-six years. The twenty-fifth anniversary of the Battle of Roanoke and the defeat of the Terrible Five will be this coming Walpurgisnacht and May Day. Our parents were married the previous year, just after they graduated from Roanoke Academy."

"Time flows differently on different worlds," Amber replied.

"I say, what are the... Twelve, was it?" asked Peter.

"My emperor's elite bodyguard," Amber replied. "More than that, I may not say. I dare not share any information that might fall into the hands of the enemies."

"You can't think we'd blab to your enemies," objected Laurel. "We're your family."

Amber bowed her head gravely, "Demons are very powerful and can read minds. All information that could aid their cause must be guarded."

"What about you?" challenged Sigfried. "You know it."

"That's right," said Lucky. "Do demons look into your head?"

"Do they need a torch for that?" asked Siggy, "And by torch, I mean flashlight, not a flamey thing. That would set your head on fire. Or is that how you produce your eyebeams?"

"I could set her head on fire," offered Lucky, helpfully. "I mean, if she wanted."

Amber replied seriously. "I have been taught Atlantean mental techniques by the fighting monks of Mt. Shu to protect my mind, though I am not as adept at it as my master, Chianglong."

Laurel murmured, "I'm impressed. Siggy failed to derail her."

Peter crossed his arms sternly. "Where have you been all this time? I don't mean what secret base. I mean, in general, what happened to you?"

"Yes!" Laurel chimed in. "Tell us more about yourself."

"I grew up in a barracks with my ninety-nine brothers," Amber swallowed, as if to dislodge a lump in her throat. "In addition to our military training, I was, as I mentioned, personally trained by Master Chianglong, who is a disciple of Mount Shu, in both their mystic and their fighting techniques. Master Chianglong emphasized calmness, concentration, and fortitude."

"So, a martial artist?" asked Gaius.

Amber nodded. She turned to Sigfried: "You look a little bit like someone I know."

"Who?" asked Siggy.

"The General. Another one of my emperor's Twelve."

"I wonder if the two of them could be related," Rachel said.

"Can robots have relations?" Turning to Amber, Siggy asked curiously, "Was he made by the Emperor of All Things, too?"

"Is that a religious question?" Amber asked dismissively. "I am not a practitioner of angel magic."

"Angel magic?" Rachel leaned forward.

"My emperor believes angel magic to be unreliable."

"Why?" pressed Gaius.

"The previous emperor had an alliance with the angels. During the second war against our current enemies, in the middle of a battle, they deserted. Without a word."

Rachel did not know what to make of that.

Gaius asked, "It sounds as if you have active duties. How long will you be staying here?"

"I came to answer the question of what power tried to draw me here. Once I know, I will return to my duties as one of the Twelve."

"Duties? Didn't you grow up without a family?" asked Sigfried, who was scowling. "Aren't you overjoyed to finally meet your family? Don't you want to stay here with them?"

A crack appeared in Amber's utter calm; she seemed almost offended. "Of course, I had a family. I already mentioned my ninety-nine brothers, who..." her voice caught slightly, "... who helped me carry out my destiny. Every necessary effort was made. Many other people made great sacrifices as well, not just the Griffin family."

"But those were not your real family," Sigfried insisted. "Don't you care about your real family?"

"They *were* my real family," Amber's voice was even, but her eyes flashed. "Closer than family. Biological connections are insignificant in comparison."

"Blood is thicker than all other connections," Sigfried replied fiercely.

Amber did not move, but her expression became more set.

Rachel took Sigfried's arm. "Siggy, I know how you feel about family, but Amber has just met us. She hasn't had a chance to get to know us yet. Why don't you and I go off and enjoy the ball and give Peter and Laurel a chance to get to know our sister, so she can have more evidence to make a judgment on the matter."

Sigfried shook her off. "It's not a matter that can be debated. Family is not a random group of people you happen to hang out with. Only those you are related to are your family."

"I thought you were my sister's blood-brother, and you used the same term for your dragon. Are your connections to them unimportant?" asked Amber.

"Lucky is my brother. I hatched him from an egg," replied Siggy. "But you were hatched... er, born... from Rachel's mother. Don't you owe her a greater duty than the man who stole you from her?"

"Sigfried...." Rachel began.

"It's all right," Amber interrupted, holding up a hand as if to signal that the interview was at a close. "I need to return to my duties guarding Nastasia."

"Wait! Before you go!" Laurel stepped forward and hugged her.

Rachel hesitated, shocked. It had not even occurred to her to brave such familiarities. She dashed forward and hugged her new sister, too. If Amber struck Laurel down for her impertinence, Rachel would not let her fall alone. She was surprised to discover Amber wore form-fitting chain mail under her robe, which made hugging her less satisfying.

Amber endured this. When Laurel and Rachel let go, she stated stiffly, "It was nice to have met you all." With that, she turned and walked away.

As soon as Amber was halfway across the ballroom—hopefully, even her new sister could not hear that far—Rachel burst out, sputtering, "Guarding Nastasia! The princess doesn't need guarding on the dance floor! How...."

Gaius laid a calming hand on Rachel's arm, but Siggy was growling in anger.

"How dare she ignore her own family," cried Sigfried, "after you went out of your way to welcome her! We should go beat her up."

"I could eat her head," Lucky offered, "or at least light her hair on fire."

"I can't attack her. She's my sister," Rachel sighed. "Besides, she would vaporize us with her eye beams. She could vaporize all of us. We would be nothing but vapor."

Lucky nodded sadly. "You would be a Vapor Rachel."

"Then you would be a ghost, and ghosts are even scarier. Ghosts are the only scary thing there is," replied Sigfried. "You could terrify her as Vapor Rachel."

"Sadly, or perhaps for the best," Rachel replied, "I don't think Amber is the kind to be afraid of Vapor Rachel."

Gaius shook his head with mock sadness. "Poor, poor Vapor Rachel."

Chapter Twenty-Five: Dancing with Dread

Rachel and Gaius returned to the dance floor, waltzing around the room to the romantic strains of Tchaikovsky's "Sleeping Beauty Waltz." At first, they danced, just looking at each other, both wide-eyed with a mixture of relief and wonder, too overwhelmed by all that they had avoided or learned to speak.

Then, Gaius leaned toward Rachel and whispered in her ear, "Your sister knows… a great deal. She knows about…." He looked nervously over his shoulder. "Never mind about that. Um, she knows about how worlds are regulated. Did she mean that this emperor regulates them? Or did she mean that the worlds are controlled by the constellations, in the sense that the tides are controlled by gravity?"

"I don't know." Rachel was quiet for a moment. "The whole thing is so amazing and yet I…." She glanced over her shoulder, trying to assure herself that Amber was far enough away. Lowering her voice until it barely audible, she whispered, "I dare not say too much now, but it's all wonderful. And terrifying." She perked up. "Maybe we could ask Nastasia to ask her!" Then she sighed. "Though, somehow, I doubt she'd share what she found out with us."

Gaius squeezed her hand. For a time, they were both silent, wanting to say so much but not knowing what might be unwise to voice.

Finally, as the end of the dance approached, Gaius mused, "Yes, the princess is a problem. Yes, your sister is not what we expected. Yes, the Master of the World is going to have to be dealt with. But we can handle all this. It's better to know your sister exists than not. It gives us a place to start. And your parents, your father's memory…. We can figure that out, too. I have no doubt whatsoever we can do this."

Some of the weight oppressing Rachel's spirit lifted. Much cheered, she smiled up at her boyfriend gratefully. Gaius's ability to lift her spirits was one reason she liked him so much.

Rachel reached up and gratefully touched his cheek. "If I haven't said how much I appreciate you recently, I just want you to know that I doubt I could have gotten through these last six months without you. You make everything crazy inside of me go all calm."

"Happy to help, milady," he replied graciously. "Happy to help."

She danced with Gaius twice in a row, grateful for his comforting presence, and then, for the next dance, yielded him to little Magdalene Chase, who looked adorable dressed as her fetch, the China doll. She had the little porcelain-faced doll in tow. It was dressed in a tiny black academic robe with a tiny mortarboard cap. Gaius kindly arranged them so that he waltzed with both of their hands in his. It made dancing awkward, but Magdalene could not have been more pleased.

Rachel headed to the refreshments table near the musicians for a glass of punch. The other table, near the door, sold champagne for college students and offered a supply of temperance charms, made by the alchemy students, that protected the wearer from becoming more than tipsy. The nearer table offered a spread of food as well as a giant crystal punch bowl with a glass scoop for serving oneself and stacks of glasses. She tried a pastry, which turned out to be crisp and sweet.

Sipping the fizzy punch, she gazed out over the ball, drinking in the red lanterns, the lilting music, the bright costumes and gorgeous gowns. It was enjoyable just to watch the dancers, watching pirates dance with pumpkins and fairy princesses dance with living versions of famous works of art. The whole affair was so splendid that Rachel's anxiety over the troubles of her family began to slip into the background. She knew they were still there, like a dark shadow one could not make out on a cloudy day, but she deliberately turned her attention to the present.

Farther off, Jenny Dare waltzed by with the creepy, intense Abraham Van Helsing, captain of the Dare Hall Vampire Hunters Club, who had come in his vampire-hunting leathers. Jenny wore a dress that was half sparkling black satin and half thin air. Like her bathing suit, it was demure in front but cut very low in the back, with large diamond-shaped openings exposing bare skin on the side. She looked very sultry with her long black gloves and her high boots. In one hand, she carried a long black cigarette holder, much like Laurel's, except Jenny's was empty. Rachel could see it poking up from behind Van Helsing's shoulder as they danced.

Rachel had only recently added Jenny to her list of admirable upperclassmen girls, but she still felt uneasy about her. The laughing young woman seemed fascinating, and Sandra liked her, which was a big point in her favor, but Rachel feared that her family's dissembling tricks might not work on Jenny, which terrified her. What might Jenny have already noticed about Rachel that she would prefer nobody ever discover?

As Rachel drained her glass, she noted that in true Magical Australian fashion, Nastasia's brother, Alex Romanov, had come dressed as an emu. To one side, near a small table, his twin, the newly-engaged Alexis—who was dressed as the fairy Lady Cobweb, in an ethereal gown that practically looked like woven cobwebs with pearls caught like drops of water in among the lacy cloth—sat in a chair, watching the dancing wistfully and looking bored. Rachel wondered why Alexis's new fiancé, Wulfgang's older brother Romulus, was not dancing with her.

From the dais where the tutors played came the sweet strains of "The Skater's Waltz." Rachel's heart leapt. Even though it had only been two songs since they had last danced together, she looked eagerly for Gaius, hoping against hope that he would remember, from the Dead Man's Ball, that this was her favorite waltz. Even as she did so, she chided herself. She knew enough to know that girls wanted boys to remember this sort of trivia, and boys never did.

Her level-headed cynicism was countered by her discomfort at the very idea of forgetting—especially forgetting something so important to her.

Only he did remember!

Gaius was a most gallant boyfriend.

From across the ballroom, he caught her eye and grinned. Then he winced and made a kind of apologetic gesture with his head to his left. Beside him, waiting for the next dance to start, stood Colleen MacDannan, the red-haired cousin of Ian and Oonagh who was hopelessly in love with Gaius. She was dressed as a fox with a fox-eared headband, a furry, rust-colored dress that matched her hair, and a fluffy, white-tipped tail. Gaius threw Rachel an apologetic sorry-I-already-asked-her shrug and took his position to wait out the waltz's long introduction.

Rachel sighed and let her eyes roam over the ballroom. Surely, there must be someone….

She froze, her heart simultaneously leaping and skipping a beat. A familiar figure stood in the doorway of the ballroom, lit by the light of the hall beyond, a tall figure wearing a cloak of black swan feathers.

Vlad.

A longing overcame her so powerful that it was as if there were no room left within her for any other thought or emotion. She wanted to dance with him. Just once. Just tonight, during this marvelous, magical masquerade.

But it would not occur. Heavily sought-after college juniors with two entire competing bevies of older girls devoted to dancing with them did not dance with little freshmen girls, no matter how much they might admire her older sister. These things did not happen. There was such a queue of young women waiting, Dread would be lucky if he had a single dance free to breathe before the night was over. Rachel sighed and began looking about again. There must be *somebody* she could dance with for this, her favorite waltz.

A dozen young women — some in clever costume, others in lovely gowns—swarmed around the doorway, smiling at Dread. He brushed past them without so much as a glance, heading into the midst of the dancing, and he was looking directly at Rachel.

In half a dozen strides, Vladimir Von Dread crossed the ballroom and stood before her, offering his hand. Rachel swallowed, unable to breathe. She stood transfixed for the space of half a breath. He looked so handsome, like some Germanic god, she feared her heart would fail altogether.

Then her heartbeat grew steady, and she found she could breathe again. Of course, he had come directly to her. He wanted to meet her new sister and get a chance to worm out of Amber the secrets of the greater universe. She slipped her hand into his and walked beside him, ready to perform the required introductions. Maybe, if she did so particularly quickly, she could still find a partner for the second half of "The Skater's Waltz."

Only Vlad did not walk toward where Amber stood attentively beside Nastasia, who was speaking animatedly with her brother Alex. Instead, he led her to the dance floor. Holding her right hand in his left, he slipped his other arm behind her, his fingers lightly supporting her upper back. Thankfully, years of dancing lessons took over as she was too frightened to think. She laid her free hand on his armored bicep, beneath the cloak, and waited, her body as taut as a violin string.

Then the song's introduction finished, and they began to waltz.

It was like dancing in a dream.

Von Dread stood very straight as he twirled her round—his hand firm against her back—without coming near any of the other dancers, even the bad ones who tended to be unpredictable. His cloak of swan feathers floated around him like a dark cloud. Beneath it, he wore his armor, which was darker than midnight. He had not worn his winged helmet or even his customary dueling gloves. His hand, clasping hers, was strong and yet gentle, with fencer's calluses. He glanced slightly to the left and right as he moved, alert to the other dancers, but otherwise gazed down at Rachel, a slight smile gracing his lips.

He was dancing with her. For her favorite waltz. It had really happened.

Could one die of happiness?

She might be about to find out.

Rachel spun across the floor to the strains of her favorite waltz, enjoying being so close to him. She was glad that he did not treat her as a small child or offer to let her stand on his feet, or any other rubbish that adults often did. Rather, he danced with her as if she were a proper lady. That was one of the first things she had come to like about Vlad, before she had discovered the many other qualities she admired. He was the only "big person" she knew who had never talked down to her.

Her heart seemed to beat in time with the music, so loudly that she was almost surprised he did not object. She tried very hard to tell herself that the extraordinarily powerful emotions churning within her were hero-worship, future-sisterly affection, and that maybe she had not fallen completely head-over-heels in love with her sister's future husband. Surely, the flutterings in her heart were just a silly school girl crush. Staunchly, she resolved to wall out this assault on her devotion to her most deserving boyfriend.

She pulled her thoughts away from the wonder of the dance and began to speak, catching him up on all that had occurred that day: Xandra and her voices, Amber and the redcap, the conversation between Amber and the rest of their family. She spoke to him over his bracelet, so that she hardly even had to whisper, and he could still hear every word clearly in his ear. She faced him directly as she talked—her head ducked just a little so that no one but Vlad could see her lips move—just in case her sister could lip read. Vlad listened with complete concentration, his gaze trained on her face.

At one point as they spun and spoke of Amber, Rachel glanced at Nastasia's bodyguard out of the corner of her eye. For the first time, her sister was not standing motionlessly and expressionlessly. Instead, Amber had pushed back her hood and stood watching Rachel dance. She seemed slightly sad, and she shifted a bit on her feet, as if swaying to the music. A few twirls of the dance later, however, when Rachel caught sight of her, Amber had raised her hood, and she again was completely still. When the waltz ended, Vladimir remained where they were, in the center of the floor—still holding her right hand with his other hand resting against her back. He neither released her nor ceased to attend to her words. Rachel continued to speak of all that had occurred. The thrill of sharing secrets—especially with the one person in her life who most appreciated hearing them—enthralled her even more than the dancing and music. An audience of this caliber, who cared about the information she had carefully gathered and might put it to a good use, was precisely what the girl-who-wanted-to-know-everything dreamt of and what made her efforts worthwhile.

He remained standing, listening, through the entire pause in the music and the introduction for the next piece, which was appropriately "The Emperor Waltz." When the dance started, he began to waltz again, still listening carefully. When she mentioned Amber's extraordinary hearing, he murmured a quiet order to his subordinates to speak of any sensitive matter only over the black bracelets and, even then, not to assume that communications were secure.

When Rachel finally finished reciting all that had occurred, the second waltz was still playing. Reluctantly, as she wished the dance would never end, she gestured with her head toward where Amber stood in her dark hood.

"Would you like to meet her now? My sister?"

"She can wait." Vladimir gazed down at Rachel, his eyes dark and intense and focused upon only her. "I am enjoying my chance to dance with my future sister-in-law."

Rachel's lips parted. A fracture formed in the hastily-constructed wall around her heart, spreading like a fissure through ice. The emotions inside her grew too great to be named, too great to be masked. She gazed up at his face, her eyes shining with adoration. She did not speak again but waltzed, safe in the circle of his arms.

He was dancing with her, just with her, and it was glorious. Most glorious of all, Vladimir seemed happy. *He was happy to be dancing with her.*

Nothing more wonderful was even imaginable.

As the second waltz ended, he bowed over her hand and said. "I should meet your new older sister. This should be... interesting."

Rachel, eyes still alight, led him across the ballroom to meet Amber. He strode beside her, cool and impassive. Amber looked up and regarded him calmly. He in turn studied her face. Then he walked around her, examining her. She stood just a tiny bit straighter.

"Amber, I am Prince Vladimir Von Dread," he stated. "It is a pleasure to meet you."

"Your Highness." She bowed to him from the waist about forty-five degrees.

"Even I, who know not to judge someone from their size, am given pause by you. Tell me, little tiger, how many campaigns have you taken part in?"

Amber opened her mouth and then closed it. "I cannot disclose such information, sir."

A shiver went through Rachel. Up until this moment, she had felt utterly safe with Vlad. It was one of the joys of being in his presence. It suddenly occurred to her, however, that Amber, with her demon-killing powers, was far more powerful that Vladimir. If she were to attack, there would be nothing Vlad could do to protect her. In addition to the frisson of fear that ran through her, the thought made her a bit sad.

Dread nodded, "Very well. Can you tell me who your commanding officer is?"

Amber straightened. "I am one of The Twelve. I serve my emperor."

He crossed his arms. "Of the Twelve, is there a commander? Are you all equals? How is it decided who joins this group? Why were you chosen?"

"I will not answer any other questions about our military and its composition, our recruiting strategies or training. My apologies, sir."

It broke Rachel's heart to see the girl, whom she had so hoped she could rescue, turn out to be so distant. She longed to break through to Amber, to reach her heart. At the very least, she wished Amber to understand how important Vlad was, that he was not just another stranger.

She stepped forward. "Vlad is going to marry our sister Sandra, once they work things out with Father. He's going to be our brother-in-law."

Dread raised an eyebrow, a slight smile at his lips. "Thank you, Miss Griffin." Turning back to Amber, he asked, "Will you be able to come to the wedding? How would we send you an invitation, should you wish to join us?"

"The princess's father can contact my emperor," Amber replied. "I cannot promise I will be available." She paused. "I... will try to come. If I can."

"You should definitely come," Rachel insisted.

Amber's brow slightly furrowed. "Did you say Vladimir Von Dread? That's an... interesting name."

"It has been in our family for generations."

"So, no relation to...."

"To whom?" Rachel leaned forward with interest.

"There was a king by that name, in the greater world, a conqueror."

"What did he look like?" Rachel asked curiously. "Did he look anything like Vlad?"

She figured it was a safe question, since Amber had said that it was normal for people in different worlds to resemble each other.

Amber shook her head. "Nobody knows. He only ever appeared as a black suit of armor with a winged helm. To my knowledge, no one ever saw his face."

"What was his character?" Von Dread asked casually, running a hand over his black hair with its red highlights. Rachel wondered if he was glad that he had not worn his helmet.

"He was violent and vicious and a formidable enemy, though he was known for protecting the poor and the needy."

"An admirable quality," stated Vlad.

"Perhaps, but he was not kind to anyone else."

Rachel sucked her bottom lip between her teeth and bit it lightly. She wanted to ask more questions about the Dread King, to inquire about other Outsiders here at the school, but she was afraid of drawing attention where she should not. She would have loved to ask if her sister had ever heard of Cassandra March, since Jariel had indicated that there was some relationship between the Grand Inquisitor's wife and Rachel's family but would not answer any additional questions on the subject. She recalled, however, the voice, speaking through Xandra Black, that had asked them to hide Cassandra's daughter Eve from the Outside forces that were hunting her and how Jariel, too, had implied that Evelyn March deserved protecting.

She remained silent.

Gaius came by to collect her for the next dance. Rachel said good-bye to Amber, leaving her still speaking with Dread. Gaius peppered her with questions about the meeting between her new sister and his boss. Rachel answered him by repeating the entire conversation back to him over the black bracelets, including everyone's voice intonations, which Gaius declared to be both disturbing and amusing.

CHAPTER TWENTY-SIX:
TARNISHED KNIGHTS
AND CRAZY KINGS

For the next two hours, Rachel danced and danced and danced.

The specter of her long-missing sister haunted her every step. Despite this, she strove to live up to her promise to herself that she would not let this put a damper on her enjoyment of her first masquerade ball.

A part of her heart felt as if it were bleeding out her life blood, and yet, in a strange way, this secret grief heightened her experience, making her joys more intense due to the depth of her sorrow. Her hidden heartbreak added a strange sparkle to the evening, which she could see reflected in the eyes of her partners. It was as if a special bond were forged between her and each young man, an unbreakable bond because she knew that for the rest of her life, this evening would come to mind each time she spoke to one of them.

She waltzed with friends, with strangers, with boys she knew from the Knights of Walpurgis, and with boys she knew from class. When they played a polka, she danced with Sigfried, which may have been a mistake, as polkas were the runaway horses of the dance world, and Sigfried was the least-restrained boy she knew. He rocketed her around the floor and nearly careened her into the furniture. Still, it was great fun.

Occasionally, they played a swing tune. Rachel had the opportunity to dance two of these with Gaius. She was delighted to discover that he was better at swing than he was at waltzing, and he knew several snazzy moves, such as the pretzel and the overhead slide. Both times, by the end, she was panting and laughing. Both times, he dipped her.

Rachel waltzed with some young men from her own class: David Jordan, Enoch Smithwyck, Jarius Knight—now the only boy in Dee Hall, as his dorm mates, Juma O'Malley and Mortimer Egg, Jr., had both left school after their parents were arrested. She danced with Siggy's friend, Seth Peregrine, who looked quite authentic as one of the fairy king Finvarra's hurling players. All of them inquired about Nastasia's new bodyguard.

Remington Blake, the goofy young man from Marlowe whom Hildy's friend Rowan Vanderdecken fancied, bowed before her and requested a dance. He looked splendid dressed as one of Odin's Einherjar. He complimented her on her cat ears. When she gave all credit to Jenny Dare, he looked impressed. Apparently, Jenny was much admired among the freshman boys.

She danced with William Locke, who was dressed as a mad scientist, and Topher Evans, who had come as a superhero, clad in blue spandex. As she spun around the ballroom, she kept an eye out for Michael Cameron but could not find him. Of course, there were numerous costumes such as the big chess piece or the giant crystal ball —which didn't even have arms, just legs. It was dancing off to one side by itself—that entirely covered the wearer; so Michael could be here, and she would never know it.

She talked the blind boy, Hod Odinson, into standing up with her. She found him sitting alone against the wall. He explained he liked to dance but the floor was too crowded for him to safely negotiate; so she made a circle of chairs to one side to give them a safe place and waltzed with him quietly, away from the madding crowds.

After that, she danced with the Drake brothers, Solon and Solomon, the sons of a famous judge. The two brothers, though young —Solon was in Rachel's class and Solomon was but two years older —were universally acknowledged to have the best knowledge of the Original Tongue of anyone on campus, tutors included.

Next she sought out the Powers twins, first Sebastian and then Napoleon, and their older brother, Nicodemus—their father represented South America at the Parliament of the Wise. All three boys asked her difficult questions about why her friend was suddenly accompanied by a servant, questions that made Rachel grind her teeth, especially when she felt honor bound to defend the princess from some particularly choice phrases. Nicodemus mentioned that he had asked Nastasia directly, but she had stonewalled him. He clearly thought her behavior had been impolite.

Occasionally, as she waltzed, she caught Gaius's gaze across the floor. When it happened, she smiled, and he winked back. Gaius was always dancing, always cordial to his partner. He danced primarily with girls from Drake Hall: the sarcastic Tessa Dauntless, who so obviously had a crush on him; Molly Bannerman, the granddaughter of the man whose abandoned mansion had housed the Dead Men's Ball; Samantha Streiga, the girl with a scarred throat whose brother had tried to kill Joy. He also danced with some girls of his acquaintance who were not from Drake. Rachel recognized Jenny Dare, Xandra Black, and two of Joy's sisters.

His casual charm had all his partners laughing. The mean girls whom Rachel despised, such as Belladonna Marley, Charybdis Nutt, and Zenobia Jones, were transformed by his attentions until their happy faces almost looked like normal people. Even Lola Spong— the ugly sophomore who, along with Cydney Graves, had attacked Rachel during the first week of school—looked so cheerful dancing with Gaius that her toadlike features almost appeared pleasant.

Still, Rachel was very pleased to note that while Gaius was outgoing and chivalrous to each of these young ladies, he did not share with them that special, admiring look he had in his eye when he was with her. It made her happy to see him spreading cheer among other girls, so long as there was a special part of him that belonged only to her.

She danced with Gaius again. As they spun about, Rachel had an epiphany. Mr. Chanson had only said that she could not fly her broom in and out of windows. He had not said that she was forbidden to fly to the roof. People flew to the roof all the time. So what was to stop Rachel and Gaius from flying to the roof and then slipping into her secret room? True, the windows would be above her head if she were standing on the roof, but Gaius could lift her up. Then they could snuggle together on the couch, maybe even fall asleep. The idea that had come to her, first while they were tracking the water horse and then more strongly as she sat alone in the steam bath—of curling up next to him, just sleeping, nothing inappropriate—seemed more and more appealing. Things had been so wild, so disturbing, in her life of late. It would be a great comfort to have someone steady hold her for a bit.

A little voice in the back of her mind, that sounded suspiciously like Amelia, Lady Devon, asked if doing such a thing would *be safe?* Her grandmother had hammered home so completely the dangers young men posed that, even though Rachel trusted Gaius, she still felt cautious. Boys were dangerous, even good boys. She did not want to sneak off with him if he was going to take it as license to try things they had not done before. She just wanted to curl up with her head on his chest. She did not even want to snog; well, not really. There was always an underlying desire to snog nowadays, a huge cry from where she had started in September when the very idea terrified her. In this case, however, that was not what she had in mind.

She thought about Gaius, how calm and steady he was, how little he had pushed her in the past. He had never forced her to do anything. She was pretty sure that, even if they sneaked off together for a little while, she could trust him not to act inappropriately.

When that dance ended, however, she had still not yet found the courage to suggest that they slip off to the roof.

After that, Rachel managed to convince her favorite proctor, Mr. Fuentes, to dance with her, though he was attending the ball in his official capacity as a chaperone. He looked quite athletic in his maroon and white flying polo jersey and his black domino mask. They chatted about the wide variety of costumes at the ball and about the exploits of her sister Sandra. It made Rachel feel quite grown up to be dancing with a proctor, especially such a charming, handsome one. She basked in the admiration of other girls as they twirled by.

"Did you always want to be an Agent?" she asked him as they danced, recalling that he had told her that he was working as a proctor in hopes of eventually being accepted into the Wisecraft.

Carlos Fuentes shook his head. "Nah, I wanted to be a flying polo player when I was young—closest thing to the street hockey I played as a kid. I worked at it really hard, too. I don't like to toot my own horn, but I was one of the best broom jockeys to ever graduate from

Roanoke. I won a few serious races. Came in second at the Internationals once. Even got into the minor leagues—which is quite a feat for a kid who went to a college that didn't field an intercollegiate team." He flashed her a dazzling grin. "I was on a team called the Flying Pegasi, which feeds into the Windcolts. Had a good shot at the big leagues, too," he ended wistfully.

"Which is why the Windcolts are your favorite professional team," she smiled at him. "What happened?"

"Big race. Another racer lost control of his broom. I could have piled forward and knocked him out of the way pretty easily, but he would have been seriously hurt. Instead, I swerved—into a wall. I was seriously injured. Even the nuns of Asclepius had trouble putting my shoulder back together." He rotated his shoulder and winced slightly. "Still bothers me, sometimes."

"So you gave up?"

"Me? Nah," he laughed. "I'm made of sterner stuff than that. But, while I was in the hospital, someone gave me a huge pile of *James Darling, Agent* comics. As I read about his fight against the Terrible Five, I started thinking that maybe there was something more important I could do with my life than just play ball. I came back here and made a deal with Mr. Badger that if I worked as a proctor, a couple of the tutors would give me private instruction to fill in the areas that Agents usually study that I hadn't bothered with, back in my jock days. And here I am."

"That's quite impressive, Mr. Fuentes," Rachel replied sincerely.

As the music came to an end, he bowed and she curtsied. She started to turn away, but Mr. Fuentes called her back.

"Miss Griffin. You're friends with the youngest Romanov girl, right?" He did that thing men do that perfectly combined a smile and a scowl. It made him look even more handsome. "You might want to let her know that her new bodyguard is causing all sorts of headaches." His expression deepened into a true scowl. "Roanoke really isn't the place to bring your servants."

Servant again. Rachel felt the blood drain from her face, but she merely murmured, "Headaches?"

"She's only had that person following her around for a few hours now, but there has already been a constant stream of visitors coming by the dean's office to complain."

"Complain… about personal servants on Roanoke grounds?" Rachel asked.

"A few, maybe." He shrugged. "Mostly it's been people demanding that if she gets servants, why can't they? So far, we've had," he counted them off on his fingers, "the Countess Grimaldi; a couple of Starkadder princes; that Moravian archduchess; the Irish girl, Lady Lacy Farnsworth; Miss Pamela Jorden-Foxx—think she's an earl's daughter; the Rothschild kid; the Ishizuka brothers; one of Chancellor Ko's daughters; the Schmitt triplets; and two of the three Powers boys. That's fifteen people, and this is just the first day! I think if anyone else asks, poor Dean Moth is gonna lose it. Heck, practically the only person with royal blood who hasn't come by is Dread." His expression betrayed his low opinion of the Crown Prince of Bavaria.

"I… will let her know." Rachel curtsied again, pleased to hear that Vlad was above such things. "Thank you for your concern."

"Hey, I figured the girl should know that trouble is brewing." He grinned his handsomest, causing her knees to go just a little weak. "You take care of yourself."

The only dance that went awry was with Kitten's middle brother, Robert, whom everyone called Bobcat. He was a cheerful young man, slender and dark-haired, a year older than Kitten, who had come to the dance in the helmet and breastplate of a knight. He seemed quite good-hearted but had a bit of a bad reputation. Things went wrong when he was around. Whenever a lab station burst into flame or all the ingredients on a top shelf in the Warding Tower fell to the ground, spreading flour and pepper everywhere and causing a fit of sneezing, Bobcat Fabian was somewhere nearby. Whether he instigated these events or whether he was just accident-prone, nobody seemed to know, but Siggy looked up to him as an inspiration.

As they stepped onto the floor, another couple—who did not understand the difference between an introduction and the dance *propre* —nearly careened into them. Bobcat's response was shockingly rude. In her memory, Rachel could hear her grandmother's imperious voice snapping out, "Language!" but Rachel settled for something a bit subtler.

Pantomiming the action of rubbing a cloth against the side of his helmet, she intoned, "A bit of tarnish there on your shining armor, sir knight."

Bobcat laughed. "I love knights, but, it's just a costume. No knightly derring-do needed at a ball."

"On the contrary," Rachel replied regally, in a tone that would have earned even her grandmother's approval, "a ball is an ideal place for chivalry. What about all the wallflowers in need of partners?"

"Wallflowers are often...."

"There's more to life than a pretty face," Rachel interrupted tartly.

"I was going to say 'bad dancers,'" he replied, grinning.

Then, the dance began, and Rachel forgave him, because anyone who danced this divinely would not want to waste his time on beginners.

Dancing the "Gold and Silver Waltz" with Bobcat was great fun. He waltzed so excellently that they attempted a Viennese waltz, which required more precision as it was danced at twice the speed of the regular waltz. Everything went well, until they spun around a particularly tight turn and had to duck quickly to the left to avoid Lola Spong and Arcturus Steele, who were careening around the floor in an almost drunken fashion. Avoiding the troublemakers from Drake Hall, they slammed bodily into the pompous and imperious Romulus Starkadder, who was currently dancing with the prince-hunting Countess Jasmine Grimaldi. The older students were not happy with the youngsters, who grabbed hands and ran, screaming, across the ballroom until they were far, far away from the scowling visages of the wrathful college students.

Once safely away, they both dissolved into laughter.

Next, she danced with her brother's best friend, with whom he shared a first name. Peter Komarek wore a skin-tight red, white, and blue garment with a big A on his chest. Over one arm, he carried a round shield. When Rachel asked if he was a knight like her brother, Peter K. laughed and said that it was similar, but American instead of British.

Salome's boyfriend, Ethan Warhol, asked her to dance. Then he spent the entire waltz trying to catch her unawares and stomp on her feet. Still, she did not mind as she credited her training from duel-ing with him for the reflexes that had allowed her to save Laurel from falling under the *each-uisge.* A living sister was worth an occasional sore toe, though she did quite well at avoiding his feet. After that, she danced with his best friend, Carl Iscariot, a surprisingly normal young man, considering the wildness of his younger sister. He was dressed as Hendrick Vanderdecken, captain of the Flying Dutchman, with lace at his collar and an ostrich plume in his broad-brimmed cavalier's hat.

"You look quite dashing tonight, Younger Mr. Iscariot." Rachel smiled as they danced to spirited strains of "Danse Macabre," which she thought a rather odd choice for a ball. "Are you having a nice evening?"

He smiled down at her. "Why, yes, Miss Griffin, I'm having a great time. Besides the constant embarrassment of my sister Salome, that is. But, having a friend like Ethan Warhol, I get used to it. How about you? It looks like exciting things are afoot for the Griffins...." He glanced over at Amber.

Alarm bells rang in Rachel's head, but she tried to deflect the question with obtuse cheer.

"Yes," she chirped. "Isn't it delightful? Nastasia's bodyguard is also part Korean and part English. We think we may have some rela-tives in common. Probably named Kim."

He looked skeptical. "Relatives in common? Like, I don't know, *your parents?* Seriously, are you saying she's not your sister? I thought she *was you.* She's a little more, uh, a little kinda, uh... She's different. Than you. But she's definitely your sister. Or I'm the King of Crazy Town."

"Towns don't usually have kings. I believe they have mayors," Rachel replied blithely.

She glanced at Amber again. It was hard to tell, since her sister was draped from head to toe in a robe, but Rachel was reasonably sure that Amber was curvier than she was. She was also reasonably sure that this was what Carl Iscariot meant by "different." She fought the desire to pout.

"She does look like a cross between my mother and me," Rachel allowed, "but then I have a cousin named Lily who's practically a twin for Mummy, only... smaller."

"If you say so," Carl shrugged, changing the subject. "Anyway, I am pushing for Gaius to take over the Knights. He's a good guy. Ethan's on board, too. And probably Salome. Probably."

"Me, too, of course," Rachel said quickly. "And Siggy. And Dread and his team. Problem is: his opponent for the second-in-command position, Freka, is currently running on the platform of 'Keep the Knights exactly as they are,' which is a hard platform for Gaius to beat—since he rather represents the same thing, being the protégé of the current leader."

"Good point." Carl gave that some thought as they swirled around the brightly-lit ballroom. "Maybe Gaius should propose something new."

"Something new?" Rachel's eyes widened, taken aback. "Um. What?"

"I don't know. He'd have to think of something."

"Well, I can suggest it to him."

Carl grinned. "You do that."

"Hello, Rachel, want to join us?" Kris Serenity Wright called, peering out from the dragon-head of her red and gold Lucky the Dragon costume. "We're opening red envelopes."

Rachel turned to find a number of her friends sitting together on the ubiquitous straight-backed chairs, which they had pulled into a semicircle. With Kris were her two roommates and also Astrid, Kitten, and Joy.

"What are we doing?" Rachel asked, bending down to hear better over the strains of a waltz called "Wine, Women and Song."

"The red envelopes," said Rhiannon, who had come dressed as the phoenix that was the familiar of Kitten's older brother, Squirrel. "They have some kind of money in them."

"It says they're Roanoke Bucks." Hekpa was rather plain, unlike many of the other girls at the school, but she looked quite lovely in her iridescent red and blue dragon outfit, representing the tiny shoulder-dragon who was the familiar of senior, Norse god look-alike, Donner Virgil. "Good for use at the café, bookstore, or the Alchemical Shoppe."

She held up an ornate lavender and green bill showing the dean's smiling face. Eagerly, the girls pulled the envelopes off the orange tree, pocketing the bills. Rachel took a single red envelope from one of the pleasant-smelling boughs and sat down. Astrid sat down beside her, smiling with delight as she pulled out a Roanoke Buck of a large denomination. Astrid gave a happy little laugh and hugged the red envelope to her chest.

"You seem happy," Rachel said. "Do you have a plan for it?"

Astrid nodded shyly. "I dropped my history manual in the reflecting lake by accident. Some of the pages are stuck together. I couldn't bear the thought of having to use my own money to buy another one. This will just cover it."

"Yes, it will! And you might even have enough left over to buy a rose soda at the café." Rachel glanced at her own envelope. "That's what I intend to do with mine."

"Rose soda? I didn't know they made such a thing. Do you like it?"

"It's heavenly," Rachel assured her.

"I've never actually been to the café," Astrid said. Despite her lab robes and pen protectors, she was wearing teardrop pearl earrings and a touch of peach lipstick. It should have made her look more sophisticated, but instead it made her look delicate and vulnerable. "I mean, I've seen it when I check my mail, but I've never eaten there."

"What? That is an outrage against Roanoke culture," Rachel replied, grinning. "You must come. I will treat you to a rose soda."

"With the largess of your New Year's money?" Astrid gestured expansively in the direction of Rachel's red envelope.

Rachel's eyes twinkled. "I plan to live dangerously and spend it all in one place."

The two girls laughed.

Suddenly, Astrid leaned forward, her elbows on her knees, and gazed directly at Rachel with her dark, doe-like eyes. "Rachel, that woman following our roommate around: Where is she going to sleep? Are we supposed to put her up in our room?"

Rachel hadn't thought about that. "I... don't know."

"Nastasia hasn't confided in you? I thought the two of you shared everything."

Rachel sighed. "Not everything."

Astrid lowered her voice. "I think life at school is very difficult for our princess. She's been trained to keep her thoughts and feelings to herself. That doesn't mix well with life at Roanoke. It must be very hard to see everyone else having fun and feel too well-bred to join them. I wonder if that is why her family sent this person."

"You may be right," Rachel said slowly, glancing at where Nastasia was dancing.

"She's rather like you in that way, isn't she?"

Rachel's head shot up, but Astrid did not seem to be mocking her. Rather, her expression was a mix of kindness and concern.

"What do you mean?" Rachel asked carefully.

"Trying to hide your emotions and keeping your feelings to yourself. It's something the two of you have in common. I figured that was one reason you two are such good friends."

Rachel's mask of calm slid over her face. Astrid was right. It had been their aristocratic upbringing that had drawn Rachel and Nastasia together. It also was part of what kept pushing them apart. They understood each other's struggle, but they both balked at sharing their own.

There was no time to say anything more because the other girls returned.

Kitten was saying, "Hekpa, I saw you dance several times with the elusive and mysterious Fortinbras Thorn, the Boy-Who-Works-Everywhere. Do you like him?"

"Yep," Hekpa answered, smiling.

The others all grinned at her and then at each other and then at her again. Hekpa just kept smiling. Rachel admired her aplomb.

"Oh, that's sweet," said Hekpa, pointing with her elbow. "No one has spoken to that girl all night. Good of your brother, Kitten."

Rachel turned and looked.

In one corner, all alone, her head hanging dejectedly within the beaked hood of her eagle costume, sat Rachel's old rival, Cydney Graves. She had been by herself a great deal this year, ever since Salome had worked her whatever-she-did to convince Cydney to challenge Rachel to a duel during the opening Knights of Walpurgis meeting in September—the same duel for which Rachel still wanted to thank Michael Cameron.

As the girls watched, Bobcat Fabian walked up and bowed before Cydney, holding out his hand in a gesture of invitation. Jerking her head up in surprise, Cydney accepted awkwardly. The two of them then walked to the dance floor, Cydney trembling with a shy joy.

"Good for Bobcat." Kitten gave a little happy sigh. "There might be hope for him yet."

Rachel allowed herself a secret smile.

Gaius found her for yet another swing number. Then she danced Strauss's "Treasure Waltz" with Max Weatherby, the big-chinned boy who was a member of the vampire-hunter's club, and Chopin's "Grande Valse Brillante" with Mr. Fisher's teaching assistant, Varo Varovitch, the Russian college student with a forked beard. At seven feet tall, he towered above her by more than two feet. It made dancing an exciting challenge, especially when he lifted her up around the waist, and her feet were no longer anywhere in the vicinity of the ground. He told her of a recurring dream he had had about a girl who lived behind a waterfall.

Recalling the glimpse of such a person that she had seen once when she was in dreamland with Zoë, Rachel replied, "Did the dream girl look a bit like Wendy Darling?"

Varo gawked at her, amazed, "How came you to know dis thing? She does! But girl in dream does not act like Miss Darling. Miss Darling is," he paused, perhaps searching for an English word, "how shall I say, sophisticated? Dream girl is giddy. Naïve."

"So alike, but not alike," mused Rachel.

Varo raised his head and gazed at something over her shoulder. "*Da*. Same vay you and new girl in cloak look alike, and, yet, not alike at all."

Chapter Twenty-Seven:
The Other Princess
of Magical Australia

Her next partner was Nastasia's eldest brother. Two weeks ago, Rachel had hated Ivan so passionately that she could hardly stand to look at him. Now that she had forgiven him, however, he seemed quite pleasant, almost dear.

The Crown Prince of Magical Australia was over six feet tall with dirty blond hair and dark brown eyes. Tonight, he was dressed as Moth, the fairy progenitor of the most numerous family on the planet. He looked quite dashing in his tight silver stockings, his sparkling waistcoat and voluminous shirt sleeves, his lacy cravat, and his spiky silver wig.

Rachel complimented him on his look, adding, "I am surprised that you did not come as a kangaroo."

"Well, I did consider coming as the noble platypus," Ivan replied cheerfully. "As it is, I must have accidentally chosen an outfit that overlaps some Unwary character. At least three people have asked me if I am dressed as the Goblin King."

"Are they daft?" Rachel looked him over. "You don't look anything like a goblin."

The musicians struck up "The Blue Danube," and Rachel and Ivan waltzed around the ballroom beneath the red lanterns and dragons. Ivan was an excellent dancer. Dancing with him was a true joy. Rachel felt even happier when he complimented her on her footwork. All those dance lessons had been worth it.

"I say," she asked suddenly, as they spun by a different section of the ballroom and her gaze fell on the elder of Ivan's two sisters. "Ivan, would you and Alex go dance with Alexis? She seems to be sitting by herself a great deal. She's been over at that table looking bored every time I've seen her tonight. There's nothing improper about a girl, even an engaged girl, standing up with her own brother."

Ivan sighed. "She's... not dancing with anyone."

"Why not?" Rachel asked, puzzled. "Isn't she at least dancing with her fiancé? Why is she here, all dressed up, if she doesn't want to dance?"

"She did dance with Prince Starkadder." Ivan made a strange face which Rachel, who knew about the trials of the aristocracy, read as I-want-to-scowl-at-my-future-brother-in-law-but-I-am-too-well-bred. "Listen, if you have questions about her, you should address them to her directly. I cannot fathom her crazy princess logic."

Rachel laughed, then her laughter trailed off. "I do not know what she thinks, but I know what I would think if my father declared my sister could not be married until fifty and then sold me to Transylvania at eighteen. I would think I was not as important as some other people."

Ivan opened his mouth and then closed it. He did not say anything else.

Rachel added apologetically, "Maybe she doesn't think that. Nastasia seemed to believe that Alexis was not upset. Your lives are very different from mine. It's hard for me to understand Nastasia. Alexis might be as different from me as she is." Rachel glanced at Alexis Romanov. She still sat alone, looking annoyed and bored. As Nastasia was dancing, her hooded bodyguard stood near Alexis. "At least, Amber's keeping her company. If you can call standing next to someone and doing nothing at all keeping them company."

"I've been to talk to her a number of times," Ivan said. "You could go speak to her."

"I will," Rachel replied quietly. She glanced at the elder princess in her silver and black ball gown and sighed. "She looks so lovely there."

She gave Ivan a very long thoughtful look. Her face was calm, but her eyes filled with sadness. They danced a bit longer. At the end of the dance, she rose to her tiptoes and pulled on his arm until he leaned down. Then she kissed him very lightly on the cheek.

Some students who were watching from the sidelines went, "Awwwwwwww."

Ivan rolled his eyes.

Taking her leave, Rachel stopped at the refreshments table and picked up a pastry. Crossing the room, she presented it to Alexis, who looked utterly lovely in the gossamer sables and silvers of one of Queen Titania's fairy companions.

"Here," Rachel said. Luckily, Alexis had chosen a chair far from the musicians' dais, so it was actually possible to speak and be heard. "I brought you something sweet."

Alexis took the pastry, smiling sweetly. "That's kind. Thank you, Rachel."

She took a bite and then looked out on the dance floor at Romulus Starkadder, where he danced with the Archduchess "Daisy" Kveta Vesela, a svelte blond who was the leader of the group Rachel had mentally dubbed the "Dee Girls," a bevy of prince-hunting girls who were the rivals of Countess Jasmine and her "Drake Girls."

For just a moment, Rachel had the strange impression that Alexis was about to shoot fire out of her eyes or maybe those lines of jagged star-lightning of Amber's. But that was just foolish. Nonetheless, Rachel peered carefully at Romulus' back searching for possible singe marks.

There were no singe marks. Yet.

Rachel sat down beside the elder Princess of Magical Australia. "Why don't you dance with your brothers? No one would murmur against it, even in the most elite of circles."

"No, that's okay," said Alexis. "They are busy. And I am fine sitting here, looking pretty, obeying my intended's orders that I prove, to his satisfaction, that I will be an obedient wife—by sitting for six hours surrounded by music and cheer but dancing with only him— while my betrothed has a wonderful time waltzing with whomever he wishes. I do care for him so. I am really looking forward to marrying him and having babies." She spoke with a completely straight face, though there was a slight twitch in her jaw.

Rachel gazed out at Romulus and imagined what choice words Amelia, Lady Devon might have shared upon the subject of the manners of such a prince. As she gazed across the floor at the Crown Prince of Transylvania, she was struck by how like Vladimir Von Dread he was and also how unlike. Vlad would never have treated any young woman with so little courtesy, much less his own fiancée.

She wished she could do something for Alexis; merely day-dreaming about her august grandmother giving the young man a dressing down would not help. Turning to Nastasia's sister, Rachel sought to put some of Lady Devon's wisdom into words. "He doesn't know you yet. You may have to seduce him. Men don't know how to do these things on their own. Women have to lure them in, by being mysterious. Particularly men like him, who are arrogant intellectuals."

Alexis made a face that might have been questioning the prince's intellectual prowess.

"He wouldn't be in Dee Hall, if he weren't interested in learning." Rachel paused, glancing at Alexis's expression. "Unless you don't like him and don't want to wow him, in which case, the only thing I can offer is to wait outside your bridal window with a very fast broom."

Alexis straightened her back, which brought out her resemblance to Nastasia. "Thank you for your advice, Rachel. I will consider it carefully."

Rachel again glanced across the floor at the young woman's intended. She had compared him to Vlad and found him wanting, but what about her grandfather? Blaise Griffin was gruffer than Vlad. While he probably would never have treated a fiancée this way, she could easily imagine him ignoring a young lady who was expectant of his attentions. While the situations were quite different, what would she herself have done, if Grandfather had ignored her? She would not have allowed him to humiliate her. That would have encouraged him to overlook her in the future. He had been that sort of man. But openly disobeying him would not have been the right thing either. Grandfather had abhorred disobedience.

Cleverness would have been required, ideally something that showed him up a bit but without violating the wording of his orders.

"If you do want his attention," Rachel said slowly, recalling her grandmother's lessons again, "you need to do something to impress him with your worth. Otherwise, he'll continue taking you for granted. The key's to find out what he's interested in and then demonstrate to him that you know more information about the subject than he does. That makes you valuable. If you can discover what he's interested in, I'm certain Nastasia and I can find more about that subject than he currently knows and give you some information with which to wow him."

Alexis spoke graciously, "Those are rather old-fashioned ideas, Rachel. I believe we know better now than to treat people as if they have more or less 'value.' A woman should be able to be herself. The man should appreciate her for who she is, without her needing to show off."

Rachel could not help herself. She laughed out loud.

"A charming fancy," she replied, sounding particularly British, even to her own ear. "Too bad these modern notions have made no headway towards changing the reality that is the nature of boys."

Then she bit her lip. Perhaps, she should not have said that. It was not very nice.

Alexis eyed her speculatively. "From where did such a young freshman gather so many cynical ideas about how to attract men?"

"My Victorian grandmother," Rachel replied honestly. "She used to speak about these things. I should add, there may well be boys such as you describe in the world—ones whom you could get to know slowly, who would cherish you for the good qualities you possess— but the Crown Prince of Transylvania is not such a one."

"You may be right about that," Alexis sighed.

"I am right," Rachel stated with complete confidence.

She was taken aback by the realization that Alexis could not look at Romulus and see how one would need to approach him. Rachel could do it. She felt strangely certain of it. She could draw the attention of Romulus Starkadder, if she put her mind to it. It would be a matter of finding the right secrets and dangling them before him like a lure. She did not wish to. She did not personally find the Transylvanian prince appealing—though he was physically handsome. She did, however, recognize his type. It was the one type of boy she had a bit of insight into.

If Alexis was unable to figure out what was needed to draw the attention of her intended, her marriage was doomed. He would continue to treat her this way—pushing her off on the sidelines, while he enjoyed himself—for the rest of their lives. Whether she approved or not, Alexis needed to do something to raise her worth in his eyes and fast. *But what?*

"It might help," Rachel mused, "if a large number of boys came over here in a constant stream and asked you to dance. You could turn them all down but seeing them come might impress upon him that you are a young lady to be held in some esteem. Would you like that? I believe I could arrange it."

She mentally counted the boys from her class or from the Knights of Walpurgis whom she could most likely convince to oblige her in this matter and concluded that it was not a small number.

"No, that's okay," replied Alexis, gesturing toward the bodyguard. "I am having a perfectly lovely conversation with Amber here."

Amber, who was standing perfectly still in her dark cloak about ten feet away, looked skeptical for an instant; then she went back to her customary state of complete calmness.

Rachel drummed her fingers on the chair arm, contemplating what she knew about Romulus from the Knights meetings. *Oh. Of course.*

"Very good," she curtsied to indicate she would take her leave, "Then we shall settle for one extremely important boy. Romulus is bound to take notice of that. I'll send him by."

Alexis gave her a sweet but sad smile, "That is exceedingly kind, Rachel. Only I doubt either Sigfried Smith or your brother — cute though Peter may be — would impress the likes of Romulus Starkadder."

Rachel who had begun to walk away, paused and smiled ever so slightly. "Indeed not, your highness, but I fear you severely underestimate that of which I am capable."

As soon as she was a good distance away, Rachel said aloud, "Vlad, could you ask the elder Princess of Magical Australia to dance? She'll turn you down... but her fiancé is ignoring her, and she's quite sad. He's bound to take note if you pay attention to her."

"What? Alexis Romanov? Um... as you will."

Rachel did not reply, but she grinned like a fiend. *This was bound to work.*

Vladimir Von Dread turned and strode across the floor. His black swan-feather cloak flared out around him. Superheroes, pixies, shepherd girls, and walking fruit scattered before him like lambs before a tiger. Alexis had been gazing down at her hands. When she looked up and saw him coming toward her, her pupils grew wide.

Dread had not turned off his black bracelet. Rachel could hear every word.

"Princess Romanov," his voice spoke in her ear, "allow me the honor of this dance."

Without skipping a beat, Alexis replied, "Why, Prince Von Dread, it would be my pleasure."

"Oops," mouthed Rachel.

Alexis was supposed to say no.

The elder Princess of Magical Australia offered Vlad her hand. He took it and led her on the dance floor as the musicians struck up "The Waltz of the Flowers." He looked very, very calm, but then, Rachel was reasonably sure that he could not shoot beams from his eyes, either.

Rachel murmured, very softly and gratefully, "Thank you, F.B."

Secretly, she hoped that Alexis was impressed. Not every thirteen-year-old could snap her fingers and produce Vladimir Von Dread. Turning, Rachel strolled past Prince Ivan, caught his eye, glanced at his sister on the dance floor, and winked.

Then, a frisson of fear shot through her as a terrifying thought occurred to her: *Would Vlad think Rachel had set him up? She dearly hoped not.*

Romulus, who was now standing among some other young men, caught sight of Alexis stepping onto the dance floor with Dread and straightened. He did not do anything except look annoyed. That, however, he did extraordinarily well.

The bracelet on her wrist was still vibrating. Rachel decided to sit the dance out and listen in on the two of them. She headed for the refreshments table and filled a small plate with snacks. It amazed her that she was so hungry, considering how much she had eaten at the New Year ceremony, but the flaky pastries and veggies with dip looked inviting and tasted divine.

She was eating her third cream puff when Alexis spoke again.

"So, your highness..." the elder Princess of Magical Australia's voice was both cheerful and plaintive, "... are you engaged to anyone?"

Dread replied, "... Not at this time."

Alexis was quiet for a moment. Then she spoke rather quickly, "Well, it's just that if Bavaria was to put in a request for my hand, my mother might be convinced. Bavaria is very wealthy and powerful. And I would be a good wife. I really would."

Rachel was pretty sure she could *hear* Vlad blink.

"Alexis," He paused only a moment before continuing smoothly, "you are a very sweet and very beautiful young woman. And, because you are a scholar in Dee Hall, I am sure that you are very intelligent as well. You would make me a very good wife, I am sure. Had I not already promised someone else that I would marry her, I would seriously consider risking the insult to Transylvania. But, if you wish, I will duel him for you to release you from this obligation. You should not marry the boy if he does not treasure you."

"No, it's okay," Alexis said, sniffling. "It wouldn't work unless I was able to find someone else who could make my parents a similar offer."

It was too bad. Rachel had liked Alexis. Now she was going to have to kill her.

It was bad enough having to share Vlad with her own sister. On the other hand, maybe she had nothing to fear. Had not Vlad himself told her that if he and she had met first, they might have ended up together? Rachel decided that meant that she was second in line behind Sandra. Alexis would have to settle for being third in the marrying-Vlad queue.

She would spare Alexis, this time, but maybe she should develop star-lightning beams like Amber's, just in case. Maybe Romulus would still be willing to marry Vapor Alexis.

Chapter Twenty-Eight: Dangerous Vows of Silence

The ballroom suddenly seemed stifling. Seeking a breath of fresh air, Rachel left the gym by an open back door and stood shivering on the stoop in the late February night, breathing deeply. The night was beautiful. Light poured out of the door and windows, creating golden blazes across the otherwise dark snow. The strains of the Tchaikovsky waltz could be heard behind her. To her right, a red and golden glow —shining from around the corner, where the proctors and the Sacred Days club were setting up for the Lantern Ceremony—added a festive cheer.

Looking out into the darkness, a daring idea occurred to her. Before she could change her mind, she ran forward, pelting across the snow in her dancing shoes. Leaving the shadow of the gym, she could see the full moon shining like a silver shield in the sky and sending silvery light and shadows across the snow. When she reached the brick path that ran behind the gym, she paused and opened her mouth. Then she closed it again, suddenly shy.

What is the worst that could happen? He could say no? Actually, the worst that could happen would be that he would Vapor Rachel her— but nothing ventured, nothing gained.

Feeling exceptionally bold, Rachel called aloud, "Jariel, do you dance?"

Her black bracelet vibrated. The Raven's voice spoke in her ear. "I have not in quite some time. If you are asking me, I am sad to say I must refuse. Perhaps we will have the chance later."

"I was asking you," she admitted with a sad smile. "Maybe another time."

Walking back toward the gym, she felt unexpectedly foolish, so foolish that she flushed with embarrassment, her cheeks suddenly uncomfortably hot despite the biting cold. *Of course, he would not want to appear where Amber might see him!* Rachel, of all people, should not be luring him into the open. She had thought of outside the gym as safe, out of sight, but who knew what kind of strange sense impressions Amber might possess. Also, he probably needed to keep a close eye on things as long as Amber was here.

At least, he had not Vapor-Racheled her.

She walked back inside, happy for the heat of the ballroom after the chill of the night. Gaius came up beside her, ready for the next dance. As they waited for the current song to end, Rachel caught a glimpse of Romulus. He was staring at his fiancée and Von Dread, a look of extreme anger on his face. Glancing toward the dancing couple, Rachel realized that nobody, not even the Crown Prince of Transylvania, could miss the fact that Alexis was crying.

Gaius nudged her shoulder and gestured toward Romulus, who had caught his attention now as well. The Crown Prince of Transylvania began walking across the dance floor. From his expression, he clearly thought that Dread was the cause of her tears. Romulus stalked across the floor, raising the hand that bore the ring within which the purple Kadder Star twinkled. Dread must have spotted him, for his fulgurator's wand was suddenly in his hand. With his other arm, he gently pushed Alexis behind him, so that he stood between her and her approaching fiancé.

Immediately, the dean and the two assistant deans began moving out of the crowd, heading toward the two princes. With dismay, Rachel realized that when she had spoken to the Guardian over the bracelet, the link to Dread's bracelet had been broken, so she could not hear what the two young men said to each other. Within moments, the dean and Mr. Gideon were between them. Mr. Chanson was there as well, though Rachel had not seen him arrive. She knew he was supernaturally fast, but she had not expected him to be able to move that fast.

Von Dread turned and spoke to Alexis, possibly asking her again if she wished him to duel Romulus. When she shook her head, he stepped back and raised his hands to show that they were empty, his wand had vanishing back into his sleeve. Romulus turned toward Alexis, but Amber reached her before him. The bodyguard put an arm around the elder Princess of Magical Australia and led her gently from the dance floor. Romulus scowled and stalked away. Dread stood watching them depart. Then he bowed to the dean and the other tutors, clicked his heels, and departed.

Beside her, Gaius let out his breath. Glancing at him, Rachel saw that he, too, had his wand in his hand. Slipping it back into its holster, which hung from his belt, he grinned at her.

"Better to be ready than not," he drawled, and, as the musicians struck up opening notes of Strauss's "Artist's Life Waltz." He held out his hand. "Shall we, Miss Griffin?"

"We shall, Mr. Valiant. We most certainly shall." Rachel put her hand in his, and, together, they walked out onto the dance floor.

Yet again, Gaius dipped her, bowed, and departed without Rachel gathering the courage to ask him about sneaking off together to the secret room. She so much wanted to spend some time alone with him, to be able to sit down and have a proper discussion, but a certain part of her feared that he would turn her down—either because he would think it was improper or because he was enjoying being here at the ball and dancing with so many other pretty girls. If she asked him and he refused her, she would be devastated. Better to wait until later, when the ball was winding down, and there were fewer distractions.

Out of the corner of her eye, she noticed Dread dancing with Magdalene Chase, the only student at Roanoke who was shorter than Rachel. Magdalene looked so blissfully happy waltzing in his arms that Rachel penciled her into the fourth slot in the marrying-Vlad queue.

Rachel stopped by the refreshments table for punch. As she ladled the fizzy liquid into her glass, she happened to catch, across the dance floor, the moment when John Darling—who, she had to admit grudgingly, was looking quite handsome in his Agent costume, with his huge, flowing Inverness cloak and his tricorne hat—approached Ameka Okeke. She had come as the missing Pleiades sister, with an elaborate headdress that included a gem that shone like a star. Bowing graciously, he asked her to dance.

Ameka turned him down flat.

Rachel could not help grinning. Thinking back, she giggled over his shocked expression several times, until she remembered that she was supposed to be forgiving him. Then she sighed and returned to sipping her drink.

As she made her way towards a boy she knew from her classes, she spied a flustered Nastasia standing beneath a large red Chinese fan decorated with phoenixes and dragons. Three older girls surrounded the princess. Rachel recognized two of them from the Knights of Walpurgis. Upper school junior, Natalie Armstrong, was dressed in what looked to Rachel's eye like tattered rags, though the rock stars in Zoë's posters were often dressed similarly, and the snide blonde Tessa Dauntless looked irritatingly fetching in a low-cut, off-the-shoulder princess dress of flowing golden satin. The third girl was a shrewd-looking redhead whom Rachel did not know, though she vaguely recalled that the young woman was a thaumaturgy student in Gaius's year. The redhead was dressed as a teapot, with one arm akimbo and the other held up to imitate a spout.

The three girls seemed to be pestering Nastasia with questions. As Rachel approached, she could hear their conversation. Tessa was saying, waspishly, "How come you get a servant? Why can't the rest of us have servants?"

The redhead spoke in a low, sultry drawl. "I bet that makes you feel pretty special, doesn't it? Having your very own bodyguard to protect your precious little body? Must be nice to set yourself above your peers in glory."

Natalie put her fists on her hips and rolled her eyes at her two friends. "Oh, come on. It's just a costume. That's actually Mini Griffin under the hood of the cloak."

The redhead put her fist against her teapot side. "Is there going to be a war now that your sister was roughed up on the dance floor? Or is your father too much of a coward to stand up to a bully like Bavaria?"

Natalie snickered. "Maybe he will send an army of emus to avenge her honor."

All three upperclassmen laughed.

To an unpracticed eye, Nastasia looked composed, but to Rachel, her friend had a shy, frozen-in-a-flash hex look. The princess hated to lie or even to dissemble, but she clearly felt that she was not free to speak openly about why Amber was there. Recalling Astrid's comments about the princess suffering here at school increased Rachel's desire to come to her friend's aid.

Seeing Joy nearby, Rachel stepped up beside her. "Let's go rescue the princess."

"Let's do it!" cried Joy, practically bubbling over with delight at the idea.

The two of them moved up, flanking Nastasia. Natalie Armstrong looked rapidly back and forth between Amber, who stood some ten feet away—a mysterious figure hidden beneath her voluminous hood—and Rachel in her cat costume.

"Look, she's never going to answer. I'm done here," announced Tessa. "Let's blow this Popsicle stand."

She turned, sending her golden skirts flaring out around her, and stalked off, followed by the two other girls. As they left, the redhead threw back her head, laughing at a comment of Tessa's. A shock of recognition went through Rachel's entire body. It was her!

"Is something wrong, Rachel?" Nastasia, whose face had broken into a welcoming smile when Rachel and Joy arrived, now gazed at Rachel with friendly concern.

"I recognize her," Rachel whispered. "The redhead was the one who laughed when the Heer of Dunderberg escaped. Everyone else was terrified or trying to help, and she just stood in the middle of the commons and laughed, as Stony Tor caved in and the storm goblin went free."

"That's creepy," Joy muttered.

"What's creepy?" asked Valerie, who had come up behind them. With her were Sigfried and, to Rachel's surprise, Zoë Forrest, who sauntered up looking bored and sipping something that looked suspiciously like champagne.

Joy burst out, "There was an upperclassman girl who laughed when the tor blew up."

Valerie ground her teeth, unexpectedly angry. "You mean while the Elf was dying?"

"Y-yes," Rachel replied, startled at the thought.

Zoë murmured sourly, "What a loser."

Valerie's jaw tightened. "The Elf I killed?"

Rachel thought silently: *You did not kill the Elf. I did.*

Sigfried elbowed his girlfriend in the ribs. "You didn't kill the Elf, Goldilocks. I told you. It was ripples. Ripples did it. The Elf was killed by ripples."

Valerie rolled her eyes sardonically. "Let's not have this argument again."

Joy shifted uneasily, trying not to be too obvious about her extreme interest in what might be causing tension between her beloved Siggy and his girlfriend.

Nastasia had regained her composure, now that she did not need to dodge unwanted questions. She drew herself up. "Speaking of that, it turns out that Rachel was correct. The Wall is important. I asked my family, and they confirmed it. It is all that stands between us and the utter chaos Outside. We must protect it with our lives."

"It wasn't my idea; it was the Raven's," murmured Rachel.

"I have no reason to believe the Guardian," replied Nastasia, primly, "especially as my family confirmed that Guardians, while useful, are dangerous and not to be trusted. But my gra... my family were very particular about the importance of protecting the Wall. Many things can damage this Wall, including sudden changes to what the inhabitants of the world believe."

"I told you we should be careful whom we told," said Rachel, unable to keep a certain amount of snideness from slipping into her voice. The princess's dismissal of Jariel irritated her.

Siggy leaned forward and hissed behind his hand. "It's unknightly to say, 'I told you so.'"

"What?" Rachel asked, confused.

"You're not supposed to say 'I told you so,'" he repeated. "It's not knightly."

"You have to be kidding," objected Rachel hotly. "Being able to point out that something you said, that was not believed, is actually true is one of the great pleasures of the intellectually-inclined. Such a thing could not be wrong. No god could be so cruel."

Zoë yawned. "I'm inclined to agree with Griffin. What girl would not want to say, 'I told you so'? It's one of our secret powers."

"It's a girl thing," said Valerie. "Boys don't do it. It's unmanly."

Siggy pointed at his girlfriend with great pride. "See, she gets us real men. That's what I like about you, Babe."

"I understand more than you know, Sir Goofs-a-lot," Valerie said with a smirk.

"If men think it's a bad thing, how come girls can do it?" Joy asked.

"We are not men," Rachel replied primly, gazing at Sigfried as if to make sure that he had not suddenly sprouted another head. Not say, "I told you so!" The very idea!

"Who said what when is not the issue," declared Nastasia. "Rachel is right. We should not be sharing the secrets we know. In fact, I believe we should take a vow not to share the information we have with anyone beyond those who currently know now. Who is with me?"

"I am," said Valerie, emphatically. "I don't want to be responsible for any more dead elves, ripples or no ripples."

"Me, too," said Joy. "If the princess wants us to keep secrets, I'm in!"

"Sure, whatever," Sigfried said glumly, glancing at Valerie. "I want to tell the world... but not if it will destroy the world."

The others, except for Zoë, were all nodding at one another in agreement. Rachel stood stock still, not moving a muscle. She neither smiled nor nodded nor did anything that might be construed as consent. What in the world was she going to do now?

True, she wanted to protect the world. In general, keeping what they knew secret was a good idea. But she had given Wulfgang her word that she would share information with him. If she agreed now, she would either have to back out of that agreement or admit to the others that she planned to tell him. While Sigfried would be on her side, Nastasia would not—and it would ruin her whole plan for trying to provide Nastasia with an additional friend.

Gah! How had her life become so complicated? When she made her deal with Wulfgang, Vlad had not yet had his run-in with Ro-mulus—a run-in that was entirely her fault. If Wulfgang did join their group, or at least befriend Nastasia, would that mean that there would be yet another person who refused to work with Von Dread and his people? That would be excruciating!

On the other hand, this arrangement with Wulfgang was entirely about a friend for Nastasia and not about her. She refused to hesitate merely because it might make her own life more difficult. Better to tell him first and only then agree to keep secrets, but how?

"Princess, may I speak to you for a moment?" came Amber's calm, military-like voice.

Rachel gave a silent sigh of relief. Saved by the sister.

"Certainly, Miss Praetor. What can I do for you?" Nastasia smiled at her sweetly.

"As the situation seems stable and you have friends around you, I wonder if I might take an hour to pursue some other mission goals."

"Most certainly. Take all the time that you like," the princess replied graciously.

"I will be back in precisely one hour." Amber nodded once and departed. Rachel watched her go. Other mission goals?

Nastasia turned back toward the group. Rachel found herself on the edge of panic.

Noticing that the current waltz was ending, she blurted out, "Oh, this is Gaius's dance. I've got to go. This is my first masquerade ball! I want to enjoy it. Let's discuss this tomorrow."

Hurrying away before anyone could object, she resolved to find an opportunity to speak to Wulfgang before someone could raise the subject again.

Chapter Twenty-Nine:
No Lantern for the Living

Half a dozen dances later, Rachel noticed that the floor was growing much less crowded. Glancing around, she realized that, as midnight approached, people were departing to prepare their sky lanterns. When the dance came to an end, she thanked her partner with a curtsey and quickly ran to find a lantern.

Rachel knew that sky lanterns were prepared differently in the World of the Wise than among the Unwary. Among the mundane, the Lantern Festival was a romantic celebration. Historically, in the East, it had been the one evening when unmarried women were allowed to go out unchaperoned. Among the Wise, on the other hand, it was more about asking for blessings for the dead. Or rather, one asked for blessings for dead relatives and hoped that they then would send blessings to you in return.

Rachel picked a nice lantern with four distinct sides. It looked a bit like an upside-down paper bag, only with fewer creases and a more parchment-like color. Inside the lantern was an instruction card. She glanced at it quickly, memorizing it, and then left it on a table.

Carrying the lantern outside, she found that, in addition to the brightness of the full moon, the commons were now lit up with huge paper lamps shaped like red dragons and orange goldfish. An area was cordoned off by velvet cords. Inside this perimeter, enchantments had been cast to warm the air. The snow was gone. Somehow, this had been accomplished without leaving behind a muddy, slushy mess. Despite this effort, the air was still chillier than felt comfortable in her thin bodysuit; however, it was not nearly as cold as the true February night she was forced to dash through to cover the short distance from the gym to the enclosure.

Rachel found a place at one of the tall tables that had been conjured for this occasion. Atop it, a large pot of India ink held a dozen calligraphy brushes. She chose one and shivered as she carefully painted her grandparents' names onto the first side of the sky lantern.

On the second, she wrote: *Thunderfrost's Boy, Myrddyn Griffin.* She had lit candles for him on previous occasions, but it was more meaningful to her since the two of them had helped save the world together back in October. She smiled as she recalled the ghostly boy on the grounds of Beaumont Castle in Transylvania, who had encouraged her as she faced down the demon Azrael in order to stop Azrael from pulling down the Walls that protected the world and to save her family and friends. In the past, when she had known him only from their wild rides across Dartmoor, she had just written Thunderfrost's Boy. Now, she now knew his name.

On the third side, she carefully painted: *Emrys Griffin & Ambie Benson.* Had it been only a week ago that she and Siggy had rounded the eastern shore of the island and seen the place where Emrys and Ambie had made their last stand? As she drew their names onto the papery surface, she wondered what the two of them had been like.

That left the fourth side. On the spur of the moment, she painted the name of her long-dead great-grandmother: *Kim Sun Li.*

A hush fell over the lawn, and a wind began to blow. An eerie tingle spread from her scalp to the soles of her feet. Rachel knew this feeling. Something supernatural was approaching. Cautiously, she peered this way and that, but she could not make out anything significant, even when she thought back over the last minute.

The wind picked up, and the words she had just written began to sparkle. The tiny sparks left the paper and flew into the air, swirling like embers above a bonfire. Rachel batted at them in alarm, trying to keep them from getting caught in her hair. Then, with a swish, they vanished.

She looked around, her body tingling with holy terror. There was nothing unusual to see. Everything looked normal, except the fourth side of her lantern was blank again.

What did that mean? Was it the lantern or the name? She decided to try another name, but whose? She considered Old Thom, the sailor ghost she had helped last fall, but she had seen him ascend a beam of light with her own eyes. She did not feel that he needed her prayers. Who did that leave? Her Elf?

A shiver passed through her body. There was one dead soul whom she knew for certain was not in a good place. Dipping her brush again, she wrote on the fourth side:

Lion's Father,
Please help
Remus Starkadder

If anyone could help him, it would be the Emperor of All Things Seen and Unseen.

She gave her lantern a few moments to dry and then began walking among the other students looking for someone she knew. A familiar grunt of masculine annoyance caught her ear. Rachel turned to see an armored figure down on one knee, a cloak of black swan feathers flowing from his shoulders. Dread's gaze was fixed upon the large circular lantern before him. Her heart pounding, Rachel approached him.

Without looking up, he asked coolly, "Did you know she would accept?"

"No!" Rachel cried. "She said she would only dance with her fiancé."

A note of humor crept into Vlad's voice. "I see even you do not know everything."

"I am so sorry!" She bowed her head in contrition. "I had no idea she would do that."

"It is not your fault, Miss Griffin," he replied mildly. "Think nothing of it."

He sounded so practical, so sincere, that the burden weighing upon Rachel lightened. Inwardly, however, she sighed. *Would he ever call her by her given name?*

He continued to kneel and gaze at his lantern. Rachel tilted her head sideways, regarding it. Then she walked around it. On the far side, a bold hand had written:

Esmeralda Von Dread

Vlad raised his head and regarded her. "Ordinarily, during the Spring Lantern Ceremony, I put the names of my mother and my uncle on my lantern. This time," he frowned back down at the lantern, his brow dark, "something strange keeps happening when I add my uncle's name."

The hairs on the back of Rachel's neck began to rise, as if anticipating what was about to come next. "Can you show me?"

He dipped his brush and painted upon the lantern:

Stefano Lovari

A hush fell. A wind began to blow, and the air grew pregnant with promise. The letters Vlad had drawn started to glow. Then they turned to fiery sparks and drifted away from the lantern.

The two of them held absolutely still. Finally, Rachel shook herself slightly.

"That happened to me, too, when I tried to add the name of my great-grandmother who fell asleep one day and never...." Rachel's voice drifted off.

Vlad cocked his head, gazing up at her from where he knelt. "Tell me, Miss Griffin, you who know so many hidden secrets—even if you cannot predict the whims of the elder Princess of Magical Australia— can you explain why this is happening?"

Could she? Rachel thought back, reading again the name on his lantern. Stefano. She remembered the name. It was the name of the uncle who conjured the black swan for young Prince Vlad, the black swan who had vanished after a day.

"I think I understand," Rachel whispered back.

"Indeed?"

"*They're not dead.*"

"I beg your pardon."

"Your uncle. My great-grandmother... Look, Vlad, you're from Outside, right? Well, how might the presence of an important person in your life, who is still alive Outside, be accounted for in your memory?"

"You think we remember them as someone who has died?"

"It's possible," she whispered back.

"But why now? Why could I add his name before and not today?"

Her voice still hushed, she whispered, "I think maybe there is a presence here now who was not attentive other years."

"You mean the Gu...."

"Shhh!" She put her finger to her lips. Amber might return at any moment. She could be anywhere, listening.

Vlad nodded. Then he put up his arms, like wings, and hunched his head, in a sort of a charades version of a Raven.

Overcome with amusement, Rachel put up a valiant fight and lost. Vlad stoically bore the indignity of being giggled at by a nearly-fourteen-year-old.

Then the hush came again. This time the wind was soft as a lullaby. Rachel glanced around but could see nothing out of place. She stared into the dark so intently that she started seeing red spots before her eyes. No, those were not spots.

Those were sparks of fire.

A swirl of flame-orange and candle-yellow embers circled around the nearer side of Vlad's lantern. They gathered upon it, etching dark letters into its surface. The eerie hush grew more powerful, until a tingle ran all along Rachel's limbs.

Gasping, she dropped to her knees. She did her best to stay motionless, though she was trembling, gazing in anticipation at the words that were forming. Chills ran up her spine and down again. Her hand clung to Dread's, firm in his grip, as they moved closer to each other, both staring at the lantern. Even thinking back with her perfect memory, she could not remember if he had grabbed her hand or she had grabbed his.

The two of them knelt with bated breath. Warmth radiated from Vlad. Rachel moved closer to him, letting the swan feathers of his cloak fall over her shoulders. The letters that burned into the paper began to form words. Rachel and Vlad squeezed each other's hands even more tightly as they watched in awe. Then the last of the sparks sank into the lantern. The words read:

Fortune
smiles
upon
his
nephew

"Wha—" Rachel swallowed and tried again. "Wh-what does that mean?"

Vlad said gravely. "My uncle used the Wheel of Fortune card as his personal symbol."

"Is he... sending you a message?"

"I... do not know."

The two of them looked around, but nothing visible in the red and orange light of the many large paper lanterns offered any answer to their questions. Rachel remained still for a time, luxuriating in the firmness of Vlad's grasp and contemplating the ramifications of all that had just happened.

"Oh my gosh!" she cried, leaping to her feet. "There's something I need to try!"

So arresting was the idea that had come to her that she was off and running across the quad before she remembered that Vlad had been holding her hand, and she had just bolted away.

"Sigfried, where's your lantern?" Rachel cried, sliding to a stop beside her blood brother outside the roped perimeter, where he stood tossing snowballs to Lucky, which the dragon cheerfully incinerated, adding to the red and orange lighting.

Sigfried shrugged. "What do I care about stupid festivals. I ain't got no relatives."

"Siggy!" She grabbed his arm. "There's a special enchantment tonight. It makes names disappear from the lanterns if you write the name of someone who's alive."

"Yeah, and that and a sandwich will get you a sandwich."

"A big sandwich?" asked Lucky, hopefully. "Or just a little flat one, with a single slice of baloney and a single piece of cheese?"

Rachel pulled on her blood brother. "Sigfried Smith, think! This is your chance!"

"To do what?" He looked genuinely puzzled.

"To find out if your parents are alive!"

Siggy was dubious, but to humor her he went and fetched a lantern and brought it to one of the tables inside the velvet cords. With a quick hand, he drew a brush from a pot and rather sloppily painted *Mother* on one side and *Father* on the other. Valerie came by while they were doing this, and the two of them explained what was going on.

Finally, he was done. The four of them waited eagerly, Lucky bobbing his head back and forth, constantly checking one side of the lantern and then the other. Rachel's heart seemed to be running a race. Nothing happened.

"Oh, I am so sorry, Siggy," Rachel whispered. "I guess they really are dead. Or you never had foster parents and are just an android."

"Sorry!" Siggy whooped.

He was grinning, not his usual crazy-boy grin, but the decent, cheerful grin of a happy young man. Rachel could not recall having ever seen him look so... normal.

"What are you sorry for? This is the best news I've heard since.... This is the best news I have *ever* heard."

His girlfriend stared at him as if he had gone batty. "You're *happy* your parents are dead?"

"Don't you get it?" Siggy insisted. "If they're dead, maybe they didn't abandon me!"

And with that, he lifted first one girl and then the other off her feet and twirled her in a circle, whooping with pure joy. Putting the dazed and laughing Rachel and Valerie back on their feet, he waltzed around the table with Lucky.

"Or he really is a robot," quipped Valerie. Turning to Rachel, she asked, "Does the maker of a robot count as its parent?"

"I don't know." Rachel replied solemnly. "Only... well, Amber thought Sigfried looked like someone she knew. Maybe he really does have relatives."

"Or the guy Amber knows is also a robot," Valerie said dryly.

A strange expression came over Valerie's face. She rushed over, grabbed her boyfriend's arm, and yanked. "Come on! You, too, Lucky! This might be our chance to find out something... very important."

Valerie dragged the other three, two of them carrying lanterns, across the commons to where Salome was sitting on one of the tables. She wore a French maid's outfit so tight it looked as if it had been painted on. A little lace headpiece was perched upon her blond curls, and in one hand she held a feather duster, with which she was dusting behind the ear of a college boy, who stood too close, gazing up at her as he spoke to her. Valerie drove off the upperclassman and explained to her friend what Rachel and Sigfried had told her.

"So?" Salome shrugged, a motion that did things to her body that were too pleasant for Sigfried, who studiously looked away. She brushed the feather duster across her fancy black-and-white nails. "I can't think of anyone who's dead who I care about enough to ask."

"Not someone *else*," Valerie's voice was unusually husky with some suppressed emotion.

Salome became instantly attentive, her huge luminous eyes glistening. "You mean, you think we could find out—you know what—once and for all?"

"Find out what?" asked Rachel, curiously.

Salome hesitated and then she said quite seriously, "Whether or not I'm a zombie."

"Zombie?" Sigfried looked at her in surprise and then remembered why he had not been doing that and glanced away again.

"I can tell you're not a zombie," announced Lucky. "If you were a zombie, you would smell bad." The red and gold dragon swooped around Salome, sniffing her shoulder and her hair, which made her giggle. "Nope. Not a zombie."

But Rachel understood. "You mean because of the princess's vision at the beginning of the year—when she saw your name on a gravestone?"

The other two girls exchanged glances, and then they nodded warily.

"We've been wondering all this time," admitted Salome. Her tone was cheerful, but her overly-large eyes looked wide enough to be small moons.

Valerie pulled a brush from the pot beside Salome. "If you're undead, you'd be dead, right? If you're alive, then you aren't. Aren't undead, I mean. Let's find out."

Ever so slowly, Valerie began painting words upon her lantern with the calligraphy brush. She did not slop them on as Siggy had done but wrote each one with care. As Valerie worked, Rachel stood quietly, waiting. Sigfried had already wandered off. He stood near a giant, glowing goldfish, shadowboxing with Lucky. Salome, however, looked younger and more nervous than Rachel had ever seen her.

"There!" Valerie put her brush down. The lantern read:

Salome Delilah Iscariot

They waited. Salome stared at the lantern, transfixed, nervously chewing on her nails, the whites of her eyes shining orangey in the lantern-light.

A hush fell over the small group. Sigfried froze and turned around slowly. The wind, when it came, was not a gentle breeze, as it had been the other times, but a gale that blew Salome's hair straight out behind her and sent her lace hairpiece tumbling through the air. Eerie tingles ran up and down Rachel's entire body. She felt as if her hair was standing straight up, despite it being wound tightly into cat ears.

The letters on the lantern began to glitter. Each one burned up with a *phhhwwp* sound, like a flame being snuffed. Then the lantern was blank again.

Salome slid from the table and stood on shaky legs, before collapsing slowly to the ground. Lantern-light glittered off the tears spilling from her eyes. "Oh, that's good!"

Then, she threw her head back and, with a loud wailing sound, burst into tears. Valerie ran to her, kneeling and hugging her. She was crying tears of joy herself, though more quietly.

Rachel shifted her weight awkwardly, not sure what to do. She was happy for this girl that her fear of being undead had been put to rest, but she felt like a third wheel. Sigfried had run and caught Salome's headpiece; he returned, looking down with puzzlement at the weeping girls. Stepping backwards, first one step, then two, then three, Rachel took this chance to depart.

Behind her, Salome gave a little shriek of astonished dismay. She stared down at her chewed fingernails. "Oh! Look what I did to my polish! That hasn't happened in years."

Rachel set off across the commons, avoiding tables, trees, and other students, searching for Laurel and Peter. She figured when the clock struck midnight and they lit the lanterns and sent them flying up into the sky, it might be appropriate to be with her siblings. She was not the only one who had had this thought. Joy, still in her banana costume, waved from where she stood with her fruit bowl of sisters.

Their lanterns bore the names of relatives who had died during the Terrible Years, including their grandfather, General Ernest O'Keefe, who had met his end fighting Koschai the Deathless at the Battle of Detroit.

The Starkadder princes and princesses stood together around one lantern, and Nastasia was with her siblings around another. The princess studiously painted names from a list she held in her hand onto the Romanov's large lantern. A little ball of *lux*-light hung over her paper. Rachel glanced it and saw: *Ivan the Magnificent, Anatol Romanov, Andrei the First.* When Nastasia saw her, she shot Rachel a sweet smile that made her look more like Alexis than usual. Rachel noted that Alexis stood with Ivan, Alex, and Nastasia, not with her fiancé. Rachel also noted that all of Nastasia's names stayed securely on the lantern.

Rachel passed the Fabians, the four siblings huddling together as befit their close-knit relationship. From Panther's robes, her two long braids, and the silver comb tucked into her belt, Rachel guessed that she was meant to be Vasilisa the Wise, the heroine who bested Baba Yaga the first time—before the evil Russian witch became one of the Terrible Five. Beside Panther, her large black panther slunk close to her leg, gazing out at the proceedings with surprising intelligence. Next to her was Bobcat, and beside him sat a funny, fat, little creature that Rachel recognized from Daring Northwest's illustrations as the Psammead, a sand fairy, a creature said to be capable of granting wishes. She knew from Kitten that it was shy and ill-tempered and seldom came out in public. Squirrel's fierce and fiery phoenix rode upon his shoulder, its brilliant flaming feathers blending nicely with the red and orange of the lanterns. The only one without a familiar was Kitten herself. Rachel saw no sign of the little Lion. When she paused and inquired, Kitten smiled and said, "What, Leander? He had to go visit his Father."

Rachel continued across the commons. Just then, the most beautiful singing rose above the general chatter. All around, students lowered their brushes and turned to listen, captivated. Over by the red dragon lanterns stood two boys, singing together. One was Sigfried's roommate, Ian MacDannan, dressed in his father's Red Ryder costume, a dark blue outfit shot through with glittering flickers of bright red flame. The other was Marble Moth, Jr., the college sophomore from Spenser Hall, dressed in the flowing gray and white silks that his father wore in concert. Marble Moth, Sr., famous for his ballads and folk songs, was popular among the Wise and all but unknown among the Unwary, unlike Ian's father, who was a superstar to both.

The two young men, one tall and easygoing with longish blond hair and a soulful gaze, the other short and fiery-haired with a mischievous gleam in his eyes, were singing the requiem from the end of Kit Marlowe's *The Rise of Arthur Pendragon and His Tragic Fall*, a play only known to the Wise. Their voices combined to produce such pure and perfect tones that Rachel could hardly believe this music came from mortals.

It was said that the first time this play was performed at the Globe Theater in London, the fairies themselves, led by Lady Cobweb and Lord Moth, appeared and sang this piece. A chance meeting that evening, between Lord Moth and a mortal maid, led to the establishment of the Stone branch of the Moth Family—the branch of the family to which the tall, cowboy hat-wearing proctor, Coal Moth, his brother Ignatius, Rachel's second cousins, Beryl and Blackie, and Marble Moth, Jr. himself all belonged. The singing of the fairies, as they mourned the briefness of the lives of human kind, was said to have been so exquisite that all who heard it that night claimed later that their lives had never again been the same.

Listening to it now, sung by two boys, one of whom owed his very existence to this song, Rachel found it easy to believe. Nor was she the only one. A number of girls and even a few boys wept openly.

Rachel stood absolutely still, listening, until the requiem came to an end. Even afterwards, she remained rooted in place, contemplating the fate of King Arthur, who had performed such great feats of kingship only to meet his death at the hand of his own son, even as he slew him. Arthur's nobility was legendary, but it had not protected him from the collapse of his own family. Tears pricked at Rachel's eyes. Now that she had dared to open the Pandora's Box that was Amber, would something similar happen to her family?

Chapter Thirty:
The Hour of the Angels

Rachel headed across the commons in search of her siblings. She walked slowly through a darker area towards the middle of the enclosure, far from the lanterns that ringed the perimeter. Under the branches of a wide old tree, the light of the full moon did not penetrate. Someone grabbed her arm. She let out a shriek.

"Griffin! Something strange's going on." Zoë's face was a pale oval in the darkness.

"Let me guess," Rachel replied, when she had gathered up her scattered daylights. "A name keeps disappearing when you are writing on your lantern?"

"Yeah, nah, I didn't bother with that lantern claptrap," replied Zoë. "This is something else entirely."

"Oh?" Rachel was shivering again. She had forgotten the cold when Vlad held her hand. Now it came rushing back with a vengeance. Also, she was struck again by how tall Zoë was. The other girl hardly looked like a high school student. Talking to her was like speaking to Laurel or Sandra.

Zoë leaned over until she could whisper into Rachel's ear. "Somethin's follovin' me."

"Some *thing?*" Rachel asked.

"Yeah. Like a little, ugly, cloppy thing."

"Oh." Rachel thought about this. "You mean something fey."

"Could be fey." Zoë perked up, now looking more interested and less terrified.

Rachel put her hands on her hips. "If you had taken the notes I wrote out for you, you would know it was an urisk and wouldn't have had to scare yourself half to death."

"All right, Miss Told-You-So," Zoë countered, "how do you know it's an urisk?"

"Only small fey on my list that clops," Rachel replied. When Zoë stared at her, she added, "You did say cloppy, right? Like goat legs?"

Out of the corner of her eye, Rachel caught a motion in the dark, something small. A feeling came over her like spider legs climbing up and down her arms.

"There it is," Rachel murmured.

"Don't look directly at it, or it shifts out of sight," Zoë whispered back.

Rachel nodded. Many fey were like that.

"What do we do now?" Zoë asked.

"Don't know. They eat rabbits and fish. But I don't have any."

The middle of the lantern festival did not seem like the right time to bring up the idea of dragging Siggy up to the alchemy lab to make more mock-fish or maybe some Welsh rarebit, though that thought made her hungry. It occurred to Rachel that she had been so full after the New Year ceremony, she had not eaten dinner.

Zoë whispered back, "I've one of those red-thread befuddlers we made in class, but this guy doesn't strike me as smart enough for that. Doesn't it catch the clever ones?"

Rachel nodded, chewing on her lip while she thought. The little form slipped from behind a tree and crept closer. It was an ugly little thing, less than three feet tall, with goat legs and a mop of bristly hair —long, coppery, and of various thicknesses. Ugly, Rachel decided, and yet endearing at the same time.

She squatted down and looked slightly to the side of the little creature. Zoë followed suit and came down beside her. From the darkness, the little goat-legged urisk spoke a string of liquid-sounding syllables that made no sense to Rachel.

"What language is that, Griffin?" Zoë whispered.

"No idea," Rachel whispered back. She recalled the words several times, listening for something she recognized. Finally, she said quietly, "I think... guessing, mind you... this might be Gaelic. But I know only a half dozen words of Gaelic. Or, rather, I have read quite a few, here and there, in books, but I don't know what any of them sound like. I've heard only a few of them."

"Big help you are, Griffin," muttered Zoë, sounding faintly amused.

The little creature spoke again. It pointed down towards Zoë's feet. Then, it pointed up.

Rachel and Zoë looked at each other. Then, at exactly the same time, they blurted out:

"It wants me to take it to Dreamland!"

"It wants to get back into the fey realm. It thinks you can get it there."

Zoë smacked her forehead. "Of course. Why else come to me? Wish I had my sandals!"

"Oh, that's right. You can't get into dreamland without them, can you? Did the dean say when she would give them back?"

"Probably after school ends. Maybe spring break."

"Oh, that's too bad." Rachel tilted her head. The little fey was sitting still, squatting on its goat legs. It did not look as if it would skitter off if she looked straight at it, so she did. It gazed back with odd protruding eyeballs.

She said, "Hallo."

It said something back.

Rachel said, "Do you understand me?"

The little thing nodded its very bushy head. Rachel and Zoë exchanged glances.

Rachel moved onto her knees and spoke directly to the urisk, even though the hairs on the nape of her neck were now standing up straight.

"Zoë can't help you now. Can we just help you off campus?"

It spoke again.

Zoë said, "He says he has no place to go."

"H-how do you know?" Rachel started.

"I... don't know. I think I'm dreaming it. It would be easier if I had Aardvark with me, but I can kind of see on my own, even without the shoes or my familiar. I think it's part of the familiar gift I get for having a quoll, the same way that people who have cats get 'can't die by falling.'"

Rachel thought about this. She turned to the urisk. "The ogre cave is empty. You could go there for a time. Until Zoë gets her shoes back."

The little creature nodded its head rapidly.

Zoë squinted. "*Dream Thief?* Who's the Dream Thief?"

Even before the urisk responded, Zoë's expression changed to one of eerie horror.

"Oh," she whispered, swallowing.

"Who?" Rachel asked eagerly. "Is it someone we've heard of?"

"Sorta," Zoë muttered. Aloud she said, "Don't trouble your head about it, Griffin. Look, I'll get the little bugger to the docks. Once he's outside the wards, I'm sure he can find his way from there."

"It's several miles," Rachel objected.

She shrugged. "He's a fey. He'll manage."

"Let's ask Lucky to accompany him. He'll get him there safely."

"That's a good idea," Zoë stood up. "You call Lucks. I'll pick up the pipsqueak."

She knelt and, as she had once done for Rachel, indicated that the little fey should hop on, piggyback. The funny, ugly thing trotted forward and climbed onto her back. Rachel was impressed that Zoë seemed unaffected by the proximity of the fey creature. All the hair on Rachel's body was standing up, and it was still several feet away from her.

Rachel pulled out her calling card and called Siggy. Convincing Lucky to come was easy. Convincing the two of them that the urisk was not for eating or for mounting on the clubhouse wall took more time. Eventually, however, all was arranged. Zoë would walk to the tree-lined pathway that led to the docks, and Lucky would join her there as soon as the lantern ceremony was over and accompany the little fey on his trek to the far side of the island.

With the urisk safely on her back, Zoë ran her hands over her hair, until her hair shone with a faint phosphorescence. Rachel gawked. She had not known the other girl could do that. As Zoë slid her hand down her forelock braid so that it too shone with phosphorescence, she hesitated, where the feather her dying mother had given her used to reside, and then, sighing, continued.

Gazing down at her forelock braid, she muttered glumly, "I miss my feather."

Rachel's heart wrenched in sympathetic pain. Then, with the urisk riding piggy-back, Zoë set off at a jog for the path to the docks and vanished into the darkness.

In the end, Rachel stood with Astrid as they lit their lanterns. Laurel had turned out to be busy with her own friends, and she could not find Peter. She had also stopped by where Gaius was holding a lantern bearing his mother's name and that of a dead little sister, the existence of whom Rachel had not previously known. But he had been chatting happily with other upper school seniors, and she had not wanted to intrude. He grinned at her and promised to see her for the next dance when the lantern ceremony was over.

So Rachel had joined Astrid, who was standing by herself. Siggy and Valerie and Salome stood a little way away. The two girls joined them as they all let Lucky set fire to their foot-long matches. These they then used to light their lanterns. Once lit, the lanterns began to bob upwards. Standing beside her roommate, Rachel gently let hers go, gazing at it in quiet joy as it floated slowly up towards the velvety blackness of the star-strewn sky.

First one or two gold-white lanterns floated up, a bright heart of candle flame glowing within each one. Then half a dozen, then three dozen, then a hundred. Soon, lanterns filled the dark night sky, shimmering umber and gold shapes floating slowly upwards. It was too beautiful to put into words, almost too beautiful to behold. Where they drifted towards Roanoke Hall, they were reflected in the lake, so the beauty seemed to come from above and below.

As if that were not exquisite enough, it began to snow. Powdery flakes drifted lazily down, catching the golden light as the lanterns floated skyward. The two girls stood side-by-side, gazing upwards, lips parted in wonder.

There was only one strange occurrence during this final part of the festival. Every single lantern floated upwards, except Siggy's. Once airborne, Sigfried's lantern made a diagonal beeline across the commons, as if being drawn by a string or a magnet. Some twenty feet above the ground, it knocked into a second lantern that was also moving at a diagonal. As if stuck to each other, the two then ascended together. Running around beneath them, Rachel could see the word *Father* on the outside of Sigfried's and no words on the far side of the second lantern. The only thing written on it had been on the side that now seemed to be stuck to Siggy's lantern. Even looking back through her memory, Rachel could not read it. It was just too far away.

"Should I go after it, boss?" asked Lucky. "I could eat the offending intruder. Or burninate it."

"No, don't," said Rachel. "Maybe it's not an intruder."

"You grasp things no one else can, Griffin. What do you think's going on?" asked Sigfried.

The girls looked at her as well. Rachel squirmed, uncomfortable under the scrutiny.

"Well, I don't know, really, but I thought..." she blushed, feeling suddenly on the spot, "... what if someone else on campus had written down the same name?"

"You mean maybe they wrote *Mother*?'" asked Siggy. He tapped his chest, above his all-seeing eye, and continued without even turning his head. "They didn't. It says: *Felicity*."

"What does that mean?" asked Salome.

"It means *happiness*," replied Valerie, who had her camera out and was snapping pictures. "Why would someone write happiness on their lantern? Do they think happiness is dead? That's sick."

"It can also be a girl's name," murmured Astrid shyly.

Rachel turned to her blood-brother. "Maybe that's your mother's name, Siggy."

Suddenly alert, Siggy stared into the crowd. "You think I might have a relative here?"

They all looked, but, in the faint reddish-gold lamplight, they could not see anyone who seemed to be acting as if something was amiss. Silently, they stared upwards again, watching the flickering, golden lanterns float higher and higher as the snow swirled earthward.

Lucky departed to meet up with Zoë and help conduct the little urisk north to the ogre's cave, until such time as Zoë could retrieve her shoes and return the creature to dreamland. The rest of them went inside.

Returning to the brilliantly-lit ballroom, Gaius and Rachel opened the first dance of the next set together. Afterwards, Rachel danced to Shostakovich's "The Second Waltz," which she happened

to know was her father's favorite, with a beautiful young man wearing a domino mask who had the most brilliant blue eyes she had ever seen. There must have been sorcery involved because she was certain that she would have remembered those eyes had she seen them before.

When they parted, a finger tapped her shoulder. Rachel turned and stifled a cry. Death stared her in the face, or, at least, a student dressed like death. She knew there had to be some enchantment to it, but it looked like a real skull gazed back at her, not a mask.

"WOULD YOU LIKE TO DANCE?" boomed the skull.

Rachel curtsied and held out her arms in acceptance. Death handed his scythe to some random person walking by and twirled her out onto the dance floor. He was a rather good dancer.

"Do you get the night off?" she teased. "No, I don't suppose you do, but still, awfully nice of all those sick and injured people to wait around while you dance with me. I am honored."

The skull nodded in its voluminous hood.

Rachel recalled his voice and speech patterns, checking it against her memory of everyone she had spoken to at the school, but she could not find a match. She glanced at him again, and an eerie tingle crept up the back of her neck. His voice sounded different, but his cloak and, when she checked her memory, his scythe, looked exactly like that of the skeletal figure on a pale horse who had appeared in the princess's vision the time Dread's hand had touched Nastasia's brow. Rachel raised her head to address him, but the dance ended. With a slight bow, he was gone, sweeping off into the crowd, possibly in search of his scythe.

Unnerved, Rachel looked around, her eyes playing over the crowd. *What was happening?*

A hush had fallen over the entire room, a strange eeriness that reminded her of standing on Gryphon Tor at dawn, gazing over the fog-shrouded moors. It left her breathless and terrified and in awe all at the same time.

The rousing tune of Khachaturian's "Masquerade Waltz" contributed to the odd impression that the dancers were floating. Amidst these dancers were a number of figures who Rachel's memory told her had not been there earlier in the evening. A figure in red armor, nearly ten feet tall, waltzed with Ameka Okeke. Another figure, this one only seven feet, had red hair that cascaded down her barely-covered back and curves that would put even Rachel's mother to shame. This nigh-goddess sauntered across the floor, smirking at the gawking boys with a slow, mocking smile. There were other unfamiliar figures as well. To one side, Rachel thought she glimpsed Gaius dancing with an unusually-tall Tessa Dauntless, but when she turned that way again, a large black fox with red eyes and a white-tipped tail sat in the spot gazing back at her.

A shiver traveled through her entire body. Taking a ragged breath, she thought back over the last minute or two and nearly cried out. In her memory, the newcomers were different.

The armored figure dancing with Ameka was *fifty feet tall*. From his back, enormous wings stretched across the entire ballroom. Each glowing feather contained a burning light that seemed to hold an entire world. Just looking at those feathers made her feel humbled, as if her pride had been ripped away from her and she were stripped bare of any shield or disguise. As she watched him swirl about the dance floor, the word that came to her mind was *meek*, but not meek like spineless, meek like a warhorse—one with the strength and spirit to dash any rider to the rocks and trample him to death in an instant but who deigned to accept the saddle and bit, who chose, of his own will, to yield to the will of his rider.

That kind of meek.

The sultry seductress was still seven feet tall, but she seemed even more alluring, disturbingly so. Rachel averted her gaze, discomforted, but not before she noticed that wings sprang from this woman's back, wings of smoke that swirled in the shape of peacock feathers.

Rachel took a step backward. She knew that wing! She had seen it before—well, a portion of it. During the fight against Veltdammerung and Mortimer Egg, back in late September, her memory had caught part of a peacock-feathered wing made of smoke that she had unknowingly glimpsed from the corner of her eye. That segment of wing fit this one. Who was this being who struck Rachel as so disturbing, and why had she been present at the battle between the Agents and Veltdammerung?

Rachel's gaze roamed over more of the chamber. She thought back again. Other winged figures danced among the masqueraders. The boy with the domino mask and the brilliant blue eyes sported seagull wings as he danced with Nastasia, speaking intently to her. An enormous black wolf with red eyes slipped through the crowd, his head low, as if he wished to avoid interacting with anyone. A white-winged girl laughed at a joke one of the students told her.

The hair on the back of Rachel's neck stood straight up. Her grandmother had been right about masquerades. The students were not the only ones attending this ball.

Angels.

She was surrounded by angels, or at least some of them were angels. Some of them might be the other kind. *Why were they here?*

When the dance ended, Rachel walked slowly towards the fifty-foot-tall being, who was gazing at Ameka with somber gentleness. Ameka looked so happy to be there with him that Rachel faltered, not certain that she should interrupt. Then Ameka hugged him, what she could reach of him, and departed, and the titanic angel turned to gaze at her.

Ah. Rachel Griffin.

"Y-you know me?" she gasped.

He nodded his great head.

"Who are you?" Her voice was barely above a whisper.

I am Saint Michael.

His voice was so fierce and so vibrant that Rachel had trouble understanding why everyone was not turning to stare at him. Perhaps there was a masking enchantment, such as whatever it was that made it seem to the eye as if he were a mere ten feet tall. She heard his words with complete clarity, but his mouth had not moved. Perhaps, he was not speaking aloud at all but rather directly into her thoughts.

"Like Roland Saint Michael?" she asked, recalling the name that the King of Magical Australia had once called her boss, Mr. Chanson. She pointed at him, where he had temporarily left his chaperoning duties to dance with Astrid Hollywell, which Rachel thought was just delightful. She knew Astrid had a huge crush on their P.E. tutor.

The angel's features were solemn, yet a hint of affection twinkled deep within his eyes. *He bears that title because he is one who carries out my will.*

Similar to the way one knew things in dreams, Rachel felt certain that there was more to the link between this being and Mr. Chanson than had been conveyed by those simple words.

"Why are you here? All of you, I mean," she gestured at the blue-eyed boy and the enormous furtive black Wolf.

My Father spoke here. All dreams fell quiet. All demons contemplate his words.

"You mean—" awe spread through her with a tremble like a hundred-thousand feathers brushing against her body "—when the Lion's Father spoke through Laurel?"

He nodded solemnly. *This peace will last a long time, unless mankind chooses to break it.*

"Please," she asked softly, "What is a saint? It's one of the orphaned words. We don't know where it came from."

A saint is one who is close to my Father.

"Your father? You mean the Emperor of All Things Seen and Unseen?"

Saint Michael nodded solemnly. *We are His children, for He made all things; but we are not His Son. That title belongs to Another. Nor are we angels made in His image and likeness, as are the children of men. We are His thoughts, brought to life. Each of us is a good thought: courage, truth, mercy, hope, fortitude. And our fallen brothers are such thoughts turned awry, twisted and sullied. They have become bad thoughts.*

"Your fallen brothers... demons?"

He did not speak, but he frowned at the sultry woman with the smoky peacock wings. The seven-foot-tall woman turned slowly, a lascivious expression smoldering in her half-lidded eyes. Then, she started, as if she had only just noticed that there was a titan present. Sheer naked terror darted across her face. Crying out softly, she fled, vanishing before Rachel's eyes. Even when Rachel looked back in her memory, all she could see was the terrified demoness dissolving into a blur.

"Who was...." Rachel turned back, but Saint Michael was gone.

Looking again around the room, she saw that the other strange figures had vanished, as well: the Fox, the Wolf, the blue-eyed boy, the laughing blond girl. The odd hush had departed, and all seemed normal again. Only now, a new cloaked figure stood silhouetted in the doorway leading in from outside.

Amber was back.

Chapter Thirty-One: One Step Forward, Four Steps Back

After her next dance with Gaius, Rachel approached Agravaine Stormhenge, the boys' RA for Dare Hall, whom she felt looked just a bit like Sigfried—good looking with curly blond hair—and asked him, through a series of indirect questions, if he had any dead relatives named Felicity. Sadly, he did not, though he did invite her to dance.

When that dance ended, Rachel tried to catch Wulfgang Starkadder, to let him know that she wished to speak to him later tonight, if possible. However, he was busy dancing, and she was not able to catch him between partners.

It was getting late, Rachel realized with a start. She looked around for Gaius, but he was dancing. If she wanted some time alone with him, she would have to act quickly. She knew the ball officially ended at two-thirty a.m., but if enough students departed, the proctors would feel that they all needed to stop chaperoning in order to head out on their regular patrols, which meant that they would have to call an end to the ball. If she wanted to make it to the roof without being spotted, she would have to leave soon. The next time they met to dance, she needed to ask him. With a happy leap of her heart, she realized that maybe they did not even need to dance again. Maybe she could whisper her idea to him, and they could slip away, before anyone noticed they were gone.

Caught up in her thoughts, Rachel accidentally walked into a dancing couple, nearly knocking over Winifred Powell of the Vampire Hunters' Club, who was dressed as a cute mushroom in glasses. Luckily, her dance partner caught her. He was a tall young man dressed in a costume that resembled a cross between a spoon and a fork but wearing a fedora. When Rachel complimented the two of them on the creativity of their costumes, they claimed to be dressed as Codex and Quizzer, a webcomic artist and writer, respectively. Rachel gave them a friendly smile, but she could not help wondering if she were so dazed after the evening's events that she misunderstood them, or if they were tipsy and had somehow failed to discern the difference between a comic and its creators.

Making her way to the refreshment table, she met up with Nastasia and Joy. The food was nearly gone. The dip bowls were empty. The large silver trays—which most likely had been conjured for the occasion for ease of clean-up—held a few lone grapes and some remaining celery sticks; however, the punch bowl had been recently refilled. Joy was sipping a glass of the bubbly punch and giggling about being bubbly and punchy herself. Amber stood a short distance from Nastasia, her face hidden beneath her ubiquitous hood.

"Do you realize that it's after one in the morning?" asked Joy, giggling helplessly. Sweat was running down her face. Rachel guessed that the banana costume was not well-ventilated. "I don't think I've ever stayed up this late before."

"That's not true, Joy," Nastasia replied graciously, practically floating in her fairy princess gown and her tiny, glittery domino mask. "We stayed up later than this back in November, when we fell into Transylvania out of dreamland."

Some of the giddiness left Joy's features. "Oh, that's true. But that was kind of different. It didn't seem late cause it was day there already."

"Perhaps, but as far as how many hours we were awake, it's the same thing," Nastasia replied cheerfully.

"Have you stayed up this late?" asked Joy, "I mean more than that one other time?"

Nastasia nodded serenely. "My father occasionally sets the clocks to the times of other cities. He will declare it 'Paris Week' or 'Tokyo Week' or 'New York Week,' and, suddenly, we are expected to live on the time and eat the food of this foreign place. Quite educational, to be sure. I could wax eloquent about the food and culture of Kathmandu or Odessa, but it did tend to lead to some late nights on the days of the switch."

She ladled punch out of the bowl and into her cup, ending up with a bit of raspberry sherbet in her glass. She gave it a stern glance and then shrugged and began to drink. As she had feared, a bit of red ice ended up on her nose. She patted it off with a napkin, careful not to spill anything on her splendid dress.

Rachel watched this, but her mind was elsewhere, wrestling with the desire to tell her friends about Amber, about what had happened to her family, about how horrible it was to have her own sister waiting on the princess. Would Nastasia tattle to her family that Rachel knew? Would she be horrified? Or would she defend her family on some flimsy pretext? *That would be the worst of all.*

Unable to bear the temptation, Rachel moved until she stood with Amber behind her. This way, at least her sister was not in front of her eyes, mocking her with her presence.

"Did you enjoy your first Roanoke dance?" asked Joy, waving her glass wildly.

Nastasia's face lit up. "Indeed. It has been most pleasant. Much more pleasant than the balls at home. The young men have been true gentlemen, for the most part, and those who were not, I did not allow to ruin my enjoyment of such an altogether splendid evening."

Joy practically glowed. "Me, too! I danced with Siggy *three* times!"

"What made this more pleasant than balls back in Magical Australia?" Rachel asked curiously, as she served herself punch, deliberately scooping up some of the sherbet.

She was not particularly worried about staining her black jumpsuit. The punch was sweet and tingly in her mouth—the limeade blending perfectly with the cherry and watermelon juice, and the ginger beer coming out in the aftertaste, along with the hints of mint and clover—and so refreshing after the exertion of dancing.

Nastasia considered the question. "I believe it is because I am dancing with people my own age. I feel more like a participant and less like part of a display."

"I can understand that." Rachel nodded as she recalled how very pleasant it had been to dance with Vlad, who treated her as an equal, compared with adults she had danced with at Yule parties and such in the past.

"And you got to dance with Gaius, didn't you?" Joy poked Rachel in the stomach with her elbow. "He may be evil, but he sure is cute."

"Why, thank you, Joy," Rachel replied, amused. "I think that's the nicest thing any of you has said about him."

Joy shrugged. "I don't mind Gaius. He's always nice to me, and he helped with Zo... a-a thing."

Joy shot a furtive glance at the princess, who Rachel realized, still did not know about Zoë's scars. Nastasia had turned around, however, and was gazing across the floor toward where Gaius waltzed with the incomparable Rory Wednesday.

"I suppose he may not be as bad as I first took him to be," the princess admitted. "Perhaps, it would do no harm to invite him to join us, occasionally."

Rachel sighed contentedly and sipped her punch. Finally, a step in the right direction. So much of the hardship in her daily life came from wanting to spend time with Gaius without alienating her other friends. Coming from Nastasia, this was a victory of massive proportions.

The princess stiffened. "As long as he agrees not to share anything he learns from us with his vile employer." Turning slightly, Nastasia addressed both Rachel and Joy. "Did you see what happened tonight? Von Dread dragged my sister onto the dance floor, even though she is engaged to be married to another." The princess's voice wobbled, but then she spoke calmly again. "Apparently, he wished to humiliate his rival by brutalizing the other prince's fiancée."

Rachel opened her mouth to explain and froze. Explain... how? She could say that she asked Vlad to approach Alexis, but she could not tell Nastasia what really happened without revealing the existence of her black bracelet, which she was not willing to do.

"I saw that!" Joy cried. "He made her cry, in front of everyone and nearly got into a duel with Romulus Starkadder."

The princess nodded graciously. "And this is not the only time that he has acted shamefully, bullying a young woman. Do you recall how he shouted at the elder Miss Chase on the ice? I still do not understand why Salome thought such an unpleasant display was boastworthy."

Rachel's jaw dropped. *Bullied?* Did Nastasia understand nothing of what had happen when Salome spurred Eunice Chase to publicly confronting Dread? Vlad's response had been the epitome of self-control.

"Does your sister really like Romulus?" Joy asked.

"She will do her duty," Nastasia replied mildly.

Rachel pushed aside the Vlad issue for the time being. There was no point in arguing about that now. Maybe Alexis would set her sister straight.

She popped one of the last grapes in her mouth, suddenly realizing that she was ravenously hungry.

Joy and the princess were discussing with whom they had danced and which partners had been the most pleasant and the most challenging.

After listening for a bit, Rachel asked casually, "Did you dance with Wulfgang?"

"Me?" Joy gave her an odd look. "Certainly not! He's rude and mean."

"I did," Nastasia replied, "though I am not certain why that should be of significance. I do note, however, that the prince knows how to dance, which is not the case for at least three quarters of the male population of Roanoke Academy. Perhaps, we should consider offering dancing lessons to a wider variety of students."

"That's a good idea, actually," Rachel replied, admiringly.

Turning to regard her friend, she gazed at the yards and yards of shimmering, satiny, pale peach cloth—was it silk or an unknown material?—cascading down from the princess's tiny waist, and the puffs of the most delicate lace covering her shoulders. A more elegant and intricate gown she had never seen.

"Nastasia, that's truly a splendid dress," Rachel said.

"Apparently, it belonged to my great-great-grandmother, the Eter...." Her eyes flicked toward Joy and around the room, as if gauging who was listening.

"There you are, you silly-pilly." Dark-haired and perky Faith O'Keefe had shed her cherry costume and was wearing a simple black gown. She put an arm around Joy, reaching under the top of the banana and mussed her sister's hair. "Off to bed with you."

Joy giggled and whined and insisted that she could go for hours, but Faith dragged her off to where she had corralled Mercy, Charity, and Patience, the other high schoolers among the O'Keefe sisters. Hope and their eldest sister Temperance then shepherded the younger ones back to their dorms, leaving Faith free to continue to enjoy herself. From her bright-eyed grin, she was having an excellent evening. She had been on the dance floor for nearly every dance, and yet Rachel could not recall having seen her dance with the same boy twice.

As Joy departed, the current dance was coming to an end. Now was a perfect time to catch Gaius. Rachel turned to take her leave of the princess, but Nastasia stepped closer, inclining her head toward Rachel. "I have spoken with my family, as I am sure you have discerned. They filled me in on many things—much of which I am, unfortunately, not at liberty to repeat. They shared with me a basic description of the greater universe and the war that my family has been fighting for centuries. I can tell you a little of that, the basics."

If every cell of Rachel's body had been lit on fire, she could not have burned as hot as her longing to know what Nastasia had learned. She abandoned any plan to slip away before the next dance started and leaned forward, torn between extreme curiosity and a sneaking suspicion that this was not going to end with her receiving any answers.

"What are you allowed to share?" she asked breathlessly.

"Very little, I am afraid." Nastasia, who, like Sigfried, hated keeping secrets, looked desolate. Rachel gave her friend's hand a little squeeze of sympathy. Nastasia's smile brightened. "But my father did tell me that our method of traveling is extremely dangerous, especially for someone like me who only has a bit of our power. When I am older, I can undergo a ritual that will unlock the full power. Until then, he has told me not to travel without guards."

"Can we travel with guards?" Rachel asked eagerly.

The princess's lip quivered slightly, and Rachel knew she was thinking of the time she had lost Zoë in the darkness.

"I... do not think it wise," the princess replied. She took a last sip of her punch, put down her glass, and adjusted her domino mask. "There will be plenty of opportunity to do such things when we are older."

Will there? Rachel thought glumly as she took another sip of her punch and finished off the last lonely piece of celery. *Will we even live that long?*

It was too late to catch Gaius. He was waltzing with Oonagh MacDannan to the strains of Eugen Doga's "Gramophone Waltz." Rachel would have to wait until this dance ended.

As she glanced around the ballroom, her gaze fell upon Amber, standing draped in her cloak. Suddenly, she could bear it all no longer. Rachel downed her second glass of punch. Leaning close to Nastasia, she whispered, "Do you know that your bodyguard is my sister?"

The princess inclined her head. "Yes."

Rachel's heart constricted into a single pulse of pain. Her friend had known and not told her.

Beside her, Nastasia's voice was filled with disappointment. "I didn't know that you knew. I thought I was going to surprise you."

"But you haven't said anything," Rachel tried to keep her own voice from rising.

"That was her choice," said the princess sadly. "I wanted to tell you right off, but she requested an opportunity to examine the situation before I informed you. She had agreed that I could tell you tomorrow morning."

Rachel let out her breath slowly. "I guess that makes sense."

She had great sympathy for Nastasia. She herself had been in a similar position several times this year. Still, she felt betrayed. *Again.*

She turned her back to Amber and returned to the subject that was near and dear to her heart. "If we did want to travel, this would be a good time. Things out there are safer than they have been for quite some years."

Nastasia peered at her through her glittering mask, "What makes you say that?"

Rachel filled her punch glass a third time, managing to make it half sherbet. She took a few bites of it and then put her glass down and took a deep breath. "I was talking to my sister Laurel the day of the skating party. All of a sudden, her eyes began glowing with a beautiful golden and warm light, like the Comfort Lion, but even more so. She said—*Do not despair. Despair is a weapon of your enemies. They have embedded it deep in your heart. Know you that with a wave of My hand, I have calmed the oceans. With a wave of My hand, I parted the darkness from the light. With a whisper, I called forth all of creation. Now I cleanse you of your inner wounds. Only I, young Rachel Griffin, can see the beginning and end of all things. Remember this when you have doubts.*"

"Then, in my vision, I was outside the universe," Rachel continued, her voice hushed and filled with awe. "The darkness bubbling below me started to rise up towards the world. But there was a flash of golden light from the heavens that lit up everything. The darkness receded far, far below. It inched back up, but when it stopped, it was a bit farther away than it had been when I first saw it."

Rachel fell quiet for a moment, and then she lied blithely, "After that, I had another vision in which I saw my sister Amber and how she came to not be part of our family. In that vision, I saw that my parents had been changed so that they would agree to give up their daughter and then changed again to forget her. Amber has heard another version, though."

Nastasia reached over and laid a gentle hand on Rachel's shoulder. "I don't want you to panic or act rashly," the princess spoke quietly, as if wishing not to be overheard. "but I think we need to do something to help your sister, quickly. I think she's in danger."

"In danger?" Rachel spun until she could see Amber, standing absolutely still. Her heart began to pound. She had been afraid of this. "Y-you think your grandfather will hurt her?"

Nastasia shook her head. "Your sister Laurel, I mean."

Rachel took a step back, her brow drawing together. "*What?*"

The princess continued, "I'm rather in the habit of believing visions—so normally I would just accept one—but the one this creature gave your sister is demonstrably false."

"False?"

"Not the part about a sister named Amber. Obviously, that's true—although I would consider that version quite suspect. But I mean the earlier part about our enemies already being defeated. Truly? Is the danger over? Can we stop worrying about the Walls and tell what we know? Unless the situation in the greater universe has changed radically in the last few hours, no.

"The best interpretation I can think of," Nastasia continued, "is that the creature that spoke through your sister is a benevolent entity that was trying to comfort you but was willing to use fiction and fairy tales to do so. The worst is that it might be something malevolent."

Rachel was so shocked that she did not know what to say.

"Unfortunately, Leander's away," Nastasia continued thoughtfully, "but perhaps there is another creature who can help us. You seem to be on good terms with the Raven, who is the Guardian here. Much as I hesitate to trust him, he may be our only hope. Do you think he would be willing to examine your sister?"

Oh the tangled webs....

"The Raven already came and talked to Laurel," Rachel replied, slightly annoyed at the direction of Nastasia's suspicions. "He said that his Father had spoken to her, and she's now holy. Then, earlier tonight, Saint Michael, an angel, told me that not just our world but all the worlds are quieter right now, because the demons are contemplating what happened, and that this peace will last a long time, unless we humans break it."

The princess gave no response. Rachel could not tell what she was thinking.

At last, Nastasia said, "I don't know how to react to your news. Your information about the state of the universe is very different—almost the exact opposite—from the information I received. Unfortunately, I'm not supposed to talk about the particulars. Apparently, if too many people know, it can attract attention from the enemies Outside. A situation with which I believe you can sympathize."

"Yes. I do understand," Rachel replied glumly, picking up her glass again and swallowing the last of the sherbet before it melted. "Knowing too much can attract things."

Rachel knew that she herself was protected from this effect, but she did not want to explain that to the princess, lest that draw undue attention to the Raven.

"Either way," Rachel concluded, waving her glass, "What I am telling you just happened. It's new—not part of the normal state of things. If your family has not checked on the demons in the last two weeks, they would not know about this."

Nastasia frowned with disbelief. "My information was from last night. I find it hard to imagine that a blow against the enemy like that wouldn't have been at least mentioned."

Rachel sighed and resisted the desire to grab her own head, which threatened to ache if this conversation went on any longer. She did not know why the possibility that there might be newer information her family did not have yet was so hard for Nastasia to grasp. Rachel recalled again the moment when the Master of the World had come into her bedroom and ordered the Raven to change her memories. A shudder passed through her body.

Leaning in, her hand over her mouth, in case her long-lost sister could lip read, she whispered into the princess's ear very quietly, "You know, when I first asked you and Siggy to keep my, er, secret, I did it on a bit of a whim, to placate my mum. I'm so glad I did! It may have saved my life—even though Amber says that your grandfather is not as terrible as I believe him to be. Thank you for keeping that secret."

"Rachel, someone Outside does know. I'm sorry," the princess said sorrowfully. "They wanted to send Amber to meet her—your—family. Afterwards, they planned to alter the memories of all of you—so that you would forget her again." Nastasia looked suddenly quite young and lost. "I-I didn't want them to send her if it was going to cause your family to have their memories altered, because I'd seen how upset you were after it happened to your father. I-I let it slip that your memory couldn't be changed."

Chapter Thirty-Two: Watch Griffin, Wait for My Word

He knew. *He knew!* Rachel's expression did not falter, but something beyond terror seized her. She felt the blood drain away from around her eyes and mouth. Her head seemed to be floating, and the paper dragons were suddenly blurry.

Don't faint, she repeated to herself furiously. *Don't faint.*

She had been so frightened, fearing that the Master of the World might spy out her secret, and he had known... because her supposed best friend had betrayed her.

"I won't make any excuses," Nastasia's eyes filled with sadness, but she spoke with dignity. "I realize it was a betrayal of your trust, though that was not my intention. I will more than understand if you are wroth with me and no longer wish to associate with me. Although, it will make me quite sad to lose your friendship."

"Oh." Rachel shook her head, as if that could dispel her fear and confusion. She was not entirely sure of what she was saying. "Maybe it will be all right."

She poured yet another glass of punch, downed it, and then poured a fourth one. She was not entirely sure that she tasted the last one, though it left a sickly-sweetness in her mouth.

In a way, it was a relief that the Master of the World had known for at least twenty-four hours, and she was still alive. The fact that he had not killed her yet was encouraging.

The princess looked on, her own face pale. Finally, Rachel managed a smile and laid a hand on the princess's arm.

"Thank you for trying to defend our memories," she said, "That was kind. You are entirely right that having more of our memories erased would upset me." Rachel's eyes pricked with unshed tears, and she could not stop herself from blurting out, "Oh, princess, you should see my mother. She's like a ghost version of herself! She's so upset by what happened to my father."

Nastasia put her other hand over Rachel's, where it lay upon her own arm, in a gesture of comfort. With her free hand, Rachel wiped at her eyes. A thought occurred to her. Nastasia wanted to make amends, did she? There was something Rachel desperately wanted from her.

Turning so her back was to her bodyguard-sister, she whispered softly, "You mentioned that you would like to make this up to me. I have to ask you something else... a favor."

"Certainly. Ask."

"I don't care who my sister is when outside our world," Rachel stated. "Here, she's a member of the Griffin family, the oldest continuous family line in the United Kingdom. We can trace our lineage all the way back to Abaris the Arimaspian, well over two thousand years ago. It is not appropriate for my sister to be acting as a maid. Even for royalty, even for a friend."

"Maid?" A frown furrowed the princess's perfect brow. "Of course not, she is not of the servant class."

"She shouldn't be waiting on you and picking up after your things," Rachel said bluntly.

The princess frowned, puzzled. "She picks up my things? ... Oh. You mean when she put up the practice dummy. I can see how it might look that way, and if it offends you, I can certainly pick up my own dummies. I have been doing so, up until today. I hadn't thought of it that way, though. It had seemed more like an older student helping a younger with her training, particularly as, just before that, she had been offering me advice on how to enhance my progress with a new spell I was attempting to create. Unfortunately, it is not working as it should."

New spell?

Nastasia continued more severely, "But she is my bodyguard, assigned by my family, and I can't help if that seems servant-like to you."

Rachel had to clench her jaw so tightly that it hurt. "It's humiliating to the rest of my family," she ground out. "Could you ask her not to do that? Those aren't bodyguard duties."

"I confess that, even in such a short time, I've begun to enjoy having her about," allowed Nastasia almost shyly. "I have been wondering if she might be able to be something like a lady-in-waiting, which is a perfectly respectable position for even the most well-placed noble families. Even princesses have served in such roles, to queens or higher placed royalty."

Fireworks exploded in Rachel's brain, bouncing around inside her skull, knocking things out of place. She was too furious to speak.

"But that is impossible," sighed Nastasia. "She will go back to her true duties soon."

Rachel drew herself up, speaking with great reserve, "Griffins have served as ladies-in-waiting for English princesses, it is true. But, Nastasia, you are not an *English* princess. Outside, she may serve your family. But here, she is a Griffin, and she should behave as a Griffin."

Her sister. A lady-in-waiting, to Nastasia. *Maybe she should kill the princess now. Maybe if she concentrated hard enough, she could develop eye beams and vaporize both Romanov sisters simultaneously.*

"Keep in mind," Rachel continued, amazed at how calm her own voice sounded in her ears, "we are presently at Roanoke Academy. Students do not wait on each other here. Even Dread's people do not wait on him. While my sister is here, she should act accordingly. Since we both know you don't really need a bodyguard, why don't you ask her to just act like a friend? By being so obvious, she's making it even harder for you to fit in with the other students."

"I will consider what you have said," Nastasia allowed, inclining her head respectfully.

With a struggle, Rachel mentally shoved her mask of calm over her features. It was unusually difficult. Her facial muscles wanted to scowl. "Amber spied on my conversation with my family and now knows some things I wish she did not. But it means I can share what she overheard: Your grandfather came into our dorm room, back in January, while we were sleeping. He did not wake you and introduce himself and say hello. He just tried to change my memory. I received a whole set of fake memories that did not agree with the memories the rest of you have… and I spent a couple of weeks living in sheer terror, during which I hardly ate, fearing that if he found out his attempts to change my memories had failed, he would come back and kill me.

"Amber said he won't kill me," Rachel allowed. She decided not to mention that altering her or her mother's memory would effectively be the same thing. "I hope she's right. But I think you should know that he did this. Also, my father did not have an accident. Your grandfather took his memories away." Her voice wavered with sadness. "I realize that what happened was my father's fault. He broke his word to your family, but since he did it out of love for me—even if he misunderstood the situation—I feel responsible." She lowered her voice. "To tell you the truth, I am still terrified—because my life is not the only one at stake here. But I feel better than I did."

She had spoken too soon. Amber, still with her hood over her face, was suddenly beside them. "Princess, may I interrupt? I do not wish to be rude."

Rachel's heartbeat raced from sudden shock. Not again! Then, with a sigh, she turned to hear what her eavesdropping sister had to say. "Yes?"

Amber ignored her. She stood, automaton-like, waiting for Nastasia's permission. Fury seized Rachel. How dare her sister—her own sister—talk only to Nastasia. How dare she come here and treat her family as if they were inconsequential. Rachel was so angry that she could hardly see. She was going to break her sister's insipid calmness, if it was the last thing she did.

She leapt forward until she stood so close to Amber that her sister could no longer pretend she was not there. She was tired of her sister ignoring her. Maybe if she treated her the way she treated her other older siblings, Amber would act more like a sibling. With that in mind, she deliberately let slip the reigns of her anger and railed at Amber as she might have railed at Laurel.

Bursting out with the first thing that came to mind, Rachel cried, "Sister, I don't know what things are like Outside, but here, things are different! Here, you are a Griffin, a member of one of the most ancient families on this world. Here, the princess is not our superior. She is a visiting foreigner from a country some people don't even believe in."

Amber said nothing.

"You cannot act like Nastasia's maid," Rachel cried. "You are shaming us."

Was that a trick of the light or had Amber's pupils flickered?

Any reaction was better than none; Rachel forged ahead. "And stop acting like Miss-Super-Bodyguard! Maybe standing alone with your hood over your face like a scary specter is how Outside bodyguards do it, but we are not Outside. You are making Nastasia's life harder!"

"Harder?" Amber's brows drew together. "I fail to see how."

Look, her eyebrows moved! Inside, Rachel crowed.

Aloud, she blurted out perhaps more truth than she should have voiced in front of Nastasia, "People already think the princess is standoffish. You are drawing attention to this. This makes them dislike her even more. All night, I've been defending her from people saying less and less pleasant things about her. Even worse, your very presence here results in people asking a million questions she isn't allowed to answer. So now, she's even shyer than usual."

Nastasia looked startled, but she was too well-bred to interrupt. The princess stepped back slightly, as if to give the two sisters space. From her expression, however, Rachel guessed that she agreed about the extra questions increasing her shyness.

"The princess doesn't need a bodyguard—not here at the dance with the tutors and proctors all around her," Rachel insisted angrily, "but she could use a friend. You are the only person with whom she can talk about the secrets her family shared with her. As someone who knows a lot of secrets, I can tell you that having someone to discuss them with can be the difference between sanity and insanity. So, why don't you stop frightening the other students, take off your hood, and talk to Nastasia like a normal person. Then maybe your visit can bring some good to our lives, instead of making everything worse." She paused, panting, and then added, "Which would be nice for us and probably nice for you, too."

Amber's cheeks had turned slightly pink. Her iridescent mother-of-pearl butterflies had sprung out of her robes and fluttered around her head and shoulders, leaving trails of starlight in the air that hovered for an instant before vanishing.

Despite this, Amber spoke coolly. "I will act as the princess instructs. As her bodyguard, needed or unneeded, I am hers to command. If I have alternate orders for this assignment, they shall be carried out as well, but they do not change what I was instructed to do.

I think you and I do not define danger in the same way. I have heard more than one person say inappropriate, close to threatening, comments about Her Highness. I do not believe she is as safe as you think she is."

"Inappropriate? Close to threatening?" Rachel could not stop herself. She rolled her eyes. "Good grief! Is a big tough member-of-the-Twelve frightened because a bunch of kids say mean things? Is there anyone here you can't kill with a glance? Literally? Hasn't anyone ever told you that 'sticks and stones may break my bones, but words will never hurt me?'"

"Actually," Amber replied pedantically, "this is one of the few places in Siderea where words cause physical harm. Even you children speak the Forbidden Tongue of the Hidden City, speaking light and commanding fire."

Rachel scoffed, "That is not what I mean, and you know it."

Forbidden Tongue of the Hidden City? What was that? And what did it have to do with cantrips?

Amber remained standing, silent as a clam.

"I do not say this for myself," Rachel growled. A lopsided smile hijacked her face as she recalled the princess's most recent betrayal. "What is one more cut among a thousand?" Taking a deep breath, she readjusted her mask of calm. "But your actions still have power to hurt Laurel and Peter. If you want to pretend you aren't their sister —please do not say it to them!"

Amber pushed back her hood. Her ears were rather red. "I am not shaming your family. I am not a part of it. I am Amber Praetor of the Twelve."

"We can't control our families, Amber," Rachel pressed even closer, until she stared directly into her sister's face. "We can expand our family circle, but we cannot contract it. Our families are our families, even when they make us cry, make our hearts break. You are a Griffin, and you always will be a Griffin. No matter who steals you away!"

"Your parents may not remember," Amber replied, "but the fact remains they gave me away. Should I be offended you want to pretend my life with my true family is meaningless?"

True family? Rachel had never felt so angry and so helpless at the same time. She waited for Amber to respond, but Amber did nothing. She merely stood absolutely still, like a soldier at attention. Even her butterflies had settled down again.

Rachel wanted to scream. They were back where they started.

"The point is, you *are* part of our family!" she nearly shouted.

"I am not," Amber spoke emotionlessly. "Our parents gave me away and forgot me."

Rachel threw up her hands, balled them into fists, and let out an exasperated howl. "Because they were *made* to forget you! Because they were *changed* against their proper nature. And they were changed, or they would never have given you up! You were told a lie!"

"There is no proof of that." Amber had straightened slightly. "I need nothing from them, and my presence in their lives would just be a disruption." She put her hands into her sleeves.

Rachel's black bracelet vibrated.

"Watch Griffin," Dread's voice sounded in Rachel's ear. "Prepare yourselves. Wait for my word."

Out of the corner of her eye, Rachel could see Jenny Dare where she stood chatting with a group of boys. She held her cigarette holder between her fingers in a familiar manner. With a start, Rachel realized that the decorative length must be concealing her fulgurator's wand. No wonder the upperclassman had not added a cigarette to her holder.

Dread had put his hands behind his back. He was on the other side of the room. Locke was with him. He also had drawn his wand. He still talked with Vlad, but he now faced Rachel's direction.

Gaius's voice sounded in her ear, "Jenny, you, Topher, and I will try indirect attacks. Vlad, William, and Naomi will assault her directly. We do not know what defenses she has. Assume she is as tough as Egg."

The hair was standing straight up on the back of Rachel's neck. *What was going on?*

Von Dread's voice continued, confident and commanding, "Hold unless I give the word. Just prepare in case their conversation goes badly. According to Jenny, Miss Griffin has struck a nerve with the young woman. I want to make sure we're ready."

Rachel's face remained absolutely calm, but inside her mind whirled with awe. He was going to fight Amber, the super-warrior death doll, risking his life and that of his people to take on an enemy that he knew they probably could not survive. *To protect her.*

All Rachel's anger melted away. A warmth, like a balm, spread through her soul. Maybe she was not as alone as she feared. Then, she nearly groaned out loud. She would give anything to fight *beside* Vlad's people, but, under the circumstance, her obligation was to her family.

Touching her chest, where her wand was hidden in the neck pouch under her jumpsuit, she turned slightly away from Amber and said very, very softly. "If you attack her, Vlad, I'm going to have to *defend* her. She's my sister."

She realized that, with her extraordinary hearing, Amber was probably listening, but at least she would overhear that Rachel was loyal to her.

Dread's voice replied, "We will not attack, except to defend you. If she remains passive, there is no threat."

Without turning her head, Rachel glanced at Dread's people again. All resolved, all determined to fight despite the overwhelming odds. Rachel's eyes pricked with unshed tears. *They were so insanely brave.*

"Thank you," she murmured over the lump forming in her throat.

Suddenly, she felt safe again. The sense of unease that had come over her when she realized that Amber could handily defeat her protectors vanished.

Yet, no matter what the others said, Rachel was not afraid of Amber herself. She had absolutely no fear that her sister would harm her. She was not sure why. Looking at the princess's bodyguard, she saw a cold, battle-hardened exterior but underneath was a lost girl, possibly more lost than Rachel herself felt.

"Rachel, sweetie," came the voice of Jenny, Dread's mistress of *kumihotoushi*. "Whatever you are saying to her, she is reluctant to believe you. It looks like she is getting ready to dismiss anything you say. You might not want to continue because, honestly, it can be really hard to regain the respect of someone after their first impression of you is really bad."

The heat in Rachel's cheeks rose to ten thousand degrees, or at least it felt that way. The idea of being dismissed beyond redemption made her feel so small, she could have passed under Amber's boot and not hit the sole of it. Yet, the humiliation of someone else seeing her in such a situation was a million times worse.

Then, suddenly, it hit her. What had she been thinking? Amber was not like Laurel! Speaking to this young super-soldier as if she were a frivolous young woman was ridiculous. Amber was calm, focused, and mission-oriented *just like... Grandfather.*

And Vlad.

Just like that, Rachel knew precisely how to speak to her new sister. She had been doing exactly the wrong thing.

"I am not Sigfried,"—this time, Rachel spoke calmly, in the same detached manner as Amber herself—"who insists blood is stronger than all other ties. Of course, those you grew up with are important, too. But you cannot escape being our sister." Her voice grew gentler. "You don't know us yet, Amber. Of course, we don't feel very important to you, but you will come to know us, with time! We have years to make up for what has been lost."

Amber pulled her hood over her face, "The matter is most likely moot. I have achieved my primary goal. I will depart as soon as I am contacted, most likely tomorrow. I do not believe I will be returning here," Amber continued, "unless my emperor sends me to guard the princess again, of course."

The words hit Rachel like a punch to the solar plexus. It was the only thing keeping her from crying. Fear slashed her heart. Amber to leave *tomorrow? Her sister did not care about her at all.*

So much for having claimed that one more cut among a thousand did not hurt.

"B-but what about our p-parents?" Rachel stuttered. Keeping her voice even proved a Herculean chore.

What about her wish?

"I will meet with them, once." Amber turned to Nastasia. "I still think it would be better if their memories were wiped afterwards, though. I do not wish to disrupt their lives."

Inside Rachel's head, explosions ignited again, even more violently than before. Also in her head, someone was screaming—with her own voice. That was not how her wish was supposed to unfold—her family meets Amber and then they forget her? *Was all this worth the pain?*

Nobody wanted Amber back in their lives, nobody but her. Peter and Laurel would probably be happier not knowing about her. Her parents had problems enough. Amber herself had no desire to return to her family. Worse, Rachel had to admit, heartbreakingly, that she was not even sure that she liked Amber. The other girl was so cold and emotionless. *A death doll.*

And yet.... Rachel gritted her teeth. It was not an issue of *like*. It mattered not one whit if she *liked* her sister or not. Family was not about *liking* each other. Family was about love, about sacrifice. She might not like Amber, but she was willing to die for her. *Amber was her sister.*

She wanted her missing sister back.

Amber continued. "Changing memories is a disturbing practice, but it is necessary at times. Your father works for the Wisecraft. They change the memories of those who are without magic on this world daily. There are enchantments around this school that make people forget they have seen it. Are you all evil for doing such things?"

"We were wondering about that ourselves," Rachel replied. She glanced at the princess, recalling their conversations on how uncomfortable they felt about the Wisecraft's use of memory-altering magic.

Nastasia met her gaze. In a moment of solidarity, both girls nodded solemnly.

Amber stood still again, waiting for orders. Rachel's heart ached. Her missing sister whom she had so longed to see was here. She would meet the family, and then she would be gone, forever. *There had to be a way to stop her, to make her come back. But how?*

Rachel forced herself to think calmly. Jenny Dare and her *kumihotoushi* had given her a valuable insight. She dared not waste it. What if it had been Grandfather? What would Rachel have said to convince him to stay?

"You say our parents did not want you." The words were out Rachel's mouth before she had a chance to think them through. "I say that they did. What we need is proof. If I can offer proof that I am right—that our parents did not voluntarily give away their baby girl—will you give me your word that you will not break off contact with us, that you will come visit us again?"

"You cannot prove it," replied Amber evenly, but Rachel could tell that there was a change in her demeanor. She seemed more attentive, less distant.

"But if I could?"

Amber considered. "If it were true—that I was not given up freely—I would feel I had an obligation to my original family, when my duties allowed."

"Consider yourself under such an obligation, because I will prove it," Rachel replied, crossing her arms, her voice as cool and even as the ice on the reflecting lake.

She had not even the slightest idea how such a thing could be done, and yet she felt an absolute conviction that she could find a way to prove that their parents loved Amber.

Gazing into Amber's eyes, Rachel stepped forward and put her hand on her sister's shoulder. Even through the armor, she could feel that the young woman was trembling slightly. *Maybe Amber really believed she had been abandoned—the way Sigfried believed he had been thrown into a dumpster.*

She put her arms around her sister and hugged her for the second time that night, whispering in her ear, "I love you. No matter what."

Amber stopped trembling. Rachel stepped back.

Dread's voice sounded in Rachel's ear. "She seems to have changed her demeanor. I think the threat is over. Be ready just in case."

Jenny responded. "Yeah, she's returned to her normal unreadable state, which, in this case, is a good thing."

Meanwhile, Amber turned to Nastasia. "Princess, how would you have me act?"

Nastasia had been standing a few feet away so as not to come between the two siblings. She looked gracious and collected, despite having been subjected to overhearing an argument in which she herself had been mentioned in not entirely flattering terms. Now, she floated forward, her yards of satin and silk, or perhaps some more rare and enchanted cloth, floating around her.

"Act as you think is best," the princess answered regally, "and most in accord with your duty and station."

Amber nodded and straightened, resuming her guarding position.

Rachel gaped. *What was wrong with Nastasia?* Wasn't she supposed to be Rachel's *friend?* Why couldn't she tell Amber to behave as the other students did? *They were right back where they had started.*

Rachel felt lightheaded. Also, the punch she had drunk was catching up with her. Turning to the other two young women, she blurted out, "I have to use the loo. I'll leave you two to work out whatever you think best."

With a nod to her friend and her sister, she headed off to the ladies' room. As she crossed the ballroom, she noticed that the members of Dread's group had shifted back to much less aggressive stances, though they were still watching her, alert. Rachel said nothing, but, in her heart, she made a silent vow to move the universe, if necessary, in order to aid the six people who had just so bravely come to her defense.

CHAPTER THIRTY-THREE: INTERLUDE AT THE LOO

It was all too much. Suddenly overcome by nausea, Rachel ran for the ladies' room. Throwing open a stall door, she knelt and vomited. The toilet and walls revolved around her, and the ground rocked back and forth like a ship in a storm—though she was fairly sure that these were subjective sensations, and the gym was not actually rocking.

At least, she was reasonably sure.

The horror of discovering that a girl who might have grown up to be like Laurel or Sandra was now a death doll, as Joshua March had called her, an emotionless killing machine of the Master of the World, slowly sank in. Rachel did not cry, but she stayed in the stall, her head resting against the cold wall, trembling and hugging her knees.

Sometime later, the outer door to the ladies' room opened. A knock came on her stall.

"Rach?" came Laurel's voice. "Are you in there? Gaius said you've been gone for a bit. Are you okay? Have you come down with the dreadful lurgy? If so, I'm here to help, but be a dear and try not to cough on me."

A noise something like *umph* was all Rachel could manage. Laurel pushed open the stall door, which Rachel had left unlocked in her rush, and came to sit next to her. It was hard for the tall leggy young woman to fit in beside her little sister, especially considering the tightness of her flapper gown, but she found a way.

She put her arms around Rachel and hugged her, saying, "It's a lot to take in."

Rachel whispered hoarsely, "I hate him... so much! But the Comfort Lion told me I shouldn't hate people. How could anyone forgive such a horrible man? He's done such terrible things to us!"

"I dunno. I've been having an awfully hard time feeling angry about *anything*, since the day I met your *tengu* friend. Even so, I'm really annoyed that this emperor man hurt Daddy." Laurel paused.

"We can find a way to fix them though, right? Amber and Daddy, I mean?"

Rachel smiled slightly, in spite of her misery, at Laurel's nickname for Jariel, even if he did not have much in common with a Japanese raven spirit.

"I think we can, with time. It's my *tengu* friend whom I'm most concerned about." She paused and then blurted out what was weighing upon her heart. "I'm so afraid that I will say the wrong thing, and he'll get in trouble. Xandra Black had a vision that some spirit being might be harmed, and I keep being afraid it's going to be him. I wish...." She shut her eyes, hard and whispered, "What I wish more than anything else... more than all the other things I've ever wanted... is that I could find a way to free him from the domination of this Master of the World. But I suspect that wish will never be granted."

"I want to tell Mummy and Father," said Laurel, "but I'm afraid this might be too much for them."

"Oh, *unni*! What do we do now?" Rachel cried suddenly, regaining some of her composure. "I wanted to get our sister back... but this is like discovering that one of us was carried off by a cult and brainwashed. I can't see how we can ever have her back!"

How could she prove that her family had not relinquished Amber willingly without putting Jariel at risk? Was the danger to her beloved Raven so great that she needed to sacrifice the future wholeness of her family and just let Amber go? *Could she do such a thing, even for him?* She was not sure that he would want her to. He was the one who had pointed out that the Griffins were willing to sacrifice their own lives for each other. *And how could she possibly find out anything useful tonight, before Amber departed on the morrow?*

"*Dongsaeng*, I don't know what to do about Amber or Peter," said Laurel. "I think he's going bonkers. Not really, but he's frustrated. He doesn't know what's going on, why we suddenly have a new sister, or why Father has amnesia, and Mummy, who is usually his calm anchor, is flipping out. I'm glad I know what's going on. Or, at least, some of what is going on."

Rachel nodded numbly, thinking of how very little her sister knew.

"Maybe it's magic?" continued Laurel. "Maybe we can de-geas her, or something."

"Wh-what if it's not magic?" whispered Rachel, swallowing.

Laurel did not answer. She hugged her little sister tightly. Rachel shivered, suddenly aware of the coldness of the metal wall and the hardness of the tiles. With Laurel's help, she stood up shakily and went over to the sink where she rinsed out her mouth and washed her face. To her surprise, the cat ears Jenny had devised for her still held. This may have been the longest that her hair had ever stayed put in her entire life. Perhaps Miss Dare had used sorcery. Could one hex just one's hair and make it freeze in place? The idea merited further research.

As she reapplied her nose and whisker makeup, her thoughts returned to the current dilemma. *She had to act tonight, or Amber might be lost to them forever. But how?*

An idea came to her. Then, her heart thumped oddly. If she acted upon it, she would lose her chance to sneak off with Gaius. She might also miss her opportunity to speak to Wulfgang before she met up with her friends again tomorrow, and she still had not had a chance to thank Michael Cameron, that annoying eejit. She had not even seen him tonight. Rachel pushed these thoughts aside, chagrined. A chance to snuggle with her boyfriend? Was that more important than saving her family? As for Wulfgang, what if she did miss her chance to speak to him, and he disliked her even more. That was hardly so terrible.

Rachel patted her face with a red terrycloth towel from a stack of clean ones, most likely conjured, lying on the counter. She was impressed by the quality of it. Cloth was hard to conjure, a complicated weave like terrycloth doubly so.

"There is one thing we can do," she said aloud, as she put down the towel. "Walk down to the glass room with me. I want to call Sandra, or at least send her a letter. Oh, but that won't get to her tonight, will it? Oh! I know! Let's ask Vlad to take her a note."

"Vlad? Is he the proctor you hang around?" Laurel began. Then she rolled her eyes. "Oh, wait. I remember, now. My crazy little sister thinks she's on a first-name basis with Mr. Von-Dreadfully-Hot. Yeesssss," Laurel drawled skeptically, amused. "Let's ask the Prince of Bavaria to run errands for us." She wiggled her fingers as if to indicate the act of sending a servant scurrying. "Always nice to have a proper evil overlord at your beck and call."

Ignoring the smirking Laurel, Rachel pulled paper from her neck pouch and wrote a note:

> *Dear Sandra,*
> *Please come to the school right away. Laurel, Peter, and I*
> *need you. No one is hurt, so don't be frightened, but come as*
> *soon as you can.*
> *Love,*
> *Rachel.*

"Maybe we should tell Peter some more of what is going on." Rachel sighed. "Let's go find him." With a sudden giggle, she added, "Peter must be really freaked out. He stood there next to Gaius for twenty minutes and didn't even notice or glare at him or anything."

Laurel whispered, "Don't say anything to him! Maybe this is your chance to actually get somewhere with those two."

Holding Laurel's hand, Rachel went back to the ball, looking for either Peter or Vlad. She could not make out Peter among the dancers. He was growing taller but had not yet achieved their father's impressive height. Vlad, on the other hand, towered above many of the other dancers. She spotted him at once, waltzing with Yolanda Debussy. The pale-orange-haired college junior usually danced with exquisite grace, but now she stood stiffly, as if trying to hold her partner at arm's length. The young woman watched Von Dread like a hawk, as if convinced that he might commit an act of dastardly evil right there on the dance floor.

As Rachel watched, the waltz came to an end. Vlad bowed to his partner, looking calm and noble despite her evident distrust, and turned away.

"Wait here, *unni*." She squeezed her sister's hand. "Just a sec."

Rachel pelted across the floor to where Vlad walked toward William, who stood to one side with a glass of punch in his hand. Sliding to a stop before the prince, she held out the note, panting.

"F.B. Could you sneak away and give this to Sandra and bring her here? Or would that get you in too much trouble? I think Sandra will really regret it if she doesn't meet Amber, and I don't know how long we will get away with keeping her here."

Vladimir Von Dread clicked his heels together and bowed. "It would be my pleasure."

He took the note and headed for the door. She saw him pause and speak to the dean before departing. Across the ballroom, Laurel gaped; if her jaw had fallen to the floor, bounced, and yo-yoed back up to her face, she could not have looked more astonished.

Rachel ran back to Laurel, grabbing her hand again. "Okay, let's find Peter."

Laurel stood stock still, as if rooted to the floor. She watched Dread depart, her mouth still hanging open. She turned to Rachel, her face alive with curiosity. "Hang on! How did you...?"

"Come on. I think I see him." Rachel tugged on her arm.

Her sister refused to budge. "No, really. How did you get him to do that?"

Rachel rolled her eyes.

Laurel tugged back on Rachel's hand. "I am serious, *dongsaeng*! How?"

"No secret can be revealed." Rachel waved her fingers, copying one of Siggy's gestures.

"Let me guess," Laurel leaned over and asked with sarcastic glee, "Did you catch him murdering someone, and you're blackmailing him? If so, shouldn't you turn him over to the police, or the Agents, or at least Daddy? Yes, it's fun to have a powerful, evil, ungodly handsome, unapproachable prince at your beck and call as your personal errand boy, but isn't justice for the victim more important? Or did the person he murdered deserve it? Because I am not sure that a thirteen-year-old is fully equipped to make that call."

"No one was murdered, *unni*."

"Are you sure? Because I can't think of any other reason the Prince of Bavaria would run errands for my little sister. Did I mention evil? Did I mention ungodly handsome and *evil?*"

Rachel sighed. She had been working hard to protect Vlad and Sandra's secret, but Laurel was about to find out when Sandra came walking in on Vlad's arm.

She said, "You are looking at this backwards."

"What do you mean?" Laurel asked suspiciously.

"It's not about who sent him. It's about whom he went to fetch."

Rachel watched Laurel's face carefully. Her sister had been giving her a skeptical eye. Then her expression faltered. The skepticism was replaced by "What the...?" and then by suspicion, followed by alarm, followed by amazement, followed by shock, as her lips parted in realization.

It was one of the most satisfying moments of Rachel's life.

Finally, a look of utter disgust settled over Laurel's features. "Don't tell me: He's been bitten by the Sandra bug."

Rachel grinned. "He wants to marry her."

"Blimey!" Laurel went goggle-eyed. She glanced at the door where the prince had departed and then back at her sister. "Big Sister Sandra has a chance to be Queen of Bavaria?"

"Someday."

"Does she fancy him?"

"Yes."

"Really? I thought she was dating Billy Locke! Do Mummy and Daddy know?"

Rachel winced. "Yes."

"So everyone knows but me?"

"Yes," Rachel nodded, adding, "and Peter. I think."

"Well, at least I found out before Peter," Laurel replied with mock gravity. "Had it been otherwise, the very laws of the universe might have thrown in the towel and gone home. Come on. There's Peter."

Laurel dragged Rachel towards Peter, who stood in a corner next to a giant paper goldfish, gazing across the room at the Princess and her bodyguard and scowling. As she followed her sister, Rachel basked in the joy of having been able to tell Laurel about Sandra and Vlad. She planned to recall that moment and watch the expressions change on Laurel's face over and over and over. To her surprise, however, she also felt a tiny bit disappointed. Telling the secret had been utterly gratifying, but now Laurel understood that it was Sandra who had power over the Prince of Bavaria. The short period when Laurel had believed that she, Rachel, had some kind of secret power over Dread had been particularly sweet.

From another part of the hall, Gaius walked toward Rachel and Laurel, an inquiring look upon his face, perhaps wishing to make sure she was all right. Seeing him, Rachel slipped away from Laurel and ran to him. She took his hand, smiling up at him.

"Laurel and I are going to go talk to Peter," she said. "He's having a hard time."

Gaius nodded understandingly. "I should think so. I... don't know how I would react. Not well, that's for certain."

Rachel smiled at Gaius. "You've been a trooper so far. Thank you."

She kissed him lightly on the cheek. Behind her, Laurel gave a snort of sisterly amusement. The three of them then walked up beside Peter. He did not even look their way. He just continued to stare at Amber.

"She's awfully short," Peter said presently. "Shorter than Mother. I think even you are going to be taller than her, Rach."

Rachel stepped up beside her brother and hugged him, hard, which was less effective than she might have hoped since he was wearing costume armor. She rested her cheek against his chest. He patted her back absently.

"Yeah. She's cute, though," Rachel said, adding, "I sent for Sandra."

Still staring, Peter said, "So, are we going to be able to talk to her again without that princess there? Are we going to tell Mother and Father? I am not sure Mummy would take this too well right now. Jolly good idea, sending for Sandra. She'll know what to do."

Rachel did not want to tell her siblings how little regard Amber had for their family. Instead, she said, "Vlad invited her to his and Sandra's wedding... that is assuming that Daddy gives his permission, and they get married. Amber said she'd try to come."

Peter murmured, "Yes. Vlad and Sandra's wedding. Yes. Good."

Rachel hugged him tighter. "Oh, Peter."

She looked at Laurel for help, but Laurel was shaking her head in disgust, most likely at the idea of Sandra becoming the future Queen of Bavaria. Rachel leaned toward her and whispered teasingly, "You could have been a queen, too, you know."

Laurel drew her head away from Rachel at a diagonal, as if moving back from a dangerous maniac. Then, suddenly, she blinked and glanced across the floor to where Ivan Romanov was dancing with Jenny Dare. Poor Ivan, who was usually rather smooth, looked as if he felt he was a bit out of his league with Miss Dare.

Turning back to Rachel, Laurel mouthed, *You know, you're right!* Then, she smirked and added, "It's okay. I prefer Charlie."

Laurel turned to their brother. "Peter, *dongsaeng*, it's okay." Laurel patted his arm. "I understand there is a lot going on for the hamsters that run your brain-wheels to process, but we are going to handle this. As a family. And everything will turn out smashing. Really!"

Peter was still staring. "Yes. Vladimir Von Dread and Gaius Valiant are going to be my brothers. Awesome. Laurel, please make sure to raise Koschai the Deathless or Simon Magus from the dead to marry. Or, better yet, both of them."

A thrill of girlish delight went through Rachel at the first part of Peter's pronouncement. Yes, that was exactly how it was going to be. Sandra would marry Vlad, and she would marry Gaius. She wanted to peek up at her boyfriend and smile at him, but she suddenly felt too shy.

Laurel arched an eyebrow. "Eww, no. Peter, please snap out of it. I know you have a tiny brain, and it can only hold one thought at a time. Like a goldfish!" She patted a glowing goldfish lantern that stood beside her. "I don't even think there are hamsters in there. But we need to deal with this situation. Or are we going to let our thirteen-year-old sister do all the work *again*?"

Just like that, Peter snapped out of it.

"You're right." He straightened. "I'll fix this. We need an Agent or two to de-geas Amber. Then we can deal with the new enemy, Snorflbarten."

Laurel scrunched up her face. "Uh, wha?"

Peter said, with his hand over his mouth as if to hide his words from lipreaders, "You know, the new enemy."

"Lost me. *Dongsaeng*," Laurel drawled. "I think you may be off your nut."

"Snorfbarten? Do you mean the Master of the World?" Rachel did not know whether she should cry or laugh. "An Agent won't do it, *oppa*. She isn't under a spell. She's just been raised wrong, for years, decades. Our parents gave up their first born—because they were ensorcelled—and she was raised to be a crazed, supernatural death doll."

He left his hand over his mouth. "Yes, the Master of the World. I mean him and his little granddaughter. Look at her over there, looking all pompous and cute. Curse her!"

Laurel squeezed his arm. "Poor, poor, Peter. You really are a doofus, aren't you? It's okay. You can't help how you are. We will all still love you." She looked at Rachel. "He's really blood related to us, right? Daddy isn't a doofus. Maybe it skips a generation?"

"He didn't get it from Grandfather," Rachel defended her beloved grandparent.

Laurel shrugged. "Maybe it comes from Mother's side."

Peter ignored Laurel. "And you know what the worst thing about this is? Wait, no, don't answer that. *One of* the worst things about this is that our sister," he pointed at Amber, "is some totally kickbutt death-ninja-superhero who I bet could beat up Vladimir Von Dread *and* Valiant at the same time, and I can't even get her to do it." He paused, adding thoughtfully, "Or maybe she would, if I asked."

Gaius sighed. "I would honestly appreciate it if you wouldn't."

Laurel shook her head, sadly. "I don't think there's any saving my little brother. He's suffering from boyness."

"You could ask her, *oppa*," Rachel agreed solemnly, "but if she did, I would cry."

Gaius shot her a look. He was struggling not to burst out laughing, probably at Peter. Rachel nodded her appreciation of his Herculean efforts.

She glanced at the princess and turned back to her brother. "You never did go try to befriend Nastasia, *oppa*, did you? Like you promised me you would? Too bad!"

"Sorry," Peter said, sounding particularly British, "but she's a freaking Ice Queen. Everybody agrees. The stick up that girl's arse has a stick up its arse."

Laurel put her hand over her mouth. Gaius's expression became even odder, as if he were almost successfully managing not to choke with laughter. His face had gone a bit purple. In Rachel's mind, her grandmother exclaimed: *Language!* Appalled by Peter, Rachel started to frown sternly, but it did not work. To her embarrassment, she burst into giggles. Once she started, she could not stop. Soon, she was bent over, tears of laughter running down her cheeks.

"Oh, Peter! That's not nice! Funny, yes, but not nice!"

Her brother shook his head. "I know she's royalty, but Ivan and Alex and Alexis don't act like that. Even the Starkadder clan doesn't act like her, and some of them are.... Well, there are ladies present, so I shall not say. I mean, they're plenty cheeky to people who they don't like, but you can talk to them. Freka is really nice, and Wulfgang seems like a decent kid."

Rachel sighed. It was true. Nastasia had placed Rachel's most precious secret into the hands of the person most suited to use it to Rachel's disadvantage. Chastened, the princess had offered her a favor, but when Rachel tried to take her up on it; Nastasia had refused her request.

Rachel was certain that her friend's betrayals were unwitting and came from ignorance rather than malice, but it still hurt to be betrayed by someone you trusted. *The princess had endangered Rachel placing her in jeopardy, and then, instead of a favor, had made her life more difficult; how much did the bonds of friendship require Rachel to endure?*

Just like that, Rachel came to a decision. In some ways, it was a snap decision, but, in others, it had been coming ever since the chestnut roast. While Nastasia would remain her friend, she was no longer Rachel's best friend. That position was now open. Maybe there was someone else at Roanoke who would prove to be a real friend to Rachel. Maybe even, if the chestnuts were to be believed, someone who needed a friend as much as she did. *Maybe Astrid Hollywell?*

Peter continued, "It annoys me to no end to see O'Keefe's little sister following her around and being all nice to her, and yet your princess treats the girl as if she's not even there. I'm not blind. I see how she acts around everyone. She's not even nice to you. Why are you friends with her? Look at where it's gotten us. Our sister is her lap dog."

"Yeah. I mean. A bodyguard is one thing...." Rachel trailed off.

The reality of the situation struck her like a blow to the solar plexus. She felt as if she might be ill again. Beside her, Laurel and Peter simultaneously frowned in annoyance. Gaius gazed at the princess thoughtfully.

Rachel spoke up suddenly, "Laurel, could you take care of Peter? This is my very first masquerade ball. Before Sandra comes, I'd like to dance one last time with my boyfriend."

"I suppose I could try to take care of him." Laurel eyed Peter as if she were contemplating a method of taking care of him that involved a sledge hammer.

"Not just him," said Rachel, realizing for the first time that when her family was with her, she did not need to do everything herself. "Amber, too. Go explain to her than Sandra's coming, and we're all going home together."

Laurel glanced across the ballroom, giving Amber a very dubious look. "Right. On it."

Gaius put out his hand. Rachel accepted with a happy smile, and he led her out on to the dance floor. He spun her into his arms, twirling her around the ballroom rather nicely, which was much easier now that the floor was not as crowded. They danced to the strains of Strauss's "Fairy Tale Waltz," and for the space of that single waltz, the world fell away, and everything was all right again.

As the music ended, Rachel waited for Gaius to dip her, but he had paused, staring off into the distance.

"Look!" Gaius's face lit up.

He pointed toward the door. Across the ballroom, framed in a doorway, stood Sandra.

Chapter Thirty-Four: Griffin Family Reunion

Sandra glided into the ballroom on Vlad's arm, looking radiant, despite the fact that it was not yet dawn in London. She detached herself from her escort and began to walk forward, heading toward her siblings, but if she had hoped to move unnoticed across the dance floor, she was sadly mistaken.

A whisper spread through the room. Heads turned. Dancers paused mid-dance. Voices cried out in joy.

"Look! It's Sandra Griffin!"

"Sandra's here! Sandra's here!"

"Sandra, *senpai!*"

The last voice sounded like Iolanthe Towers, who, despite her Japanese heritage, Rachel had never before heard use an actual Japanese word.

The dancers parted, opening a way before Sandra as she glided forward. The music stopped as the tutors on the dais paused to wave to her. The few freshmen who had not left yet stared around in confusion, but almost everyone else cheered, with many rushing forward to surround the elder Miss Griffin.

Mr. Chanson was already beside Sandra, greeting her cheerfully. Rachel recalled that they were friends. Mr. Fuentes did not have the gym tutor's supernatural speed, but he crossed the room waving, a big grin on his face. Sandra spotted him and waved back with a happy smile of her own. Junior and senior college boys, such as Agravaine and Veli, who seemed so impressive and cool to Rachel, eagerly circled around her sister, looking young and hopeful. Even the elegant Yolanda Debussy rushed eagerly to join those gathering around the new arrival. Sandra greeted each one of them warmly, shaking hands and kissing cheeks.

Among the older college boys present in the ballroom, only Romulus Starkadder and his cronies did not rush to crowd around her sister. They watched the spectacle of Sandra's arrival with amused disdain and then went back to whatever they had been discussing.

From behind Rachel, Donner Virgil walked up to the semi-circular crowd around Sandra. He frowned at the press of people. Then, he nodded at the little, iridescent red and blue dragon on his shoulder and backed up. Spreading his arms, he took several running steps forward and leapt.

He soared over the entire crowd, somersaulting ten feet in the air. He landed lightly behind Sandra's shoulder, his arms outstretched like a gymnast, left hand open, the right with fingers curled. Gasps of astonishment accompanied his landing, followed by applause. Rachel knew that every familiar gave its owner a special gift. She suspected that his tiny shoulder dragon lent him some ability that was the secret to his astonishing feat—which was interesting, because when Siggy had asked him, back in September, what gift his dragon familiar granted, Donner claimed he did not know.

Sandra turned and smiled warmly at Donner, lightly touching his cheek as if rewarding him for his daring. Then she turned away and greeted the next person with equal equipose. Glancing over his shoulder, Donner tilted his head and squinted, eyeing Dread, who still stood by the door. Dread crossed his arms and met the other young man's gaze head on, and the two young men took each other's measure. Watching all this, Rachel wondered how differently this exchange would have gone if either boy had possessed the dreaded eye beams.

Watching her sister greeting the eager crowd like a reigning princess returning to her subjects, Rachel suddenly understood how Vladimir must see her: a young woman suited to be queen. Sandra had all the qualities a future king needed in a wife, among others, someone who could greet the public with grace, who could charm the hearts of his people.

Rachel's own heart fell. She herself was nothing like that. As she had told Ivan Romanov in September, she was more of a power behind the throne type, a spy mistress rather than a queen. An unexpected stab of embarrassment coursed through her. All those times last fall when she had daydreamed about what it would be like to use her gifts on the behalf of a prince, she had neglected to consider that a monarch would have no need to marry a person such as herself. Maybe Ambassador Cavendish had benefited from marrying Great-Aunt Jin, but why would a prince need to do so? Or the Master of the World? Why not merely hire the girl with the perfect memory or, in the case of Amber, kidnap a child and keep her around as a servant-retainer.

Ashamed, Rachel roughly pushed aside her feelings for Vladimir yet again and renewed her support for the Vladimir-Sandra match. Gazing at the eager students pressing around her sister, it occurred to her that maybe the *Sandra Uber Alles* Club had a much larger membership than she had first thought.

Sandra, meanwhile, raised a hand, gaily calling the crowd to attention. "It is so lovely to see you all. It pains me to make this short, but family duty calls. I am here to gather my siblings and take them back home." Her eyes fell on Amber, standing silently behind Nastasia in another part of the ballroom and, while her expression did not falter, Rachel thought she saw her lose a bit of the color in her cheeks. "All of them."

Sandra herded her siblings together and down to the docks. Even Amber came with them. When Sandra approached her, she agreed to come speak to their parents tonight, and as Nastasia announced she was off to bed, Amber felt there was no reason not to accompany her siblings.

Once at the docks, beyond the wards of the school, Laurel put the broom that she and Sandra had ridden across into her kenomanced backpack, and the two of them jumped to the Glass Hall, dissolving into a towering beam of white light and then forming back into themselves on the far side of the Hudson. Amber flew up into the air and across the water, to cries of awe from all her siblings. Too young to jump, Peter and Rachel continued on Vroomie across the dark waters, meeting up with the others at the small cottage that served as Roanoke Academy's Glass Hall.

The five siblings followed the same route Rachel and the prince had taken two weeks earlier, arriving in Devon in the morning, though at this time of the year, it was still dark. At the Gryphon's Nest, Rachel recalled Vlad's question and suggested that Amber try opening the door sealed with the ducal crest. Amber looked skeptical and murmured that, since she had never been this way, the spell could not have been crafted to include her, but when they all urged her to try, she brushed her fingers across the griffin on the crest. She nodded impassively when there was no response.

Then the door swung slowly open. Amber stared at it a moment and then followed the rest of them, a faint frown troubling her brow.

They reached the front door of Gryphon Park Manor. Tennyson glided down the main staircase to greet them. At Sandra's request, he departed, saying that he would let the duke and duchess know that their children had arrived along with a guest, to which Rachel replied that this was not correct. There was no guest, just their children. A puzzled Tennyson nodded and went off to carry out their bidding.

Five minutes later, the Griffin children entered the Lavender-Green Drawing Room, which four of them were in the habit of calling the Dilly-Dilly room. It was a spacious airy chamber near the center of the main wing. Paintings of the Gryphon Park Lavender Farm in bloom graced the walls, along with dried sprigs of the flower pressed behind glass. Armchairs and divans, upholstered in violet and green, were arranged around a hand-carved, two-toned Moroccan coffee table. To one side, against the wall, stood another Moroccan piece, a long black sideboard with silver fittings that looked like unicorns. Above it, an antique lantern clock ticked regularly as its pendulum swung. A matching, six-sided Moroccan coffee table fit snugly in a bay window, displaying a black and gold chess set. In the opposite corner, set in the shadows where the wisps were few and far between, sat an antique billiards table.

The room was chilly when they first entered, but Tennyson saw to that, before departing along with Laurel, leaving a young salamander cavorting in the hearth enclosure. The odor of cinnamon, emanating from the salamander, was only just beginning to overpower the room's normal scent of lavender.

The duke and duchess arrived shortly after their children. Ambrose was dressed in a black shirt and black slacks, but their mother was still in her nightgown, an Edwardian-style gown in Black Watch flannel. They were smiling when they came in, but their expressions changed when they saw Amber. The duke looked extremely curious, but the duchess's expression was harder to read. Lady Devon's face was very pale, as pale as Rachel had ever seen it. Rachel was not as good at judging others as Sandra was, but if she had been forced to guess, she would have said her mother was terrified.

After the initial introductions, Ambrose indicated that everyone should take a seat. Rachel climbed onto a lilac loveseat to the left of the leaf-green overstuffed armchair Peter had chosen. Beside Peter, Sandra sat cross-legged on the green and purple carpet with its designs of ferns and grapevines, watching their parents and Amber closely. She looked actually relaxed, not her dissembled calm. Rachel suspected this was because their father was in the room. Sandra was always calmer when she felt Father was in charge.

Rachel herself had once trusted their father that unconditionally. Had that truly been only six months ago? It seemed like a lifetime.

Across from Rachel, Amber sat in the middle of a green velvet couch with their parents to either side of her. She rested there calmly with her hands folded in her lap, but, to Rachel's shock, her cheeks were wet with tears. Their mother reached out and pulled back Amber's hood, so they could see her face clearly. Amber's resolve cracked more. She hung her head, gazing at the floor.

As it was not yet dawn here, the forest green velvet curtains were still drawn over the windows. The will-o'-the-wisps in this chamber had not been maintained properly, or perhaps they were reluctant to come out of their nighthoods at such an early hour. Either way, there were fewer of them than usual, so that the light in the chamber was a dim creamy golden glow. Rachel's father gestured, and the will-o'-the-wisps came closer together, casting more light onto the family's faces, but this left the greater drawing room around them in shadow.

Under her breath, Rachel whispered Vlad's and Gaius's names. She had promised her boyfriend that he could listen in on what Amber had to say. Her black bracelet began to vibrate, and she heard Vlad say softly, "We are listening but will remain silent."

Ambrose Griffin sat very close to his long-lost daughter, gazing down at her. "Amber, I'm sorry this is uncomfortable for you. Please understand no one here is upset with you. We are so glad to have this chance to meet you. You are my beautiful girl. I am just so proud of you. We are proud of you, all of us."

Laurel came in again with Tennyson, both carrying trays with tea and juice and brandy. They placed the trays on the coffee table, and Laurel served.

Tennyson bowed towards their new addition. "Lady Amber, it is wonderful to have you here. Please let me know if you are in need of anything at all."

He offered her a silver silk handkerchief, which she took, dabbing her eyes. Laurel thanked him. Nodding, he told her he would be awaiting her call, should anything be needed, and walked out, closing the doors behind him. Laurel poured a small amount of brandy into three snifters, which she served to their parents and Sandra. She then poured tea for herself and for Peter, who rolled his eyes and put it on an end table by his chair.

She glanced at Rachel, as if to ask if she preferred juice or tea. Rachel chose tea. Finally, Laurel looked at Amber, holding out the teapot and, after Amber gave a slight nod, poured her a cup. Then she crossed to the loveseat and squished in beside Rachel, wrapping her arms around her littlest sister, hugging her. It was hard for Rachel to drink tea with her sister squeezing her so tightly at seemingly random intervals, but it was lovely to drink real tea again, not what passed for tea at school.

"Tell us about yourself. Please," the duchess said to Amber, her voice soft and beautiful.

Rachel could see that her mother was trying very hard not to touch Amber or put her arms around her. Several times, she started to lean toward her newly-restored daughter and caught herself. Somehow, that sight created a larger lump in Rachel's throat than anything else that had happened that day. Her mother seemed so hopeful and so lost at the same time. How was she going to feel when she discovered that Amber was not planning to return?

Amber spoke dutifully, "I was raised in the barracks of the Praetorian Guard of my emperor, Andre the Second. It may sound bad to you all, but it was not. I had many brothers. We trained together, learned together, ate together, and only were separated at night, when I had a room alone. The guard does not mix sexes; usually, they are all male. It was...." She paused briefly. Was that her voice catching before she stopped? Rachel could not tell. "... an honor to be raised with my brothers. And my emperor came and visited me many times, as did other members of the Twelve. The Twelve are the greatest of his warriors. Heroes. Men and women whose skills were beyond even that of my brother Praetorians.

"I was told when I was very young, I had been picked to be of the Twelve. I had a destiny. It was a great deal of pressure, but I studied and trained daily to be worthy of the honor. Other members of the Twelve came and trained me directly at times. I had to learn the art of war with a sword and shield and spear. Tactics and endurance and patience. I also had to learn mental disciplines. I had a very good teacher. He is patient and very kind. I think you would like him.

"Shortly after my fifteenth birthday," she continued, "I took part in a ritual.... I am not allowed to describe it. I'm sorry. But the ritual prepares you for great tasks. And it stops you from aging—which is why, today, more than a decade later, I still look as I did then. So this is how I shall look until I am cut down in battle."

Peter winced. Their mother made a soft, pained sound. Ambrose listened calmly, nodding encouragingly to Amber whenever she glanced in his direction. Their mother reached out hesitantly and lightly touched Amber's back. She looked a tiny bit happier when Amber did not push her hand away.

Rachel took another sip of her tea and stared down at the delicate porcelain cup. What a strange and busy evening this had been. She still had to find some way of proving to Amber that their parents had wanted her, so that she would visit again—otherwise, they would have no chance of reclaiming what had been stolen from them. *But how?*

Something painful was poking her back. It took her a moment to realize it was the wire tail of her cat costume. It was hard to move her arm freely with Laurel hugging her so tightly, but she eventually was able to reach back and pull it to the side.

Amber continued, "I went out with the Twelve for the first time that very day. We traveled with my emperor to a place and fought there. It was my first true battle. The enemy were of the Legion of Everlasting Fire, Elysians who had mixed their substance with a lord from the Pit and his troops—and before you ask," she raised a hand as if to forestall questions, "that day, I was able to fulfill part of my destiny. I cannot say more about what this means."

She smiled slightly, looking down at her hands. Then, looking up at their mother, she said, "I know you are hurting. I am sorry. I do not want to cause you pain. I just wanted to see you. I knew all along that I was adopted. I-I... wanted to see you."

Amber started crying harder, dabbing futilely at her eyes with Tennyson's handkerchief.

The duke put an arm around her, murmuring quietly, "It's all right. Shhh. It's okay."

The duchess's face had become very still. Rachel noticed that their mother's quietness seemed to have had a calming effect on Peter. He lay back in his chair now and did not look as shell shocked as he had earlier. He sipped his tea and even smiled slightly. Laurel, on the other hand, hugged Rachel so tightly that Rachel began to have trouble breathing. She felt her sister's hot splashes of tears on her neck and back and heard Laurel sniffing quietly.

Rachel herself, who had been so upset earlier in the evening, felt calm. Now that her family knew about Amber, much of the weight had been lifted from her shoulders. She hugged Laurel in return, hoping to comfort her and that Tennyson had the necessary healing herbs in the medicine cabinet because her ribcage felt as if it were threatening to crack. There were a number of things she wished she could say to Laurel, but this did not seem like the time.

Their mother asked softly, "So... how did you find your way back here?"

"Something in this world tried to change my mind and draw me back," Amber said. "I told my emperor that something on this world was using fate magic to try and draw me here." Her features softened unexpectedly. "I-I also was curious about you. So I asked him to please let me come and investigate. He said he could arrange it so I could stay with his granddaughter and investigate the matter. He also asked me to watch her while I was here. I have other standing orders that I must follow as well, as long as they do not interfere with my primary goals. I have done my best to follow them."

Rachel started to speak up but then fell silent. She wished she could tell her family that she had discovered Amber's existence and arranged to bring her here. She knew her father would be impressed. However, she did not want to blurt out something that would cause more trouble.

Amber looked at Rachel, "I know there's confusion over the reasons for the pain inflicted upon this family. I promise you, my emperor acted for the good of the universe. I apologize for what happened to you. If you are going to be angry, please do not be angry with my emperor."

Rachel nodded expressionlessly, but inside her anger kindled more hotly. Her father and her other siblings were nodding, as if they accepted Amber's explanation, but to Rachel's surprise, for just an instant, she saw her own sentiments burning even more brightly in the eyes of her mother. Apparently, the duchess was not buying the notion that the Master of the World was not the source of their woes.

"My emperor," continued Amber, "would not have done such things, if he did not believe it was to protect this world. I am not a madwoman. I am not under a compulsion. I serve my emperor because he is a good man, and he does his best with the very little he has. He is under attack by mighty powers who threaten to overrun the few worlds that are left. There are... circumstances present here of which I think he might not have been aware. I think if it were explained to him what is going on and how the changing of memories here is causing such disruption, he would listen. I know he would."

Is that so? Rachel thought skeptically, her face expressionless. *And this from the person who was certain that their parents could not have been changed.*

The duke leaned forward. "Worlds that are left?"

Amber inclined her head. "I can share this, because it is well-known to our enemy. Far too well known. Once there were millions of worlds. Billions, maybe. Now there are fifty known worlds, and maybe a few more that can still be salvaged."

"I say! That is...." Their father drew a deep breath.

"Not good." Amber nodded expressionlessly.

There was a moment of silence. Then Rachel spoke up, her voice low. "Even if you are right about our parents, the Master of the World did come into *my* bedroom and try to change my memories. It terrified me."

The duke frowned, clearly not too keen on this idea. Peter had an odd look on his face. Sandra still looked calm. Laurel squeezed Rachel so tightly that she saw spots before her eyes.

The duchess laid her hand on Amber's arm, "We can discuss that later. How long can you stay? Can you take leave? Stay for some time?" Their mother's voice rose hopefully. "Forever?"

Chapter Thirty-Five:
One Last Hope

Above her, Rachel could hear the soft whisper of the wisps. From the hearth came the noises of the salamander at play. The scent of cinnamon now fully perfumed the chamber. The pendulum of the lantern clock swung back and forth.

Tick. Tock. Tick. Tock.

Rachel bit her lip, hoping against hope that Amber had changed her mind and would not break their mother's heart.

Amber shook her head. "I have achieved my primary goal. I will report back as soon as I am contacted."

Rachel could bear it no more. The truth came tumbling out of her. "I brought her here. I wanted to meet her, so I arranged that she would come."

Peter's eyelids were closed, and the duchess's entire attention was focused on Amber, but Sandra's head shot up, and she gazed at Rachel in surprise. From the couch beside Amber, their father was eyeing Rachel curiously. Since her father had forgotten everything that had happened since September, he might not even be aware of Rachel's friendship with the Raven. If so, such a claim upon her part must seem quite mysterious.

"What, you did?" Laurel cried, astonished. She squeezed Rachel even more tightly. "*Dongsaeng*! But how did you…. Oh! You had had a vision about her. You mentioned that."

Rachel took a sip of her sweet, milky tea, not wanting to lie to her parents about the source of her information; however, she was spared from making any additional comment upon the subject by Amber who spoke up.

"The Guardian brought me," her eldest sister said. "I spoke with him, and I felt him use his powers as we traveled around this world. It was clear he was the cause of it. I am glad that it was him and you, Rachel. I was… concerned at first that it might be a trap. I was wondering though... Actually, forget it. Best not to ask, I think. Thank you for arranging it."

"You're welcome." Rachel replied softly.

Amber paused, then she asked timidly, "What does *dongsaeng* mean?"

Laurel answered first. "It's Korean—the language of the country our mother's family came from. It means 'younger sibling.' So, I am your *dongsaeng*, and you are my *unni*—my big sister."

Amber's pupils widened ever so slightly. The effect was so small that Rachel had to remember back to confirm that it had happened at all. Outwardly, Rachel showed no reaction, but inwardly, she smiled. Amber had come here knowing that she was their sister, but that was not the same as having a younger sibling refer to her as "big sister." Big sisters had responsibilities toward their younger siblings.

Good. Maybe this knowledge would grow on her. Even if it did not sink in now, maybe it would eventually draw her back.

Rachel glanced at her mother, who had lost all semblance of formality. She sat with her legs folded under her, looking as if she were itching to hug her long-lost daughter. Her hands were on Amber's arm, and she kept bouncing slightly, shifting her weight as if she were about to spring forward.

Rachel tried to catch her mother's eye and encourage her. Their father was hugging Amber. Why shouldn't their mother?

The duke noticed his wife's distress. His arm around his eldest daughter's shoulders, he spoke gently to her, "Amber, you have to understand we raised our children in a peacetime environment. We're going to be more affectionate than you are used to. I don't want you to feel uncomfortable but please accept that we're going to act differently than you are accustomed to."

Amber ducked her head. "I will do my best."

He smiled and winked at his wife. The duchess grabbed her long-lost daughter and hugged her very tightly. Then she drew back slightly in surprise, most likely because she had just discovered that she had wrapped her arms around armor rather than flesh. Amber, meanwhile, tensed for a moment and then relaxed. Lady Devon kissed her on the top of her head, whispering to her reassuringly.

Peter's voice startled Rachel. "Laurel! I can hear Rachel's ribs creaking from here. Are you trying to kill her? Let the poor girl breathe, at least!"

Laurel relaxed her grip, which was a good thing, because when their mother finally hugged Amber, Laurel had started squeezing even tighter—if such a thing were possible. Rachel had begun to feel light-headed again. She threw Peter a thankful look and let out her pent-up breath and then inhaled inhaling deeply.

Kissing Laurel on the cheek, Rachel whispered in her ear very quietly. "Should we tell Mum and Daddy that Amber was told they gave her up willingly?"

Laurel whispered back, "Uhhhhh. Good question. Should we leave it for another time or get it over with now?"

Meanwhile, Amber was saying, "I haven't told you anything the enemy does not know. I will ask my emperor to please not use the Guardian on you all again. Unless it is to fix your memories. If that is what you all wish."

The duke straightened and nodded. "Having my memory re-stored would be preferable. Not having us interfered with again would be acceptable, though."

"It would be very good," Rachel murmured softly. "Would you like to go upstairs to see the gallery—with portraits of Griffins going back hundreds of years? I am so glad that we actually are Griffins. For a time—from something father said—I thought we were Outsiders, and the gallery was false."

Amber frowned slightly. "I have only ever heard of locals having their memories changed. I am not sure that the Guardian would do such a thing to Outsiders...."

"Um...." Rachel stopped.

Had the Master of the World not told Amber that the Guardian had been rescuing people and changing their memories for a long time? Or did he not know?

Rachel glanced at her father and then back at Amber. "You told me that our parents took vows to serve the Cause. I guess that is why Father had his memory changed to make him believe he was an Out-sider. Do any locals know?"

Amber shrugged. "I don't know. I don't think the emperor knows exactly what's going on here. Not fully...."

A faint frown appeared on Rachel's brow. "That doesn't quite make sense. When I spoke to him in his office, just before he lost his memory, Father said that it was the Romanovs who enforced the covenants that he had agreed to when he came here. And it was definitely the Master of the World who came to take our memories away."

Sandra ran her finger along the designs in the Moroccan coffee table, her head tilted as if she were listening to something. Rachel wondered if she had an object like the black bracelet, and if someone else—maybe even Vlad—were speaking to her.

Amber wiped her face and sat up straight, gently disentangling herself from their parents. The duke released her, but their mother was reluctant to let go. As she slowly released her first born, she now looked extremely unhappy and unsure, and surprisingly young.

Amber rose to her feet. "It is very late. I wish to return to the school and the Princess now. It was... I thank you for the chance to meet you all."

Their mother looked utterly crushed. She cried out, "You don't have to go, Amber! You can stay for a while, can't you? We can show you the house, and you can tell us more about yourself. You just arrived!"

Amber shook her head. "I must go." She paused and then added, "I tried to remember you. I couldn't though. My first memory is of playing in the barracks. Before that point, my memories are confused, and I can't get them to line up in a way that makes sense. So, I wanted a clear memory of what you were like. I wanted to thank you for what you did for me. For my existence. For allowing me to serve my emperor and letting me follow my destiny. I'm sorry you are in pain. I... want you to see something."

Stepping in front of their mother, Amber gazed into the duchess's eyes. She leaned forward until their foreheads were practically touching. Her eyes glittered brightly, as if reflecting a light source that were not present in the room. Her iridescent butterflies rose up from under her cloak and fluttered around the two of them, leaving slightly glittery silvery trails in the air. She stood thus for a time, forehead to forehead, looking into her mother's eyes. Lady Devon relaxed noticeably. She stared back, unblinking, for minutes.

The duke rose and stepped closer to his wife and daughter, looking thoughtful and slightly concerned. Sandra, who now relaxed against a large throw pillow, looked attentive.

Peter's eyelids had fluttered closed several times, but his mock armor kept poking him and waking him up again. Finally, he rose and began stripping off his costume. However, he must have decided that whatever he wore underneath was not appropriate for the occasion, because he came and knelt beside Rachel and asked in a low voice if he could borrow Vroomie. She nodded, and he flew out of the room, presumably heading for the west wing and his bedroom to change his clothes.

Laurel had rested her sharp chin on Rachel's shoulder. Now she rose, picked up the tray with the tea service, and followed Peter out into the hallway, shutting the door behind her. Rachel took advantage of the calm to finish the last of her tea, savoring the flavor. As the sweet, woody-tasting liquid slid down her throat, she closed her eyes for a moment, thinking back an hour, remembering the dancing, the lights, and the music. The Year of the Dragon Ball now seemed like another world, another lifetime.

Peter returned after a few minutes, floating into the room seated sideways on Rachel's steeplechaser, which he handed back to her. He was now dressed similarly to their father, in a black shirt and slacks. He wandered over beside the duke, gazing at the duchess and Amber. Seeing the two male Griffins standing together, now that Peter had finally begun to grow taller, Rachel was struck by how much they looked like each other. Peter was more slender than their father, and his eyes resembled their mother's, but their hair, their brows, their straight, long noses, and their lips were nearly identical. They even stood the same way, with their weight more on their right leg than their left. Rachel, who had always associated Peter with their mother, as those two were very close, found this similarity quite interesting.

Laurel returned with a fresh pot of tea. Rachel rose and poured herself another cup, adding cream. Sandra, too, rose and poured herself some tea. Apparently, she had finished her brandy. The three younger Griffin girls stood together, teacups in hand, mutely watching their mother commune with their new-found oldest sibling.

Their father returned to his seat on the couch, apparently coming to the conclusion that his wife was in good hands. After a few minutes, Amber and her mother both blinked. Amber hugged her and straightened. Lady Devon seemed slightly dazed. She sat back on the couch and stared at the coffee table with a thoughtful look.

Laurel glanced at Rachel and began to snicker. Looking down, Rachel realized that the wire cat tail still stuck out sideways from her hip. Her cheeks growing warm, she quickly pushed it behind her again. Laurel's snicker turned into an outright giggle, which earned her a shushing glance form Sandra.

Sandra gave Amber a tight-lipped smile. "It was nice to meet you, Amber. I hope we'll get a chance to speak again soon."

Amber straightened. "I am not sure that would be wise. I am very busy."

The duke's head had shot up, surprised, and their mother's face crumbled, wrenching Rachel's heart to near the breaking point. Rachel moved her cup away from her as if it were scalding. She quickly set it back on the tray. What had she been thinking, sipping tea and daydreaming of sky lanterns and dancing with Gaius? She was supposed to be figuring out how to make Amber keep her word and return. Terror gripped her like a vise. *Had she failed? Was it too late now?*

Rachel wracked her brain, searching for something she could say. There must be something. Could it be she was wrong? Was Amber really taken away at birth with no fight from their parents? And then, suddenly, she loved the Raven even more than she had before, because he had given her the one piece of knowledge she needed to answer that question.

"Amber, are you sure you don't want to look around before you go?" Rachel asked cheerily. "It might help jog your memory. You know you lived here when you were little, right? Don't you remember the house at all?"

"Lived here?" Amber frowned severely, smoothing her cloak. "I was given up as a newborn. I am not sure I ever even entered this house before tonight."

"No, you lived here," Rachel spoke more confidently. "You weren't given up as a newborn. You lived here until you were at least two." She turned to her parents. "Father, how does the ducal door in the Gryphon's Nest work? Will it automatically open for any family member, or does each individual have to be keyed into the spell?"

"A person has to be keyed in," the duke replied.

Sandra spoke up. "When Amber touched the crest, the door opened."

There was a moment of silence. Rachel grinned. There, she had won.

Amber said coldly, "Perhaps, I have been to this house—when I was a week-old infant—but that proves nothing."

"You said you had not been here. We now know for certain you were wrong," Rachel replied. "Maybe some of your other ideas are wrong, as well."

"Either way, I never lived here," Amber replied coolly. "My first memories are of the barracks."

Rachel's father was frowning at her and rubbing his forehead. Peter, who had been pouring himself tea, paused to frown at both of his sisters. Laurel watched curiously. Sandra moved away from Laurel to sit beside their mother, squeezing her hand. Sandra looked weary, but their mother was staring at Rachel, a very strange, alert look on her face—something halfway between a terrified deer facing hunters and intense hope.

"Rachel, let it go for now," their father said gently, rising to his feet again. "It's late. Let's see Amber to the door and hope she will see fit to return again."

Rachel moistened her lips. She wanted to please her father, but she could not let it go. *Her father did not understand.* If she did not prove that their parents had not given away their newborn daughter without any resistance, that they had not surrendered her willingly, his newly-discovered daughter would not be coming back. And much as she did not quite know what to think about her new sister, she knew one thing: *Amber was her sister.*

Rachel was never going to give up on her family. Besides, she was now certain that Amber had lived here. She just did not know how to prove it.

"You did grow up here, Amber." Rachel crossed her arms stubbornly, ignoring her father. "If you don't remember it at all, someone changed your memory."

Anger flashed across Amber's face, a reaction with which Rachel sympathized. Had someone said that to her, she would have been angry, too. However, Amber did not lose her temper. She just took a deep breath and stood calmly.

"Absolutely not," replied Amber.

Rachel walked around the coffee table to stand in front of her sister. Amber was barely taller than she was. It was easy to look into her eyes. "You promised—if I can prove that you were not given up without concern, that our parents cared about you—that you would return to us again. I can't let you go until you at least give me a chance to prove this."

Several family members gasped. Rachel could not sort out which ones without thinking back, which she did not want to take the time to do.

Amber sighed. "I have given my word. If you prove it, I will return. But you cannot."

Rachel glanced desperately around the airy green and lavender room. Outside, the sky was lightening, with a faint dawn glow coming over the top of the curtains. An almanac in her mental library told her that sunrise would be at seven-ten a.m., local time. Her mind ranged from the drawing room, picturing the rest of the house, recalling backwards the last several times she had been here: the Red and Gold Drawing Room where she had entertained Vlad; the dining hall where the family had eaten their Yule Tide feast; the Blue and White Drawing Room, where they had held some of their family festivities and exchanged presents Yule morning; her bedroom with its pink canopy bed, its pile of plushy bed buddies, and the balcony overlooking the hedge maze; her parents' bedroom as it had looked when she sneaked into it to look in her mother's ornate jewelry box; the main library; the east library; her grandfather's library.

Surely, there was something....

The duke frowned openly at his youngest daughter. "Rachel, I have already asked you: Please let it go. We can discuss this next time."

"Next time!" Rachel turned on him, shouting. "What next time?"

Ambrose raised an eyebrow, his face entirely calm. His frown darkened. "Rachel...."

"Right," Rachel glared at him fiercely, the horse of her anger having grabbed the bit in its teeth and taken off at a gallop. "Because you know everything, Daddy. And you are so smart that you don't need to listen to your daughter, which is how you lost your memory!"

"Rachel," their mother gasped. "You shouldn't speak to your father like that."

Her siblings were looking at her aghast. Sandra, particularly, was frowning at her.

"It's true!" she cried wildly, turning from one to another. "He wouldn't listen to me! If he had only listened. If he had only believed me, none of it would have happened!"

"I am listening now," said Ambrose Griffin, his voice soothing and even. "What is it that I need to know?"

"Don't you understand, there *will be* no later!" Rachel gestured toward the door of the room, her arm outstretched. "If she walks out that door before I have proven that you did not freely give her up, as a newborn, that's it. She's not planning to come back. We'll never see her again, and our family remains shattered. Forever. Is that what you want? This is our last hope!"

The duke's pupils widened ever so slightly. He turned to Amber, his expression alert. Rachel's siblings were all staring at her. Peter looked faintly annoyed. Laurel watched her intently. Sandra pressed a hand against her heart.

"I have many duties," Amber stated. "And I have my own family I grew up with. I... just came to meet you."

Rachel cried, "She planned to come meet us and then have our memories erased, so that we would not remember that we met her! That is what would be happening right now, if it were not for my friend the princess!"

"Please thank the princess for us," replied the duke, gazing at Amber. "Daughter, would you really do such a thing to us? Rob us of what little we have of you?"

Amber's ears turned red. She pulled up her hood.

"If that is the way she feels, maybe she should not come back," Peter spoke sternly.

"Peter," gasped their mother.

If he had stabbed her with a knife, she could not have sounded more pained.

"I am sorry, Mum," he turned to her, "but look what disruption her visit brings to us and to her. Is it kind of us to want to continue to cause her this kind of pain?"

Ellen Griffin covered her face with her hands and burst into tears. Peter watched her helplessly, but his face remained set.

"Is that what you all want? To give up?" Rachel cried, spinning around to look at each of them. "What happened to 'Griffins will die for each other'?"

Of course it had been Jariel who had said that of them, but Rachel felt in her bones that it was true. She knew, she just knew, that her family would do such a thing. She just had to convince them that Amber was truly one of them.

"I say, who said that?" asked Peter, looking a bit chagrinned.

Rachel swallowed with some difficulty and murmured, "The Raven."

"Who?" asked Ambrose.

"Mr. Tengu!" Laurel cried simultaneously.

"She means the Guardian, Father," said Sandra simply.

Sandra, of course, had not forgotten the events of the last two years, and Father had probably discussed with her his visit to Roanoke in September, where he had instructed Rachel to avoid the Guardian. He forgot that now, but Sandra had not. Besides, Rachel had told her some of her adventures herself.

"The Guardian?" Ambrose gazed at Rachel, his face alert. "When did the Guardian speak to you?"

Rachel sighed. Right now, she hated the Master of the World more than anything else in the universe. Yet, what hope did she have of stopping him, of punishing him for his crimes against her family? Find his name, like Rumpelstiltskin? She doubted real life would be so simple.

Peter's words, however, had begun to work their way into her thoughts. Was he right? Was it too much of a burden for all of them for Amber to keep up her acquaintance with the rest of her family? After all, a little voice whispered, *it was not as if Amber was pleasant to be around. She was cold and a bit mean and didn't seem to care about the rest of them at all. Maybe it would be best to let her go. True, there was a rip in the family, but it would scar over. They had gotten along this long without Amber. Surely they could do so again.*

To her left, her mother made a soft, painful sound. Rachel glanced toward her, and their gazes met. Her mother's eyes were filled with such anguish that she seemed unable to move, but as Rachel watched, subtle changes came over the duchess's features. Her eyebrows moved in and then up. Her pupils widened ever so slightly. Her mouth, too, changed subtly, her lips parting very slightly. These changes might have meant nothing to Rachel were it not for two things. One, they looked so deliberate, and two, she had seen that exact sequence of changes upon her mother's face once before.

Her mother was sending her a message with *kumihotoushi*. Rachel may not have learned enough *kumihotoushi* to read people's emotions under normal circumstances, but these were not normal circumstances. She had no need to *interpret* her mother's poses, she merely had to *remember*. Because this was her mother, the person who had taught her this art.

Rachel closed her eyes for an instant, remembering. In the mansion of her memory, they stood in the winter garden, surrounded by the fragrance of lovely blooms from all seasons. Lily of the valley, daffodils, and peonies bloomed next to dahlia, cock's comb, and goldenrod. Above each section of the Victorian-style greenhouse hung orreries displaying the constellations and planets for different seasons. With the alchemical influences shed by these mini stars and constellations, their mother could grow out-of-season flowers all year round.

Rachel recalled her four-year-old self standing dutifully next to eleven-year-old Sandra. Laurel was there, too, but she had wandered off and was pulling petals off of a daisy while singing a rhyme. Peter had been with their grandparents that day. Her mother had been drilling them on the poses. She paused to display for them some of the lesser poses. Just after *weary* and before *annoyed*, she went through the exact, specific sequence of expressions and body language changes Rachel had just beheld. There had been two poses involved: *supplication* and *hope*.

As clearly as if she were speaking aloud, Rachel understood that her mother was saying, *Please, if there is any hope....*

Suddenly, Sandra was beside her, her hand gripping Rachel's shoulder. Bending down, she whispered in her littlest sister's ear, "Mummy needs help. We can't let Amber just walk out of our lives. Think hard. We must do something."

Rachel gritted her teeth. *She would not let the Master of the World win.*

Leaning forward, she balled her fists and shouted at the top of her voice, as much at the voices in her head as at those in the room. "Amber is *my sister*, and I will *never* let her go!"

Ambrose, who had not caught this secret exchange, took a sudden step back, perhaps from surprise, perhaps to spare his eardrums, but Amber stood absolutely still, like a soldier at attention. Her butterflies, however, flew about her in an agitated, silvery cloud. The lovely insects fluttered around her sister, glittering bits of living mother-of-pearl, each one unique.

No, wait....

Rachel peered closer. The glowing, mother-of-pearl butterflies were not unique. There were maybe a dozen different patterns, but these repeated over and over. She spotted three of one design, four of another. There were even two that looked, strangely enough, as if the butterflies had exactly the same chip out of their left wings.

Rachel's world slowed. In the mansion of her memory, she was back at the night of her parents' annual Yule Ball, standing in her parents' room, staring down at an identical butterfly with an identical missing chip.

Despite a sudden dryness of her throat, she whispered, "I can prove it. Wait here."

Chapter Thirty-Six:
The Duchess of Devon's Secret Sorrow

Rachel barreled out of the Dilly-Dilly Room on her steeplechaser, flying down the halls and up the staircases of Gryphon Park Manor towards the wing of the house that held her parents' bedroom, the tail of her Mistletoe costume streaming out behind her. Then, balancing a large object wrapped in a blanket, she zoomed back the way she had come. Flying back into the drawing room, she stumbled from the broom and carefully placed the object she was carrying on the Moroccan coffee table.

Straightening, she pointed at the two-toned squares of the table next to the blanket-covered object. "Amber, put your butterflies right here."

"Butterflies?" Amber looked confused for a split second. "Oh! My questing beasts."

Iridescent silvery butterflies that had been hovering around her head and shoulders swarmed over to the coffee table and landed on its surface, glistening like mother-of-pearl.

"Rachel, what are you doing?" the duke asked firmly. "We don't have time for theatrics."

He stopped speaking when his wife grabbed him, her fingers sinking into his flesh. She was staring at the butterflies on the table. Rachel was certain that she recognized them, too. Stepping forward, Rachel yanked away the blanket.

On the table rested her mother's jewelry box. The black-lacquered Oriental antique was inlaid with mother-of-pearl in the shape of roses and butterflies—very familiar butterflies. One even had a chip out of the left wing. The family looked back and forth between the jewelry case and the iridescent, glowing forms that Amber had called questing beasts.

They were exactly the same.

"See?" Rachel met Amber's gaze and pointed. "You do remember."

Amber stared at the butterflies on the box. She blinked thrice, a confused look on her face. The duke sucked in his breath as he grasped what Rachel was saying. The duchess had lost all her color and now pressed her free hand against her face. Sandra stepped forward and went down on one knee, regarding all the objects on the table with interest. Peter was squinting at Amber's questing beasts, studying them carefully. Laurel slid to her knees on the carpet beside the coffee table and leaned forward, tracing one of the mother-of-pearl butterflies on the box with her finger. Then she gently poked one of Amber's butterflies. Whatever the sensation this produced, she quickly pulled her hand away and then giggled.

Rachel flipped up the top of the jewelry box, revealing three little drawers. She opened the bottom drawer and pulled out from the back a silver rattle marked with an *A*. Holding it up high, she shook the rattle. It rang with a high, sweet tinkling sound.

Ting-a-ling-a-ling.

Amber gasped. She took a step, reaching out as if to grab onto something, but there was nothing in front of her. Ambrose and Sandra moved to support her, but she waved them away.

"I've..." Amber whispered, her voice soft and breathy, "... I've heard that before. I remember...."

"Of course, you do," Rachel replied softly, mentally thanking the Raven again for giving her the hint she needed. "They took you for your memory. That's *why* you were taken from us. Because of your memory, which is like Mummy's and like mine." There was no point in being secretive now. The Master of the World already knew all about her memory, thanks to Nastasia. "You were not taken from this house until after it was certain that you had inherited our gift."

The duchess slowly lowered her hand, her eyes locked on Rachel's face. Beads of sweat were forming on her brow. Again, she had that same very strange expression, like a cross between hope and utter despair. Rachel met her eyes and gave the tiniest nod.

"But we don't develop our perfect memories until after we develop language," she continued, "usually between the ages of one and two. So our mother bore you and raised you and cared for you and loved you. Probably, for at least two years. Only once you showed evidence of our family gift did your emperor come and take advantage of the oath of loyalty our parents had been manipulated into swearing, and force them to give you up.

"You lived here! And these butterflies," she pointed at them dramatically, "that look exactly like the ones from Mummy's case—are the proof. You might not remember her consciously, but you remembered her subconsciously!"

Rachel gazed directly at Amber, who stared back. Everyone else watched their confrontation. In the silence, the salamander's feet could be heard scampering around the hearth.

Absolutely expressionlessly, Amber spoke out loud, "Guardian."

Pure terror coursed through Rachel. No! *What had she done?*

A flicker of black feathers, and the Raven stood in the room, towering above even her father. He was in his man shape, shirtless, black pants, and holding his halo. Huge raven wings spread from his back. His eyes gleamed, red as blood. Upon seeing him, Lady Devon threw her hands in front of her face in fear and screamed. Sandra and Peter both ran to her side. Ambrose stepped back and shouted out a cantrip. Moments later, his fulgurator's staff—a length of wood topped with a diamond the size of a man's fist—came flying through the door and into his hand.

Rachel pressed both hands against her mouth to keep from screaming. Would Amber hurt the Raven? Would her father? *That would not go well. Look what happened last time.*

"Mr. Tengu!" Laurel exclaimed happily, clapping her hands with joy. That earned her an odd look from their father.

The Guardian spoke in his harsh, croaking Raven voice. "I am here."

Amber had resumed her martial bearing, standing without moving a single muscle. She asked simply, "Please explain to my sister the events that resulted in my being taken from my family."

The Raven cocked his head in a birdlike gesture, regarding Rachel, who knew that her face was as pale as the mother-of-pearl butterflies. The red drained from his eyes, leaving them a pearly gray, which reassured her a little. When he spoke, it was in his melodic, angelic voice. Rachel's father watched this transformation curiously.

Her mother, who had been hiding behind her hands, began peeking through her fingers, and even Amber made a slight noise in her throat, as if such a change in the Guardian were something new.

"Andre the Second asked me how likely it was that a future could be found where your parents would agree to swear an oath of obedience to him."

"What did you tell him?" asked Amber.

"I told him that I saw no futures where Ambrose Griffin swore such an oath."

"None?" Amber's voice wavered ever so slightly.

The duke was listening with great interest. He lowered his staff but still held it ready.

"None," replied the Raven.

"What did my emperor say?" asked Amber.

"He asked if I could make it become possible."

"And what did you say?"

The Raven's eyes grew dark as storm clouds. "I said that Ivan would not have asked such a thing of me."

"Ivan?" Laurel rubbed her eyes. "But he wasn't even born yet?"

Jariel looked faintly amused. "Ivan the Magnificent. Andre the Second's grandfather."

Amber asked impassively, "What did my emperor say?"

"He said, though not in so few words, that desperate times called for desperate actions."

"So you...." Amber faltered. She tried again. "You changed my father?"

A look of sorrow came over the face of the Raven. "I gave him false memories that he had come from Outside in order to raise his family in safety. In the memories, he had already sworn such an oath in order to be allowed to come. So when the man he thought of as his friend—the King of Magical Australia, Andre the Third—asked him and his young wife to swear again, he thought he was merely renewing a vow he had already made."

Ambrose stood calmly, but a muscle in the side of his jaw had begun to twitch rhythmically. No wonder he did not like the Raven, Rachel thought with a shiver.

The duke asked, "Why would you do such a thing?"

The Raven turned toward her father, his face as inhumanly perfect as a porcelain mask. "All Guardians are under an oath of obedience to the Eternal Emperor."

"You mean," Rachel swallowed, "you could not disobey?"

The Raven did not answer.

Amber stood motionlessly, but her butterflies left the table and began circling her head and shoulders as if agitated. Rachel's eldest sister closed her eyes, breathing slowly and deeply, until the flittering forms grew calm. Some retreated inside her robe. Others settled on her head and shoulders, their silvery glow gleaming brightly in the dimly-lit room.

Ambrose asked, "Why did you remove our memory of Amber?"

The Raven replied, "Andre the Second felt this was necessary."

Amber asked, "You removed my mother's memory of me because she was becoming too distraught?"

The Raven turned his head and stared at Ellen, who stared back at him. Her hands were shaking, and she swallowed convulsively. For the first time, Rachel wondered what her mother had been so afraid of all evening. She had a look as if the thing she feared had come upon her.

The Raven turned back to Amber. "No."

Amber faltered. "No?"

"At the Eternal Emperor's orders, I changed the memories of the family and servants so that you were forgotten by them."

A thought struck Rachel, a terrible thought.

"B-but..." she cried, her voice cracking from terror. "Wait!"

The Raven cocked his head to look at her. "Yes, Rachel Griffin."

Out of the corner of her eyes, Rachel noticed her father give her a thoughtful look, perhaps wondering why the Guardian called her by name.

Rachel opened her mouth to speak, but the thing she wanted to ask was so terrifying that it took a few tries to find her voice. "Y-you told me once that if you changed my memories, because of my perfect memory, it would harm me. K-kill me."

"I did." There was a tremendous sadness in the voice of the Raven.

Ambrose looked back and forth between Rachel and Jariel. His voice dangerously low, he asked, "Guardian, what do you mean?"

The Raven addressed her father. "The act of changing memories causes confusion, but the soul recovers. The only case where this is not so is for those, like your wife and daughter, whose memories are so closely-knit that changing them would require changing everything about them. For all practical purposes, to alter their memories is to turn them into someone new."

"And d-did you…?" Rachel whispered hoarsely, not wanting to hear the answer. "… k-kill my mother?"

"I…." The Raven paused suddenly and bowed his head, as if he were in pain. He placed his hand upon his chest.

Ambrose slowly raised his staff again, the glittering diamond pointed at the Guardian. Peter had raised his hands menacingly, preparing to form a cantrip. Sandra left their mother and moved to their father's side, raising her hands, the gems of her five rings of mastery glittering.

Time stopped.

Rachel's parents and siblings, even Amber, were absolutely still, motionless, hands partially raised; eyes half blinked. Even the salamander in the hearth had halted mid-slither.

The Raven met Rachel's eyes and lifted a finger to his mouth, indicating silence. Rachel nodded wordlessly, her heart beating painfully. He laid his golden halo on the coffee table. Then, tipping his head back slightly, he opened his mouth and reached toward it.

Despite her efforts to be quiet, Rachel gasped.

Against all laws of physics, the Raven drew from his mouth a second halo. This second hoop, as large around as his head, was a thousand times more beautiful than the first, if such a thing were possible. It shimmered with silver moonlight that flickered from it as flames flicker from a candle. From this silvery fire came such a feeling of forgiveness and mercy that, despite the dire accusations, Rachel found herself smiling.

Whatever the Raven had done, she would find it in her heart to forgive him. She was suddenly sure of this.

Jariel touched this new halo with one finger. The silvery moonfire stuck to his skin, flickering about his outstretched hand like living flame. He pressed his finger to his lips and then against his chest, above his heart. When he touched the silvery flame to the bare skin of his chest, a ripple of silver ran though his black hair and his feathers, vanishing again as quickly as it had appeared. He smiled faintly.

Then, he stepped forward and touched the same finger to the diminutive duchess's lips and her nightgown above her heart. Rachel thought she saw her mother stir slightly.

Returning to the coffee table, Jariel put the moonlight halo back into his mouth—a feat Rachel's eyes could not explain. Once this was done, he retrieved the other halo from the table, holding it in his hand as he had before.

With a gesture of his head, he indicated that Rachel should return to the position she had held when time stopped. She did so quickly, using her memory to recall exactly where she had been. He, too, resumed his previous stance.

Time started.

The Raven spoke, his voice ringing out in the drawing room. "No. I did not."

A wave of relief swept across those in the room. The duke lowered his staff. Sandra stuck her hands into the pockets of her coat. Peter, however, continued to stand ready, his eyes not leaving the Guardian.

Amber frowned. "Then what did you do? To my mother, I mean."

"I did nothing."

As one, everyone in the room turned and looked at Lady Devon. The tiny duchess was staring at the carpet, her cheeks pink.

"I could not bear to change her." Jariel lowered his head, feather-dark hair falling over his face. "I left her as she was."

Ambrose gazed intently at his wife. "You mean, all this time...."

"I told her that she must not speak of it, and she did not." The Raven spun, turning on Amber, his gaze fierce. "You have claimed that your mother was weak and unable to bear the separation. Ellen Kim Griffin has been anything but weak. All this time—raising her children, enduring the slings and arrows of the disdain of her in-laws, never complaining, not even to her husband—" Ambrose's head swiveled to stare at the Guardian and then back at his wife, startled.

"—she has remembered. And she has done so in silence, to safeguard her family."

"Ellen?" asked Ambrose, brows beetling.

Rachel's mother nodded wordlessly.

Suddenly, Rachel understood what had so puzzled her earlier in the evening: why her mother had seemed so terrified. Lady Devon had promised never to speak of her lost eldest daughter, and she had been tremendously afraid that she would accidentally blurt something out that would reveal the truth. Now the truth had been revealed; relief was flooding her mother's features.

"Mum, all this time?" burst forth from Sandra, who rushed forward and hugged their mother. The duchess rested her head against her much taller daughter.

Even Laurel looked cowed. "To think that I gave her such a rotten time."

Leaping to her feet, Laurel ran to her mother, too, throwing her arms around both of them. Peter had not lowered his hands, but he looked as if *crestfallen* had rushed headlong into *angry* and both were vying for ownership of his face. He moved closer to his mother as if to protect her.

Ambrose and Rachel and Amber kept their gaze pinned on the Raven.

Amber's brows drew together, troubled. "I don't understand. If my mother was not so distraught that she was a danger to herself, why did my emperor ask you to make her forget me?"

The Raven replied. "It was not the mother who could not bear the separation."

Sandra, Laurel, and Peter glanced at their father.

"You cannot mean it was Father..." began Peter, angrily.

"That's not what he meant," whispered Rachel, who understood.

"I... don't understand," said Amber.

Rachel replied bluntly, "He means it was *you*. That little you was too upset when you were parted from our mother."

Amber turned to the angel plaintively. "Guardian, is that what you mean?"

Jariel nodded. He turned towards her with exquisite grace. "With your perfect memory, you could not be coaxed to stop focusing on your mother and concentrate on your new life. With a heavy heart, Andre decided that it would be better if your family stopped disrupting your training."

Amber closed her eyes and took a deep breath. Instantly, her body calmed. "But... why don't I remember any of this?"

"Perhaps your previous memories have been blocked. If so, it was not my doing."

Amber frowned uncertainly. The Raven looked off into the distance, as if he had heard something. Then, he was gone.

"Wait." Amber looked faintly surprised, glancing around. "How did he just...."

Peter shot across the room to where their mother stood hugging Sandra. He stared at her, horrified, "Mummy, is it true? You've known? All this time?"

Their mother looked up, tears in her eyes, and whispered, "What could I do?"

Gently, almost like a wounded creature, she pushed away from Sandra and stepped toward Amber, stretching out her arms toward her long-lost daughter.

"Gave you away? Is that what you thought?" Her voice broke painfully. "We never gave you away, Amber. Never! They had to drag you from us. We could not resist because our oaths were killing us. Ambrose tried to fight Andre, and the oath brought him so close to death that I feared I had lost him."

Rachel's mother stepped forward and took the rattle from Rachel, examining it, turning it this way and that. She shook it twice, the silvery sound of it ringing through the drawing room.

Ting-a-ling-a-ling. Ting-a-ling-a-ling.

"A winged woman came, all silvery and bright," Rachel's mother continued, tears glistening on her lashes, "She said the Guardian had sent her. She taught me to hide my memories. Not forget them, just temporarily veil them." The duchess looked up again at Amber. "So every day, for twenty-two years, five months, and thirteen days, I have gone about my day with my memories of you hidden away, so that I only thought of you if something arose to remind me. And every night —every single night—before I slept, I brought them out again and remembered you. Remembered your actions, your laugh, your little face."

Ellen Griffin stroked her eldest daughter's cheek. "I remember you," she whispered, her eyes wide and luminescent. "I remember how you used to giggle when the puppies licked your face. I remember how one of your first words was ball. You used to toddle around crying, 'Ball, ball.' You were so sweet when you said it that everyone —your father, myself, the staff, even your stiff, cold grandparents— rushed to buy them for you, so they could hear your cry of delight and see the joy on your face. You owned big beach balls, little itty ones, red ones, white ones, green ones, and when you saw them, your face would light up. You would reach out your little hand and cry, 'Ball, ball!' When they took you away, there were twenty-nine of them in the house, twenty nine different balls. And every time...."

The duchess began to weep more openly, tears cascading her cheeks. Her husband stepped forward to comfort her, trying to gently shush her. She pushed him aside. Laurel and Peter were weeping, too. Rachel's own cheeks were wet, though she had not noticed when she began crying. Sandra pressed her hand against her mouth, and her eyes were filled with sorrow.

"They were all over the house," Ellen continued, hiccuping. "It took over a year to gather them. Some had rolled under things: furniture, couches, beds. Every time I found one, as I rounded them up, I would hear again that sweet, little cry of, 'Ball, ball,' and I would remember...." She was now weeping so hard that tears were streaming down her cheeks like two tiny waterfalls, dripping from her chin and forming a wet spot on her Black Watch nightgown. "I would remember...." Her voice rose into a wail of anguish and she grabbed Amber, holding her very close. "They stole her! They took my little girl away to turn her into a killing machine! My baby! My daughter!"

Ambrose stepped forward again to comfort her. Ellen did not push him away this time, but she continued hugging her diminutive eldest daughter.

"Every day," she whispered. "Every day, before I fall asleep, I think about you, Amber." Her hands balled into fists. "And then I think about how to kill the monster who stole you."

Chapter Thirty-Seven: In Defense of Dread

Laurel sank to the floor again and sat on the green and purple carpet beside the coffee table. "Amber, what *is* your first memory? You don't remember Mummy? What do you remember?"

"She already told us," Rachel looked down at Laurel and then up at Amber, who was standing absolutely still in her hood and robe. "You said you were playing in the barracks?"

"Yes," Amber replied, calm and emotionless. "I was sitting in a beam of sunlight in the barracks playing with a...." Her voice broke abruptly. "W-with a ball."

Rachel's mother let out a long, low, sorrowful cry.

Amber backed away from them all. She looked back and forth between her family members with frantic little motions that reminded Rachel of a wounded animal.

She said, "I will keep my word and return—when I am allowed to. I'm going now."

With that, Amber ran from the room.

"Does she need to be shown out?" Peter dropped to the couch, resting his eyes against his palms.

Rachel shook her head, "No. She's like Mummy and me. She remembers the way."

"Oh. Right." Peter's eye drifted closed.

Laurel rose to her feet and yawned. "I'm really tired, too. It is the wee hours of the morning for us. I think I'm going to sleep here and head back to school after I wake up. I'll see everyone in the morning? Er, night. Er... whatever."

She made a round of the room, hugging each person, even Sandra, and kissing their mother gently on the cheek. Then she left with a wave, her teacup in her hand.

Ambrose's brows drew together, gazing at Rachel's cat outfit. "Wait. Have you lot not been to bed yet? It must be well past midnight there. What happened?"

Rachel, who felt strangely awake, even though she could tell that her fatigue was beginning to catch up with her, replied, "It was Year of the Dragon Ball."

"Ah. Masquerade." The duke smiled, perhaps remembering his own days at Roanoke.

He walked over and gathered his wife into his arms. She was still weeping. The two of them sat down together on the couch, her curling up with her head in his lap. He sighed, playing with her hair, and then looked at Sandra and Rachel.

"Are you girls going to be staying or heading back?" he asked.

Rachel crossed to the loveseat and sank back against the velvet cushions, trying to decide if she should sleep here at home or head back to school. She was tired and loved seeing her family, but there were a great many things she still wanted to do at school, including talking to Wulfgang, which she needed to do before she met up with her friends again. On the other hand, there were things she really wanted to tell her father. Some of them should wait until he regained his memory, but there was one thing that she had been wishing she could say to him for the last two weeks.

Sandra said, "I should head back to my apartment. I can take Rachel to school if she wants to go."

"I don't know," Rachel sighed, not wanting to hold Sandra up or further burden her mother. "I... I probably should. There was something I wanted to say to Father and Mummy, but it is about other subjects entirely. I think it'll have to wait."

The duke said, "Out with it. If it is important, you should let me know now."

Rachel waved her hand back and forth in a negating gesture. "No. No. It's not that kind of thing. Really." She looked at her mother. "It's the kind of thing that will wait. I'll write it down and send it in a letter. I think Mummy has had enough bother tonight."

Ambrose said, "As you will. Let me know when you're ready to speak of it."

Zzzzzzzz. Her mother had fallen asleep. The duchess looked very young, curled up next to her husband.

Sandra went over and kissed their father on the forehead. "Love you, Daddy." She leaned down and gently kissed her sleeping mother on the cheek.

The duke smiled up at her. "And I you, my beloved girl."

Sandra stepped back. "Ready when you are, Rach."

Rachel turned to her father, "I could tell you now, since Mummy's asleep. Sandra might actually like to hear this."

Her father smiled at her. "Go ahead."

Sandra nodded. "Sure, *dongsaeng.* Whatever you wish."

Rachel thought about how best to frame what she wished to say. "I was just remembering the moment when Serena O'Malley came through the door of Sandra's apartment and how utterly helpless I felt, as if there was nothing I could do, and no one to turn to...."

"*Dongsaeng,* I am so sorry." Sandra grabbed Rachel's hands. "I shouldn't have left you alone there. I should have taken off from work."

Rachel smiled and squeezed her sister's fingers. "It's okay. There's no way you could have known. That's... not what this is about."

The duke leaned back. "I, too, am sorry to hear this, though I currently have no memory of this incident, but... go on."

Rachel continued, "A great many people expressed regret or told me to be more careful, but only two people actually did something about the situation."

"I... gather I wasn't one of them," her father said with chagrin.

Rachel shook her head slowly. "Sorry, Daddy. No. The first was Peter." She held up her aquamarine necklace, gesturing with a smile toward her brother who was now gently-snoring. "He gave this to me for Yule. It protects you from being caught by the paralysis hex. Works, too."

"How did you find out? Do you little freshmen go around casting hexes on each other?" asked Sandra, wiggling her fingers to indicate hex casting. "How cute."

"It protected me from redcaps," Rachel responded blithely.

"You faced a redcap?" Sandra asked dubiously.

"Four, actually," replied Rachel, rather pleased with herself.

"By yourself?"

"With Sigfried. We took down two of them. The rest ran, the cowardly blighters."

Her father squeezed his eyes shut and then opened them again. "When did this happen?"

"About two weeks ago."

"So recently? Why didn't I hear about this?" asked her father, watching her carefully. "Has Dean Moth decided that I am too daft in my current state to learn about the dangers my daughter faces? If so, why didn't she tell your mother?"

Oops.

"Um.... About that," Rachel said awkwardly.

"Yes...." The duke waited.

She twitched. "The dean does not know. We didn't mention it to anyone."

"You fought a rank five dangerous fey—on campus, I assume—and you didn't report it to anyone?" her father asked skeptically.

"We... weren't supposed to be out."

"And why were you? Out, that is?" He crossed his arms.

Rachel squirmed. She did not want to tell the truth. Her father already disliked the Raven. "Siggy snuck out to go collect the loot from the cave of the ogre he slew, before the adults could get to it. He didn't tell anyone. He just snuck off. But then he got into trouble, with redcaps. Someone told me, so I went to rescue him."

"By yourself?"

Rachel shrugged. "It was the middle of the night."

"Oh, that makes it so much better." Her father rolled his eyes, muttering under his breath, "Why am I beginning to suspect that not remembering what you have been up to of late is a blessing in disguise?"

"Anyway, back to what I was saying...." Rachel pointedly ignored his comment.

"Yes, yes," he waved his hand again. "By all means. Go on."

"The other person who actually did something to protect me was..." she paused a moment for emphasis, "... Vladimir Von Dread."

Sandra, who had been standing by with just a hint of a sisterly smirk, looked suddenly attentive. So did their father.

"You see," she continued, "after I was kidnapped, the next time I showed up at a meeting of the Knights...."

"The who?" her father leaned forward. He looked at Sandra. "Is this a new club?"

Rachel replied first, "The Knights of Walpurgis."

The duke blinked, twice. "What were you doing at a meeting of the Knights of Walpurgis?"

"I'm a member," Rachel replied, slightly confused, since he had been the one to send her the wand that had once belonged to her grandmother—until it occurred to her that, of course, he no longer remembered having done this.

"My daughter, a member of...." Her father rubbed his temples. He turned and gestured to Sandra. "Did I know this?"

Sandra nodded gravely. "Yes, Father, but neither of us was happy about it."

"I should say!" He turned back to Rachel. "Proceed."

"As I was saying," Rachel said dryly, "at that meeting, Dread came forward, in front of everyone, went down on one knee, and apologized for allowing Sandra's little sister to fall into danger. He seemed to think that he should have figured out that I was in trouble and rescued me."

Ambrose was paying close attention now. She could not tell for sure, but she thought he seemed pleased that the prince had looked out for his youngest. Sandra was standing very still, as if not trying to draw any attention to herself, but she too was listening raptly. On their father's lap, their mother moaned softly in her sleep. Peter, who was sitting at an odd angle with his head over the back of the armchair, had begun to snore more loudly.

"But he wasn't just talk. He gave me this." She pulled from her neck pouch the card Dread had given her and held it up. "It has a number, for mundane phones, to call for help, but if I crumple or tear the card, they come automatically."

"Who comes?" Sandra interrupted, intrigued.

Rachel turned to her older sister. "People from Ouroboros Industries. Vlad and William have people permanently assigned to protect me, if I need help."

"That seems like a cushy job," murmured her older sister.

"Sandra!" interrupted their father, holding up his hand in a "stop" gesture, "don't encourage her to put them to work."

"Right, Daddy. Good point," Sandra replied smoothly, smirking again.

Rachel snorted at them both but then continued, "He also made sure I had a way to reach Gaius if I needed help."

Okay, that was not the *entire* truth, but she did not feel right leaking the secret of the black bracelets. Either Sandra knew about them, or she did not.

"And what would Gaius do?" the duke asked dubiously.

Rachel threw him an arch look. "When Agent Bridges and Mrs. MacDannan came to escort me to your office, I called him—to let him know I was being dragged away against my will—and they showed up—Gaius and the whole lot of them—ready to rescue me."

Her father leaned forward. "They were going to *fight* the *Agents?*"

She nodded proudly. Sandra whistled, a long low sound. Rachel peeked sideways, but her sister's whistle did not produce any sparks. Apparently, she was not attempting to cast a spell.

"The 'whole lot?' Who was it that came?" asked her father.

"Vladimir Von Dread, William Locke, Naomi Coils...."

"Ahhh," murmured the duke. "I see."

Rachel continued, "Gaius, Jenny Dare...."

Her father gave an amused snort. "I know her parents. If she is anything like them, she must be a hoot."

"She's one of Sandra's friends," said Rachel.

The two of them looked at Sandra, who smiled and nodded. "She's a protégé of mine."

"You have protégés? Good for you!" their father said, pleased.

From Sandra's expression, Rachel gathered that her father had known this before he lost his memory.

"... and a boy named Topher Evans from Alaska," finished Rachel. "Lucy Westenra, too, but she wasn't there that time."

"That's a rather formidable line up," her father allowed. "Westenra—you mean a vampiress?"

Rachel nodded. Ambrose whistled. He also produced no magical sparks.

"They're a rather rough bunch," Sandra drawled, sounding rather pleased with Rachel's information. Then, more cheerfully, she added, "Except for Gaius. He's a sweetie."

Rachel peered at Sandra to see if she was mocking her, but she looked entirely serious.

In answer to their father's silent query, Sandra added. "Lovely manners. Very charming young man."

The duke rolled his eyes at this description of his underage daughter's boyfriend, but he said aloud, "I'm not sure that even the Prince of Bavaria and his band of young ruffians could have taken Templeton and Scarlett."

Rachel's lips twitched with mirth. She said primly, "That is quite not the point."

"As you say," he made a gesture for her to continue. "I will allow that they might have been able to give the Agents a hard time."

Rachel thought her father was seriously underestimating Dread and his cronies, but she kept that to herself. Aloud she said sadly, "I should have told them to go ahead and fight. You might still have your memory."

Her father cleared his throat. "Yes. Well. But something else might have gone severely wrong instead." He paused, peering at her, "Was that it?"

"Not at all," Rachel objected hotly. "I'm not nearly done."

"Continue." He leaned back against the cushions behind him.

"I felt safe after that," Rachel explained almost shyly, "until tonight, when I watched Vlad size up Amber, and I realized how scary Amber was. I realized that the person I had been relying on couldn't actually keep me safe. Only...." She picked up her teacup, took a sip of cold tea, made a face, and then continued, "At one point, Amber became upset and put her hand under her cloak. Vlad and his people thought that she might attack me. They did not hesitate for one second. Immediately—despite knowing that Amber was a demon-killing death doll—they moved into position to defend me, if needed.

"This support has made a great difference to me. It lifted my spirits and made me feel safer again. And it's not just me."

"Not just you...." Ambrose rubbed the bridge of his nose. "I am not sure I...."

Rachel said, "At my request, Vlad came to the defense of Magdalene Chase, the only girl at Roanoke who's smaller than I am, and kept her from being beaten. Someone goaded the person who had been abusing her into publicly confronting Vlad, and he answered extremely well. Also, at my request, he came to Princess Alexis Romanov's defense, just tonight—offering to duel her fiancé, Romulus Starkadder, on her behalf, because—and I quote—" she lowered her voice, copying Dread's intonation, "'no girl should have to marry a boy who does not treasure her.'"

Sandra's eyebrows leapt up. Vlad must not have mentioned this incident to her when he fetched her from London. Rachel did not include the part about Alexis asking to marry him. That did not seem like something she should repeat in front of Vlad's beloved.

"I've talked with him at length, Father," Rachel continued, "and he's done quite a few other things that have impressed me. He is extremely intelligent. He is extremely brave. He is devoted to protecting the school, the world, Sandra—whom he loves very, very much—me, and everyone else he is in a position to protect. I'm also impressed by the caliber of the students he's gathered around him, all of whom serve him out of loyalty and respect. He also treats me as an equal and never talks down to me, which I appreciate tremendously.

"I know that Von Dread has a bad reputation, Father," she continued, "but I thought you should know some of the things he's done —not just the things people think he will do—and how he has looked after me... before you make any decision involving his suit for Sandra's hand. My girlfriends think he's evil, and, at first, I thought they might be right. But they are wrong. They think he is self-serving, but he isn't. They think he just puts his interests before what is good and right, and he doesn't—or at least, I've seen him have opportunities to do so, and he has not. He really is a very fine boy."

"Boy?" Sandra objected. "He's nineteen-years-old and six-foot-five."

Rachel shrugged. "He's not yet twenty-one. And in Bavaria," she checked an encyclopedia in her mental library, "the age of majority is twenty-five."

"I can't imagine he would appreciate being called a boy," Sandra replied, eyes sparkling.

Rachel arched a single eyebrow. "I hardly think that matters, as he is not here."

In her ear, she heard a faint snort. To her shock, she realized that her black bracelet was still vibrating. The boys had been so quiet that she had assumed that they had wandered off or gone to bed. The snort was clearly Gaius, but, Vlad must have heard all this, too.

Little tingles of electricity seemed to run up and down her body. The thought that Vlad, and, more importantly, Gaius, had heard everything she had said made her slightly uncomfortable but also a little bit pleased. For the first time, she realized that almost all of her personal interactions with Dread, except the public attempts to defend her, had been entirely private. It was possible that even Gaius had no idea how often she had spoken to Vladimir or what they had said to each other.

What she did not say aloud—to her father or to Vlad—was that it made her feel safer to refer to Gaius and Vladimir as boys. She could not say exactly why. It was a ridiculous term for a six-foot-five nineteen-year-old who, once, in a previous life, had been a conqueror controlling sixty-five worlds, and yet, it comforted her to remind herself that, currently, he really was a boy.

"There's a lot more I could say," Rachel concluded, "but it's late, and I think I've said enough. I hope you'll tell Mummy when you think she's ready to hear it, and one of us should tell Peter at some point. He only knows Vlad's outward reputation, which includes incidents such as the one on the dance floor tonight—where Vlad walked away looking the villain, even though he was entirely gallant and noble, and Romulus was a total jackass," she paused, "which I fear is an insult to the noble donkey."

"That is quite a bit to take in, Rachel," her father acknowledged. "I shall think on it, and I shall share it with your mother." He peered at her closely. "Are... you done?"

Rachel thought for a moment and then nodded. She still had not had the conversation she most longed for—to tell her father how she had saved him and the world at Beaumont last fall—but that needed to wait until he regained his memory or, at least, read more of his letters and notes. At least, she had seized this chance to defend Vladimir Von Dread.

It had been very satisfying indeed.

The duke said, "Thank you, Rachel, for the glowing report on his behavior. I had never heard much about Vladimir himself, but his father is known for being… heavy-handed. It sounds as if Vladimir could be very good for Bavaria. I hope so."

He turned to Sandra. Her cheeks grew slightly red, but she held her head proudly. Their father said, "So, you should bring him by, sooner rather than later."

She smiled and nodded. "You're not going to yell at him again, right?"

Her father gazed at her keenly. "No, I am not going to yell at him. But, you need to make sure that whatever Vladimir comes to ask us is what you want, all right?"

She nodded again, meeting his eyes steadily. Then, she turned to Rachel with a kind smile. "So, back to Roanoke?"

Rachel embraced her father. He hugged her back and then rubbed her nose with a napkin. Rachel realized that, this whole time, she had been wearing a white nose and cat whiskers. She sighed.

"I'm ready to go now, *unni*," she said simply, turning to Sandra.

Sandra said goodbye to their father one more time, and the two of them started to leave the room.

Peter woke with a start. "Wait, *dongsaeng, unn*—er, *nuna*. I want to head back, too. Give me a moment. I'll meet you lot in the foyer."

Rachel and Sandra walked the long corridors to the foyer. When they arrived, the soft glow of dawn light was coming through the frosted windows. Sandra dropped on her knees, so her head was closer to Rachel's, and hugged her tightly, almost more tightly than Laurel had, which Rachel felt she had only barely lived through.

"Thank you, Rachel," Sandra whispered.

"My pleasure," replied Rachel sincerely, when she could breathe again. She stilled her black bracelet, breaking the connection, just in case Sandra said anything that either of them would not want the boys to hear. "You can always return the favor for me, if Daddy and

Mummy ever get around to remembering that they wanted to object to me having a boyfriend."

Sandra rose gracefully to her feet. "I will try my hardest. Though even I think you're rather young to be dating. Daddy wasn't objecting to Gaius. He was objecting to a sixteen-year-old dating his thirteen-year-old. A sixteen-year-old thaumaturge at that."

"Nonetheless," Rachel replied regally, "I shall expect support."

"We shall see," Sandra ran a hand over Rachel's head, playing with her cat-ears, which, thanks to the amazing hair skills of Jenny Dare, still held.

Rachel sighed again.

Chapter Thirty-Eight:
A Promise to Kill

Upon arriving at the Roanoke Glass Hall, Rachel, Peter, and Sandra were surprised to find Amber still on the grounds. The cottage sat among the pines on a short promontory of land on the far side of the railroad tracks that curled around the foot of Storm King Mountain. Amber stood near the tracks, speaking into a calling card. Rachel tried to catch a glimpse of the person on the other side of Amber's card, but her sister was holding it at the wrong angle.

"*Dongsaengs*," said Sandra to the other two, turning the word into a plural that Rachel knew was not grammatically correct, "you go ahead. I want to speak to Amber."

Rachel would have waited for her, but Peter was exhausted and yanked her along, as she was the one with the broom. The two of them climbed onto Vroomie and set off across the Hudson. It was still dark here in New York; however, the night was clear, and the full moon was bright. The stars twinkled silvery and crisp overhead and then twinkled a second time in the dark waters beneath them. Peter sat behind her as they flew, his head nodding slightly from fatigue. Rachel, however, was awake; the February air sliced through her thin bodysuit, biting to the bone.

From high on Storm King, a gust of wind blew down the slopes and over the Hudson with such fury that the bristleless tumbled end over end. Rachel held onto Vroomie for dear life. She dared not work the levers until she knew which direction was down, lest she fly into the ice at high speeds. The moment she caught a glimpse of starry sky and could orient herself, she began manipulating levers and calling out commands to Peter, who, unlike Sigfried and Gaius, understood the workings of a steeplechaser. Acting together, they righted the broom.

Once upright, Rachel flipped on her new becalming enchantments, courtesy of the Chansons, and was delighted by the sudden sensation of warmth. Not only did the gusts of wind stop buffeting them, but the biting cold also receded. Behind her, Peter sighed in pleasure. She took a deep breath and looked around. Above shone the moon and stars. Below....

Rachel sucked in her breath in alarm. The gust of wind had thrown the broom high into the sky. Some thirty feet below her was the forest of Roanoke Island and, more importantly, a mere half a dozen feet to the right grew the wall of trees that made up the wards of Roanoke Academy for the Sorcerous Arts.

The wall of trees were five feet away. Now, four feet away.

To Rachel, it was like *déjà vu*. Had she not been in a similar situation with Sigfried only a few months ago—careening toward the wards of the school while operating becalming enchantments? That excursion had not ended well, and they had been just above the branches. If she and Peter went over the wards now, the drop would be dreadful indeed.

There was no time to switch off the becalming enchantments. She threw her whole body into banking, flipping levers and shouting instructions to Peter. Then she held her breath, because they did not have the radius she needed for such a turn. To her utter astonishment, the steeplechaser pivoted with near perfect precision. It was almost as if the becalming enchantments were not there. Whatever the Chansons had done to her broom might have just saved their lives.

Rachel whooped, and Peter let out a sigh of relief.

"That was close, *dongsaeng*," Peter began, as Rachel soared away from the wards and back toward the Hudson. He paused and looked around. "Where are we?"

They had been blown at least half a mile upriver. In the light of the full moon, she could make out enough of the shoreline to recognize where she was. The place was quite familiar to Rachel, since she had made so many trips around the island, but it was likely that Peter had never seen it. When would he have ever flown this far north of the campus entrance?

"The ruined castle is over there." She pointed south.

Peter peered over her head. "Are you sure?"

"Positive."

They flew south, toward the docks and the ruined castle. Rachel decided to fly above the middle of the icy river. True, it put them out in the open, but her chances of being swept over the warding wall were much reduced. She also flew lower, only ten feet above the ice.

A crackle of lightning whipped past them, glimmering all electric blue-white.

"Lightning imp!" she yelled.

"Dear Jove, protect us." Peter's arms tightened about her waist, as if he could somehow protect her from lightning with his body. "The Heer of Dunderberg. We're going to die."

"Why should we die?" Rachel asked, pulling from her neck pouch the oak key Sigfried had given her and the spare piece of nettle cake, wrapped in its napkin. "We're properly grounded!"

"What?"

"Er, sorry, something Sigfried says. Don't you have your anti-lightning charm?"

"Sure, but those don't really work," said Peter. "Or rather, they work against natural lightning, but not against the Heer—not against a direct hit, anyway. The tutors only have us make them because they're better than nothing, and most of us won't ever take a direct hit."

"What makes you say that?" Rachel asked, surprised. "That they don't work?"

"Loads of things," replied Peter.

That was… strange. *Why had Sigfried's worked so well? Could it be the Elf heros?*

On second thought, Peter might be correct that not all of them worked as well. She thought back to the mid-air fight between the Heer and Vladimir Von Dread, the day the demon broke the storm goblin out of its prison. Dread had looked charred after a while. Rachel had not stopped to think about it before, but if the full force of the lightning had been hitting him, he would have been dead. He must have had some kind of protective charm, but one that was not strong enough to protect him completely.

The Agents of the Wisecraft, on the other hand, had seemed to be able to protect themselves, the time Rachel and Sigfried came upon them fighting the Heer on Storm King Mountain. So Peter was not entirely correct.

"Take this." Rachel handed hers to Peter and pulled the spare Siggy had given her from the pouch. "I have another."

"No offense, Rach, but not sure a charm made by a freshman will cut it against the Heer."

He thought she had made it. Peter might not know enough to trust Sigfried's craftsmanship, but there was another name he would trust.

"Mr. Fisher helped Sigfried Smith make them," she said simply. "They work."

"Oh, well. That's all right then," said Peter, slipping it on.

Was it the oak key that had done such a good job of protecting her and Siggy, she wondered, or the nettle cake? That actually had been Mr. Fisher's recipe.

"And eat this." She pulled the extra nettle cake Sigfried had given her from her neck pouch, unwrapped it, and broke it in half, wondering if it, too, contained herbs Siggy had received from their Elf. Maybe that was why it was so effective. She handed half to Peter and popped the other half in her mouth, enjoying the lemony sponginess.

Two boulders came barreling down from Storm King, breaking the surface where they fell. The *crackling* noise of fissures spreading through sheet ice ricocheted off the hills.

Suddenly, the air was filled with creatures made of living lines of blue-white electricity, all buzzing and bright. They danced and leapt, darting back and forth more rapidly than Rachel's eye could follow, leaving a glow on her retina that continued for a moment after she closed her eyes. Some held lightning javelins. Others merely danced in the night air, their eyes gleaming with malicious glee, issuing eerie sounds that might have been mocking laughter.

"Lightning imps!" she cried again. "They're everywhere!"

"I guess this is as good a time as any to find out if Mr. Fisher's charms work," Peter called back, his voice rising unexpectedly at the end as a lightning javelin flew right at them.

At the last minute, it swerved away, followed by a clap of thunder.

"Blimey," murmured Peter, impressed. "Father needs to hear about this! Mr. Fisher's work is to be commended."

Rachel smiled on Sigfried's behalf, but she was too busy to speak. Drawing her wand, she let go of the bristleless, gripping the seat tightly with her thighs. Assuming a dueling pose, she parried a rock with her left hand using a cantrip, sent a second spinning directly at a lightning imp with her right, using one of the *tiathelu* charges in her wand, and whistled a hex.

The boulder smashed through the chest of the imp, its blue-white electricity splashing wildly. Blue sparkles from her paralysis hex struck another imp, causing it to freeze and fall.

"Rach, that was jolly amazing!" Peter exclaimed. "Three separate actions at once, four if you count that you redirected a boulder into an attack. I had no idea you were so good."

"I give all credit to the Knights of Walpurgis," Rachel replied primly.

The lightning imp that had been struck by the boulder reformed and threw another javelin at them, which swerved, crackling. The frozen imp only fell a short distance before the blue sparks shot out of the blue-white ones, and it was moving freely again.

"Aw!" Rachel cried, disappointed. "Except none of it did anything."

"Leave it to me," replied Peter.

Straightening on the seat behind her, Peter cast two Glepnir bands in a row. Each glowing band ensnared a lightning imp. Rachel stared in awe. It was not easy to direct a Glepnir band without a wand, much less do so while flying, at night. She was lucky if she could get one around the trashcan in the private hallway where she practiced. Peter must have excellent reflexes. As both imps plummeted downward, Rachel thought that it was a shame that her brother was not in the Knights. He would make an excellent duelist.

The two lightning imps struck the ice below, bouncing several times. Their feet were free but apparently they were unable to fly while constrained. The two imps zipped pell-mell across the ice, so the glowing golden bands entrapping them could be seen flashing here and there and then back across the Hudson again. They looked so comical rushing frantically to and fro that Rachel and Peter burst into laughter.

The lightning imps darted away, giving wide berth to Peter and his Glepnir bands.

"Looks like they're leaving us in peace," Peter stated. "Good. Let's get back to campus."

An eerie horripilation ran over Rachel's entire body.

"Peter," she whispered, "Last time... they caught the Heer of Dunderberg with Glepnir bands. You and I are immune to his lightning. You seem to have a fair hand with the bands. I can deflect the boulders...."

"*Dongsaeng*," Peter replied in hushed tones, "Can you imagine what it would mean if we caught him! No more lockdowns, no more fearing the fey, no more proctors or Agents getting charred. No worrying about Father coming out here with his crew."

"Let's do it!" cried Rachel.

Mist rose from the west bank and moved across the ice. In a matter of moments, it had enclosed them. The whole world was a faint silvery whiteness, with thick fog moist against their faces. Moving slowly, Rachel flew west and down until they were only a few feet above the ice. They were less likely to run into something if they were in the middle of the Hudson.

Off to the east, there came a crash and a cracking. Another boulder had struck the frozen surface of the river, breaking the ice.

"*Oppa*, this isn't good," Rachel whispered, trying to peer around her but seeing only moonlit mist. "I want to fly upward, toward the peak, but in this fog, they could throw a boulder at us, and we would not see it coming."

"It's mist sprites," Peter said grimly. "I just saw you do that whistle thing Mummy can do. Can you whistle the song for dispelling mist?"

Rachel shook her head, chagrinned. "I'm only good at hexes."

"Don't apologize, *dongsaeng*, whistling hexes is pretty amazing for a freshman. But in this case, leave it to me."

Peter reached into a kenomanced pouch he carried somewhere on his person and pulled out his silver flute. He played the song for dispelling mist with such eerie beauty that it brought tears to Rachel's eyes. Full of faith in her brother's prowess, she angled her steeplechaser upward, ready to head for the peak of Storm King Mountain and the storm goblin.

The mist began to thin. The first thing they could see was the silver trail that the moonlight left on the ice. Only....

That was not right.

The silvery trail, which became clearer and clearer though the mist, was too far to the west. It seemed to be on the shore, by the Glass Hall, which was now beneath them and to their left. She glanced towards the Glass Hall, curious as to Sandra's progress, and gasped.

The silvery light was not moonlight on the water. It was a glowing silvery trail, the exact color of the thin rails the princess walked on to travel from world to world, but as wide as a sidewalk. It stretched over the promontory on the far side of the train tracks that ran around Storm King Mountain, where the Glass Hall stood. Following the silvery path, it led to the feet of....

The Master of the World. Nastasia's grandfather stood a bit up the slope from the docks, speaking to Amber, who gazed up at him, listening. Then, she turned and walked back to the Glass Hall, where Rachel saw her disappear inside with Sandra.

Hatred blossomed within Rachel like a blood red rose. *How dare the Master of the World damage her family!* How dare he manipulate her parents, playing with their minds like so many toddler's blocks!

Fueled by anger, she increased the speed of her bristleless, soaring up the slope of Storm King. Above, she could see the lightning imps jumping about, and, beyond that, a childlike form, head thrown back in laughter, a trumpet in its hand—the Heer of Dunderberg!

"Bring us in closer," Peter cried. "He's just out of my range."

Rachel flew higher. Right above her was the cut in the side of the mountain where the road ran, farther up above the road was sheer rocky cliff, and then the peak. Even higher than that, strutting about in mid-air, was a young Dutch boy dressed in doublet and hose, the light of the silver moon illuminating his pure white sugarloaf cap— the storm goblin!

Dwerg, the Heer of Dunderberg, stood with arms akimbo in the air atop Storm King Mountain, shouting into his speaking horn. At his signal, the lightning imps threw their javelins toward the Griffin children, and a boulder sailed their way as well. Thunder echoed off the slopes of Storm King.

Rachel deflected them all. Behind her, Peter tensed on the seat. Then, swift as a mongoose, he cast the cantrip.

The golden band flew true, but the storm goblin was so quick that Peter's Glepnir band merely snagged the boy's ankle. He hovered in mid-air, one ankle glowing golden, like a glow-in-the dark ankle bracelet.

"Missed," Peter hissed.

"Missed!" Rachel cried. "You struck him! And that was your first time! Try again!"

"Can you get any closer?" asked Peter. "This is way beyond my normal range."

"Rather!"

Rachel flew up the slope. Peter took control of the footrests and stood up, casting again. Again, his spell flew true, but a lightning imp dashed in front of its master, knocking the Heer out of the way. The Glepnir band snagged it, and the little electric creature plummeted downward with a long, sorrowful moan.

Peter grunted in frustration.

A flurry of lightning javelins came their way, attempting to overwhelm their defenses with their numbers. Using her wand, Rachel easily deflected them, mentally crossing off her charges of *nothor*, the cantrip that allowed her to parry, as she used them. Behind her, Peter waiting for an opening.

"*Argos!*" he cried, casting another Glepnir band.

A shining band of golden light encircled the Heer's shoulders and upper body. It trapped the hand with the speaking-horn against his chest, but he was so nimble that he managed to pull his other hand free. Now one band glowed on his ankle and another trapped one arm to his body.

"Are you sure this will work?" Peter cried.

She called back, "The Spriggan said that is how they caught him before. I think you have to trap both arms and pin his legs together."

"Very good. On it!" Peter declared.

The Heer ducked out of sight.

"Sly little blighter," Peter murmured, raising his hands for the cantrip. "Just you wait. When you come back, I'll be ready for you."

Ahead of her, a motion caught her eye. Flying higher, she saw an odd sight.

On the side of the cliff, two squat little fey men of a variety she could not identify—storm trolls, maybe? Real storm goblins that had not been combined with the ghost of a Duchman?—reached into the rock of the hillside and dug out a large rock the way a child might take a pinch of clay. Boulder in hand, they passed it up to a larger, squatter creature of their same order, who, drawing back his arm, then threw it with tremendous force, so that it sailed into the air.

The great stone crashed onto the Hudson. A lightning javelin whizzed by. It was a good thing Siggy was not there. He would expect her to repeat her feat from the night of the skating....

All the hairs stood up across Rachel's entire body—*her second wish!*

She glanced at the Glass Hall, which was still clearly visible beneath them. *He* was still there, standing by himself, no doubt waiting for Amber. Rachel looked upward at the dark shapes of boulders and the lightning imps darting to and fro. *She could do it.* If she set herself up properly, if the trolls kept hurling rocks and the imps kept throwing javelins....

She could kill the Master of the World.

A flush of sheer glee coursed through her veins. She imagined the approval in Vlad's eyes and the admiration of her father when they discovered that she had taken out this despicable villain without their help's. Sigfried would be disappointed that he did not get to participate, of course, but he would still be impressed.

A thought caught her up. This man was her best friend's grandfather. *Could she really going to kill Nastasia's grandfather? Why? Because she and Siggy spat in their hands and shook?* True, she had given her word to Sigfried, but, as annoying as she could be, the princess was her friend, too. It was unlikely they could remain friends if Rachel murdered Nastasia's grandfather.

Yes, she wanted the Master of the World to suffer for his crimes. *But murder him?*

Nastasia was not always a good friend, but Rachel truly felt that the princess meant well. She had spoken up for Rachel's family, saving them from having their memory wiped. That would not have gone well, no matter how it had played out.

Sparing the life of her friend's grandfather, even a friend who had recently betrayed her, had to be more important than her vow to Sigfried. Besides, she had only agreed with Sigfried to "do whatever was necessary." That did not require her to commit murder.

But what about her duty to her mother?

In all the twenty-two years her mother had spent imagining different ways that the Master of the World might die, Rachel suspected that she had never once considered that her youngest daughter might accomplish the task for her.

Rachel gritted her teeth. Sorry, Nastasia, but her loyalty to her family outweighed her loyalty to her friends, especially a friend who had squealed on her.

"Who's that?" Behind her, Peter pointed. "That man surrounded by moonlight."

"That's him," her voice sounded hoarse. "That's the Master of the World."

"The one who stole Amber? The one whose death our mother dreams about every single day?" Peter replied, his voice steely with determination. "Let's kill him."

"Rather!" Rachel cried again. "I think I can do it from here."

"You?" Peter asked, astonished. "You can't murder somebody. Let me do it."

She had promised Sigfried. They had shaken on it. With spit.

"I killed my Elf," Rachel replied. Inside, she felt hollow and haunted, but her voice was hard as flint. "I can kill this man."

Chapter Thirty-Nine:
The Roar of the Lion

A lightning javelin flashed farther up the slope. Moonlight glinted, whiter than white, off a sugar loaf cap.

"Rachel!" cried Peter. "The Heer!"

Standing, her brother cast the cantrip with exquisite precision. It encircled the Heer, who tried to scoot out of it before it tightened. The result was that it closed around his middle. He now wore the glowing golden band as a belt.

"So close," murmured Peter. "Still too much of a lag, though. Bring me closer."

"Will do."

Far up the slope, she caught the dark shape of a boulder as it left the peak and sailed through the air. Could this be the one? There were two lightning javelins in the air. Would they be close enough when the boulder came into range? No. That boulder was too far south. Hopefully, the next one would come farther north. Otherwise, she was going to have to reposition herself to the south of the Glass House.

"This blighter who stole our sister," Peter called as they flew, "What's your plan?"

"I know something that will work," Rachel called back, her voice tight. "But I have to set it up perfectly. It may take me a few minutes."

"Right." Peter nodded. "Carry on. I'll look for another opening to capture the Heer."

Rachel nodded absently, gazing at the moonlit sky and the dark silhouette of Storm King. She had spoken so confidently to Peter, but now the reality of what she had promised was hitting home.

"Incoming!" Peter cried.

Four boulders headed toward them all at once. She was not in position yet to try her trick. Nor were there any lightning javelins nearby. Rachel pivoted the broom, again thankful for the new becalming enchantments, without which the Heer would have blown them away with his wind gusts seven times over. She would have to find a way to show her gratitude to the Chansons.

Together, she and Peter raised their hands and parried the onslaught of boulders with cantrips.

Flying higher, her thoughts returned to the duchess. Her mother had suffered so. Rachel could not imagine living—for decades—knowing that her daughter had been stolen and not being able to even discuss the matter with anyone, not even her husband.

It was time to set up the shot.

"Look there!" called Peter. "Those little buggers are causing our boulder troubles."

Above them, Rachel saw the squat troll-men digging another boulder from the rocky mountainside. They pulled a large boulder from a slab of rock. A bevy of lightning imps were preparing to launch their javelins.

If she timed it correctly....

Du-du-du! The Heer blew into his speaking-horn like a trumpet. The entire sky lit up with lighting imps dancing an eerie, wild dance. Lightning arced across the sky all the way from the peak of Storm King to Breakneck Ridge on the far side of the Hudson.

Booooom! Thunder echoed among the Hudson Highlands, shaking both Griffin siblings.

Peter cast another cantrip, but the nimble Heer barely dodged out of the way, flying upward again, like a leaf on the wind.

"Drat. He's out of range," Peter growled. "Can we fly closer?"

"Do you want to go after the Heer or the Master of the World?" Rachel asked.

"Oh, right," Peter said. "Definitely, the fiend below. The one who harmed Mummy. Let's get this World Master before he leaves or something. Then we can come back after the Heer."

Rachel dived farther down still. Below her, the Master of the World still stood by himself, looking down at a rectangle of silvery light that he held in his hand. Perhaps, he was speaking with someone on a calling card? Amber was still safely inside the Glass Hall, farther away than the edges of the crater on the spriggan's land had been from its center.

As she flew back down past the cut where the road ran around Storm King, Rachel called up her memory of the Master of the World again, forcing herself to examine the man she planned to kill. Her grandfather would have expected at least that of her, to look into the face of the man she planned to murder. She recalled how Andre the Second as he had looked while he was talking to Amber. She took in his dusty armor, travel-worn loden cloak, his salt and pepper hair, the white at his temples. As she examined the memory, something else struck her.

In her mind's eye, Amber stood staring up at the Master of the World, her eyes wide and soft and filled with... *Oh, no!*

Rachel knew that expression, the one that transfixed Amber's face, her entire being. It was the expression she often felt come over her own face when she was with Gaius, the one that, if truth be told, had shanghaied her face only tonight during "The Skater's Waltz," when she danced in the arms of her future brother-in-law.

Amber was in love with the Master of the World.

Above her, the storm trolls threw their latest boulder. Two lightning imps zipped by. One threw a javelin toward the river, and the other threw one toward Rachel and Peter. Narrowing her eyes, Rachel traced the trajectories in her mind and moved her broom until she was in the perfect position. She raised her wand. In a moment, everything would be in range.

The pounding of her heart was shaking her ribcage. Her mother hated the Master of the World, but would she want to break the heart of her eldest? Would she want him dead now, while Amber was still entirely attached to him? Or would she rather than wait in the hopes of wooing her lost daughter away from him before they attacked him? If Amber loved him, and Rachel killed him, that would be the end of her dream of reuniting their family in the future.

Did Amber's love trump her mother's hatred?

A lightning javelin flew into range, blue-white electricity dancing along its length. Rachel glanced down at her target. What could Amber possibly see in this monster, this destroyer of families? *Nothing. Amber was deceived. He was evil.*

With a flick of her wrist, Rachel waved her wand, casting *turlu*.

Roooaaarrr!

The noise shook Rachel to her bones. Spooked, she looked left and right, searching for the source of the sound. Meanwhile, the boulder flew past before she had a chance to aim.

"What was that?" she yelped.

"What was what?" Peter called from behind her.

"That sound."

"I didn't hear anything. Maybe it was a boulder hitting the ice?"

"How could you not? It was so loud!" Rachel cried. She thought back, hearing it again from her memory.

A second horripilation passed over her.

Oh no.

She could recall the sound, but two things alarmed her. The first was that it did not seem to have any particular eerie quality, which meant that the eeriness had to be experienced. The second thing was that she recognized the sound. *It was the roar of a lion.*

Despite the bitter cold, Rachel began to sweat.

Surely, the Comfort Lion did not expect her to forgive the Master of the World. This monster had stolen her sister. He had taken her father's memory. He had caused immeasurable pain to her mother. She had wished upon a star for an opportunity for revenge, and now it had come. She was not going to let it slip through her fingers.

And yet....

Her limbs trembled so hard that she could hardly maneuver the steeplechaser, much less line up a delicate billiards strike of boulders and javelins.

"Can you do it?" Peter asked, his voice tight.

"I can, but the Lion doesn't want me to," she called back.

"Screw some animal," Peter snarled, followed by several other expletives. "Have you forgotten what this *monster* did to our mother?"

"Peter!" Rachel snapped over her shoulder. "Language!"

She was relieved that he had the good breeding to wince, chagrined.

"Sorry, *dongsaeng,*" he said meekly. "I guess today has shown that I'm an unreliable rotter who can't keep his cool under fire."

"It's all right," Rachel replied, glad to have something to distract her from deciding what to do about the Master of the World. "You've been under a great deal of pressure."

"But that's just it," he replied sincerely. "If my manners are not ingrained deeply enough for me to maintain them in times of trouble, I cannot, in truth, call myself a gentleman. I need to improve if I am to be worthy of my future rank." He paused and then asked, his voice cold as steel on ice, "Are you going to do it?"

She looked over her shoulder again, meeting his calm, steady gaze. She could not bear to let him down. "Yes."

She dived, swooping above the steep slope of Storm King, and maneuvered into a better position as she waited for the next boulder. Her heart was beating so loudly that, twice, she mistook the roaring in her ears for the Lion, but no real second roar came.

Did that mean the Lion did not mind if she went ahead? Or that he had given up on her? *Surely*, she thought again, *he did not expect her to forgive the Master of the World*. Such a thing could not be possible.

As she waited to make the shot, Rachel's thoughts spun. The Lion had promised her some kind of a gift if she forgave people. She had done so well with everyone except John Darling. Did she want to break her record now?

But she could not forgive the Master of the World, not even for the Lion.

Rachel steadied her steeplechaser. As another boulder plummet down the slope, she thought back, recalling the cold November afternoon in the Memorial Garden, standing before the Shrine to the Unknown God. At its foot sat the tiny Lion, just as it had every other time she had recalled this scene. Only this time, the Lion appeared very stern indeed.

"Why?" Rachel cried in her imagination. "This man did such terrible things to us!"

Gazing back steadily, the Lion replied, *"Do unto others as you would have them do unto you."*

What did that mean? Rachel was struck by the concept. Treating others as you wanted them to treat you seemed cleverly wise, but what did it mean in this case? Would she want someone who had a grudge against her to kill her, without a trial? But the cases were not equivalent. She had never stolen a child or changed a man's memories.

She thought back to Amber. How could her sister love this vile man? Couldn't she see how appalling he was? How he had abused her and her family?

He must die!

A lightning javelin flashed through the sky. Rachel pointed her wand and cast *turlu*, moving the inertia from the mini lightning bolt to the plummeting stone, so that the force of the bolt struck the rock at just the angle necessary to place the billiard ball in the correct pocket —if by ball, she meant the flying boulder and if by pocket, she meant the Master of the World.

The boulder sped downward at incredible speed, almost too fast to see. In less than a second, he would be struck by all the force of a lightning bolt added to the mass of the plummeting rock.

Do unto others as you would have them do unto you.

Time slowed.

It was almost as if she herself was moving as quickly as the lightning javelin. Suddenly, her thoughts were racing with unexpected clarity. What if the Master of the World was not the *others*? What if her sister were the *others*? How would she want Amber to treat a man she loved? With a sudden shiver, Rachel realized that this question was not as theoretical as she might have wished. What if Amber found out that Vlad was the Dread King or that Gaius was *that* Gaius Valiant? *Rachel certainly would not want her sister to kill them!*

Could she love this vile man for her sister's sake, merely because her sister loved him? Was that possible? One last time, Rachel regarded the Master of the World, looking at him with new eyes. She tried to see him as Amber did: calm, regal, stern, proud, keenly intelligent. He reminded her a bit of her grandfather, or....

From her memory echoed words that had been spoken on her way to visit her father two weeks ago: *I cannot have someone altering my thoughts. It is a terrible thing and should be used only on criminals or the Unwary. And even then, only in the most dire circumstances.*

All in a single instance, much like a vision, a scenario unfolded before her. In this imaginary alternate life, it was Dread who had received a prophecy that an Unwary child, if raised among the Wise, would save the world from burning. She pictured Vladimir Von Dread very clearly. She saw him approaching a farm in rural England, his face calm and resolved, solemn, despite his regret. He gave the command to have the memories of the Unwary parents erased, so that they would not remember their little one. *Would he hesitate?*

No. She was reasonably certain that he would not.

Would she still love him? Of course, she would. She already knew he had once been a conqueror of worlds. She might disapprove. She might very well try to talk him out of it, but she would not stop loving him, especially since she would know that he thought he was doing what was necessary—for the good of the world.

If she could still love Vlad under such circumstances, then Amber could love the Master of the World, whom she believed to be fighting bravely against vastly overwhelming forces.

Like ice being struck by one of the Heer's boulders, a crack ricocheted through the hatred in her heart.

But she couldn't give up her grudge! cried a little voice in the back of her mind. *She would have to give up her solidarity with Vlad. They were going to work together to destroy the Master of the World! They were a team!*

Really? Was *that* her reason for not forgiving, something so frivolous?

A rush of peace spread through her, so powerful that it felt almost like joy. It was as if a tremendous burden lifted from her shoulders, leaving her feeling so light that she feared she would float right off her bristleless. The anger and hatred that had bound a certain part of her melted away.

Time returned to normal.

The boulder rocketed away from her at tremendous speed, headed directly for the Master of the World. Only he no longer seemed vile to her. Rather, he reminded her of Vladimir, of her grandfather, a regal and fierce man willing to do what it took to save the world.

To her amazement, she felt no hatred toward him, none at all.

"*Tiathelu!*" she shouted at the top of her lungs, gesturing at the boulder and swinging her hand to the left.

It proved extremely difficult to dislodge the boulder from its chosen path. She grabbed her wand with both hands and pulled with all her might. At the last moment, the boulder veered east. Passing over the head of the Master of the World, it smashed into the Hudson, a few hundred feet south of Roanoke Island.

Chapter Forty: The Last Wish

Kaboom!

The boulder struck the river. An enormous geyser erupted from the Hudson, splashing freezing water and chunks of ice in all directions. Rachel and Peter were far enough away that they merely felt the spray of icy water. A chunk or two of ice flew by them.

In her mind's eye, Rachel recalled standing by the shrine of the Unknown God. The little Lion rubbed against her leg, purring. She recalled this so clearly, the pressure of his fur against her leg, the warm and cheering vibration of his purr. She knew it had never happened, but she remembered it perfectly... almost as if it were happening right at that moment.

Rachel smiled, happy despite the cold. A warm feeling was spreading through her, driving back the cold. It came with the growing sense of joyous wonder and freedom. The feeling seemed oddly familiar. With a start, Rachel realized that it was similar to the sensation she had experienced in the presence of Jariel's secret second halo with its moonfire.

"You missed!" exclaimed Peter.

"I changed my mind," replied Rachel.

"Trust a girl to go soft at the last minute," he said, his voice filled with disgust. "I should have done it myself."

Rachel opened her mouth to explain and then shut it again, sighing. Below, Amber had come out of the Glass Hall in time to see the Master of the World coolly gazing at the hundred-foot column of ice and water that had exploded from the river.

Amber frowned up at the peak of Storm King. Butterflies of starlight gathered around her, forming clouds of living light. They dissolved into glitter and then formed two glowing points, one in front of each eye. Jagged lightning the color of starlight shot from her eyes and up the slope of the mountain.

The star-lightning beams returned, wrapped around a little Dutch boy dressed in orange and green doublet and hose and with a white sugarloaf cap. Bands of glowing gold still encircled his ankle, his waist, and his chest, trapping one arm.

"Oh, look!" Peter cried with delight. "She caught him! The Heer! Good for Amber!"

The last wish! Rachel gazed in wonder. It had happened, and it was Amber who caught him, though Rachel liked to think that she and Peter had helped a bit, perhaps slowing him down. Their father was going to be so pleased.

Despite the bands constricting his chest—of both golden light and star-lightning—the Dutch boy threw back his head and laughed, a high, eerie sound. Rachel was too far away to hear what the storm goblin was saying, but clearly the Heer taunted his captor.

Amber's star-lightning beams began to tighten.

"Nooooooooooooooooo!" Rachel put the steeplechaser into a nosedive. Behind her, Peter was shouting something very similar.

On the ground, Rachel could see Sandra, who had just come out of the Glass Hall, racing across the grounds towards Amber, shouting.

They were all too late.

Before Rachel could reach Amber, or even get close enough for her sister to hear her, Amber tightened her beams, constricting the storm goblin's chest. The creature's mouth opened in agony. His face contorted. It no longer looked like the face of a child. Now it was old and gnomish.

Then, with a sensation like waking from a dream, the storm goblin dissolved. A tiny glint of gold flickered in the air, and the Heer was gone.

"Blimey," whispered Peter again, "That's... not good!"

Rachel slowed her dive. Below them, Sandra had stopped and stood with her hands over her mouth. Amber turned to speak to the Master of the World again, her face lit by the silvery path behind him.

Numbly, Rachel realized that this was what Xandra's spirits had been trying to warn her about. With the death of Dwerg, the Heer of Dunderberg, the Roanoke Concords became null and void. Without the presence of the storm goblin to terrify the other fey into submission, the agreements that had kept the campus safe for well over a hundred years were no longer in force.

Rachel thought back, recalling the moment that the storm goblin met his end. To her astonishment, there was someone else present in her memory. A man hung in the air above where Amber had slain the goblin. He was dark-haired and dressed in old-fashioned clothing of the Dutch style. He wore a black hat with a large plume, and a thick white ruff surrounded his neck.

He was translucent. Rachel could see the train tracks and the slope of Storm King Mountain behind him, through his body. As she watched, a beam of glorious light descended from far above. The man looked up. Far, far, far above, through a hole in the sky, the man's friends beckoned to him. They, too, were dressed like Dutchmen with plumes in their hats. The translucent man, presumably John Colman, saw them above him, waving. His face lit up.

Then it grew too bright for Rachel to see, even though, to her real eyes, it was still night.

Sandra met Peter and Rachel on the docks on Roanoke Island, after Amber and the Master of the World departed along the silver pathway. She let them know that she had spoken to Father and told him about the Heer's demise. He, in turn, had promised to contact the dean, the Master Warder, and Mr. Badger. Since Sandra had not thought to bring a broom, the three of them walked back through the ruined castle and down the tree-lined path to the campus *propre*.

Dread and Gaius were waiting for them under the wisp-powered street lamp that stood beside the stone bench next to the opening to the tree-lined path that led to the docks. They looked tired. Gaius was still in his now-rumpled suit. Dread was no longer wearing his armor, but his black swan feather cloak fell from his shoulders. It gave him a regal air.

Peter mumbled a goodnight and headed on to Dare Hall, but Rachel still felt as if she were walking on air, lifted up by the joy of having let go of her hatred and anger. She ran and hugged Gaius, who embraced her tightly. Vlad swept Sandra up into his arms and kissed her.

After a moment, Sandra asked coyly, "So, are you really going to wait for my father's permission to actually propose?"

Dread replied, "Yes."

Sandra pouted prettily, which made Rachel giggle. She ordinarily did not get to see this side of her sister. Then, she stepped back and curtsied to the young men.

"Thank you, gentlemen, for providing backup."

"Any time, milady!" Gaius bowed. He tried to stifle a yawn but failed. "Sorry, it's been a long night,"

"And it's not over yet," Rachel sighed.

Briefly, she explained to the two young men about the death of the storm goblin.

"I need to return home," Sandra said. "I already told my father, but there will be more work to be done."

"I will escort you," stated Vlad.

"Th-they'll close the school now, won't they?" asked Rachel, her voice shaking. "I mean... for good. Or at least for weeks, maybe months?"

Sandra smiled at her. "Actually, they won't. Father saw how upset you were at the idea of the academy closing when you visited him two weeks ago. He contacted the dean. Together, they came up with a plan that was approved by the Board of Visitors and Governors. It had been meant as a contingency plan, but, well, I guess this is the contingency."

"What is it?" Rachel cried.

Sandra poked her little sister's nose. "Oh, ho, Miss-Impatient-Pants. You'll just have to wait and see. And now, missy, you are off to bed." Then she turned back to Vlad, murmuring something Rachel could not hear.

Shivering Rachel moved close to Gaius, basking in his warmth. He gallantly took off his suit jacket and put it around her shivering shoulders.

"See, that's why you keep me around." Gaius grinned sleepily at her.

Meanwhile, beside them, Dread and Sandra were being rather inappropriate, by Rachel's way of thinking. Particularly, in front of Sandra's younger sister, who felt very... strange... watching some other girl kiss Vlad, even if that girl was Sandra. She swallowed, trying not to let unexpected misery ruin her buoyant mood.

Vlad stopped. "Enough. It is late." He turned to Rachel, "I will make sure your sister arrives home safely."

Rachel shot Dread a grateful smile. "Thank you for looking after Sandra."

"Goodnight, Rachel," Sandra gave her little sister a quick hug and a kiss on her cheek, which Rachel returned. "Try not to go too crazy, okay?"

"By the way," Gaius drawled wryly, "I finally remembered where I had heard the name Wyllt before. I have been trying to remember why it sounded so familiar, ever since Laurel mentioned it after the Lily and Thorn thing. We'd covered it in class, of course, but I had not made a note of it." He turned to Vlad, gestured airily. "Did you realize that the Griffin sisters have been holding out on us? They're descended from Merlin."

"No, I did not." Vlad looked pleased.

Rachel wondered if this news pleased the prince because descended from Merlin was the kind of lineage that might impress the King of Bavaria. Sandra must have been thinking the same thing because she gazed at him through her lashes, giving him a half-lidded, smoldering look.

Uncomfortable, Rachel averted her eyes. She turned back to Gaius, smiled up at him and, reaching up, ruffled his hair.

"You're so cute when you're tired," she sighed. "Maybe you should have gone to bed rather than waiting up. That way one of us could have been good for something tomorrow."

Gaius kissed her, sweetly and gently. "You're always good."

Sandra cleared her throat. "Right then, watching Gaius kiss my thirteen-year-old sister is too weird."

Rachel was glad that the darkness hid her startled expression. How ironic that each sister found the other's behavior so disturbing.

Sandra gestured dramatically. "Take me from this place, Vlad!"

Vladimir Von Dread swept Sandra Griffin up into his arms and walked towards the docks, his black feather cloak flaring out behind him as he strode. Sandra waved good-bye over his shoulder.

Once they were alone, Gaius kissed Rachel again, a rather nice kiss. His hands ran along her ribs and down to the small of her back, but no farther.

He whispered in her ear, "Did I mention how adorable you are? The costume is cute, but I just want to be clear it's unnecessary. I mean," he flushed suddenly, as if realizing his words could be misconstrued, "you're cute no matter what you wear."

Rachel made a soft purring sound. "You know," she murmured in Gaius's ear, "My original plan for this evening, or morning as the case may be, was to try to talk you into spending the rest of the night snuggled up on the couch in the upper tower with me.... Nothing inappropriate, mind you," she wagged a finger at him, "just curled up together... but," she lowered her lashes, "then I chickened out and was too shy to ask."

Even in the moonlight, she could tell that he had turned rather red. "Curse your sister Amber, not really, for showing up tonight! Ah well. I am sure we will have plenty of chances to have some alone time in the future. It would have been nice, though."

Rachel allowed herself a small happy smile. She was so relieved that he had not mocked her idea.

"Finally, my lady," Gaius bowed charmingly, "we can call this very, very long evening a night."

"I still have something I have to do." Rachel muttered. "Or at least, I have to do it before I see my friends tomorrow."

Gaius yawned again. "Isn't whatever you need to do right now something you can do eight hours from now?"

She gave a long drawn out sigh. "I promised Wulfgang Starkadder I would bring him in on some of our secrets, but then my friends decided we should all vow that we won't tell anyone new—so I have to find him and tell him before they wake up."

"Ah, that's rough." He yawned yet again. "I'm beat. This is it for me."

The sound of footsteps echoed from the tree-lined lane. Out into the wisp-light tromped four Agents of the Wisecraft, looking splendid, despite the early hour, in their tricorne hats and their Inverness cloaks. Each held a tall staff tipped with a gem the size of her fist.

While they did not pause, they looked surprised to see her. Two of them waved.

"Who are they?" Gaius whispered when they had passed.

"Agents from the London branch," Rachel replied. "No doubt my father sent them in response to Sandra's call."

"Ah. Makes sense to send them from London—where it's daytime now—rather than to take the extra time to wake up the American Agents," said Gaius. "I really have to sleep," Gaius admitted, yawning yet again. "Call if you need assistance. Locke is away, and Vlad is, as you have seen, indisposed. Topher, Naomi, and Jenny and I are all still available, though. And Naomi could always drag Lucy along. I'm not sure she even sleeps. And, of course, Vlad could be back rather quickly should you need help. Just be careful, okay?"

"I'll be careful," she promised solemnly, "just for you."

With a roguish grin, Gaius swept her into his arms. Rachel yelped, fearing she would be too heavy for the overly tired boy, but he did not seem to have any trouble. He carried her, broom and all, across campus, which she appreciated, seeing as she did not have a coat.

She leaned against his shoulder, enjoying his warmth and the strength of his arms. As she rested, eyes half open, she thought about all that had occurred in so short a time. Had it only been this morning that she had dressed up in her *hanbok* and learned about her mother's year in Korea? That seemed worlds away from facing off against the Heer and the Master of the World, or even from their family gathering back at Gryphon Park, or from the Year of the Dragon Ball with its dancing and lanterns, even though each event remained crisp and pristine in her memory.

So much had changed. Her family now knew about Sandra and Vladimir. That was a relief. She hated keeping secrets from them. She had been to her first masquerade. She had spoken to an angel and danced with a skeleton, who, she realized with a shiver of awe, might actually have been Death, and she was now reasonably sure, after seeing great grandmother name disappear from a lantern, that Sun Li was still alive somewhere in the great world Outside.

Had it only been a little over two weeks ago that she had first learned about Amber's existence? It seemed both as if it had happened only a breath ago and as if the Rachel Griffin who had not known about Amber was an entirely different person.

As she shivered against the chill of the night, her face buried against her boyfriend's shoulder, she realized that, in one way, she was not the same girl she had been two weeks ago. That girl had viewed her memory as an unadulterated good, a gift that gave an advantage to help her keep up with those who were bigger, stronger, and more powerful than she. But now....

Her sister Amber had been stolen because of her perfect recall. Her family had been torn apart because of this gift. Terrible as it was to have the memory of one's own child ripped from one's mind, was it really better to suffer as her mother had suffered, twenty-two years of misery and heartbreak that the passage of time did not diminish? Reluctantly, Rachel was forced to admit that Astrid had been right, this family talent that she had seen as such a blessing could also be a heavy burden, at times unbearably heavy.

Gaius carried Rachel up the stairs to the door of Dare Hall and deposited her on the porch outside the dorm with a gentlemanly bow.

"Good night, Rachel Griffin," he drawled charmingly.

"Good night, Gaius Valiant," she replied, equally elegantly. She handed him his suit jacket. Then with a wave goodbye and a *brrrrr* at the cold, she ran into the dorm.

Rachel closed the great oak doors behind her and ran across the black and white marble squares to stand before the grate of golden bars, behind which the young salamander, who normally cavorted in this habitat of brick and glowing bronze, was snoozing. She was shivering so hard from the cold, in her river-splattered bodysuit, that she did not even want to move away from the heat to walk—now that she was no longer allowed to fly—the five stories up to her bed. She rested Vroomie against the wall and held her hands out over the salamander's enclosure. Standing at the grate, she basked in the waves of warmth emanating from the red-hot sleeping body, breathing in the sweet, cinnamon scent of the coal-black and ember-red lizard.

As warmth returned to her limbs, she thought again on the night's events. As she did so, a thought struck her: In this one day, *all three of her wishes had come true.*

Rachel shivered. The wishes had seemed so innocuous at the time, but each had, in one way or another way, gone terribly wrong. Did she regret having wished them? The first one, no. She would rather have Amber in her life than not. The last one, yes. The loss of the Heer of Dunderberg would be an enormous blow to the school. The middle one? It felt strange to no longer feel any hatred toward the Master of the World. She did not look forward to having to explain this to Sigfried or Dread. They had both promised to face this menace with her. Would they feel that she was letting them down?

She probably would not tell her mother at all. Peter could tell her whatever he wished.

Had the light in the room altered in hue? Rachel frowned, suddenly alert. The change was so subtle that she almost had not noticed, but when she compared the light now with moments before, she could clearly recall the difference. The golden glow of wisps had been replaced by a silvery light, more like moonlight.

Feeling suddenly warmer, she glanced down to see if the wet spots on her jumpsuit were dry and gasped. She was no longer wearing her black jumpsuit with its white spots and wire tail. Instead, she wore the most beautiful gown she had ever seen. Even Nastasia's gown did not rival it. Layers of lace and satin appeared to be woven from moonlight and starlight with hints of the midnight sky.

Rachel could not imagine how such a thing was possible. *Was she dreaming? Had she fallen asleep in the foyer?*

An orchestra began to play the strains of her favorite waltz. As the music swelled, filling the vast foyer, a voice spoke behind her, angelic in its melodiousness.

"I believe this is our dance, Rachel Griffin."

Rachel spun, the lace and satin of the dream gown floating around her. "Jariel!"

The Raven stood there in all his glory, dressed in a dark shirt and slacks. His wings arched out to either side, and his feather-like, raven-black hair fell over his piercing gray eyes. He held out his hand, inviting her to dance.

With a cry of joy, Rachel ran forward and took his hand. He bowed low and then, leaning way over, put his other arm behind her.

To the melody of her beloved "Skater's Waltz", Rachel Griffin danced with the Guardian of the World.

Epilogue:
Dances with Ravens

They danced to the rousing waltz without speaking. After a time, the Raven turned his head and narrowed his eyes as if peering into the distance. "I foresee, barring unexpected events, that you and your sister will meet again."

"Amber, you mean? Good." Rachel sighed in relief, adding, "I would be rather cross if she did not keep her word to return."

"I also see many futures where she is able to convince her master to restore your father's memory." He moved his head slightly, as if examining something. "The most prevalent is that this will happen in September or October."

"Oh, thank goodness!" cried Rachel, though she wondered why it would take so long.

It was difficult to dance with someone so much taller, but Rachel did her best. After one turn around the floor, however, the Raven shimmered and turned into a boy a head taller than her. He drew her into his arms, holding her like a proper waltz partner. They glided around the black and white marble floor of the chamber with the grace of skaters.

This was sweet of him, but Rachel wished that he had not done it. True, he was easier to dance with this way, but it was *him* she wanted to dance with, not some unknown boy. Also, he was so ungodly handsome as a boy, with his perfect features and his intense gray eyes, that Rachel found her thoughts slipping into dangerous territory that never came up when he was eight-feet-tall. Still, it was nice to really waltz with him.

As they soared past the door to the boys' hall and the far hearth, Rachel spoke softly, putting voice to the topic that had just been on her mind. "Jariel, two weeks ago, I wished three wishes upon three stars. My wishes came true, but they were not entirely what I had wanted."

"Wishes are dangerous, Rachel Griffin," the Raven said gravely. "Not all stars are loyal to my father."

"Wh-what do you mean?"

"What did your sister Amber tell you about the stars?"

Rachel thought back. "You mean," she imitated Amber's intonation, "*'There's much more to it, but the short version is that the stars that make up the constellations are either stars of good omen that produce beneficent influences or stars of ill-omen, or dis-asters, which cause evil fates.'*"

"Indeed." His hand pressed against her back as they maneuvered a tighter turn.

"Was one of the stars I wished on evil? Which ones? More than one?" Rachel shivered slightly, despite that she no longer felt cold.

He did not answer but continued sweeping her around the foyer to the lilting notes of "The Skater's Waltz." They whirled by the great oak doors leading into the theater and then the sweeping staircase that led up to the girls' dorm.

"Jariel," Rachel cried plaintively, "if we are not supposed to wish on stars, what are we supposed to do? Life can be so hard. Isn't there some way of asking for help?"

He stared down into her face for a very long time. Rachel wanted to stare back, but they were going so fast that she had to keep turning her head to spot.

Finally, he spoke. "Would you like to learn the answer to that question, Rachel Griffin?"

"Yes!" she cried.

"Very well," he replied gravely. "I will arrange it."

The dance came to its climactic end, with the two of them spinning tightly across the entire floor. As the last note died away, he bowed over her hand.

"Thank you, little one, for the memory," said the Raven.

Then, Rachel found herself again standing in the wisp light, shivering in her black and white bodysuit. She moved closer to the grate and soaked in the heat again. *It had really happened, right? She had not just dozed off standing by the hearth, right?*

"Rachel Griffin." The Raven was suddenly behind her again. "Will you undertake a task for me?"

"Anything!" Rachel spun, her heart thumping from the surprise. "I will do anything you ask. Please! Let me help you! There must be something I can do to help!"

He took her hand and pressed something into it. "Please return this for me. I went to some effort to retrieve it."

With a bow and a flutter of black wings, he was gone. Rachel looked down. In her hand was Zoë Forrest's missing feather.

Here ends *The Unbearable Heaviness of Remembering*.

Our heroine's adventures continue in
the Sixth *Book of Unexpected Enlightenment*:

GUARDIANS OF THE TWILIGHT LANDS

Subscribe to the *Roanoke Glass* at https://goo.gl/UEdUKW
to be kept up-to-date on all things *Unexpected*
and the further adventures of Rachel Griffin.

For more information about the
Roanoke Academy for the Sorcerous Arts, see the school's website:
http://lampwright.wixsite.com/roanoke-academy
or join the Facebook group at
https://facebook.com/groups/RoanokeAcademy

GLOSSARY

Agents—Magical law enforcement. Agents fight magical foes, both human and supernatural.

Alchemy—One of the Seven Sorcerous Arts. It is the Art of putting magic into objects.

Bavaria—A country that exists in the world of the book but not in our world. It is known to both the World of the Wise and the Unwary. It is ruled by the Von Dread family.

Canticle—One of the Seven Sorcerous Arts. It is the Art of commanding the natural and supernatural world with the words and gestures of the Original Language.

Cantrip—One word in the Original Language, *i.e.* a canticle spell.

Cathay—The Democratic Republic of Cathay, a country that exists in the world of the book but not in our world. It is known to both the World of the Wise and the Unwary. It is ruled by an elected council.

Conjuring—One of the Seven Sorcerous Arts. It is the Art of drawing objects out of the dreamlands.

Core Group—A group of students, usually from the same dorm, who attend all their classes together.

Dare Hall—The dormitory at Roanoke Academy that is favored by enchanters.

De Vere Hall—The dormitory at Roanoke Academy that is favored by warders and obscurers.

Dee Hall—The dormitory at Roanoke Academy that is favored by scholars.

Drake Hall—The dormitory at Roanoke Academy that is favored by thaumaturges.

Enchantment—One of the Seven Sorcerous Arts. It is based on music and includes a number of sub-arts.

Fulgurator's wand—A wand with a spell-grade gem on the tip that is used by Soldiers of the Wise to throw lightning and to hold other kinds of spells.

Gnosis—One of the Seven Sorcerous Arts. It is the Art of knowledge and augury.

Heer of Dunderberg—Storm Goblin locked up with his Lightning Imps in a cave in Stony Tor on Roanoke Island.

Jumping—A cantrip that allows the practitioner to teleport.

Magical Australia—A country that is only known to the Wise. It is ruled by the Romanov family.

Marlowe Hall—The dormitory at Roanoke Academy that is favored by conjurers.

Morthbrood — An ancient organization of practitioners of black magic. During the Terrible Years, the Morthbrood served the Terrible Five.

Mundane—Without magic. Refers both to the modern technological world and to those who cannot use magic. It is possible to be mundane and Wise, if one has no magic but is aware of the magical world.

Obscuration—A subset of Warding. It allows for the casting of illusions that hide things and trick the Unwary.

Original Language—The original language in which all objects were named.

Parliament of the Wise—The ruling body of the World of the Wise.

Pollepel Island—The name the Unwary call the island they see in place of Roanoke Island. It is also called Bannerman Island.

Roanoke Academy for the Sorcerous Arts—A school of magic on a floating island that is currently moored in the Hudson near Storm King Mountain.

Scholars—Practitioners of the Art of Gnosis.

Sorcery—The study of magic.

Spenser Hall—The dormitory at Roanoke Academy that is favored by canticlers.

Terrible Five—The leaders of the Veltdammerung, who terrorized the World of the Wise during the Terrible Years. They consisted of: Simon Magus, Morgana le Fay, Koschei the Deathless, Baba Yaga, and Aleister Crowley.

Thaumaturgy—One of the Seven Sorcerous Arts. It is the Art of storing charges of magic in a gem.

Thule—A country that is known only to the World of the Wise. It occupies the section of Greenland that is, in our world, occupied by the world's largest national park (larger than all but 32 countries).

Transylvania—A country that exists in the world of the book but not in our world. It is known to both the World of the Wise and the Unwary. It is ruled by the Starkadder family.

Tutor—The term used for professors at Roanoke Academy.

Unwary—One who does not know about the magical world.

Veltdammerung — Twilight of the World. The organization that served the Terrible Five during the Terrible Years. It consisted of the Morthbrood and of supernatural servants.

Warding—One of the Seven Sorcerous Arts. It is the Art of protecting one's self from magical influences.

Wise—Those in the know about the magical world (as in the root of the word 'wizard').

Wisecraft—The law enforcement agency of the Wise. The Agents work for the Wisecraft.

World of the Wise—The community of those who know about the magical world.

ACKNOWLEDGEMENTS

Thank you to Mark Whipple, John C. Wright, and
William E. Burns, III, who breathed the life into the original story.

To Virginia Johnson, Erin Furby, Brian Furlough,
Bill Burns, and Jeff Zitomer, who helped iron out the bumps,
and to my sons, Orville and Justinian for playing along and
particularly to Juss, for wearing a lightning imp under his cat.

To Erin Furby for slogging through the early drafts,
and to Anthony Regan, Mark Thompson, Michael Putlack, Andrew
and Bryanna Craig, Kiara Lingenfelter, Meredith Dixon, Katherine
Peterson, Pamala Stump, Julian W. Thompson,
James Stepanek, and Paul A. Piatt
for their excellent beta reading efforts.

With special thanks to Declan Finn and Joel C. Salomon
for slogging through the awful draft.
No man should have to had suffer so!

To Anna "Firtree" Macdonald for making it readable
and to Joel C. Salomon, again,
for making it accessible to the rest of you!

To Jim Frenkel for the gift of editing,
for which Rachel will be forever grateful.

A special thanks to J. Conrad Matthews
for his expert advice on the matter of Bigfoot.

To my mother, Jane Lamplighter,
for listening as she drove to ballet class.

About the Authors

L. Jagi Lamplighter is also the author of the *Prospero's Children* series: *Prospero Lost, Prospero In Hell*, and *Prospero Regained*. She is an assistant editor with the *Bad-Ass Faeries* anthologies. She is also a founding member of the Superversive Literary Movement and maintains a weekly blog on the subject. When not writing, she switches to her secret identity as wife and stay-home mom in Centreville, VA, where she lives with her dashing husband, author John C. Wright, and their four darling children, Orville, Ping-Ping, Roland Wilbur, and Justinian Oberon.

> Her website is: http://ljagilamplighter.com
> Her blog is at: https://arhyalon.livejournal.com/
> On Twitter: @lampwright4

Mark A. Whipple grew up in Croton-on-Hudson, which is not far from Roanoke Island. He then attended St. John's College in Annapolis, the mundane sister school to Roanoke Academy. Until recently, he has spent his free time, when not busy torturing Rachel Griffin, protecting the world from video game threats. Now, however, he volunteers with Stillbrave, a charity devoted to helping the families of children with cancer.

UNEXPECTED CHARITY: 30% of the authors' proceeds from the *Unexpected Enlightenment* series goes to charity. Current charities of choice:

Mark's choice: Stillbrave Childhood Cancer Foundation—helping families of children with cancer.

Stillbrave Childhood Cancer Foundation
6731A Edsall Road
Springfield, VA 22151

https://stillbrave.org

Jagi's choices: St. John's College—a mundane branch of Roanoke Academy's Dee Hall

St. John's College
60 College Avenue
Annapolis, MD 21401

http://www.sjc.edu

and: All Girls Allowed—fighting for the rights and dignity of girls in China

All Girls Allowed
101 Huntington Avenue, Suite 2205
Boston, MA 02199

http://allgirlsallowed.org

www.ingramcontent.com/pod-product-compliance
Lightning Source LLC
Chambersburg PA
CBHW030354200726
48286CB00014B/1380